Praise for Howard Hendrix's
THE GIRLS WITH KALEIDOSCOPE EYES

"Howard Hendrix here dem ty, and heart, in story after story. He h 's from the sciences with permanent tr ıs that are quirky and memorable. Hig
—Kim Stanle …ᴜ, author of *Red Moon*

"If you read science fiction to consume and savor ideas—lots of ideas, big and small, salty, bitter and sweet—then Hendrix offers a full course meal in *The Girls with Kaleidoscope Eyes*."
—David Brin, author of *Existence*

"Howard Hendrix's work glows with imagination, compassion, and ingenuity. The characters are alive, and the science is gripping."
—Jack McDevitt, author of *The Engines of God*

"Just when you think you know where these tales are going, the floor drops out under you. The characters seem like people you might recognize—until they don't. Near future, far future, Earth or far out in space, the stories entertain and satisfy, but above all they make you think. And not all the questions asked lead to pretty answers."
—Sheila Finch, author of *Triad*

"Howard Hendrix is one of science fiction's cleverest writers—a fountain of ideas any one of which would have made Asimov or Clarke proud. Prepare to have your mind blown."
—Robert J. Sawyer, author of *Quantum Night*

"Hendrix's first book since the 2006 novel *Spears of God* collects a pleasing array of science fiction stories. While there are no explicit links between the individual stories, recurring ideas such as the Mobius strip bring a sense of unity. The history of science fiction is well represented, with "Palimpsest" and "The Infinite Manque" paying homage to Arthur C. Clarke and Daniel Keyes, respectively. Other highlights include "Whatever Became of What Might Have Been," a comparison of addictions; "Knot Your Grandfather's Knot," a poignant time travel story centered on the 1939 World's Fair; "Monuments of Unageing Intellect," an exploration of the implications of immortality; and the title novella, which combines AI and genetics to explore potential ramifications of the surveillance state. The clever mix of story length and style keeps the reader's attention. Fans of idea-driven SF will enjoy dipping in here and there or reading the collection straight through."

—*Publishers Weekly*

THE GIRLS WITH KALEIDOSCOPE EYES

ANALOG STORIES FOR A DIGITAL AGE

Also by Howard V. Hendrix:

THE GIRLS WITH KALEIDOSCOPE EYES

ANALOG STORIES FOR A DIGITAL AGE

HOWARD V. HENDRIX

FAIRWOOD PRESS
Bonney Lake, WA

THE GIRLS WITH KALEIDOSCOPE EYES:
ANALOG STORIES FOR A DIGITAL AGE

A Fairwood Press Book
August 2019
Copyright © 2019 Howard V. Hendrix

All Rights Reserved

First Edition

Fairwood Press
21528 104th Street Court East
Bonney Lake, WA 98391
www.fairwoodpress.com

Cover image © Getty Images 2019
Cover and Book Design by Patrick Swenson

ISBN: 978-1-933846-77-4
First Fairwood Press Edition: August 2019
Printed in the United States of America

To editors Stanley Schmidt, Trevor Quatri,
Emily Hockaday, Ben Bova, and Eric Choi;
to publishers Patrick Swenson and Jacob Weisman;
and to my wife Laurel—my thanks to all of you for your patience.

CONTENTS

FOREWORD:
THE CRITIC AS WRITER
BY GREGORY BENFORD

This collection ponders the vast and various. Its author has spent a lifetime to make these stories.

I have known Howard since he was working on his doctorate. I kept in touch with him at the Eaton conferences at UCR and was impressed when his fiction began appearing. Few can do both criticism and fiction (I can, but not much scifilitcrit escapes my desk). Even fewer do so as well as Howard; indeed, very nearly none. His novels have built for him a reputation for scientifically savvy fiction, with an added insight into social issues. He had melded the social aspect of science fiction with a respect for the hard driver of technology, in its many aspects.

I'm a novelist, not a critic. I enjoy Howard's deft scene-setting, his audacious imagination, and his sense of plot. I think plot is the hardest aspect of fiction, for a working writer. I have learned this the hard way myself. I am a research physicist and professor, with writing as a hobby that has rewarded me well. I have not written for the straight 'literary' market, preferring the true current of modern science fiction—fiction for people who care about the future and like to think about it. Howard is such an accomplished, lit-savvy writer. I have commissioned stories from him for the original anthologies I edited. I have also seen him speak dozens of times, and he is a commanding presence with a canny knowledge of how to shape his message to his audience—any who speak at the Eaton Conference know it's a competitive event. He holds his own.

Let me make the case for Howard as specifically a writer of science fiction. Throughout this century, conventional literature persistently avoided thinking about conceptually altered tomorrows. The rapid march of science and technology was just plain unsettling to the literati. Conventional literature retreated into a realist posture, with fiction of ever-smaller compass. Henry James and H.G. Wells engaged in a classic debate on the matter during World War I, quite a nasty affair that ruined their friendship. In the end, awash in the tides of fashion, the novel of character, foregrounding personal relations, claimed the high ground of orthodox fiction. James won his argument, but surrendered the future to the genre that would increasingly set the terms of social debate—science fiction. Though Aldous Huxley, Nevil Shute, Italo Calvino, George Orwell, and Vladimir Nabokov did impressive work along science fictional lines, they were little emulated. The real work was done in the genre. By such as Howard.

Like immense time-binding discussions, genres allow ideas to be developed and traded, and for variations to be spun down through decades. Players ring changes on each other—a steppin'-out jazz band that inventively agrees on its central tune, jivin'—not a solo concert in a plush auditorium. Contrast this with too often self-consciously solemn "serious" fiction, which supposedly proceeds from canonical classics believed to stand outside of time, deserving awe, looming great and intact by themselves.

Genre origins still carry a class burden. Some in genre fiction still worry we'll scarcely be invited to the high literary tea, if we have so many companions with such muddy boots. The difference between highbrow and low—between Eliot and Poe, between mainstream and SF—is not one that can be mapped by the conventional criteria of criticism. Poe was more a formalist than Eliot, in many ways—and less given than Eliot to overt lecturing and preachiness (two often criticized SF mannerisms). Instead, the essential difference between their works and standings is not one of aesthetics or of some subtler metaphysical nature, but of the two writers' antithetical social and economic positions. Poe was a popular, market-driven writer, a "magazinist," while Eliot was supported by a high culture with subtle, indirect patronage. And still, sf/fantasy dominates the few still-standing fiction magazines. Realist fiction blooms in the hothouses of small, funded little magazines, and a few mainstreamers like *The New Yorker*.

I digress into this history because this speaks to the structure that universities erect around literature. Science fiction is the most important market-generated genre, and it intersects with the big drivers of the last century and more—science and engineering. It has the future in its bones. That's why it has become a dominant genre in our time, with many films and novels in the public eye.

The Eaton Collection at UCR is at the fore in carrying forward a genuine revolution, directed toward the reality of how our scientific culture and literature interact. They have the world's largest and best collection of the literature of the fantastic. Howard comes from that movement and has become the foremost graduate UCR has produced from over thirty years of effort in the Eaton tradition.

Howard is a true generalist—he can write criticism, commercial fiction, articles and reviews and much else. He lectures very well, has warm personal skills, and works harder than he probably should. Most of the stories in this volume are from a single magazine, *Analog*. It is based on the assumption that hard SF must be understood primarily as an attempt to induce the feeling (if not the reality) of conceptual breakthrough. Howard's work does just that. He repeatedly seeks to use the tools and metaphors of science to evoke the splendor of breakout ideas, where our future lies.

He's a master of the form. This collection tells us how and why.

—Gregory Benford

THE GIRLS WITH KALEIDOSCOPE EYES

KNOT YOUR GRANDFATHER'S KNOT

Mike Sakler knew about chaos. In the 1950s his doctoral work in turbulent airflow dynamics eventually led to a job with a major aerospace contractor in Southern California. He'd dabbled in nonlinear dynamics throughout his career, then chaos and complexity theory in the 1980s and '90s. Since his retirement and his wife Ginny's death of lung cancer, in 1989, he'd had lots of time for dabbling.

With the kids grown and gone, he sold the family house in Southern California and moved to the central Sierra Nevada near Alder Springs, an hour outside Fresno, among tall pines and old oaks and tree-sized manzanita. He spent his days working and playing on his twenty-acre spread and in his great barracks-like, 12,000 square foot retirement "party house." Solar powered and off the grid, he built the house with his own hands, out of wood from his own land's trees.

Once the house was up, he found himself playing more than working: tossing horseshoes, bowing his fiddle, strumming his banjo, jamming with young friends, endlessly tinkering with his home sound-studio's electronics.

His fascination with the Cord 810 Beverly was much more than just play or dabbling, however. Mike considered the mothballed green 1936 Cord to be the strange attractor underlying his increasingly chaotic life.

Part of it was personal history. His own grandfather had owned a Cord exactly like the piece of automotive sculpture previously owned by Donald and Rita Batchelder: same make, model, and year. When Mike was twelve and his Grandfather Sakler about the same age as Mike himself now was, the old man took him in that very car to the 1939 World's Fair, for the first of a dozen visits.

The Batchelder Cord had a long and complex history of its own, going back to Rita's late husband Donald and his purchase of it at an estate sale in New York, years before. Time had pretty much blown the original paint job—a sort of silvery gray-green, like a spruce forest seen at high speed—but that was typical of Cords. Aside from that, the only further damage was the small scratch and dent made by Rita herself in 1955, for which crime Donald had forever after mothballed the car.

So it was that in all other respects the 810 looked the way it did the day it left the factory. The Cord emblem with its art-deco wings, still shining. The eyes of the hidden headlights blissfully sleeping away the years in the big pontoon fenders. The coffin-lid hood fronted by futuristic grillework—still giving off an impression of blunt velocity, even though the car had been parked and motionless for more than forty years when Mike found it in Rita's garage and had to have it.

Unfortunately, Mike's relationship with Rita didn't continue very long once the sale of the Cord was consummated. What with her calling him a "mercenary, self-centered, heartless old bastard," he couldn't say the affair had ended well.

Still, he reassured himself that, if he wasn't too busy, he could always find another girlfriend through either his martial arts or folk-dancing classes—"ai-ki-do, tae-kwon-do, and do-si-do," as he liked to think of them. He'd been doing all of them for so many years that he'd have blackbelts in all three if they handed out blackbelts in folkdance.

Widow Batchelder may have called him heartless, but his heart was fine—or at least as fine as years of exercise, the latest heart meds, and the occasional angioplasty could make it. Oddly, though, he took the fiasco of his break-up with Rita worse than he would have thought. Funneling all his energy into restoring the Cord had the virtue of diverting his attention to what seemed to be more tractable problems, at least at first.

He started with the car's aesthetics—smoothing out the dent and scratch, lifting off all the chrome pieces, getting them and the bare steel bumpers shined up again. He redid the paint job in its original green, working on all the detailing that would return the car to absolutely mint condition.

The body work went well. Rita claimed her husband had drained the gas and thoroughly changed the oil when he moth-balled the car in 1955, so Mike felt his odds of restoring the engine should at least be even, too.

He removed all the plugs and mystery-oiled the holes. The car wouldn't start.

He removed and cleaned the fuel system. It wouldn't start.

He rebuilt the carburetor, did a leak-down test for the rings, and checked the valves. It wouldn't start.

He hooked pulleys to an external electric motor and cranked things around a bit to check the compression. It wouldn't start.

He adjusted what didn't need replacing, brought up the fuel, water, and electrical levels, put the key in the ignition, said a fervent prayer, and still—it wouldn't start.

He would have loved to give up, but he couldn't. When he neglected to work on it, he felt guilty, as if shirking some responsibility he didn't fully understand. He returned to it again and again, often reluctantly.

He put less effort into keeping up his own health. Where before he had been more than willing to "keep active," now he avoided trips down to the valley for martial arts classes and dance performances.

He'd be damned if he'd let the sawbones put him on one of those bland rabbit-food diets. He would eat the way he wanted to, thank you. If you couldn't enjoy life while trying to stay alive, you might as well already be dead.

The same was true of his drinking—which, after long hiatus, he took up again in a big way. His young party-people friends kept visiting for a while, some even helping him with his automotive restoration work, but gradually his "drinkering and tinkering" drove them away.

A year and a half into the Cord project, after the endless big failures and small successes, Mike Sakler finally hit bottom.

He drank heavily the first part of the night, then fell asleep. Toward morning, Mike knew he was starting to wake up again when he dreamed he was drunk—and had tied a noose to hang himself.

He had hoped for months and months the drinking would turn up the stage machinery that made the fog in his brain, until it filled the theatre of his consciousness, obscuring his memory uniformly. It hadn't worked out that way.

Instead, as the months had passed, his memory had become more and more like the Tule fog that came up out of the ground in the valley below—fog thick, yet low, so that it was easier to look straight up through it and see a star shining down out of all those long lost lightyears than see the streetlamp just passed a block and a moment before.

The star that shone down on him in his foggiest darkness now was a perfect image of the Perisphere and Trylon, with the Helicline ramping down around them: the "Egg, Spike, and Ramp," the prime symbols of the 1939 World's Fair and its "World of Tomorrow" theme.

That was the future that was—yet never was yet. His childhood attempts with the Build-Your-Own New York World's Fair kits never got much beyond building scale models of the 610 foot tall Trylon obelisk, its 188 foot tall Perisphere globe companion, and the Helicline ramp linking them, but that had been all right with him. Those three were what really mattered.

How much Grandpa had loved that fair was a surprise to everyone in the family. Patriarch of a large New York Jewish clan, all the relations thought him old-fashioned, with his banjo and fiddle-playing, the same instruments he'd taught Mike to play before Mike was ten. Mike knew his grandfather wasn't old-fashioned, though. The old man had been picking up *Amazing This* and *Popular That* at the newsstand for years and sharing them with his precocious, frenetic, problem-child of a grandson.

After that first trip to the Fair, Grandpa was a quiet visionary no more—a result of the same run-in with Yorkville street toughs that had altered the old man's physiognomy, or so some in the family theorized. From whatever cause, in his last two years of life Grandfather Sakler experienced a personal Indian Summer, a blaze of fierce, bright, quirky creativity in his closing days. He began keeping a journal and corresponding with world leaders and thinkers, especially Albert Einstein, with whom he met once (by accident) at the Fair and, later, by appointment at Princeton—twice.

Now, amid his deepest fog, Mike remembered the trunkload of Fair memorabilia he inherited from the old man. Rummaging with sudden furious energy through closets and drawers in the eight empty bedrooms and the enormous party room on the top floor of his cavernous house, he found he couldn't remember where he'd stored the trunk.

He staggered down his house's great spiral staircase to the main floor and pillaged more storage spaces. Fear and frustration gnawing at him, he stumbled down one last circuit of the turning stairway. In a spare basement room he finally found it: the musty sealed steamer-trunk that was his legacy from an old man dead more than fifty years.

Inside, he found journals and correspondence and other writings, an intriguing but inexplicable device apparently handcrafted by the old man, even a full suit of what appeared to be his grandfather's clothes, smelling slightly of smoke, with fine shoes and shirts and underwear too, wrapped in a garment bag that had grown brittle with age.

All the Fair memorabilia was still there. The Trylon and Perisphere-adorned orange and blue high-modern Official Souvenir Book. Democracity clocks. Fair plates and puzzles and radios. Heinz pickle pins, and a crop of GM-Futurama "I Have Seen The Future" buttons—of which the old man had been particularly fond.

Mike hadn't looked at any of this stuff since the early Fifties and had looked at none of it thoroughly at any time. What he remembered from his previous glances through it was embarassment and fear that, in his final years, his grandfather had become a slightly crazed technobabbler, his notebooks full of inexplicable terms, diagrams, and equations.

What caught his eye now were the photos. In the shots taken before May 1939, the family resemblance that was always there was never so striking as it was in those images taken *after* that first trip to the World's Fair.

He stared at a fading color picture of himself as a boy. Beside him stood a thin, mostly bald man whose remaining hair and beard were a mix of white and gray and yellow—his grandfather, on one of their later trips to the World's Fair, with the Trylon and Perisphere in the distance behind them.

Mike knew his own visage well enough to see how close the resemblance was between the way the old man looked then and the way he himself looked now. It was almost as if the boy had grown up to become his own grandfather.

Grabbing the trunk by both handles, he hauled it upstairs. Its wdeomcdsdf forced him to pause and lean against the railings or wall of the stairwell every few feet. When he reached his office, he set the trunk down beside his eight-by-twenty foot worktable.

Clearing his Cord-related stuff from the workspace, he removed the trunk's contents and spread them out over the table's broad top. Up came the suit of clothes and other garments. The sharp leather shoes, too.

Next came all the memorabilia, the flyers, the brochures, the programs. The oxymoronic prose of the captions describing GM's futurama, "a vast miniature cross-section of America as it may conceivably appear two decades hence...."

He sat down slowly in the chair at the worktable. Looking more carefully through the correspondence and the writings again after all these years, Mike thought that the notes now seemed less demented than eerily prescient. Here, paperclipped to a page of typed notes in a binder, was a letter apparently sent from Einstein himself:

Matter can be made to 'degrade' into energy more readily than energy can be made to 'upgrade' into matter. I do not, however, believe matter and energy are just types of information, as you have suggested, or that there is a spectrum linking them such that consciousness is just a more complex form of information than matter or energy. Nor do I believe that consciousness can be made to 'degrade' more readily into matter and energy than matter and energy can be made to 'upgrade' into consciousness. Although the distinction between past, present and future is an illusion, the distinction between energy, matter, and consciousness is not.

Indeed the notes from that page on were most curious. "Planck energy for opening gap in spacetime fabric = 10^{19} billion electron volts," read one, but then that was crossed out with a large X as the writer of the notes took a different tack.

"At each bifurcation point," read the next, "flux occurs in which many potential futures are present. Iteration and amplification mean one future is chosen and others disappear. In bifurcations the past is continually recycled, held timeless in eddies or in closed timelike curves, stabilized through feedback. Time is turbulently recurrent, expressing self-similarity across different scales."

After a flurry of equations came an underlined conclusion: "Human nervous system both classical and quantum, exploits quantum scale processes to accomplish macroscale ends—solution lies in phase-locking feedback!"

Mike picked up a page with a meticulously handplotted diagram, hauntingly beautiful in its elegant simplicity. When he looked at it more closely, he found the diagram was labeled with questions: "Closed Timelike Rössler Attractor? Temporal Möbius in Phase Space?" Below the question was the note, "Always incompleteness and missing information at the center. The shape of uncertainty shapes certainty."

What pushed Mike back in his chair, however, was how much the "Temporal Möbius in Phase Space" resembled an idealized, abstract image of Perisphere, Trylon, and Helicline. Looking away from the image, he realized that the sun was up, that his head hurt with hangover, and—something else. Bifurcations? Self-similarity? Phase-locking feedback? Phase space? That was the language of chaos theory!

His hand trembled as he flipped through more and more pages of detailed notes, until he reached the inside back cover of the notebook-binder. Taped to it was an ancient envelope, with the words **MICHAEL SAKLER** written on it. With a shaky hand he pulled the envelope loose from the notebook and opened it.

LETTER TO MYSELF:

If Professor Einstein is right about what he calls a "temporal Möbius" and I am right about the role consciousness plays on the information spectrum, then reading this letter is about to stop you from drinking yourself to slow suicide. Perhaps you have by now realized that these notes are memories of the future, not only mine in 1939, but also yours. In 1997 you have not written these notes yet, but you will—in 1939.

As a boy, we first travelled with Grandfather Sakler to the Fair on May 28, 1939, to witness the opening of the Jewish Palestine Pavilion. Albert Einstein speaks there, and that day you—I—meet him for the first time. The old man whom the boy returns home with is not his grandfather. It is himself from sixty years into that boy's future.

Why must "we" go through such temporal acrobatics? I'm glad I asked. If we don't, our grandfather will be brutally murdered after running out of gas in Yorkville on the night of May 28. The very fact that this temporal Möbius exists proves that possibility.

On one timeline, embittered by our grandfather's death, one of the many possible "us" devotes his life to inventing a time-travel device and uses it to return to 1939 to save our already severely injured Grandfather by sending him into the future. He—we—I—remain in 1939, taking over the role of that grandfather. The boy is spared the suffering and grief of seeing his grandfather die from his injuries.

In creating the device and using it to alter his own timeline, however, our other self on that line creates a temporal paradox. On that timeline, Grandfather Sakler is killed and as a result one of us grows up to create the device that will allow him to travel back to 1939 to prevent Grandfather Sakler's murder. Preventing Grandpa's murder, however, means none of us ever grows up to become the man who invents the device to prevent Grandpa's murder. Therefore Grandfather Sakler is killed and one of us grows up to create the device that will allow him to . . . et cetera, et cetera.

Professor Einstein tells me the structure of the universe will not tolerate such an endless conundrum. Instead it conserves its own integrity by melding the two timelines together into "the temporal equivalent of a Möbius strip"—something both and neither loop and intersection. On such a dimension-collapsing Möbius, "either/or" (either Grandpa is saved or the device is created) becomes "not only/but also" (not only is Grandpa saved but the device is also created).

We have, in some sense, been "grandfathered into" this temporal loop-hole, but at a cost. The price of this shift to "not only/but also" is the energy of our eternal vigilance. If we want his murder to never again recur, we must never again prevent its recurrence.

I know this is difficult for you to understand at first, but if you choose to perpetuate this recurrence, you will learn that time travel is less like running a particle accelerator and more like experiencing a lucid dream or particularly vivid memory.

Utilizing the chaotic effects always present in consciousness, we can exploit time's turbulent and strange-attractive properties to burst the surface tension of spacetime at far, far less than Planck energy. I know we can, because we already have.

For us, it's not only the dream of the doing that's grandfather to the *memory of the accomplishment, but also the reverse: The memory of the accomplishment is grandfather to the dream of the doing.*

The device in the steamer trunk is only partially complete. I have done as much as I can with technology available before midcentury. The system can only be completed with technology from your era. I have enclosed a list of what you'll need. You'll have to search it out and make it all work together, if you choose to perpetuate our responsibility in this and knot your grandfather's knot—our grandfather's knot, and Einstein's knot—in that old Cord.

I hope you will do so, and will find it both a loophole that binds and a knot that frees, as I have. At all events, good luck!

—Michael Sakler

P.S.: That Cord's no hot rod, but it's crucial to the set and setting of the mental state required for this time travel experience. It also works well enough for hauling batteries and getting around New York in 1939, so treat it kindly!

Mike slowly folded the letter. Lost in thought, he stroked his beard absently for a while. *Well, it's better than the other option for a loophole that binds and a knot that frees,* he told himself, remembering his hungover dream of a hangman's noose.

He got up from the table and the chair, and stretched. Then he went downstairs, down to the garage/workshop where the Cord sat with its hood up. The sun was shining brightly just beyond the shadows. He got to work.

Focused on his work, Mike's days flew by. A certain balance had returned to his life, too: his obsession was no longer a mad one. He returned, at least sporadically, to his ai-ki-do, tae-kwon-do, do-si-do classes. He sent a card of apology to the widow, who, unfortunately, was not interested in re-establishing contact. During 1998 and early 1999 he even went to Temple a few times—something he hadn't done in years.

Maybe the prayers paid off. In June of 1998, he was able to start and run the Cord's engine for the first time—and the completed restoration cost him less than he'd expected. Such was not the case with completing the "Temporal Möbius Generator," however.

The interface synching his mind up to the machine and capable of inducing the mind-chaos needed for his time trip required state-of-the-art neuro-hookups so expensive he had to take out a second mortgage on his property. They were on the 1939 list, however, so he purchased top-of-the-line units from a "mindware" dealer operating out of a software storefront in a Marin County strip mall.

Using the system he put together, Mike experimented with low voltages to create a map of his own mind's functioning. Taking as his guide the 1939 notes—with their jargon of "ekstasis points," "temporal dissipation vortices," and "eschaton particles"—he located regions of his brain that, when stimulated, produced both "out of body experience" and vivid strange-attractor memories of the World's Fair. These, the notes indicated, were vital to the temporal voyage he was to undertake.

By May of 1999 all was in final readiness. A couple of days before his planned time-jaunt, he took the now operational and fully-equipped Cord on one lengthy test drive—but only one.

That test drive in itself narrowly missed becoming a disaster. Driving the Cord down to the Valley to see his doctor for his routine physical, he felt fine and the car was running fine, but he still almost didn't make it. Pulling off of Herndon Avenue and into the rat's maze of private medical offices surrounding St. Agnes Hospital, Mike blanked out at the wheel. Only in the last second did he catch himself—and catch the hard left turn he very nearly missed.

When he finally pulled into a parking spot, he was both shaken and relieved. He had narrowly escaped smashing into the cinder-block wall separating the parking lot of his doctor's building from the Hospital's parking lot.

Well, he reminded himself as he walked to his appointment, if I'd smashed through the wall, at least I would have practically landed in the emergency room!

The only sign of Mike's brush with Fate was a slightly elevated pulse rate. No trace of a mini-stroke or any other brain glitch that might explain his blanking out just moments earlier. His doctor declared him to be in fine shape, outside of the pulse spike—especially considering his cholesterol, his plaqued arteries, and everything else the doctor deigned to lecture him on.

Given Mike's failure to change his diet to save his ticker, the doctor warned that he would have to remain absolutely faithful in taking his heart pills and would likely still need surgery within the year to remove his blood mud.

Mike agreed politely but planned on changing nothing because, two days later, he was ready to go.

Into his winged chariot's trunk Mike loaded the big Exide storage batteries which had, until then, provided electrical storage for the solar panels atop the roof of his off-the-grid party house. Despite the fact that his house would soon be going dark, he was in a celebratory mood.

He decided to dress appropriately for the occasion. From the closet in his office Mike removed the full suit of clothes and shoes he'd taken from the trunk, so long before, and tried them on. All the clothes fit perfectly, as he somehow knew they would.

He looked at himself in the mirror, a man of not inconsiderable years, dressed in a dark suit and tie of a rather conservative cut, topped by a snapbrim hat. Yes, just what the well-dressed time traveller would be wearing in 1939.

He locked up his home. Walking toward the Cord in the driveway, he twice glanced back wistfully toward his huge handmade house. Starting up the Cord, he drove it through evening light along the deserted Forest Service gravel road until it passed directly beneath the hydroelectric powerlines, where he stopped.

Rigging up a coupling and converter, he linked power from an overhead line to the battery array in the trunk. From the system of dams and turbines on the upper San Joaquin River, he swiped enough of that clean safe Democracity energy to bring the device and the storage batteries up to maximum.

As he decoupled his power tap, he doubted the power company would much notice. A little free juice was the least they owed him, after he'd put up with this powerline eyesore all these years.

The fully restored Cord spun gravel on the last stretch of switchbacks before fishtailing up onto the blacktop of Alder Springs Road. Einstein had once contended that imagination was more important than knowledge. At this moment, Mike felt like a living embodiment of that premise.

No machine alone could do what he was going to do. The chaos of brain, the individuality of mind, the singularity of memory: all were indispensable to the reality of travel in time.

Over the blacktop he drove to the summit of the ridge, then stopped the Cord. Its engine thrummed along placidly, idling, as he watched the sun go down. Slowly, the rim of the turning world obscured the light of day. Soon the first stars began to come out.

Mike took off his hat and put on his temples the circlets containing the neuro-hookups. Checking everything one last time, he threw the switches to activate the timers and all the memory systems of all the computers on board, revved the engine as high as it would go, put the Cord in gear, then took his foot off the brake.

He was overcome by a euphoric sensation of floating upward, not unlike what he had sometimes experienced just as he drifted off to sleep and the bed beneath him seemed to fall away. This time, however, there was no hard jerk of ordinary consciousness striking to reassert control.

This time, he just kept drifting, a full-blown out of body experience bringing his body and the car with it. Faintly he heard the engine sounds breaking up, digitizing, becoming discrete, then wildly dilated, then sounding almost as if they were being played backwards.

Through the windshield and windows he saw a fog rising—a type of Bose condensate. Mike seemed to have seen it before: thick, yet low, the Tule fog of memory.

He looked up through the windshield and saw a star perched atop a great curving skybridge, like a diamond ring effect seen during a total eclipse of the sun. The bridge was a vast, slightly rainbow-shimmering catenary Möbius curve. From this angle, it looked rather like the St. Louis Gateway Arch, only countless miles high—and it wasn't so much "in" the sky as it somehow *was* the sky.

The Cord was moving in and through the skybridge, in the ultimate daredevil stunt loop. His own memories ran like cords of fog through the suspended and suspending bridge and tunnel. Particular events in his life possessed their own unique gravity, curving and warping his memoryspace in ways he could not have foretold—

—until the fogbridge did its Möbius fillip and he sat outside the 1939 World's Fair, in sunshine, in the Cord, in the parking lot that would one day become Shea Stadium. Through the windshield he saw the Trylon and Perisphere surrounded by the whole of the Fair, a candied confection of the future to be consumed by the present.

Too often, for him, black and white was the past, while the future was color. Yet here he was, in the past—and in color. Putting on his hat as he stepped out of the car, Mike was a man inside his own dream.

Might as well enjoy myself, he thought. He grabbed a frankfurter with everything at Swift & Company's streamlined superairliner building, then some ice cream over by Sealtest's triple shark-finned edifice. He paid for them with the antique liberty coins the notes had suggested he bring.

Strolling about the Fair grounds, he saw again how wind-shaped so many of the structures appeared. Buildings that looked as if they'd been designed in wind tunnels. Frank R. Paul melanges of fins and keels and flanges. Spirals, helices, and domes, their towers topped with zeppelin-mast spires. An airstream wonderland, waiting for the inevitable arrival of Northrop flying-wings and Bel Geddes tear-drop cars.

Stopping at the base of the Trylon and examining it closely, Mike rediscovered the Fair's secret. Like everything else, the Trylon was intended to look smoothly mass-produced, machine-precise and slipstream-slick. Up close, however, he saw that its surface was rough, stuccoed with all the "smoothness" of jesso over burlap. Beneath its assembly-line dreams of aerodynamic cowls and zero-drag farings, the great exhibition felt handcrafted—a prototype of the shape of things to come, not a production model.

The future is best viewed from a distance, Mike thought as he approached the Chrysler Motors Building in the Transportation Zone. Remembering its "Rocketport" display, he went inside.

Where he literally bumped into Albert Einstein.

"Pardon me, professor," Mike said quickly.

"Not a problem, not a problem," the Nobel laureate said with a distracted smile, turning back to lean on a railing. Together they watched the Rocketgun simulate another blastoff into tomorrow, with full noise-and-light special effects.

"They'll probably use it for shooting atomic bombs at each other," Mike remarked, "long before they use it for passengers."

Einstein gave him a startled look, then smiled wryly and shrugged.

This was the hard part. The only way Mike had been able to come up with to get the great man's attention was the way Klaatu had gotten Professor Barnhart's attention in *The Day The Earth Stood Still*. Mike couldn't remember how fluent Einstein's English was, but he pressed on quickly nonetheless.

"I know you've been working on unified field theory," Mike said, pulling a folded sheaf of papers and a card from his coat pocket, "so I thought you might be interested in this."

Unfolding the papers, Mike presented the sheaf to the Professor. On the pages he had diagrammed, with explanatory captions, a particularly interesting variant of what would someday be called the Einstein-Podolsky-Rosen theorem.

Einstein glanced at the pages, perfunctorily at first, just humoring him. Then the physicist's eyes grew wide as he realized the importance of what he was looking at.

"Wo— Where— ?"

"I knew you'd see their merit," Mike said, gesturing toward the thin sheaf, then handing Einstein the card with his grandfather's name, address and phone number. "It's been a pleasure meeting you in person, Professor. I can be reached at this address. Let's keep in touch."

"Ja—er, yes!" Einstein said, shuffling papers and card about in his hands so he could shake the hand Mike offered him. Tipping his hat and turning before he melted away into the crowd, Mike was pleased he'd made his Einstein contact already.

Deciding to treat himself to as much of the Fair as possible before he made his way to the Jewish Palestine Pavilion, he toured the Town of Tomorrow. Then it was on to the Immortal Well and its streamlined Time Capsule, scheduled to be opened in 6939 A.D. Next he saw the robots Elektro the Moto-Man and his Moto-Dog, Sparko, perform in the Westinghouse Building.

He felt a childlike awe at General Electric's ten-million volt indoor lightning-bolt show, and Consolidated Edison's block-long "City of Light" diorama. The line for the GM Futurama was far too long, however. His rendezvous with that tech triumph could wait for another visit.

He made his way through what felt more and more like a planetary county fair, until he at last reached the Jewish Palestine Pavilion. During the day the numbers of spectators for the pavilion's official opening ceremonies had swelled past 50,000. On the fringes of the crowd, entrepeneurs sold Jewish Palestine flags, as well as armbands and yarmulkes adorned with the Star of David.

Recalling that his grandfather—though neither Orthodox

nor Conservative—had on a lark bought such a yarmulke at the World's Fair today and all those years ago, Mike now bought one as well and put it on, in hope and remembrance.

In his accented English, Einstein himself at last pronounced the words "I am here entrusted with the high privilege of officially dedicating the building which my Palestine brethren have erected." Amid the vast cheering crowd, Mike despaired of finding the old man and boy he was seeking, but he kept looking.

By the time the ceremonies ended, however, Mike still hadn't found the boy and the old man he sought—not even after the crowd broke up.

Worry, frustration, and anxiety warred within him as he drifted like a lost ghost through the great squares and avenues of the Fair, alongside the Lagoon of Nations, past the pavilions of states and governments. He wandered beneath the closing fireworks, his hope fading like blown starshells. He came to the reflecting pool beneath the Perisphere, at just the moment the great Voice of that globe began to sound its eerie tocsin over the emptying Fair.

With other stragglers he made his way toward the parking lots, panic rising in his mind. He'd lost them somewhere in the Fair! They were no longer on the grounds anywhere! He banged his forehead with palmed fists. How to find them? How to find them?

Getting into the Cord, he sat and stared through the windshield. He felt forlorn and powerless as a lost child. Not even the play of faerie lights over the Trylon and Perisphere could alter his despondent mood. He leaned his head against the steering wheel and mourned inconsolably.

Yorkville.

The word drifted into his consciousness like a boon from a merciful god. Yes! New York's German-American section, where his grandfather had had his run-in with the street gangsters. It was only a hunch, but as he left the parking lot for the streets he could think of nowhere else to go.

He had maps, but the maps were not the city. He got lost, again and again. By memory he had successfully navigated across sixty years of time and thousands of miles of space, but now he was having difficulty finding his way around New York City!

When at last he made his way into Yorkville, streets and landmarks began to take on the faintest aura of deja-vu familiarity. He began to remember. They'd run out of gas, yes. He had waited in the car while his grandfather had gone to fill up the gas can. His grandfather had been gone a long time—

At the far edge of a streetlight, in a vacant lot, Mike saw and heard it, before he was ready for it. Four young men yelling "*Jude! Unflätig Jude! Verderber! Teufel-Jude!*" as they pummeled and kicked an old man.

Mike skidded to a stop beside the nightmare tableau and got out of the car.

At the sound of the Cord screeching to a halt, the young men stopped their heavy-booted work. Hearing the car door opening and slamming, one of the men, the smallest, took to his heels. The other three stood their ground, fists clenched.

Mike walked steadily across the lot toward them. When he was perhaps fifteen feet away, one of the three abruptly broke away toward something off to one side—a gasoline can. Mike saw the youth take matches and handkerchief rag from his pockets. He knew immediately what the boy intended to do.

While the firemaker fumbled about his work, Mike in battle-dance kata waded into the remaining two, punching and kicking.

An elderly avenging angel, he felt strangely detached, as if in a minor trance. His only barely-conscious thought was an odd little mantra—ai-ki-do, tae-kwon-do, do-si-do, again and again.

He knew he took many blows and strikes, but he gave far more, stomping insteps, roundhouse-kicking ribs, smashing noses, snapping collar bones, shattering kneecaps. Even Yorkville street toughs had never encountered such a fighting style. They fled at last, but they had done their damage.

His grandfather, doused about the neck and chest with a slosh of gasoline, was going up in slow immolation. It was all Mike could do to put out the fire with his suitcoat. The old man's pulse was thready, but the pain of his burns roused him to consciousness.

"Thank you," he whispered, coughing blood.

"Grandpa," Mike said, cradling the old man's head, "it's me, Michael."

"Michael?" asked his grandfather, confused. "How?"

"I know—I'm old," Mike said, picking his grandfather up awkwardly in a fireman's carry. He headed toward the Cord, heart pounding, talking all the while, adrenalin-delirious, trying to explain. "I know it doesn't seem to make sense. But listen, you've got to believe me. I'm sending you into the future. You'll die of your wounds and burns, here. I've come from the future to help you. Having you to save saves me, both as the boy I was, and the old man I'll be."

Mike opened the passenger side door of the Cord and propped his grandfather in the seat. Dazedly his grandfather watched him. Taking Grandpa Sakler's keys and money clip, Mike tossed his own wallet onto the seat beside his grandfather.

"All the ID you'll need to pass for me in 1999 is in that wallet and in the car," Mike told him. His grandfather nodded weakly, or perhaps he passed out. Coming around past the back of the car, Mike opened up the driver's side door. Slotting his own key on its key chain into the Cord's ignition, he started the car and turned on the temporal Möbius generator.

The car was equipped with enough computer power for a full memory of his trip here, as per the notes he had written, the notes he would write. Now, though, he would have to change its return destination.

Putting on the neuro-hookups, he fast-reversed the memory guidance record to a bifurcation point two days before he left 1999—to his last trip to the doctor's office near St. Agnes Hospital, for his physical.

This time, the Cord would miss the turn, and not miss the cinderblock retaining wall. He remembered all he could, then imagined the car through wall and total smashup, into the hospital parking lot—right in front of Emergency, where an old-fashioned man with a secret desire to see the future would finally get his wish.

Turning to his unconscious grandfather, he kissed the old man lightly atop his bloodied head.

"I love you, Grandpa."

He stood on the brake, revving the engine while in gear. At the same instant he flipped the Möbius generator's last switch, dropped his foot off the brake, and threw himself from the car, the circlets tearing free of his head.

Around him he felt the chill of death. He was every place and no place at all, every time and no time, and he was falling. . . .

He landed heavily on his hip. Around him a thin mist dissipated as a breeze blew along the street. He propped himself up on his forearm, feeling old and very tired. Something had happened to his memory. His recall of the last several hours was as hazy as a dream or nightmare dissolving on waking.

"Grandpa?" a boy's voice said, coming toward him. The boy peered into his face with evident concern. "Grandpa, is that you? You don't look right. Are you okay?"

"Just tripped and fell down, is all," Mike said, getting slowly to his feet. At last he began remembering something of the role he was supposed to play.

"Grandpa? Where's the gas can?"

For a moment Mike had no idea what the boy was talking about. The boy looked around.

"Oh, here it is," the boy said, running to pick it up from the vacant lot, then coming back, still looking at Mike. "Here. Your yarmulke fell off too."

"I'm a bit discombobalated from the fall, is all," Mike said, trying painfully to smile and joke as he took the yarmulke with its Star of David from the boy's hand. "Thank you. Lead the way back to the car. I'll follow you."

The short walk returned Mike partway to his senses. His chest hurt. He realized that, here in 1939, without medications or surgical techniques yet to be invented, he would not live very long.

So be it. Until he died he would lead a very full life. Here, in this time when the Future was beautiful and distant as Heaven, he would spend his remaining days remembering—and planning.

"Hey Grandpa!" the boy called when he'd reached his grandfather's Cord automobile. "Gimme the keys."

"What?" Mike said. He looked quizzically at the kid as he took the gas can from the boy. The can was still close to half full. Pouring its remaining contents into the fuel tank, he hoped it would be enough to restart the car.

"You know," the boy said. "Lemme drive."

"No, no," Mike said, waving his hand in a light gesture of dismissal. He put the empty gas can in the trunk, then opened the doors to let them both in. He slipped the key into the ignition and looked at the smiling boy sitting on the other side of the front seat.

"You may just be driving this road too, someday," the old man said quietly. "Maybe sooner than you think."

After a time, the engine caught and they drove away.

HABILIS

Driving my used but newly purchased Montjoy LoCat onto the fish hatchery grounds, I can hear the spatter of gravel, despite The Pharaoh and Denile's "Pi-Rat Love" blasting from the vehicle's Airpush speakers. The dusting of new snow on the road doesn't damp down the road-noise much—just makes the gravel slicker, easier for me to drift slideways, a wannabe big fish in the small pond of Planet Dolores.

Ahead, beside the hatchery's ancient Sun Dog pickup, my boss Mark Kemper is standing, a wiry man with wiry hair. The space around his head is wreathed in the steam of his breath hitting cold air and the smoke of the skankweed stick he's huffing. Chill morning notwithstanding, he's wearing the same old two-pocket, lightweight ASGuard jacket he wore offworld during the Knot War. He doesn't like wearing heavy coats, even in cold weather. The pockets bother him. Mark says a man with too many pockets soon finds he has too few hands.

The first time Mark told me the story of his lost and found hand, we were dressed in chest-high waders, sludging out the kettle of Pond 7, removing the thick, foul-smelling organic muck we had pressure-hosed from the bottom of the drained pond into the concrete-lined, boxlike depression at the pond's deepest point—the "kettle." The stinking stuff—a mix of mud, fish dung, debris, and detritus Mark called "crapioca pudding"—was too thick for the pump to suction up, so we were shoveling the mucky dregs of it by hand from the kettle's bottom.

"I should have died when the Bots turned our own AIs against us and drove us from Citadel Moon," Mark said. "My left hand was blown away, but that was among the least of my worries. I lay there, bleeding out from half a dozen wounds, among the dead and dying bodies of my comrades, in a dying spaceship, with the Bots breaking through our last bulkhead."

I power the LoCat's passenger window down. Hearing the courtship ballad of Pi-rat Susie and Pi-rat Sam blaring from my speakers, Mark shakes his head. From beneath a mustache smoke-stained the color of rusted barbed wire, he flashes me a lopsided smile.

"A ground-effector is not the kind of tuna boat I'd have chosen to drive," he says, thumping the Montjoy, "but that song reminds me of something—beyond the fact that it's ripped off from a two hundred year old pop hit."

He elaborates no further, just opens the battered blue Sun Dog's driver-side door and gets in. I kill the LoCat's engine and the music and exit my vehicle.

"I think that's why I'm still alive," Mark said, glancing down at his complex prosthetic hand, then gazing at the space above the message board in the office where we were taking our lunch break. "That *there* is why I'm still looking on the sunlight, instead of eternal night. Despite being captured by the Bots."

His gaze, I saw, had come to rest on the banner above the board. The banner was labeled with the digits 0 through 9. Next to them stood the twenty-six letters of the Roman alphabet, capitals and smalls both, from Aa to Zz. The previous fish-hatchery manager had home-schooled her kids here, and the office retained something of the air of a classroom about it.

"What? The numbers and letters?"

"Not just in themselves. The handedness of them, the chirality. Ontogeny recapitulates phylogeny, recapitulates chirogeny, recapitulates cosmogeny. Or maybe cosmogony. The Bots seem to think it's the key to human difference, however you spell it."

"I don't follow."

"Look at the ten numbers there, and hold out your right hand, palm facing away from you. Sixty per cent of them—1, 2, 3, 4, 7, 9—are right-handed, opening outward in the same direction your thumb and forefinger do from your right hand. Now hold out your left hand, palm away again. Twenty per cent of the numbers—5, and 6—are left-handed. The remaining twenty per cent—8, and 0—express mirror symmetry. You might call those numbers ambidextrous, since they face both directions and neither. See that?"

"I think so."

Opening the creaking door on the truck's passenger side and climbing in, I note the truck cab smells of beer and skankweed again this morning, as it has every morning since Mark and his wife split up, six Doloresian months back.

The tale of the wreck of his marriage is Mark's second most oft-repeated story, and he keeps telling it, though by now he knows I know it by heart: Jinny was the high school sweetheart he married before he caught a NAFAL troopship to the up and out. Quirks of near-lightspeed travel and time dilation being what they are, he aged only the two years of his tour fighting the Bots, while Jinny, planetside, aged the twelve years he was gone in her reference frame. She stayed with him five years after he came home, too. She'd long since grown up and grown away from him, though—even before she left, taking their little girl (the save-the-marriage baby that didn't—) with her.

"Jinny treated every bump in the road as if it were a cliff," Mark says, always coming to the same point in his sifting of the wreckage. "I treated every cliff as if it were a bump in the road. We just couldn't make that work together, in the long run."

"I passed out from blood loss, certain I would die," Mark said, standing knee-deep in kettle muck. He heaved a great shovelful of sludge into the wheelbarrow on the bank beside him. "Yet against all expectation I woke up again. Unsure how much time had passed, with no memory of my Bot captivity, I found myself dumped out into space, in an environment suit that couldn't sustain me for much longer. I wouldn't have bet on my chances just then, but against the odds I was spotted and picked up by a passing cruiser—one of ours, as luck or fate would have it. To this day I don't know whether the *intent* of my abandonment by the Bots was to be lost to my enemies, or to be found by my friends."

As we bump along toward the double sunrise, the Sun Dog's solar-electric motor is inaudible over the squeaking of its bad shocks. We stop at the south end of the hatchery's easternmost pond—the coldest, Pond 1. Both it and Pond 2 have spotted graithlings in them. The other twenty ponds grow a few goldengills, but mostly they're full of slant-head minnows. All three species are sacrifice fish for the EnviroLab on the hill and its LC_{50} tests, which designate a heavy metal, a prionoid seed protein, or other water pollutant "toxic" when a given concentration of the substance proves lethal (within four hours) to fifty per cent or more of the fish in the test population. Such tests were long ago banned as inhumane on Old Earth, but they're expedient on a frontier world like ours.

*

"Now look at the letters," Mark said, pointing at the banner at the back of the office. "Handedness is a bit more complicated for letters than for numbers. Hold out your left hand in front of you again, palm away, so you're looking at the back of the hand. Thumb spread away from the rest of the hand at about a ninety degree angle. See which direction the thumb points? Capitals B, C, D, E, F, G, K, L, P, R, arguably S—11 out of 26, or 42.3 per cent of the alphabet—are left handed, while only capitals J and Z—2 out of 26, or 7.7 per cent of the alphabet—are right handed. A, H, I, M, N, O, Q, T, U, V, W, X, Y—13 out of 26, or 50 per cent—are ambidextrous, although I suppose you could argue Q trends left, and N is some kind of mirror-inverted. Got it?"

"Okay . . ." I said, continuing to stare hard at the banner with its basic numbers and letters on the office wall, trying to puzzle through what he was saying.

"Good. Now, of the small letters, *b, c, e, f, h, k, p, r, s*—9 out of 26, or 34.6 per cent—are left handed, while *a, d, g, j, q, y, z*—7 out of 26, or 27 per cent—are right handed. The remaining small letters—10 out of 26, or 38 per cent—are best described as ambidextrous."

I shook my head and whistled softly.

"You've obviously thought and calculated about this a lot, Mark—and those are interesting statistics—but, well, *so what?*"

"See, the Bots have never figured out what allows the Raveleras to weave and unweave spacetime around them," Mark said, moving the wheelbarrow for me to shovel muck into it, "because it's not something you can do by figuring. Not calculable. But that didn't stop my captors from giving me this hand."

"Any idea why they did that?"

"Many ideas—even if I don't remember when this alien hand joined the rest of my body. Maybe I've kept learning so much about all this, beyond my debriefing, because—despite the memory wipe—some faint trace of my time in Bot custody still persists in my head unconsciously, still keeps prodding me to try to puzzle it out. I don't know for certain, though. I can't explain, for instance, why I absolutely will not allow my faceless 'friends' in our merc-corp government to remove this hand from my body—for their 'research.' It's not just because it's interwoven into me deep enough I might die in the process of that removal. I just refuse. That's annoyed the powers-that-be enough that I'm lucky even to have this shit-shoveling fish hatchery job."

Mark shook his head and exhaled.

"So they think me a spy, and spy on me. Maybe they're not the only ones, either. Maybe Hivist turncoats are reporting on me back to their Bot masters, too. Who knows? Maybe you too, without even knowing it, might be some kind of android, designed by the Bots to be indistinguishable from a human being. And you're recording all this for some unseen audience."

He gave me a sly, sideways look. We laughed, but even in my own ears the laughter sounded forced.

At the northern end of each pond stands a spring box. We check the boxes all summer long for any cruncher turtles that, blundering onto the gapped planking atop the sunken concrete boxes and falling between the planks, might have gotten trapped down in the boxes themselves. This morning I doubt we'll find any of those nasty-tempered little dinosaurs. They don't move as much from pond to pond once the weather gets cool.

"'So what?'" Mark laughed and took a bite of his luncherito. "That's what I thought when I was debriefed, too. It took me a while to see it. But try to think like a curious kid for a minute. Notice that the right-handed forms are the most common forms for numbers, but the least common form for letters—both capitals and smalls."

"I see that, Mark. So maybe the differences in spatial orientation of numbers and letters are *statistically* significant. But are they *truly* significant? I don't see the context."

"Neither did I, at first. Maybe that's because the context is so *big*."

"In what way?"

He stared off into a space I couldn't see into.

"People have probably realized that the brain is in two major parts—that it's in two chambers, or *bicameral*—for as long as they've been looking at the brains of their usually deceased fellow humans. A couple hundred years ago researchers started doing split-brain work with living epilepsy patients. They had the connections between the right and left hemispheres of their brains cut, in order to reduce their seizure symptoms. That research led to work on hemispheric dominance, cerebral lateralization—on the 'handedness' of human minds, if you like."

"And numbers and letters say something about that?" I asked, gesturing at the banner with my sandwich.

We decide not to check the spring boxes for wayward turtles after all, and focus instead on looking for the bank pi-rats. It's cold, but the ponds haven't iced over yet. We walk toward the north end of the first pond, each of us pacing a shoreline. As we go along we check the long-spring leghold traps we've staked into the bank and set for the 'rats, near their burrow entrances. We look for traps whose chains have been run out from the bank, to the deeper water, indicating that a foot-clamped ratty, big as a mid-size dog, has most likely dragged the device and itself into that depth, and drowned.

*

Together Mark and I pushed the wheelbarrow up the bank, toward the lowered bed of the Sun Dog. It took everything we had to lever up the handles on the barrow and tilt its load of sludge into the truck.

"This hand is a souvenir," Mark said, as we took a breather. "A scar I can't hide but don't want to lose. A reminder of the Bots' investigation into the interweaving of hands and minds—a crude experiment, for all the magnificent crafting that went into this. No prosthetic that humans have developed can match the nano-mechanics of it. I think that's one reason why the military brass still want this hand—so they can reverse-engineer it. I've let them examine its workings, again and again, but I draw the line at letting them try to sever it from my body. They'd love to disconnect it from me the same way the Bots connected it to me: without my permission."

"Right," Mark said, ignoring my sandwich. "For some time now, researchers have wondered if the right-handedness of the majority of numbers might indicate that the left side of the brain, which controls the right side of the body, dominates most in the production of numbers. At the same time, the left side of the brain also seems to be *least* powerful in influencing the production of letters. When you include the smalls, 'ambidextrous' edges left-handed out—just barely—as the most common letter-form of all, even if you include capital Q among the block of letters you might call left-handed and right-brained. Makes you wonder if hemispheric *non*-dominance—with a strong tilt to the left hand and right brain, admittedly—is in fact the most 'dominant' factor in letter production."

"That makes both sides of my brain hurt," I said, laughing, "although I guess that makes some sense. What about spatial orientations in numbering systems other than the Arabic, though?"

"In Mayan numerals, for instance? Or how spatial orientation of letters manifests in languages read not left to right, but right to left—in Hebrew, say? Or what about other systems in which the numbers are also letters and vice versa—not only Hebrew but the Roman system too, whose numerals were not part of a separate numeric system but derived from the Latin alphabet?"

"Let me guess: You've already thought about this."

Mark nodded and leaned toward me.

"I learned in my debriefing that *all* of those questions had already been asked. Neuroscientists, cognitive psychologists, linguistic anthropologists—all of them have been quietly involved in investigating whether or not the spatial orientations of letters and numbers might be evidence of patterns in the 'cultural unconscious' that mirror the evolutionary history of the human brain."

"And they found . . . ?"

"The same patterns, with some minor variations, persist across all human cultures."

That made me pause.

Mark claims his grandfather knew the First Expedition biologist who named these freshwater critters we trap "pi-rats." Although better known for naming our world Dolores after his wife, Hector Quinones was not only the mission's chief population ecologist but also a math geek of the first water—and tagged the bank-burrowers with their odd but appropriate name, given the critters' packrat thievery, giant muskrat looks, and their disproportionately long (seemingly endless) tails.

"As hatchery manager," Mark says when we get to the north end of Pond 1, "I suppose I should reiterate that, officially, we're thinning the pi-rat population because their burrows damage the levees between the ponds. It also just so happens that pi-rat fur is prime now, and bringing a good price."

*

"My hand is like those other exquisitely complex mechanisms the prionoids the Bots have been bombing our worlds with," he said, grabbing the wheelbarrow's handles. "Those D-amino transmission particles meant to morph our brain chemistry, confuse our myriad complications and defeat that thing in human consciousness that the Bots can't figure out. I guess they figured you don't have to understand something to destroy it. But all the Bots' efforts have resulted only in poisonings, and madness, and the necessity of running those LC tests on our air and water."

He lifted up on the handles.

"The poop is in the pudding. Back to it."

I followed him down the bank, and stepped with him into the kettle once more.

"But even supposing, for the moment, we accept that the pattern-thing works, more or less, for every culture—what does it have to do with the Bots allowing you to go on living?"

"Ah. Follow the logic. What started the Knot War?"

I suppose I gave him an odd look, but then shrugged and answered.

"Surprise attacks by Bot forces. Coordinated lightning raids."

"And the goal of those coordinated attacks?"

"To capture the central junction point of universe-lines known as the Big Knot, and to abduct Elena Zametis—greatest of Raveleras in the greatest line of Raveleras—and carry her to the Knot."

"Yes. Which, with aid from singularitarian Hivists, from turncoat human-sphere AIs, and from the strangely willing Elena, the Bots managed to do. So far, so good—but what made it worth going to war over?"

I was beginning to wonder where this belaboring of the obvious might be headed, but I decided to let it roll out a bit longer without comment.

*

Heading south, back toward the pickup, each of us walks the bank opposite the one he walked on the way out, hoping to catch sight of anything the other might have overlooked. At the south end we climb into the Sun Dog, move the pickup to the next pond, and park again there. Standard operating procedure: walk the levees, check the traps, move and repark the truck, pond after pond.

"I know what you're thinking," he said as we started shoveling the thick muck again. "You think, 'All this war stuff is just a mask for Mark's obsession with his lost hand and lost wife—Napoleon Blownapart mourning the loss of his Josephine. This stuff with numbers and letters, handedness and sides of the brain—hand waving at best, delusion at worst. All just seeing patterns that aren't really there.' And the paranoia about spies and spying! 'Application for membership in the Tinfoil Hat Crew—approved!' as they used to say. But you'd be wrong to believe any of those explanations is sufficient."

"Because all the leaders of the worlds of human space had already sworn to protect the Raveleras," I said, slowly chewing my sandwich.

"Yes. Why?"

"Isn't it obvious? Everybody knows the answer to that."

Mark smiled inscrutably, looked around the office, and nodded.

"Please, bear with me. Again: why?"

"Their ability to travel clewed space, of course. It's what has allowed human crews to pilot starships at velocities within a hair of the speed of light. Their ability to weave and unweave space-time about themselves. To witch the way the subspace web is woven, the way other women once witched the courses of water underground."

"Which means?"

"Which means that humans have been able to spread out beyond Earth—to settle newer home worlds on Earth-like extrasolar planets."

"Right, but that's not what I was asking. 'To weave and unweave space-time'—what does that mean? How is it done?"

I puzzled over that one a minute, before speaking.

"I gather that's kind of a trade secret among the Raveleras. The scientists theorize about 'q-net'—the quantum something or other."

"Quantum Nonlocally Entangled Tunneling. The webwork of evanescent wormhole tunnels, latent in the fabric of the cosmos."

"If you say so. But the Raveleras talk about how the universe is 'holographically conscious.' That, through the altered state of consciousness peculiar to them, they are able to locally alter the structure of space-time. To 'weave a Way out of No Way,' along that universe-infrastructure of threads or lines or tunnels they call clewed space."

"And this 'infrastructure'—what's its origin?"

Whenever we find traps that have been run out on their chains we pull them back onto the bank. Using his gripper-hook prosthetic left hand with the dexterity of a surgeon gaping an incision, Mark has shown me how to prize open like steel clamshells the sprung traps and remove from those metal jaws the beached pi-rats, slick and red-brown and stiff.

"A poet of Old Earth once said that love does not alter when it alteration finds nor bend with the remover to remove. I don't know if it's really true for love —divorce'll sure make you question *that*—but it's definitely not true for the universe. Everything the

Raveleras do, with the help of their 'entheogens,' is proof that the universe alters when it alteration finds."

Under Mark's questioning—especially in the ghost of a classroom still haunting the office—I felt like a truant student facing an oral examination every query of which was somehow a trick question.

"Presumably the substructure is a natural feature of spacetime," I explained, "although there are those who think it's an artifact created by, well, someone."

Mark gave his inscrutable inquisitor's nod-and-smile again.

"What would you say has been the greatest assurance of the human future, by your lights—and what is the greatest ongoing threat to that future?"

I had to think about that one for a moment.

"I'd say control of clewed space has been the greatest assurance, and the Bots the greatest ongoing threat." A thought suddenly occurred to me—a delayed answer to a much earlier question. "That's why, after the Bot surprise attacks, the leaders of all the worlds of human space had no choice but to raise a thousand-starship armada and go to war at the Knot."

"Very good. But what exactly *are* the Bots—and why did they launch those attacks?"

From Mark I've learned how to reset the traps, pushing the jaws fully open and dogging the trip-pan in each, priming the jaws to snap shut once the pan is depressed by the next creature's paw. For all I've learned, though, I still can't match Mark for speed or skill or experience with the traps. That may explain why, of the five pi-rats we've piled in the bed of the truck by the time we reach Pond 20, four are his work.

*

"The Knot was our Troy," Mark said, shoveling, "and Zametis our Helen. I was there for her interrogation. She *allowed* the Bots to abduct her."

"Why's that?" I asked, splashing a load into the wheelbarrow.

"Because, despite her webwork witching skills, or maybe because of them, she thought the relatively easy and rapid spread of humanity throughout space by such swift, Raveleran means put off, yet again, our species' having to face the moral hazard of our shortsightedness, when it comes to fouling our own nest. If we can always fly away to yet more new worlds, we never have to live as if the world in which we live has irreplaceable value in its own right."

"The Bots are expansionist machine intelligences," I answered, around a mouthful of my lunch. "There's a lot of debate about their origin. Most of the experts claim the origin of the Bots can be found in a human space probe that was altered as a result of an encounter with a distant machine civilization—and the transformed probe was the seed for all the myriad Bots that came after. What is certain, though, is that their spaceships are limited to significantly lower speeds than ours, due to the Bots' inability to open spacetime and weave a Way out of No Way thing, the way the human Raveleras can."

"And that's why they wanted the Knot and Elena, then?"

"Yeah. But I still don't see what it has to do with this handedness you were going on about."

At Pond 20, Mark finds something odd enough that he takes his long-ashed skankstick from his mouth and waves me over. He holds up the almost-empty trap, to show me.

"Back on Earth, they'd consider finding *these* in our traps more proof of our 'frontier barbarism'—but this ain't sophisticated Earth, kiddo. One gnawed-off paw is rare enough anyway, but look at this. Two paws, each gnawed off above the wrist."

I nod.

"And they're both left front paws. From two different animals, caught in the same trap at the same time. Hard to tell, but from the smaller size I bet this one's from a female, and the larger one is from a male."

"Maybe the Bots hooked up this prosthetic not just to see how hand and mind cross-reference each other," Mark said, watching me shovel, "but also to see if a little brute-force cybernetics might jumpstart the development of what the Raveleras murmur about. The appearance in time of a 'Ravelero' or 'Ravelator,' a male human not only capable of making and unmaking clewed space around himself, but a true tripmaster, not bound by the speed of light."

Mark pointed to the office ceiling to punctuate his point.

"Because handedness is seen everywhere! From the microcosm to the macrocosm, the quantum scale to the cosmological scale, chirality links it all. The universe is not the same in every direction. It violates parity and funhouses mirror symmetry at every scale. The whole show was born spinning about a preferred axis from the very beginning, and that angular momentum, still conserved after fourteen billion years, shows up in an excess of left-handed, counterclockwise rotating spiral galaxies. The majority of spiral galaxies are lefty-loosey, not righty-tighty!"

"Whew! Give me some of that skankweed you've been smoking! The whole universe rotating like an ice-skater—that makes my head spin!"

"As well it should, young man. And I'm not thinking *this* because I'm smoking *that*, by the way. The spin is all the way down to the smallest scales—not just galaxies and skaters, but protons and quarks as well. Nuclear beta decays, for instance, violate parity in favor of the left hand, too. The versions of molecules like amino acids found in living things—the biologically relevant versions—are overwhelmingly left-handed on Earth and every Earthlike planet we've visited, even though amino acids produced by *inorganic* reactions are equally split between right-handed and left-handed versions! Even the idea that the left-handed molecular dominance, found throughout life on Earth, might itself have been extraterrestrial in origin has been floating around a long time. At least since left-favoring enantiomer imbalances were found on the Murchison meteorite—long predating interstellar travel to extra-solar worlds."

"But why should the left hand be favored?"

Mark springs open the trap. He shakes into his cupped right hand the two paws—red-furred hands with disproportionately long fingers and nails.

"I don't know much about pi-rat love," he says, flashing me his lopsided grin again, "but this tells me all I need to know about pi-rat divorce."

We laugh. He draws back his hand to hurl the paws into the pond, then stops. He shoves the two small hands into a pocket of his workpants instead.

"Not for naught did we Nauts of the Knot," Mark sang as he shoveled, *"Teach the Bots how dearly bought was everything they stole!"*

He paused to wipe his forehead.

"You have no idea how many times I sang that song with men and women of the Astronaut Service Guard—now dead, so many of them."

*

"One great mystery, lots of great theories!" he said, working his way through his luncherito. "Some say the lopsided favoring of left-handed biological molecules—what the experts call biological homochirality—is the result of slightly different half-lives of biologically relevant molecules, stemming from that beta decay connection. Others say it's from the preferential destruction of right-handed amino acids by left-circling polarized light, blasting out of rapidly rotating stars in primordial galaxies. Or Mie scattering on aligned interstellar dust particles, triggering the formation of optical isomers in space. From all or whichever of the above, it's clear the bias in favor of the left hand is not just a local phenomenon."

"You called it a bias in *favor* of left-handedness—yet wasn't there bias *against* left-handedness, in almost all the cultures of Old Earth?"

Mark's face lit up. He had obviously thought about that, too.

Finding no pi-rats around Ponds 21 and 22—the westernmost, warmest, and smallest ponds in the hatchery—we return to the truck's cab. From under the driver's side of the front seat Mark pulls out a beer for himself and one for me, popping the stopper off each brewpak.

"To the silly songs of human freedom," he says, thudding his brewpak against mine in toast, "and what it costs to sing them."

He motioned me over to help him with the wheelbarrow.

"Alien hand notwithstanding, I had returned to duty by the time of the final battle for the Knot. I swear, something about my new situation allowed me, and my troops around me, to be everywhere at once in that battle. It was as if something had changed the hand in the mirror of my mind. Suddenly I could funhouse a universe of mirrors, alter the fundamental info-physical coding of the cosmos in my own small, unexpected—and uncontrolled—way. Maybe what the Bots had done to me had done the trick. If so, it was a trick, in my hands and mind, that I could now do to them."

Together we pushed the sludge-laden wheelbarrow up the bank.

"Bias? Oh yes!" he said, distractedly watching me eat the last of my sandwich. "The cultural slight of the left hand goes back to at least the ancient Romans, including the fact that the Latin word for 'the left side' was *sinister*, meaning 'unlucky,' among other things, and for 'the right side' was *dexter*, meaning 'skillful,' among other things. But you don't have to engage in much sleight of hand—'sleight' from Old Norse meaning 'sly,' later expressing 'deftness' and 'dexterity' and 'clever tricks'—to see that the sinister hand of letters is the dexter hand of numbers, the sinister hand of numbers is the dexter hand of letters. We're a tricksy species, lucky in that we've been so unlucky, and unlucky in that we've been so lucky."

We drink. Mark retrieves the pi-rat paws from his pants pocket. Taking a length of baling wire from the storage compartment under the dashboard, he makes a loop from the wire. He twists the ends so as to bind the paws together at the wrists, then hangs the whole assemblage from the mirror in the Sun Dog's cab.

"That's what the Bots, even in defeat, are still trying to figure out," he said as, together, we tipped the sludge-barrow's contents into the truck's bed. Finished with sludging Pond 7's kettle at last, we leaned against the truck as he smoked and finished his thought. "How the twisted mirror of our DNA has allowed human consciousness to be both chiral and chiasmatic, left handed-right brained, right handed-left brained. How that X-ing makes possible the crossing over through all scales, until all scales fall from our eyes and we see that just as the universe is 'as above, so below,' so too the infinite is closer than it appears in mirrors placed face to face. There's no need to be forgiven for Eden and the 'fall' into knowledge. No need to be acquitted of crimes never committed."

"Tricksy?" I asked, crumpling up my lunch wrapper. "Lucky that we've been so unlucky? I don't get that."

"We've probably been *habilis* as long as we've been *Homo*—handy as long as we've been human. But 150,000 to 200,000 years ago, a chance mutation—some of that same old lucky unlucky—produced a dextral allele involving the FOXP2 gene and the transcription factor POU3F2. The changes arising from that mutation not only affected synaptic plasticity and dendritic trees but also strongly biased handedness in favor of the right hand and control of speech in favor of the left cerebral hemisphere. That chance mutation interacted with an already present alternative allele that was 'chance' in another sense—directionally neutral, mirror image, ambidextrous, coin-flip, fifty-fifty."

"And that did—what?"

"The heterozygous form—neutral plus dextral—was evolutionarily advantageous: it improved information storage for learning and storing memories, and consolidated the control of both manual and verbal capabilities in the same hemisphere of the brain. Together with later changes in the regulation of FOXP2 expression, it resulted in a shift from a predominantly gestural to a predominantly vocal form of language—a major speciation event."

*

Struck by a sudden idea, Mark laughs and slaps his thigh.

"Of course!" he says, starting the truck. "Two wrongs don't make a right, but three lefts do!"

Gravel crunches beneath the wheels. The paired pi-rat hands, clasped together in inverted and disproportioned prayer, pendulum slowly from the rearview mirror as we bump along. Around us, like a dream the night forgot, the thin snow disappears in the morning suns.

"The intriguing thing about those changes affecting synaptic plasticity, however," Mark said, finishing his luncherito at last, crumpling its wrapper into a ball, and tossing that ball into the recycling can, "was that they involved right-handed, dextral forms of amino acids—even though our cells make only left-handed forms."

"So how does that happen? Doesn't sound evolutionarily efficient, to me."

"Brain cells exploit a trick by making an enzyme that flips the handedness of an amino acid—serine, say—from left-handed L to right-handed D forms, thereby *breaking the mirror-symmetry breaking* even of biological homochirality itself. Like breaking the mirror twice, or three times—for better luck, next time. It's the sort of trick we're always benefitting from. Never more so than when our peculiarly human form of consciousness arose from the breakdown of the bicamerally specialized mind—when the two 'sides' of the mind began to communicate, each by borrowing from the mirror's other side."

"But it's a delicate balancing act," I suggested, as neutrally as I could, "this contrariwise pattern-finding?"

"Yes. Very. I know what you're thinking again: that's why so many of us go mad, making impossible connections between implausible dots. And it's true that too little D-serine in the brain is a cause of schizophrenia, but too much exacerbates stroke damage. Lefty loosey, righty tighty. But *I* know the difference."

*

The sludge-filled Sun Dog moved low and slow as Mark drove it to the hatchery's compost dump—or ORGANIC NUTRIENT RECYCLING SITE, as the official sign read.

"Here we are—the Onerous ONRS. Time for you to exit."

I got out. He backed the pickup against the biggest pile. I unlatched the tailgate and got out of the way. With a nod Mark floored the accelerator on the pickup. A stinking tsunami of sludge sloshed toward the back of the bed, slammed open the tailgate and flowed out in a great vomitive heave, emptying the truck bed. Mark got out and leaned against the truck.

"A neat trick," I said, "and a dirty one, too!"

"I've picked up a few handy tricks on this rock," he said with a shrug. "A few off it, too."

"Such as?"

"Oh, things I learned from my time at the Knot, fighting the Bots. Like the idea that 'infinite' does not mean the same as 'all possible.' The set of even numbers is infinite, but also inherently incomplete: it contains no odd numbers, excluding all elements of that other infinite set. Odd and even, left and right, infinite yet incomplete. So humility is due."

I laughed.

"Anything *not* involving numbers?"

"Just that—as much as being human allows you to—strive to be free, strive to be true. That's the only wisdom I can offer you. Besides, it's about time for lunch."

As we drive, it occurs to me that maybe Mark's in his right mind and all's left with the world. If so, I don't think he will be here tomorrow. I don't know how I know—I just know. Perhaps he will become the long-awaited Ravelator, stepping through the curtain of space-time, traversing dark light-years in an instant, taking a bow in the starry footlights on the other side of forever. Maybe he will kill himself. Maybe they amount to the same thing. Or not. In any case, this report to you, my unseen audience, ends here, ends now.

THE GIRLS WITH KALEIDOSCOPE EYES

The school buses had just started unloading by the time Agent Onilongo arrived and pulled into a Visitor space. Fingering the Möbius softclock pendant on the necklace Philip Marston had given her, she watched as the girls of the Special Class walked toward their temporary replacement classroom.

She picked up the extended magazines from the seat beside her, took her recovered twin Glock pistols out of the glove compartment, slipped the magazines into the pistols and the pistols into her a holster at the small of her back. She donned her long jacket, opened the car door, and stood up. Looking into the sunshine of an early morning in late September she saw a flock of birds shape-shifting like a cloud of animate smoke. They were still distant, but growing closer by the minute. Watching and waiting, she thought back over all that had happened to lead her to this moment.

Special Agent Ciera Onilongo didn't quite know why she had been ordered to Bluffdale, Utah from the FBI office in Sacramento, California. Her usual work within the Bureau was cybersecurity—particularly cyberterrorism and cyberespionage, in the context of foreign and domestic events linked to state and corporate actors. The case of Philip Waypoint Marston was not the sort of thing Onilongo was accustomed to working on.

A high school biology teacher in his late fifties, Marston stood accused of the attempted mass killing of sixteen students. Nothing in his actions suggested he had been specifically motivated by politics or corporate espionage. Judging by the all-too-brief briefing Onilongo had received before coming to Bluffdale, there also appeared to be very little that was "digital" or "cyber" about the Marston case. Given the type of crime, even Marston's *age* harkened back to the pre-digital era, when mass murderers had most often been men of middle years who had endured decades of frustration before "going off." Since the advent of social media, though, the average age of mass murderers had been falling sharply, year by year.

About all Onilongo could say in favor of her taking the case was that at least she had been brought in on it early. She had received her perfunctory briefing about the same time the first reports of "The Terror Teacher" began breaking in the media. Given the choice, Ciera Onilongo preferred to approach her cases in an interview-driven fashion, a circuitous and somewhat slow approach but also one which, more often than not, helped her get a more in-depth sense of what had actually occurred, especially when it came to the question of motive.

On her flight to Salt Lake, Onilongo had pored over the slim briefing materials she *had* received. Initially she thought Marston's attempted mass murder might be some sort of hate crime. He didn't seem prompted by race, though—all of Marston's would-be victims were as lily-white as Marston himself. Perhaps he was motivated by some sex-and-power hate kink, given that all the intended victims were young and female. Or perhaps the trigger had been something religious: all of the students involved came from families who were members of a polygamous Mormon splinter movement headquartered in Bluffdale, the Apostolic United Brethren, who referred to themselves variously as the Work, or the Group, or the Priesthood.

Onilongo discovered that, though Marston was now what the locals called "Jack Mormon," he had himself been raised AUB, and had seemed to harbor no ill will toward the Group. That just didn't fit the profile of someone whose actions had been motivated by sectarian hate. Nothing in his record indicated any particular tendencies toward pedophilia or violent misogyny, either. Marston and his wife Melinda, although they had no children themselves, had been Aunt Mel and Uncle Phil to the kids in their community. They had also, by all accounts, been happily married for thirty years, until Melinda passed away from ovarian cancer, five years back.

Once on the ground in Bluffdale—on the ride into town from the airport, in fact—Ciera came across what *might* be a possible digital connection for the case, however remote. What her initial briefers had neglected to remind her about was the other source of notoriety (beyond the AUB) that this small white-bread town twenty miles south of Salt Lake City might lay claim to: namely, that Bluffdale was also the home dirt of the National Security Agency's Utah Data Center, or the "Intelligence Community Comprehensive National Cybersecurity Initiative Data Center," as it was officially known.

Onilongo thought it strange that no one who briefed her had bothered to mention this particular black hole at the center of the local galaxy. Had they presumed she would already know? She didn't want to look stupid, but still, her first afternoon in town, she raised the issue with the Bureau's local field officers. Agents Robinson and Gediman were an undistinguished and almost indistinguishable pair of time-serving functionaries she couldn't help but think of as "Rosencrantz and Guildenstern." The two field boys, in response to her query, admitted that Marston's wife Melinda had worked at the Center in a low-level position almost up to the day of her death. But Phil Marston himself (they claimed) had no known current connections to the NSA's global/local cloud and code-cracking operations.

That struck Onilongo as both fortunate and unfortunate. She would have appreciated a solid cyber-linked lead for helping her understand why she had been given this case. Yet she also knew from experience how persnickety No Such Agency could be when it came to Never Saying Anything about their projects and person-

nel. If Ciera was going to have to talk to someone at the Center—
and she thought she probably would—it might be best to start the
ball rolling that way, ASAP, via inquiries and requests.

That evening, once she had settled into the small apartment she
alternately called her "crash pad" and her "uchi," she phoned her
husband Mark and eight-year-old daughter Geneva in California.
She brought them up to speed on her situation—at least as much as
federal law would allow. Shortly thereafter, she started contacting
her higher-ups about the possibility of meeting with NSA staff at
the Center, in the event such a meeting became necessary.

From boredom, curiosity, and homesickness, she began poking
around on the public web to see what she could learn about the
respective roles and goals of the Data Center and the Group. She
hoped there might be some overlap. Popping a temp implant into
her head plug, she had hoped she could start browsing immediately. First, though, she had to push past a barrage of neural implant
anti-hack ads—"Are you and yours neurosecure? Make sure, with
NeuroLockPure!" Gradually she realized the ads, so persistent and
dense, were for a company headquartered here in town—and were
probably more inconvenient than most of the potential hacks the
company's product was intended to counter.

The public net revealed little connection between the Group
and the NSA, other than the fact that a not-inconsiderable number of members in the former were also employees of the latter.
Onilongo's level of access to classified material in the governmental
deep net didn't get her much further than that, although she *did*
learn that the AUB now had three times as many members and
four times as many multiple-marriage households as it had half
a century earlier. In terms of the percentage of Bluffdale's land it
owned and Bluffdale's population it employed, the Group was second only to what the locals called "the spy center."

The Group and the Utah Data Center were clearly the two

biggest things going between the Oquirrh Mountains and the Wasatch Range, but information about the Center was, if anything, more spotty and arid than background for the Group. She plowed through stats about the Center's data hall—square footages, maps featuring the locations of tech and admin support facilities, specs on the visitor control unit, the sixty-five megawatt power substation, backup generators, pumps and chillers, tanks for water and fuel. All the usual non-descript descriptions of restricted access buildings—and the even more non-descript descriptions of what went on inside them.

Digging deeper into the notes on the Center, she learned it was a "million square foot archive for handling yottabytes of information pumped through the Pentagon's Global Information Grid." Behind the vagaries of the publicly disclosed information, however, Onilongo began to see the outlines of what the Center not so apparently was: the nearly invisible spider at the center of a nearly invisible ghost web of aerospace data facilities and geostationary satellites. Of secret corporate and government communications. Of domestic and overseas listening posts. Of specialist intercept and analysis facilities in Hawaii, Georgia, and Texas. Of research facilities in Oak Ridge, and headquarters in Fort Meade, where No Such Agency built supercomputers and advanced artificial intelligence systems destined for the bleeding edge of cryptanalysis. All of it seemingly dedicated to ensuring that no password-protected data or anything supposed to be "private" would by any means remain so, should that private data conceivably pose even the slightest threat to national security.

The strangest documents Onilongo stumbled upon, however, were a particular subset of blog posts, thread comments, and letters to the editor in the *Salt Lake Tribune* and the *Valley Journal*. Judging by the dates of all of them, the writer first posted his ideas through telegraphically brief online missives warning about the dangers posed by strong AI, by cross-domain optimization power, by arbitrarily super-intelligent machines. The somewhat longer newspaper letters noted that the Utah Data Center's vast accumulation of human cultural information made the optimization engines employed there more valuable for national security purposes, undeniably—but also increased the danger those optimization engines posed for a "singularitarian-style global AI takeover."

That last bit sounded rather tinfoil-hat to Onilongo, but also quite intriguing. More intriguing still was the authorship of all that material, once she figured it out. The blog posts and thread comments had been written under the internet handle "Mars Town and Gown," but after she had read two of the newspaper letters Onilongo recognized the name of the writer—P. W. Marston—and from that decoded the name behind the blogger's handle.

She rubbed her aching neck and eyes and ended her research for the day. Despite her exhaustion, as she got into bed Onilongo couldn't help but continue to puzzle herself about why a high school biology teacher should be so concerned—or even so knowledgeable—about artificial intelligence. She vowed to learn more about the man's background before she interviewed Marston the next afternoon.

As Special Agent Onilongo dressed for her day in business jacket, slacks, and dress running shoes, she thought again about Marston. Investigating public and private records further, she saw that his career trajectory seemed to have been on a downward path for a very long time.

He had started off well enough. After a stint in the Navy working for something called the Naval Security Group, he topped out as a lieutenant commander. He returned to school, where he earned a PhD in biological anthropology. An appointment to a tenure-track position followed, straight out of graduate school.

After several years in this first academic placement, however, he had been denied tenure at the university. He had then moved on to another college in the role of adjunct faculty. When that position ended, he followed up with one last career move—a return to his hometown of Bluffdale, and to teaching at Jordan Summit Charter High School. Onilongo saw too that, despite his having come down in the world of academia, he had kept up his memberships in all the loftiest professional and educational societies, as well as in local stargazing, bird-watching, and rod and gun clubs.

Onilongo was unable to determine from the available records why the first university had denied tenure to Philip Marston. All she was able to find was his published comment suggesting that "addressing economic inequality ought to be a higher priority than merely celebrating diversity." Although Onilongo didn't fully agree with that analysis—inequality and ethnicity, for instance, were often intertwined—such a political stance hardly rose to the level of hate speech. Still, Onilongo *had* heard that university tenure committees could be oddly sensitive about such things.

The second university's reasons for terminating Marston's adjunct faculty appointment were much easier to figure out, once Onilongo found Marston's "Ghost of Commencement Future" blog post—and another post discussing the subsequent end of his adjunct faculty career (both posts now over a dozen years old). Onilongo found them noteworthy enough that she launched into a second reading of the "Commencement Future" piece, with distinct interest:

Congratulations to my students graduating with this year's class. Your graduation present is this live feed from your now-virtual teacher.

Because I am old school, I am sending this non-commencement address via tweets, though I know most of you are twitterpated by newer tech.

This year I've retired my academic regalia. Given Academia's demise, I would now have to wear my cap and gown with a Scream skull mask.

Together apart, those of us listening now hear the opening strains of the second movement of Elgar's "Pomp and Circumstance" March No. 1.

If we're honest with ourselves, we should ponder the following lyrics whenever we hear this ponderous tune, but especially on this day:

"Everyone starts with a B . . . / And Cs get degrees. / No need to learn skills or con—tent; / Just smile a lot, and pretend! Dum-dum-dum."

How did we come to this pass? Our AI commencement speaker and arguably human university administrators won't tell you. But I will.

Ciera Onilongo stopped and shook her head. Marston's adjunct faculty contract was "not renewed"—big surprise. Down he fell, to another lower plateau on the descending spiral. Yet, through it all, his wife Melinda had amazingly stuck with him—for thirty-plus years. Agent Onilongo marveled at such patience, and persistence.

Glancing at her watch, Ciera saw she would have to hurry to arrive on time for the interview she had scheduled with Marston. Recovering from burns suffered during the mass-murder attempt, the former teacher lay abed in a secured ward of the county hospital. *He* was not going anywhere, but Onilongo still liked to be on time. As she made her way to her silver government car, she popped in one of her ear buds, and commanded her text-reader to continue Marston's "Commencement Future" in "aloud" mode. She ordered it to fast-forward until she reached the part she wanted to hear again.

. . . Everyone had to go! More students, spending more money, for more degrees worth less and less. Diploma assets purchased by long-term debt.

Colleges with no business being in the education "business." Digital diploma mills. Massive open online con-job academies. W.E. Scam U.

The bubble burst. Trillions in loan debt. Students walked at graduation, walked away from debt. The latter more often than the former.

Yet that was not the whole story of American higher education's collapse—a story full of truths so unpopular no one wanted to hear them. . . .

Onilongo switched off the text reader as she got into her car. Driving out of the parking structure and onto the highway past another NeuroLockPure billboard, she shook her head again. Marston's "Commencement Future" predictions, in the blog post, had been pretty much on target. The post itself had garnered enough attention to get him a contract with a small publisher for a collection of essays, *Travels in Transelitium: Ritual Humiliations of the Digital Age*, and some small fame as a satirist—but at the cost of his job.

Still, from everything she had seen on him in the public and private web, Marston had not regretted his screed. He had eagerly unsheathed the naked sword of his truth for all to see, and then proceeded to fall upon it. Again and again.

Once into the flow of traffic, Onilongo set the car's driving mode to semi-autonomous and commanded the text reader back on, fast forwarding once more.

. . . *Pass/Fail and checkmark grading. Contract grading, based on assignment quantity rather than quality. Teaching to the tech.*

The decades-long rollout of a public higher education system staffed mostly by adjunct faculty. Stress of a CEO, pay of a burger-flipper.

The growing emphasis, from college administrators and state politicians, on lower admissions standards, higher and faster graduation rates.

High academic standards in the classroom growing ever more likely to get teachers punished rather than rewarded.

(Academic standards? Insensitivity to the endless diversities of our students! To the concierge service demanded by our paying customers!) . . .

Commanding off the reader again as she took the wheel and the turn leading to the hospital, Onilongo realized such sentiments as that last one must have endeared Marston to neither the Left nor the Right, in that order. Brave words, in their way, but foolish. The man had not earned his doctorate from Self-Created Adversity University, Ciera thought, but he might as well have.

On the hospital floor where Marston was recuperating, Agent Onilongo presented her credentials to the security personnel at the nurses' station, and then to the armed Salt Lake County sheriff's deputy outside Marston's room. As the deputy opened the door, Onilongo found herself thinking of Marston's grim, head-shaved mug shots. The man in the bed before her now, with his white hair stubbling in, seemed almost frail—more "cancer survivor" than "Hannibal Lecter."

The young man standing by the window beyond the bed strode toward her. Sticking out his hand, he introduced himself as "John Hertenstein, Mister Marston's attorney." Agent Onilongo shook the proffered hand, introduced herself, and again presented her credentials. She asked Hertenstein if she might record the interview with his client, but Hertenstein demurred, saying that he preferred she restrict herself to making notes. Onilongo agreed, and turned to Phil Marston. They shook hands, then Marston gave a small nod in his attorney's direction.

"I've lawyered up, as you see, Ms. Onilongo. I suppose John's here, as usual, to make sure I don't reveal anything self-incriminating. Before I answer your questions, would you be so kind as to answer a few of mine?"

Surprised by Marston's rational and calm—even gentlemanly—demeanor, she nodded. She found him much easier to talk to than she'd expected.

"Do you have any children, Ms. Onilongo?"

"A daughter."

"And how old is she?"

"Eight years old. Geneva, but we call her Gena. She's just entered third grade this fall."

"Hmm. Not so good for me, I suppose, but be that as it may. Do you have a particular specialty in your work for the Bureau, Ms. Onilongo?"

"Cybersecurity—mostly counterterror- and counterespionage-related."

Marston flashed a quick smile.

"Neurosecurity too?

"Some, yes."

"Better, better! Could it be possible? Has *somebody* out there gotten it right—and not sent in just another beat detective with no idea what I'm talking about?"

Ciera Onilongo found she had nothing to say to that.

"Did you start in domestic or foreign counterterrorism?"

"Actually, I started in bank robbery and fraud investigation. Then domestic counterterror, followed by foreign. I did a couple of overseas stints in the Legal Attaché program, serving under State Department auspices."

Marston stared hard at her.

"You were part of the Legat program? Where were you posted?"

"Bagram/Kabul, and Islamabad. After I got married—especially after my daughter was born—I didn't want to travel as much. So I began to work more on the cyber side."

"Hmm. Interesting. Do you have permanent neural implants, Ms. Onilongo? You don't appear to. I'd have thought those would be *de rigeur* for an expert in cybersecurity."

Ciera was surprised, and vaguely embarrassed. Implants could be very small, and discreet. How had he known she had no permanents?

"They're not absolutely required. I do removables only—templants, they're called. Temporary implants. I'm a bit old-school, that way."

"I've been accused of the same thing myself, Ms. Onilongo. You'll also find I tend to be rather direct—another of my failings, but I'm nonetheless going to expect the same failing of you. So, talk to me straight. What do you want to know?"

Ciera inhaled, and then asked the question that had been niggling at her from the moment she was assigned to Marston's case.

"If you were in fact trying to kill those girls, then—why?"

"Ah, 'if.' Very good. One might almost hope that you're still open-minded enough to look at the facts. That you've not just uncritically accepted all that 'Terror Teacher' and 'Murder Professor' noise buzzing about in the media, the ignorant social chatter of a billion annoying gnats."

"I'd like to think so."

"I *hope* so, Ms. Onilongo. So I'll tell you about that 'if.'" He glanced at his attorney. "Don't give me that look, John—I'm well aware we're almost certainly being eavesdropped on, but what does it matter, at this point? Yes, Ms. Onilongo, I *was* in fact intending to kill those girls, but I changed my mind. Which is why they are largely unhurt, and I'm here recuperating from my rather nasty injuries."

"But why did you want to kill them in the first place?"

Marston gave her a direct and level look. Onilongo noticed that the man's eyes were so light a blue they looked almost gray.

"Because, Ms. Onilongo, before there can exist a world of machines that can pass for people, there first must be a world of people that can pass for machines."

"I don't think I understand."

"No, it's not an easy thing to take in. You have to know quite a few things already, to understand why I've been branded a 'heinous criminal,' a 'bloody-minded villain,' a 'monster that must be destroyed'—when all I'm guilty of is attempting to share my admittedly impolite piece of the truth, and act upon it, to save us all. So be it. If we do not come into this world for any purpose larger than the winning of popularity contests, then what's the good, eh? So—what do you think you already know? What has your research shown you—about me?"

She told him. About the NSA data center. About the Apostolic United Brethren. About his Naval and academic career history. About his deceased wife Melinda. About his blog posts and letters to the editor. About her hate crime theories, and why they hadn't seemed quite right. When she had finished, he flashed her another brief smile.

"That's a start, then. The Center, the Group, my dear wife Melinda—they are indeed part of it, but not in ways you might expect. You've left out one very important piece, however."

"What's that?"

"The girls, of course. My 'intended victims.' What do you know about them?"

"They're all ten years old. And they were all your students."

"Doesn't that strike you as odd?"

"Why should it?"

"I was teaching high school, Ms. Onilongo. Almost exclusively junior and senior year courses. Do you think ten-year-olds would normally be my students?"

"I thought they might be your students in Sunday school, or something."

"No, Ms. Onilongo. They were among my students at Jordan Summit Charter High. Among them—but apart from them."

"Maybe they were . . . advanced?"

Marston flashed his enigmatic little smile again.

"Oh, they're advanced, all right. They always have been—and I've known them almost their entire lives. You might want to visit Jordan Summit High. Ask admin and faculty and staff about the 'Special Class.' And about the local spike in youth suicides. See what answers you get."

Agent Onilongo looked up from her notes.

"All right. I will. Anything else?"

"You also might want to ask around town about the Nightshift Nodoff, a.k.a the Bluffdale Blackout. Happened about eleven years ago."

"Anything else beyond that you think I should know? About the Data Center? Or the AUB?"

"Many things—about both of them. I'll give you a couple for each, if you bend close and let me whisper them in your ear."

Overcoming her reluctance at the thought of placing her ear so close to the teeth of a would-be mass murderer, Onilongo leaned forward. Marston cupped his hand between his mouth and her ear and spoke very softly.

"At the Center, you might want to look into a tech they call the Sifter system," he said, just above a whisper. "Also the spike in female reproductive cancers, and why the Center stopped using terahertz-wave tech in security screening and ultrafast computing. As for the Group, perhaps you should look into the Adam-God

Doctrine, and its history. And here—" he said, pressing something into the palm of her hand, "wear this. It'll let each of us know when the other is in the vicinity."

Marston winked, then sank back into his pillows and spoke at a more ordinary volume once more.

"Anything else you might like to know, Ms. Onilongo?"

"Just one thing. What's Transelitium?"

"Ah. The girls were fascinated by that interesting asymmetry in translation, too. It still persists, even all these years after I found it. Go to the most popular online translation system on the web. Specifically, to its English-to-Latin variant. Input 'on the other side of the screen' as the English phrase to be translated into Latin. When the program outputs the Latin phrase, take that Latin phrase and make it, in turn, the input for a Latin-to-English translation run. Then see what English phrase it produces."

He smiled tiredly and sank more deeply into his pillows.

"That should be enough homework for today, Ms. Onilongo. I know *I'm* feeling tired, at any rate."

Onilongo shut her electronic notepad and nodded. Whatever it was Marston had pressed into her hand she palmed into her pocket without looking at it. She folded the notepad into her carry bag, and turned to leave.

"Oh, and something else, Ms. Onilongo."

"Yes?"

"As you go about your investigations, keep in mind that the strangest thing is how normal everything still is. Or how normal we pretend everything still is. Make sure you get some time out of town, too. There are some wonderful hikes in the area."

Onilongo nodded again, handed him a solar-powered wi-fi business card with all her contact info, and left. Winding her way down from the secured floor, through the hospital and back to her government car in the parking lot, she thought Marston had proven more than helpful enough, in his own way. That was just it, though: *his own way*. She didn't want to be manipulated, or sucked into some would-be mass murderer's distorted view of reality. She needed to retain her objectivity. Partly to remind herself too of just how quirky Marston's view of reality was, once she was back on the highway she commanded her text reader on again and listened as it finished reading Marston's "Commencement Future" to her.

Looking back, the edu-bubble bust now seems inevitable. And, like the housing crash before it, the post-crash reforms have changed—what?

The truth is as unpopular as ever. We keep spraying the groves of Academe with digital Agent Orange. Is it any wonder the trees are dying?

Would that we could go back to it before it was too late!

Before the edu-bubble burst and made everything worse!

But we lack a time machine.

Its message much different from mine, our commencement AI has just finished speaking, to applause and smiles from mostly ghostly people.

Soon the band will strike up "Pomp" as our recessional. The music will be familiar, but we'll have forgotten the words few dare to ponder.

Time machines, Onilongo thought as the text reader fell silent. The pseudo-tweeted essay was itself all that: a piece written in the past but looking back from a future of "Commencement AIs" that sounded a lot like the present. A document from the time before Marston's intended victims were born, yet still, Ciera sensed, somehow relevant to Marston's attempt on their lives.

She shook her head. It would all be so much easier if Marston were just an ordinary pervert twisted up by some love-hate relationship with the local Lolitas. But no—she couldn't be that lucky.

Remembering the object Marston had pressed into her hand and that she had palmed into her pocket, Onilongo took the item out to look at it. It was a necklace, the pendant of which was a strangely beautiful image of Time's arrow bent into a Möbius strip. A small Möbius-band softclock, "closed in time and non-orientable in space," as she learned once she matched it with images online. Like the temporal complexities of Marston's essay, it made Ciera's head hurt. It likewise reminded her that she would need to stay on her guard while dealing with this man. Yet she donned the necklace, nonetheless.

Finding out about the "Adam-God doctrine" was easy enough: Ciera looked it up online via a Mormon History site. The doctrine, originally preached by Brigham Young, was eventually rejected by the Church of Jesus Christ of Latter Day Saints, but was still revered by the Apostolic United Brethren and other Mormon splinter sects.

The doctrine (or theory—sources varied) held that Adam and one of his wives, Eve, came to Eden as "resurrected, exalted personages" after traveling in their celestial bodies from another world or reality. According to the doctrine, Adam not only helped make and organize Earth, but was also the Archangel Michael, the Ancient of Days, and the father of all the spirits of humanity, as well as of all physical human beings. Adam and Eve fell and became mortal so that they might create physical bodies for humanity, their spirit children. Later, Adam was also the spiritual and physical father of Jesus Christ.

That was all well and weird in a time-travelly kind of way, Onilongo thought, but she really didn't see why Marston had referred her to it. She wondered if she might have to speak to an elder or priest of the Group to figure out the theory's relevance. She also wondered if Marston might just be toying with her. Pushing down her suspicions of the latter, she posted a query to the AUB's headquarters, explaining her role in the Marston investigation and requesting an interview with an elder or bishop.

Her research into the Nightshift Nodoff was much less fruitful online—just a wry comment in a blogpost thread in the *Valley Journal*'s digital edition from eleven years back. It was, however, much more productive in person. And almost by accident.

Burnt out on her research, Ciera had touched base late with her husband in California, thankful the coast was an hour behind the mountains, time-wise. Still tired but wired, she made her late-night way to the Denny's off Bangerter Highway. Over decaf coffee and a midnight French toast breakfast—served to her by Vera, a veteran waitress who seemed to add the word "honey" to almost every question—Onilongo thought to ask her server about "this Nodoff thing."

"How long have you been working the night shift here, Vera?"

"Sixteen years, I think it is. Why do you want to know, honey?"

"Someone told me today to find out about something called the 'Nightshift Nodoff.' Ever hear of it?"

"More than heard of it," she said, keeping a poker face while pouring Ciera some coffee. "I was part of it. People call it the 'Bluff-dale Blackout,' too. Night of March 14 and early morning of the fifteenth—eleven years ago. Pretty much covered the whole town, from this Denny's right here to the Data Center up there. I remember it just as right as right ever was."

"What happened?"

"I guess it must have been not long after midnight. I had just put a chicken fried steak special in front of a customer, and I—fell asleep on my feet. Boom, down, out! Then woke up, just after one in the morning. Got to my feet again and didn't remember a thing. It happened to everyone in the restaurant. I remember watching the customer—the one I had just served—come out of it. He poked at his meal, then complained that it was cold, though the last thing I remember I had just brought it out, piping hot. My clothes were damp, and I was kinda cold myself. Strange as could be."

"And it covered the whole town, you say?" Onilongo asked, noting that one of Vera's much younger co-workers, a busboy, was eavesdropping. Ciera noted that the young man had a sort of soft Mohawk, and that the left side of his head, over which he'd flopped his hair, was in fact shaved bald and scalp-tattooed with sections and captions of some sort.

"Pretty much. Of course, we're a quiet town. It was a weeknight, so when it hit most people were already asleep anyway. About the only ones who really noticed were folks working the late shift—waitresses and waiters, busboys, janitors, night nurses. Police, fire, paramedics too. Crime was nothing during that hour, though. The only thing the firefighters and paramedics had waiting for them were a couple of accidents—involving drivers who weren't on autonomous-vehicle mode, and blacked out or fell asleep at the wheel."

"Was there any formal investigation?"

"Not much of one. The police confiscated a bunch of surveillance camera records, but there was thunder snow that evening, maybe followed by a dry lightning bust. Lots of power outages that night, anyway. I don't know how much the cameras really got. The Bluffdale police and Salt Lake County sheriff interviewed some people—including me—but not much ever came of that. Most day-people don't think it actually happened. Those of us who know it *did* happen don't much like to talk about it. Kind of an embarrassment, especially for law enforcement and safety services. What makes you bring it up, honey? You a reporter?"

"No. I'm in law enforcement myself."

"Really? What branch?"

"FBI. Investigating the case of Philip Marston."

Vera nodded, her gray-blond hair bouncing.

"Makes sense that you'd be interested in the Nodoff, then."

"Oh? How's that?"

"Those Allred Group girls, the ones they say Phil Marston was trying to kill."

"Allred Group?"

"The Allreds founded the Apostolic United Brethren, though members mainly just call it the Group, now. Those Group girls were all part of the Christmas baby rush."

"I don't see the connection."

"They were all born right around Christmas—just a bit over nine months after the Nodoff. Some of us who went through *that* think those mothers all got pregnant that same night. Another embarrassment."

"How so?"

"Because some of the mothers were very young and very un-married. More than a few claimed to be virgins. Said they had never been touched that way by a man—despite being pregnant. Others, their husbands were out of town, or overseas in the military. I remember what Lori Jenkins said, and when she said it. Her husband was a long-haul trucker then, before almost all the trucks were made self-driving. She was the first to claim she had a vision of an angel, and that's how she got pregnant while her husband was away."

"And people believed her?" Onilongo asked, disbelief in her voice.

"Oh, she wasn't the only one. Several of the mothers who were *embarazada*, as the Mexicans say—they claimed to have been visited by an angel, or visions of an angel."

"And people believed *that*?"

Vera shrugged.

"We're a visionary people, us LDS folks. All the mothers were part of the Group, but that focus on visions is true for them too—maybe more so. Of course, some of the more cynical sort thought the angel stories were all a cover up for a rape-on-the-night-shift sort of thing, but visions constitute a mark of divine approval in our church, and among those in the Allred Group, too. We don't much question the idea of it."

"So you just accept such unexplained supernatural occurrences?"

"That's not how we look at it. In our doctrine, visions aren't really supernatural. My bishop says it's like X-rays and atomic particles. You can't pick those up with your ordinary senses, but scientific instruments can spot them. In visions, the instrument is the person, who has become attuned to visions through faith and the help of God's spirit."

"Sounds more like LSD than LDS!" the eavesdropping busboy said, laughing.

"That's a very old and very tired joke, Ricky," said Vera. "Don't you listen to him, honey. He forgets that philosopher's rule he told me about: Whereof one cannot speak, thereof let one keep silent."

Ciera smiled at them both. She could see that these two had bandied such comments between them before.

"I'll keep that in mind. Thanks for the info. I appreciate it."

Onilongo finished up her meal, left a tip, then went to the front to pay her bill. After she had exited the restaurant and had almost reached her car, the young busboy sidled up to her. He was out of his busboy uniform, dressed in jeans and a shirt that bore the command "Virtualize Existence!"

"Hey! There's something Vera forgot to tell you."

"What's that?"

"A bunch of those Group people lived on the street where I grew up. They told us kids that those Christmas girl-babies all had the same father. Adam, or an archangel, or something. They were *real* protective about the girls with kaleidoscope eyes."

"The what?"

The busboy gave a surprised laugh. His Mohawk, spiked up with mousse or whatever, revealed on his head's bald side what Ciera now saw was a gridwork phrenological-head tattoo.

"The girls of the 'Special Class.' You haven't actually seen them yet, have you?"

"I'm hoping to see them tomorrow. At the high school."

"If you see them, you'll see what I'm talking about."

"And what's your name?"

"Ricky. Ricky Dwyer."

"Thank you, Mister Dwyer. I'll keep in mind what you said."

"Nobody wise messes with those girls with kaleidoscope eyes!" he said, nodding and waving. "They'll blow your mind to pretty glitter!"

He scurried back into the shadows. With a puzzled frown, Ciera watched the young man until he disappeared. In a way, she felt relieved. Even in a place as squeaky-clean and above-board as Bluffdale appeared to be, Phil Marston wasn't the only one who had secrets. Those secrets didn't seem to be of the blackmail, gambling debt, porn site, guns-for-drugs sort, but they were enough that Agent Onilongo began to feel a little less like a film-noir shamus mistakenly translated into a white picket fence, *Father Knows Best* universe.

Getting behind the wheel of her car, she felt very tired, very suddenly. She hoped she could stay awake long enough to get back to her crash pad.

Even before she left her room the following morning, Agent Onilongo remembered to do two things she had been thinking about upon awakening. First, she followed up on Marston's "Transelitium" asymmetry. She typed the words "on the other side of the screen" into the English side of the web's most ubiquitous English-to-Latin translation program. The output produced on the Latin side, "trans elit," she used as input for translation back into English by the Latin-to-English program. The English output was not "on the other side of the screen," as she had expected. Instead, the proffered translation was "beyond the classroom." That was a head-scratcher, no doubt about it.

She also ran a search on young Richard Nelson Dwyer. She found a social media page on which Dwyer was wearing the same T-shirt with the same command she had seen the previous evening. She clicked on the video and listened as Ricky proudly explained that wearing that very T-shirt was what had recently gotten him fired from his former employer, a tech company called Neuro-Shield, where he had been a coder since graduating from Jordan Summit High a few years back. Agent Onilongo shook her head, thinking that getting busted down to busboy was probably not the wisest move the young man had ever made.

As she got in her car to drive to Dwyer's alma mater, Agent Onilongo learned from a destination-triggered net ad on her phone that Jordan Summit High School claimed to be "the most STEM-intensive high school educational experience in Utah." The school and its staff were big on life sciences, physics, chemistry, engineering, mathematics, computing and robotics—all the major STEM career-path curricula.

Walking across campus, Ciera thought the grounds and buildings didn't look much different from those of any other well-funded high school facility built almost anywhere in the United States in the last twenty years—except for the charred remains of what looked like a modular classroom building, surrounded by yellow police line tape, on a hill behind campus. The scene of the crime, she knew, from the reports she had already read.

Walking through the halls, she noticed that Jordan Summit had a high ratio of labs to classrooms, and that the student body seemed a bit on the geeky side, but otherwise it could be a good public or charter high school almost anywhere. Agent Onilongo also noticed that the students and teachers were almost entirely Caucasian, overwhelmingly enough that she felt the reality of her Fillipino-Korean heritage much more keenly than she usually did.

Remembering how forthcoming Vera and Ricky had been the previous night, however, Ciera felt her "difference" might somehow be a good thing. Some people might be more willing to open up to her as an outsider, than to those who looked just like themselves and their fellow townsfolk. Maybe that difference had even helped with Marston.

Such had not always been the case. The school environs she moved through this morning reminded Ciera of a joke a seventh grade classmate had made at Ciera's expense—about Ciera looking "Mexican-Chinese" and asking her if she'd ever made a mu shu burrito. Ciera had not found it funny.

Walking into the principal's office now, she introduced herself and presented her credentials to the receptionist, then asked if she might speak with the principal regarding the Marston case. Virginia Willey, the receptionist (who promptly informed Ciera that she was actually the "management services officer") told her to wait while she spoke with Principal Tewly. Agent Onilongo took a seat and, for the first time, paid actual attention to the bespectacled, business-casual blond woman already sitting in the waiting area.

"Nancy Harlow," said the woman, extending her hand for Ciera to shake. "I already heard who you are when you introduced yourself to Ginny. I'm the school psychologist and counselor."

"You must be very busy, given what happened to those girls."

"Oh yes. Near escape from a fiery explosion is unsettling in real life, no matter how many times action heroes do it in the movies."

"Yes," Ciera said, nodding. "I saw the burnt building surrounded by crime scene tape when I drove in. Quite the mess." She was trying to figure out how to broach to Ms. Harlow the subject of her colleague Mister Marston's behavior, when Ginny opened the door to the inner office.

"Principal Tewly will see you now."

"Nice to meet you, Nancy," Ciera said, getting to her feet. She again shook the hand of the still seated Ms. Harlow, then turned to enter the principal's office.

The thin man in blue suit and red tie rose from behind a large desk of dark wood. He appeared to be about sixty years of age—white haired, blue eyed, lantern jawed. He shook her hand briskly and gestured for her to sit down, as he also returned to his seat.

"What can I do for you, Special Agent Onilongo? Is that how I should address you?"

"Ms. Onilongo will be fine."

"Very well then. How may I be of assistance, Ms. Onilongo?"

"I'd like some background on Philip Marston and his intended victims."

Tewly frowned.

"Ms. Onilongo, we're very serious about quality education here. Our families and students are also very serious about that, too. As you might guess, this whole episode is quite the black eye for us. And for me personally. I was the person most responsible for hiring Dr. Marston, nearly a dozen years ago."

"Did anything in particular make him an appealing candidate for the job?"

Tewly leaned back in his chair, thoughtful.

"Balance. We're a science-heavy school—very 'left brain,' if you like. Although his bachelor's and master's degrees were in biology, Phil's doctorate was in anthropology. He had also published a book of essays—"

"*Travels in Transelitium? Ritual Humiliations* et cetera?"

"One and the same. That came with baggage of its own, of course. The California State University system had terminated his appointment because of what he'd written, but he *was* a full-pop PhD, with many years of teaching experience. I'm just a humble EdD myself. Getting someone like him to teach in a small town high school—his own home town, no less—*that* seemed quite the coup, at the time. Even that controversial little book of his was proof to me that Phil might be a help to us, not only in the life sciences but also in the humanities."

"And was he?"

"Yes indeed. A very rigorous teacher, with very high standards. The students considered him something of a 'hard ass,' but those that valued academic rigor liked him a great deal. And even for those students who found him more than a little challenging, he could be entertaining enough—playful, eccentric, even a bit goofy."

"My grandfather used to say something about that," Agent Onilongo said, looking up from her electronic notepad. "He was a teacher himself, but he said, 'To be a great teacher, one must also be a very great fool.' He was usually talking about somebody like Socrates or Jesus or Buddha, as I recall, but I always thought he was talking a bit about himself too."

"Exactly so. Phil Marston never suffered arrogant, ignorant fools gladly, but he was more than willing to play the wise fool himself, to get a point across. That's the kind of teacher he was. In his heart of hearts I think he always saw himself as some kind of educational reformer." Tewly frowned. "Here I am, talking about him like he's already past tense—almost as if he's already dead. But in some ways the Phil Marston I knew *is* already dead. Trying to kill sixteen ten-year-old female students is a very strange brand of 'education reform.' The Phil I knew would never have done such a thing. Yet he did. Have you seen what he did to that building on the hill? And we have the surveillance camera records to prove all of it. Already turned over to the police."

Agent Onilongo nodded. She made a note, reminding herself to take a look at those records.

"And the girls? What is their background? I've heard mention that they're part of a 'Special Class'..."

Tewly looked uncomfortable for a moment, but then recovered.

"Yes, yes they are. Precocious in the extreme. Phil Marston used to liaise with the local grade schools, helping them, and us, to groom students who might be well suited to eventually enrolling here at Jordan Summit. He 'discovered' those girls. He was the one responsible for getting them tracked so that they skipped all those grades. A gifted bunch, no doubt. Gifted in another way, too."

"How so?"

"An anonymous donor put up a goodly sum of money to make sure that our best teachers would be available to work with them, especially during summers."

"Any idea who the donor might be?"

"None whatsoever. Around the office we've speculated it might be someone who's AUB, since all those girls are part of the Group. But we really don't know."

"Might I meet with the girls?"

Tewly glanced away at nothing in particular on his desk.

"I'm afraid you'll have to take that up with Nancy Harlow," Tewly said. "She's our school counselor—and the point person with the girls and their families, after all that has happened."

"I already met her, in your outer office."

"Very good, very good," Tewly said, standing and offering his hand for her to shake, concluding the interview. "I leave you in Nancy's capable hands. We wish you the best in your investigations, Ms. Onilongo. Feel free to call or stop by if you have any more questions."

Tewly sat back down. Ciera would have liked to ask him more about the girls, and about the jump in youth suicide rates Marston had mentioned, but Tewly's time for further questions seemed to have passed, at least for today. Awkwardly Ciera turned toward the door and passed into the outer office, where Ms. Harlow was still waiting.

"Principal Tewly tells me you're the person I'll have to go through, if I want to meet the girls involved in the Marston case, and learn more about them."

Harlow got to her feet, smiling.

"I can help you with the latter, but not with the former—at least not until they're back on campus, day after tomorrow. After what happened, we've been trying to strike a balance between bringing them back to school too soon, and not bringing them back to school soon enough."

"Understandable. But you *are* willing to talk to me about their background?"

Ciera noted the way Ms. Harlow's eyes darted quickly left, then right.

"I'll be happy to do that. Let me walk you to your car. We'll talk along the way."

Ciera agreed and they departed the office.

"So, what was the subject of your conversation with the principal?" Harlow asked. Ciera glanced at her own feet, walking along the shiny hallway floor as if they were somehow separate from her body.

"We talked about Philip Marston, and the girls presumed to be his intended victims. But we didn't talk that much about the girls, actually. He just said they're part of the Special Class, because they're precocious. Gifted."

Through double doors they pushed out of the Administration Building.

"They aren't 'part of' the Special Class," Harlow said quietly as they walked across a concrete path bisecting a quadrangle of lawn. "They *are* the Special Class."

Onilongo highlighted that snippet of conversation on her note-taker, and nodded.

"When I suggested to Philip Marston that they were 'advanced,' he agreed, but I don't think he was using that word in the same way I was."

"Probably not, knowing Phil. And he *would* know—especially about how that 'Special' has changed."

"Changed?"

Harlow looked down at the concrete path as they walked.

"When those girls first came to our official attention, six years ago, they were considered 'special' as in 'special education', not 'special' as in 'gifted' or 'advanced.' About the only thing they were precocious in, at that time, was their love of tech. Voracious consumers of digital media, almost from the get-go. Three of their pediatricians claimed that their patients, among the girls, had been solidly screen-addicted since the age of fourteen months. Fractured thinking, lack of focus, frantic superficiality—all off the charts, as a result. By age four, all the girls were throwing gale-force tantrums, trying to push their parents into letting them have neural implants."

"They do sound like problem children," Agent Onilongo said, stepping off the curb and onto the parking lot.

"The preferred term is 'neurologically diverse.' Because no child is ever really a 'problem' anymore, I suppose. Not that we had brain-scan evidence, back then, of any supposed neuro-diversity. Until this most recent episode, none of the families allowed the girls to be scanned."

"But you suggested there was other evidence," Ciera said, "that the girls *were* advanced?"

"Yes—that is, if you consider it 'advanced' to have a bundle of nascent identity-formation issues and other disorders more often associated with screen junkies in their late teens and early twenties."

"What sorts of issues?"

"Narcissistic personality disorder, obsessive compulsive disorder, depression, bipolarity, ADD and ADHD, paranoid schizophrenia, autistoid affect, you name it."

"How did you turn them around?"

"I didn't—we didn't. Not entirely. I came up with the description of their problem, and Phil came up with a solution to it. Or at least a partial fix."

"What was their problem? And the solution?"

Harlow glanced up at Ciera a moment before speaking.

"Since the girls spent so much time gaming and blogging and living in virtual worlds, they were engaged in a constant re-invention of identity. I suggested that the creation of that multiplicity of identities loosened the bonds that normally develop to keep the mind's autonomous psychoid processes more or less under the control of a more-or-less unitary self."

"And Marston's contribution?"

"That's where Phil's background in anthropology came into play. He began to think of each of the girls as sort of her own 'tribe of mind.' Especially after they told him about their text-empathy."

Ciera thought she might have heard that last phrase wrong.

"Do you mean telepathy?"

"No, although sometimes it seemed like that, even then. Much more so later, after they got their neural implants. Anyway, when the girls were about five years old, all of them began telling us that they could 'feel' another person's mood just from how that other person was texting. That led Phil to suggest bringing all the special girls together in a single classroom setting—one in which it was only them. He thought that change would help their little tribes of mind sort each other out, and the girls would become more socially functional overall."

Agent Onilongo and Ms. Harlow stopped beside Onilongo's car.

"And it worked?"

"In its way. They got better at code-switching, from online to offline behavior. Their rate of overall task-switching became less manic too. At about age six, they transitioned into the sort of peer-centered identity formation we usually don't begin to see until kids are in their teens. And they've done it with a vengeance, ever since."

"How do you mean?"

"The girls are adult- or family-centered almost not at all, now. Much to the chagrin of most of their parents and teachers—and more than an annoyance, to their siblings at home."

"But otherwise, the changes have been positive?"

"I suppose so, yes. The girls are like a lot of kids these days—only much more so. Probably more dopamine-jumped and amygdala-pumped from digital stimulation than most. They still treat electronically-mediated communication as more 'true' than face to face interactions, also. For them nothing is real until it's seen on a screen."

"That doesn't sound so out of the ordinary, what with everyone on social media."

"Maybe not. Then again, they're not 'on' social media—they *are* social media. I remember one of them, early on, asking me, 'Why do I have to be good with people when I'm already better with machines?' Phil claimed they interoperate better with machines than they interact with human beings. And they still demonstrate a fairly severe lack of empathy toward people outside their group."

"What are the signs of that?"

"People are 'pausable,' as one of the girls told me—especially people outside their group, and especially when the girls start communing via their implants. That's when they tend to zone out, to be pre-occupied, in a unique way—'present, but unavailable' is how Phil describes it. That was another one of his proofs for the idea that they're growing up in a hurry—taller, bigger than kids their age, as you'll see—yet *not* truly maturing. *Physically* 'prematurely mature,' he called it."

"Marston was one of the adults they were willing to work with, then?"

"Absolutely. They trusted him. He was probably their only true friend, outside of their own 'special class.'"

Ciera Onilongo opened the driver's side door.

"That makes what he tried to do to them almost *worse*."

Harlow's eyes flashed left and right again. She glanced upward, too.

"I don't quite understand that myself, but we shouldn't be so quick to judge him. Phil knows those girls better than anyone. He must have had some reason for doing what he did. Or what he was, apparently, *going* to do."

"Must be a pretty crazy reason."

Nancy Harlow colored slightly, perhaps in embarrassment, Ciera thought.

"Oh, I know he talked about some wild ideas—the whole 'Cloudbirds of Saltate City' thing, but I don't know if even *he* believed that stuff."

"Cloudbirds of Salt Lake City?"

"No, *Saltate* City. That's what Phil began to call Bluffdale, a few months back. He began researching all this crazy stuff about saltation, and xenogenesis, or machinogenesis—I forget what all."

"And cloudbirds?"

"Phil's pet name for the girls. He also used the term for those swarms of flocking birds—when they make those weird swirling and shifting clouds?" Her eyes darted swiftly around them and overhead again. "Strange as all that sounds, I can't help thinking Phil knows something about those girls that the rest of us are still trying to figure out, or refusing to see."

"Any idea what?"

Ciera watched, fascinated, as Nancy glanced around again, then literally wrung her hands.

"I'm not quite sure. A number of people at the Data Center, who knew Phil and Melinda, had questions about what happened to Phil's wife—and about some of the other women who took ill. They were sympathetic enough to funnel Phil information from the inside, I think—the Navy signals-intelligence guys, particularly."

Ciera drummed her fingers lightly on the roof of her car.

"Do you know what conclusion Marston might have come to, given such inside information?"

"No. Phil didn't take me all the way down that road with him. I do remember him saying those girls are 'birds to our dinosaurs'— and that it's not wise to anger them. He's certainly right about that last part." She tried to pass it off with a girls-will-be-girls smile and shrug, but then undercut any light-heartedness she might have been aiming for when she once more glanced around them sur- reptitiously—left, right, up, around—then looked fixedly at her own feet. "I hope that covers everything Principal Tewly wanted addressed. I've probably said too much already."

"Not at all," Ciera said, sitting down in her driver's seat but leaving the door open. "Just a couple more things. A young man I spoke with referred to the girls of the Special Class as 'the girls with the kaleidoscope eyes.' Do you know anything about that?"

Harlow gave a shy smile that looked, somehow, *relieved*.

"Oh, that's the retinal backscatter pattern, the 'iris trans-illu- mination defect' the girls all share. More a marker than a defect, if you ask me. The condition is particularly obvious when they're us- ing their implants' entoptic displays. Some in the Group think the kaleidoscope eyes are evidence the girls all share the same 'secret father.'"

Ciera nodded, suddenly struck by a thought.

"Might he be the 'anonymous donor' the Principal told me about?"

Harlow looked confused.

"What?"

"Mister Tewly told me he thought the person who put the

money into the tutorial programs for the special class might be someone in the Group, since all the mothers and daughters are members."

"I've never thought that—although I suppose that last part's true, about their all being members. But the mothers were also all employees at the spy center, too. I've always thought the anonymous donor is somehow connected with NSA."

Nancy Harlow now looked like she wanted to literally dart away at that moment—and was only restraining herself through a deep act of will.

"If you see Phil Marston, please tell him that Loretta—the girl who suffered the mild concussion, and was scanned—tell him she's okay. And tell him the brain scans show he was right. Gray matter atrophy in the striatum, and the insula. Got that?"

"Loretta's okay—right," Ciera said, looking up from her notes and further observing just how anxious Harlow was to be gone. "Atrophy in the striatum and insula. Will do. If I see him or hear from him, I'll tell him. Just one last thing, please. Phil Marston mentioned something about a jump in youth suicide rates. Do you know if that might have any relevance here?"

"I'm afraid I can't say much about that," Harlow said, her eyes doing their shifty darting again. "I heard it had something to do with online stuff—cyberbullying, I think. But I really can't say."

Nancy Harlow turned and strode rapidly away. Agent Onilongo closed her car door. She checked her rear view mirrors, but saw nothing except Harlow's retreating backside, and the burnt-out classroom building on the low hill beyond her.

Dealing with that charred crime scene would have to wait for another day. At least local law enforcement's reports on it were already in the can, so far as she knew. While it was on her mind, she sent a message to the Bluffdale Police Department over a secured channel, requesting the surveillance camera records of the explosion incident involving Marston and the girls.

As Ciera drove away, she shook her head in wonder. What was

it about this town that these people felt the need to talk to her in parking lots? First Ricky Dwyer, now Nancy Harlow. What was Harlow so guarded about, too? Why all the covert looking-about—even overhead!—to see if they were being overseen or overheard? What was the woman afraid of?

Ciera sighed. Thinking about the whole "secret father" issue, she realized that, as much as she might have hoped to avoid dealing with No Such Agency, there was nothing for it now but to follow up on the process she had already started. Once back at her rooms, she spent the rest of the afternoon and evening working the phones and contacts of her connections, bird-dogging them and pulling strings, to get inside the spy center.

It was late in the evening by the time she called her husband and daughter in California. After talking on the phone with them, she found a "Greetings and salutations!" text from Marston, funneled through his lawyer. She responded with the information Nancy Harlow had wanted her to pass along—about Loretta being okay, and her scan revealing gray matter atrophy in the insula and the striatum.

It was later still when, unable to sleep, Ciera looked up "cloudbirds," then "saltation" and "xenogenesis" and "machinogenesis." Both saltation and xenogenesis, she found, seemed to involve some sort of evolutionary leap in which offspring differed markedly from parents. "Machinogenesis" was harder to pin down: In one place—amid much discussion of self-diagnosing, self-repairing, self-reproducing von Neumann machines—it was defined as "the generation of machines from non-machine structures." In another virtual place in cyberspace, the word referred to the appearance of both living and nonliving "cognitive subjective entities," further described as "self-revising learning neural network machines capable of active evolution."

To ease the headache such research gave her, she turned back to the video loop she had found earlier while researching "cloudbirds." It was to those living lava-lamp images of bird flocks swirling in synchrony—murmurations of starlings and conjurations of cow-birds—that she fell asleep.

After going up her chain of command almost to the level of the Director of the Bureau herself, Agent Onilongo finally got clearance to enter the Utah Data Center facilities and interview both the Center's chief interagency liaison officer and an assistant to the chief technology officer, regarding the Marston case. It was with some trepidation, then, that—after passing another of the seemingly ubiquitous electronic billboards hyping NeuroLockPure—she turned down the road for Camp Williams, the National Guard training center, on one large corner of which sat the heavily fortified spy center.

She and her government car had to pass through a vehicle inspection facility just to enter the parking lot. Walking from the car to the visitor-control center, Ciera preoccupied her anxious mind with the heavy scent of sagebrush in the air, all the more aromatic after the light rain that had fallen overnight.

At first approach, the security systems rising out of the sage-brush flats didn't look all that overwhelming: mainly some closed-circuit camera housings atop a tall fence. She knew from her research, though, that all along the boundary of the facility were multiple layers of intrusion-detection tech, and that the fence itself was anti-terror grade, capable of stopping a 15,000-pound vehicle traveling at 50 miles per hour.

Military guards in ballistic vests, plainly armed and in plain sight, stood in front of and inside the visitor-control center, which itself looked to be blast proof. After presenting her badge and credentials—and California Driver License, and passport—she was granted the pleasure of submitting to a battery of biometric identification protocols: retina scans, finger and gene prints, voice ID. Those were only the overt identification checks. She did not doubt there were also other identity-scrutinizing systems running in the background.

Ciera walked under a final broad arch (which she assumed was scanning her body and clothing for weapons and explosives) before stepping forward to receive a visitor ID badge.

"Special Agent Onilongo?" said an African American woman, stepping forward out of a glassed-in waiting area. "I'm Tanisha Elliot, interagency liaison." She shook Ciera's hand, then gestured to the ginger-haired man beside her. "This is Dr. Martin Hanlan, from our chief technologist's office." The tall, thin fellow who shook Ciera's hand, perhaps too conscious of his height, maintained a bent-forward posture that made Ciera feel like she was meeting a human question mark. That impression was not lessened by the fact that his eyeglasses made his eyes look particularly large and prominent.

The three of them walked to a small electricart and boarded it. Tanisha Elliot took the wheel, and soon the vehicle was humming down a long promenade to the Administration building, passing many people along the way, all of them badged. A goodly number were in military uniform, but still more were in the non-uniform uniform of "corporate casual." Stopping at last beside a small conference room, they exited the cart and walked only a few steps before taking seats around a large oval table. Display-sharing screens popped up from the tabletop.

"How might we help you?" Tanisha Elliot asked.

"As I think you know," Ciera began, her gaze alternating between Elliot and Hanlan, "I'm investigating the case of Philip Marston, and the sixteen girls he was apparently planning to kill. I just wanted to confirm a few points that have come up in my investigation, if that's all right with you?"

Elliot and Hanlan glanced at each other, then nodded.

"I'm told that the mothers of all sixteen girls once worked here. Is that correct?"

"That's right," said Hanlan. "Some still do. Nothing unusual about that. Since we opened for business we've hired a lot of people from the area."

"But the odds that *all* the mothers would work here strike me as . . . odd. Especially since all the mothers were members of the Apostolic United Brethren, too."

"We've hired a lot of those folks as well," said Hanlan with a shrug.

"We've looked into this already, Ms. Onilongo," said Elliot. "If you'll check the table screen, you'll see I've just shared with you a pie chart. If you examine it, you'll see that the women who had what the locals call the 'Christmas rush babies' are a fairly small fraction of the total number of women who actually worked here at the time. Likewise with their AUB connection. Not all of the women who had a Christmas girl-child were practicing AUB members, either—some were former members of the Group who had left the movement, while others converted later."

"Marston's wife Melinda," Hanlan said, "who worked here as a software engineer almost to the day she died—she was one of those former Brethren people. Both AUB and an employee, but she didn't have one of those girls, see?"

Ciera nodded, then addressed them both again.

"I'd like to come back to that later. You mentioned the rush of Christmas girl-babies. Some of the people I've talked to—they interpret that as indicating that all the mothers of those girls became pregnant the same night, during something they call the Nightshift Nodoff, the Bluffdale Blackout."

"That stuff's all apocryphal," Hanlan said, waving his hand dismissively. "Both the supposed event, and the supposed result. It was a power outage, nothing more."

"Perhaps so, but there is something else that seems to be concretely verifiable and specific to the girls. A number of people in town call those Christmas babies by another name—'the girls with the kaleidoscope eyes.' Have you heard the term? Do you know to what it refers?"

Ciera watched as Elliot and Hanlan donned their poker faces and shook their heads.

"All the girls have the same prominent iris trans-illumination defect, or marker," Ciera said. "Endemic only to them and to Bluff-dale, as nearly as I can tell. I gather that some members of the Group feel it's a sign that the girls all have the same secret father."

Hanlan gave a prominent roll of his very prominent eyes, but Ciera plunged on.

"When I interviewed the principal and the school psychologist yesterday, they felt there might be some connection between the secret father and an anonymous donor—someone either AUB, or NSA, or both—who is funding special tutorial programs for the girls. Do you know of any funding from your Center here that might be underwriting programs for those girls?"

"Nothing whatsoever," said Elliot. "There's no record of any such outlay. Ms. Onilongo, our budget may be 'black' as far as most congressional and public oversight is concerned, but internally we have a very good idea of where the money goes—and it doesn't go to special tutorial programs for a group of young girls in Bluff-dale."

Hanlan laughed lightly before he spoke.

"'Secret father' and 'anonymous donor,' who may be one and the same. Sounds like an anonymous *sperm* donor! Ms. Onilongo, that's just not our look-out. Around here, 'AI' stands for 'artificial intelligence,' not 'artificial insemination'!"

All three laughed at Hanlan's witticism—Hanlan most of all. Ciera tried another tack.

"Doctor Hanlan, you mentioned that Melinda Marston worked here for years—as a software engineer, is that right?"

"That's right. Software engineer and tech support. All fairly low-security stuff, as I recall."

"Do either of you remember the cause of her death?"

"Cancer—ovarian cancer," said Tanisha Elliot, looking up from online personnel records. "Tragic."

"Were there any other instances of such cancers that you re-call?"

"Why do you ask?" Hanlan said, trying to sound casual—and failing.

"When I interviewed Philip Marston, he mentioned something about a spike in female reproductive cancers. A situation that, somehow, led to your Center discontinuing the usage of terahertz-wave technology in security screening and ultrafast computing. That's what my notes say, at least."

Hanlan, looking annoyed, ran a hand through his thinning red hair.

"Marston went on about that, after his wife died. Wrote op-eds, hired an attorney. Threatened to sue the NSA to obtain information regarding cancer rates here at the Center. He didn't get very far with *that*."

Ciera nodded. No, she supposed it wouldn't be easy to get the Agency to agree to allow itself to be investigated in that way. *She* could still ask questions, however.

"Could you explain a little bit about these 'terahertz waves'? All I know about them is that they're used in security scanners."

Hanlan, suddenly in his element, became professorial.

"Terahertz waves lie between infrared and microwaves. The lower terahertz range, just beyond the top end of gigahertz, are the ones that are the most interesting, for our purposes."

"And those purposes . . . ?"

"Security. As you said, the place where most people have encountered them is in airport security scanners. Most chemical compounds—including illegal drugs and explosives—have distinct signatures in their terahertz transmission spectra. Those signatures help scanners distinguish between legal and illegal substances, or between dangerous and harmless compounds. Terahertz waves, at the most basic level, can tell you what's inside an envelope—without your having to open that envelope."

"And they were in use here?"

"For personnel access control, yes. And for hypercomputing. THz fields are useful for monitoring and controlling ultrafast processes in semiconductors, and for producing ultrafast switching in semiconductor components. They're particularly helpful in quantum computing applications, photonics, and nanotechnology."

"Did your Center here stop using them, as Marston suggested?"

"Mostly, yes," Elliot said.

"Why?"

Elliot and Hanlan glanced at each other.

"In the scientific journals," Elliot said, "articles began appearing that suggested tuned terahertz waves might selectively affect not only genetic material but also might generate complex epigenetic effects capable of perhaps altering an individual's overall epigenomic roadmap. For those reasons—and not because there was any conclusive evidence of increased cancer incidence—the administrators of this facility felt that the use of terahertz wavelengths here should be strictly curtailed, and in many cases banned outright."

Hanlan grew abruptly agitated.

"But the heaviest use of terahertz scanning here occurred for a period of *only three months*! And *that* was almost a dozen years ago, after a terrorist attempted to smuggle explosives into this facility—in the threads of his clothing. Marston's claims about such terahertz exposures don't hold up, scientifically. You see what this is about, right?"

Ciera didn't.

"Marston blames terahertz waves, and the Data Center *and* NSA, for the cancer that, unfortunately, led to his wife's death. You've seen that stuff he's posted and published, I presume? Because we've got the deepest and broadest data library on the planet, and the most generalized AIs to analyze it—as if that's a bad thing!— Marston believes our facilities must necessarily be the 'origin point' of some big bad singularity destined to take over the whole world and wipe out humanity!"

Ciera Onilongo nodded, thoughtfully but non-commitally. Hanlan continued.

"Such a huge leap into speculation *must* make any rational person conclude that Marston's obsession with his wife's death has turned him into some sort of paranoid crazy—at least in regard to *everything* about the facility his wife worked in, when she died."

"I can't speak to that," Ciera said, "but Marston did tell me that while I'm here I should look into a technology called the Sifter system, which sounds innocuous enough." She glanced from Elliot to Hanlan, and was surprised to see their poker-faces fall. "Are you familiar with something by that name?"

"We are," said Elliot, "but Mister Marston should *not* have been. I don't believe his wife would have had clearance to that level . . . ?"

Doctor Hanlan shook his head.

"No. That was far above her need to know. Someone said something they shouldn't have. That's the danger with people like Marston. They're squirrels who gather nuts and disgruntleds around them—anyone who wants to share their little acorn of the big oak, national security be damned. Unfortunately, some of his disgruntled buddies must have a background in signals intelligence."

"I've heard he had friends with those skills," Ciera Onilongo said, "but I'm more interested in something else, at the moment. What *is* this Sifter thing?"

Tanisha Elliot looked to Hanlan, who shrugged.

"It might be best to show you," he began, "if you don't mind another ride in the cart—and if your clearance will allow it."

Elliot and Hanlan tapped in passcodes on their implant panels—a gesture that reminded Onilongo of people scratching behind their ears—then nodded.

"You're cleared for a ride-along," said Tanisha Elliot, rising from behind the table. "Shall we?"

The three of them boarded the electricart—Doctor Hanlan driving, this time—and were soon humming along in a direction Ciera thought might be east. Not long after they exited the administration building they found themselves in a great white warehouse space, passing row upon row of servers, lights blinking red and green and gold, inscrutably. One of the four vast data halls, Ciera surmised.

"SIFTER," Hanlan said, gesturing toward everything around them. "The Strategic Information Forecast Threat Evaluation and Response system. A cross-domain optimized, arbitrarily super-intelligent, self-evolving quantum machine, built on and exploiting an expanded suite of GAIA—generalized artificial intelligence algorithms."

"That sounds a lot like the sort of thing Marston warns about in his posts," Ciera said, over the cart's hum.

"And as I said, it is nothing of which to be afraid. 'Generalized' simply means that this system, instead of being a specialized tool like a stone axe, is more like a Swiss Army knife. The same can be said of the human brain."

"But what does it all *do*?"

Hanlan flashed a smile that Onilongo found a bit too rictus-like for comfort.

"It *could* do almost anything it put its mind to," he said as he drove along, clearly more interested in his own thoughts than in the particulars of their route through the data hall. "Computing power of this magnitude could explain the deeper information basis of the physical universe—why, for instance, there seems to be considerable overlap between one-way functions in mathematics, like the factoring problem, and hard-to-invert processes of the *physical* universe, like the arrow of time, and the problem *that* poses for the construction of, say, time machines. Or some of the universe's other hard-to-inverts and one-ways—like why it's so much easier to transform matter into energy than it is to transform energy into matter."

He swung around a corner—sharply enough that Ciera feared for a moment that he might tip the electricart over—and continued blithely on.

"What it's *designed* to do, though, is sift through as much of the data that humanity produces—has *ever* produced—as it possibly can. In that data it looks for patterns that enable it to 'know' —decrypt, analyze—as much as possible of everything that has ever happened, and *is* happening, so that it can make the best possible predictions of what is most likely *yet to happen*—at least in the realm of possible threats to our security, and potential responses to those threats."

"Predictive analytics—writ large?" Ciera suggested.

"Writ *very* large."

Martin Hanlan sped up, apparently sure of his way and destination, despite his erratic driving.

"To do that," he continued, "it must know *us*—human beings, individually and collectively—better than we have ever known ourselves. Its goal is to be able to see as much of the entire human picture as possible. The more complete its knowledge of all things human, all things public and private about us, the more fine-grained and accurate its sifting, and predicting, and responding."

Hanlan pulled the electricart to a stop beside a chrome railing, in what looked to be a control room of sorts—lots of throat-miked people with subtly blinking implants, seated in front of screens in what looked like an amphitheater. At the center of the bowl was something that, incongruously, reminded Ciera of the sort of large, high-backed, round sofa she had sometimes seen in hotel lobbies.

"Knowing the entire human picture—" she said, "—that's what drives the 'vast accumulation of human cultural information' Marston posted about?"

"Yes. The system—and you're at the heart of it here—has a voracious, even an insatiable, appetite for all manner of information. Before it can decide whether a piece of information is relevant or not, it first has to *know* that piece of information. That's why it 'wants' its sensors to cover as much of *everywhere* as possible, so it can know as much of *everything* as possible."

"Sounds like the old theological description of God as omnipresent and omniscient," Ciera said, then immediately wondered if her hosts might be offended by the analogy.

"You could think of it that way, if you like," Hanlan said, contemplating the idea. "But remember that this *striving* to be 'omnipresent' and 'omniscient'—that's what the SIFTER system is *designed* to do. It's *not* designed to strive for *omnipotence*, much less achieve it—which is where Marston, with his AI take-over paranoia, goes seriously astray. *Striving* toward the first two 'omnis' does not necessarily imply the *creation* of the third. The way we have designed the system, and constrained its evolutionary possibilities, is intended to make sure that last 'omni' is as close to impossible as we can possibly make it."

Hanlan turned to her.

"Ms. Onilongo, out in the world there's a lot of noise about what we do here. A lot of jokes have long been made about what our acronym stands for. Perhaps you've even made some of those jokes yourself." He stared at her quizzically, as if he somehow already *knew*, but then passed on. "For us, in the context of the tensions between privacy and security, the NSA has always stood for No Simple Answers. From our side of the looking-glass, it stands mirror-wise as ASN—Absolute Security Necessity.

"When you come down to it, that noise arises from the simple fact that there are just more mathematicians and computer scientists alive today than have ever existed before in human history —and it just so happens that more of them work for the NSA than for anyone else. We're like Medieval monks, trying to keep alive some permanent signal amid the entropy of history, the tendency of everything to descend into ephemeral noise."

Hanlan gestured toward the center of the amphitheater's bowl.

"Look down there—at that thing that looks like an ottoman on steroids. *That* is the 'super-intelligent machine' Marston is so afraid of. Doesn't look very threatening, does it?"

"No, I have to admit—it doesn't."

Hanlan glanced at Elliot, then back at Ciera.

"I think we've proven our point. I'll drive us back to Administration, then Tanisha will take you from there."

The ride out of the data halls and back to the Administration building was quiet, as was the driver hand-off to Tanisha from Martin. Tanisha waved good-bye to Ciera at the Visitor Control Center. This time, Agent Onilongo noted, no one sidled up to her in the parking lot before she left.

As she sat in her car waiting for her phone to cycle up, Ciera wondered if she might have hit another dead end. The SIFTER system was intriguing enough, but what possible connection could it have with the girls who were intended to have been Marston's victims? And of what use was knowing about the former applications of terahertz waves at the Data Center—other than their possible connection with Marston's wife's cancer, which seemed remote at best?

She drove only a short way before she found herself stopped again. Waiting for her car to be cleared through the exit at the vehicle inspection station, Ciera found that, despite her misgivings about Marston's cryptic version of things, she still wasn't convinced by the alternative description of the situation that Hanlan and Elliot had laid out before her. Hanlan's dismissal of the Nodoff—and of Marston himself as merely some sort of lightning rod for crazy static—struck her as just too pat.

Her mood lightened somewhat when, as she drove away from the Center and Camp Williams, she accessed the messages that had come in while she was behind the Data Center's wall of secrecy. The first was a thank-you from Marston, with no further comment. The second was a phone message from Nancy Harlow informing Ciera that the girls of the Special Class would be back on campus the following afternoon—and had a free period available.

The last was a text message from Bishop Richard Culver, of the Apostolic United Brethren, who said he would be happy to meet with her and address her questions the following morning at his place of work, the NeuroShield Corporation—a name she remembered from her research into Ricky Dwyer's background. When she looked up that company online, she was surprised to see that it was the maker of NeuroLockPure—and even more intrigued to see that Bishop Culver was also President and Chief Technology Officer of NeuroShield.

People in this town seemed to be connected by far fewer than six degrees of separation, she thought. The NSA door might be closed for now, but she could not deny that windows seemed to be opening on the girls and the Group—and perhaps also on Marston himself, again, soon enough.

To Agent Onilongo, the relatively small size of NeuroShield's research campus was fitting for a young company not so very far beyond the startup phase. The three pale adobe low-rise buildings currently under construction, however—beyond a bannered arch that read Visualize Excellence!—suggested to Ciera the company's ambitions were beyond its present situation.

When Richard Culver met her outside his office, the man struck Ciera as compact, energetic, ambitious—rather like his company. He pumped her right hand in greeting, ran his left hand through the executive-silver hair at his temples, then offered to show her NeuroShield's business, before they got down to her business.

"Our NeuroLockPure product is a spinoff from work originally done at the Data Center," Culver explained as they walked down a long chrome-and-white hall together. "The safe passcode system we developed is highly resistant to the usual side-band and side-channel attacks, because the user doesn't consciously know his or her passcode. What users don't know, users can't betray—not even if they're drunk, drugged, beaten with rubber hoses, or seduced by the sexiest agents!"

Culver seemed quite jaunty about the whole matter—so much so that Ciera wondered whether or not she'd be able to get any straight answers out of the man.

"But how can the user make use of the code," Ciera asked as

they entered some sort of learning lab, "if the user doesn't know what the code is?"

"Implicit learning! Do something repetitively enough, and the doing of it becomes unconscious. Like riding a bicycle—you can't exactly explain how you do it in words, and you don't need to be able to, in order to ride. Once you've learned how to ride, you are no longer really 'conscious' of how it is you ride that bike. We do the same thing here, only with codes and passwords. Here, let me show you."

Culver sat down at what looked like a virtual game console and donned a pair of VR goggles. Agent Onilongo followed suit. Culver spoke over the game as he began to play.

"This is an implicit learning game we call 'Gravities and Galileos,'" Culver said. "As you see, we've got a dozen Towers of Pisa spread across the game grid. A dozen Galileos stand ready to drop various objects—ranging from cannonballs to feathers—off each Tower's balcony. The user's job is to press a particular key, corresponding to a particular location on the game grid, every time an object dropped from a tower lands at the bottom of the tower. The user gets points for accurately 'timing' the fall of each object. Depending on how secure a code you want, the game levels up through different planets and moons with different gravitational fields and different atmospheric thicknesses."

"I don't quite see the connection."

"It's nonobvious," Culver said, smiling, "and meant to be. Playing the game trains users to enter a particular unique pattern—the user's passcode—but, because the sequence of *which* objects fall from *which* towers to land at *which* times constantly changes, the users can't consciously distinguish what their personal 'signal' is from all the added noise. Later, however—because the game contains parts of the learned pattern the users have been unknowingly taught—the user's identity is authenticated by his or her superior skill at playing those particular parts of the game."

"So," Ciera ventured, "if I get you right, it's sort of a subliminal message you send yourself—without knowing what you sent?"

"Right! You don't remember what it is you're supposed to remember, but you remember it anyway. And, because it works particularly well with entoptic displays built for neural implants, it's particularly effective against brain-hacks to those implants. Here—want to try it?"

"No, thanks. I get the gist."

"Very well, then. Let's adjourn to my office, and we can switch the subject from technology to theology, if I've got your interview request right."

Once they had entered Culver's office, he shut the door behind them, and they each sat down on the socially appropriate sides of his large desk.

"So, Ms. Onilongo, what do you want to know about the Group's beliefs?"

Ciera inhaled, and began.

"In my investigations I've come across something called the Adam-God doctrine. I think I understand what it is, but I was wondering what the importance of it might be, for members of your movement."

Culver played absently with a pen on his desk.

"We in the Group revere the doctrine not least because we feel it bolsters for us, across both time and space, the centrality of the Principle—what those outside our movement call polygamy."

"Bolsters? How so?"

"The Principle is embodied in Father God Adam. Eve was one of his wives, but not the only one. He was the original spiritual and physical father of all humanity. Later, through his wife Mary, he was also again, specifically, the spiritual *and* physical father of Jesus Christ."

Ciera jotted a note, then looked up.

"One of my informants tells me that members of your movement are particularly protective of the girls of the Special Class, the Christmas rush girls. Does that involvement have any connection with the Adam-God doctrine?"

Culver toyed still more absently with the pen on his desk.

"The verdict is still out on that, but yes, I think it does. I know there are some among us who, because of the girls' similarities to each other, believe that—though they were all born of different mothers—they are all children of the same father. One husband and father, multiple wives and mothers, and a vision of an angel remembered by most of the women involved. I think you can see how *that* might be seen as proof of the rightness of the Principle, and our upholding of it. The Archangel Michael is, after all, one of the forms Father God Adam is known to have taken."

He pushed the pen away.

"As to our protectiveness, you can probably see the need and reason for that as well. Latter Day Saints have endured a long history of persecution. These girls are uniquely God-gifted, and a special treasure to us in The Work. Despite their youth, they have also unfortunately attracted a not-inconsiderable amount of envy and enmity. The fact that Phil Marston himself—*their* good friend, and *my* long-time friend—hoped to destroy them, well, that seems to me reason enough for our special watchfulness over them."

"Do you know of any explanation for the angel or angel-vision those mothers say they saw, Bishop Culver?"

Culver leaned back in his chair, meditative.

"I have no doubt that a person of faith, and in God's spirit, can have visions. I think that, just as we take on the forms of avatars when we enter machine-generated environments, an angel is the form that higher spiritual beings take on when they enter our human perceptual environment."

Culver abruptly stood up, as if he had come to some sort of decision.

"I may not have evidence to prove the 'existence' of the angel that appeared, in vision, to each of those women, Ms. Onilongo—but I *do* have evidence for what that angel led them to do. Since I showed that evidence to Phil Marston, five or six years ago now, I suppose he will eventually tell you about it anyway. So I might as well show it to you, or all you'll hear is *his* side of it."

Culver walked toward the framed painting of a pastoral scene hanging on his wall. Swinging the painting aside, he revealed the door of a safe, hidden behind it. After entering a code much simpler than the ones NeuroLockPure traded in, he swung open the small safe's door. He reached in and removed an envelope from within.

Onto his desk he emptied the envelope's contents—older media storage, mostly thumb drives and first-generation data needles—and inserted one of the latter into a player built into his desktop. As Culver sat down to watch, display screens slid up from the desk's top, one for him and one for Ciera.

"This is a compilation of surveillance camera records—mostly closed circuit TV—taken during the Nightshift Nodoff," Culver said. "A deputy sheriff, a member of our Group, availed himself of copies of these, before they—and many other records—were appropriated by NSA on national security grounds. Now, if you say I shouldn't have this, it'll raise thorny issues of the separation of church and state, so be warned."

As the recorded material played, Ciera noted that all of it consisted of variations upon the same theme. Again and again women, in house robes, job uniforms, nightgowns, lingerie, or nude, came forward into camera range. They strode across snow—most of them barefooted, a few in house slippers or shoes, all apparently sleepwalking. In every case each came to a halt, always below power lines, and raised her arms upward. Ball lightning instantly gathered, then soared down off the lines—to bury itself in the pelvic area of each of the women, time and again. Each fell into the snow, making strange snow angels in their convulsions. Then, as if nothing had happened, each got up and headed whence she had come, apparently still asleep.

"You showed this to Philip Marston?" Ciera asked, after the last variation of the sequence had played and the record had ended. Culver stared down at the desktop.

"To my everlasting chagrin. I thought it would convince him of the reality of the visions the mothers claimed, and the miraculous reality behind the girls themselves. I reminded him of the many myths and stories—from different places throughout the world and different times throughout history—of women impregnated by divine lightning, goddesses gotten with child by thunderbolt, among other unusual examples of cosmic *raptus*."

"Jove in the form of a shower of gold impregnating Danae," Ciera said, nodding. "In the form of a flame impregnating Aegina—"

Culver gave an odd little smirk.

"Father of gods and men. Yes—you've been doing research! I thought that, given the anthropological side of his training, Phil would see the miracle those girls represented. But he would have none of it."

"How *did* he respond?"

"Like the worst sort of scientific reductionist. He insisted that everything had a physical explanation. He didn't believe the big sleep of the Nodoff or Blackout, or the angel visions themselves, were anything of spirit origin. For him, the angel that appeared to those women was nothing divine. All of it was just sprung from a sort of extremely advanced version of the unconscious coding we do here."

"In what way?"

"Messaging—implicit, subliminal—incessantly repeated to everyone around here, over all their electronic media. TV and radio, net and web, even electronic billboards! Until what the message commanded was so powerful you'd be hard pressed to distinguish that messaging from some sort of paranormal mind-control drugging everyone to sleep, then dragging those sleepwalking women out into the snow. That was Phil's explanation, anyway. All nonsense. The last redoubt of doubt in others' faith is faith in one's own doubt." He shook his head slowly. "Still, lately I've been wondering if showing this to Phil Marston might have contributed somehow to his mad attempt on the lives of those girls. But I can't see how.

Or maybe I'd prefer not to."

From behind his desk, Culver came to his feet.

"That's all I can really say about the girls and their history. Tell me, have you met them in person?"

"Not yet. I'm supposed to talk with them this afternoon, at the high school."

"Good, good. There's no substitute for meeting them in person. And you're in luck! If I'm not mistaken, one of our tech trainers will be there this afternoon too, working with the girls on their new passcodes."

Culver shook Ciera's hand then, walked her to the door, and said good-bye. Walking to her car, Agent Onilongo felt that her interview with Bishop-and-CTO Culver had been brought to a close somewhat peremptorily—as had also been the case with Principal Tewly at the high school. As she drove away from the NeuroShield campus, she reminded herself that, once she got to Jordan Summit, at least she would be dealing directly with Ms. Harlow—and the girls, not the men.

Since she would be arriving at the Jordan Summit High School campus early, Ciera Onilongo texted ahead to Nancy Harlow, suggesting that they examine the site of the burnt-out modular classroom building before going on to meet with the girls. Ms. Harlow replied promptly, agreeing to meet Ciera at the ruined structure.

Once they met—and Agent Onilongo had lifted the crime scene tape, so they could walk about the site—Nancy Harlow visibly relaxed, even as they picked through the debris of what had once been classrooms.

"You could hardly tell now," she told Ciera, "but this temporary building looked like nothing so much as a double-wide trailer parked behind campus. Even before it burned, it was something of an eye-sore."

"What was it used for?"

"Not what, so much as *who*. Originally it was parked here for home-schooled kids who were required by state law to pick up a few classes on campus. The last couple years, though, it was used almost exclusively for the Special Class. The parents insisted."

Assuming that "the parents" referred to the girls' parents, Agent Onilongo shortly found herself telling Nancy Harlow about the compilation video of sleepwalking women and ball lightning Culver had shown her—and wondering if Nancy had seen it, or heard of it, herself.

"Never saw it," Harlow said, "but I heard about it. From Phil. And Richard Culver is right, about Phil's nonspiritual explanation for all of that. It took Phil a while, but over the course of maybe six months he came up with an explanation he found satisfactory. I remember that much."

"What was his version?"

Nancy paused to more closely examine a pile of melted media and burned books.

"I think it must go back to his wife's cancer and her death. That's where Phil's obsession with all this began. He came to believe that every step we take to make ourselves more secure unintentionally also makes us more vulnerable."

"I don't follow," Ciera said, from behind a charred and scorched shelving unit.

"The increased rates of reproductive cancers among those women who worked in the Data Center—the ones who passed daily through the security scanners. Phil was certain those scanners had been reprogrammed to alter the genes of those women's eggs in specific ways. His wife Melinda, and the other women who died of those ovarian and uterine cancers—they were 'collateral damage.' Victims of a covert experiment."

"An experiment? Conducted by whom? The NSA?"

Harlow shook her head.

"No, Phil didn't blame the Agency. Not directly. Especially not in the beginning."

"Then who?"

"That's the strangest thing. It wasn't who was behind the experiment, according to Phil. It was *what*."

"And that was . . . ?" Ciera asked, staring at the shattered remains of a teacher's heavy desk.

"Some big AI machine over at the Data Center."

Ciera thought suddenly of the SIFTER system. Not knowing the full security implications of mentioning the thing, she debated with herself about whether or not she should avoid making a comment about that system, and just plunge on. But she couldn't.

"The name of this big AI—was it called the Sifter?"

"Yes," Nancy said, looking immensely relieved. "That's what Phil called it."

"He thought the Sifter was somehow involved in altering the genes of those women, then?"

"Yep. Zapping their ovaries and tweaking their eggs. He thought terahertz waves from the scanners were 'prepping' the reproductive genetics of all those women—both the mothers for whom the experiment worked, and the women for whom the experiment went wrong and led to cancer."

"Prepping? For what, exactly?"

"I don't know *exactly*. For whatever it was that happened the night of the Blackout, the Nodoff. What you said Culver showed you."

"And the strange ball lightning all those women were struck by? Did Phil Marston have any idea what that was about?"

"Induced in the grid, according to Phil. By the Sifter commandeering the internet of things. Through something called skater systems, I think it was."

"SCADA systems?" Ciera asked. "Supervisory Control and Data Acquisition?"

"Yes, that sounds right."

"That's the 'how,' then. What's the 'why'?"

Nancy Harlow paused, trying to remember something as exactly as she possibly could.

"To generate an electrical stimulus—one capable of triggering a parthenogenetic process that would result in viable offspring, in the women who had already been prepped. Phil said that's the reason they're all girls."

"*What?*"

"I know how that sounds. I didn't even think it was possible to create human offspring through parthenogenesis. But I looked it up, and what Phil said weirdly hangs together. As early as 2004 a South Korean scientist unknowingly produced human embryos via parthenogenesis—a result confirmed in 2007."

"But why would this Sifter system want to do such a thing? To what end?"

"Like I told you last time you were here, Phil kept talking about all that 'genesis' stuff. Xenogenesis, machinogenesis. I thought it was crazy, and I still want to *believe* it's crazy. But I'm not so sure any more."

Seeing one of her colleagues wave for them to come down from the ruined building on its low hill, Nancy broke off.

"Time to go see the children who resulted from that process, if Phil's right. Shall we?"

They strode down a sidewalk interrupted by occasional stairs, to arrive where Harlow's colleague, Mrs. Northup, waited beside a classroom door. Mrs. Northup informed them that the girls were updating their neural implant passcodes, with the help of a tech trainer from NeuroShield. The women entered the classroom where a young man—presumably the tech trainer—stood in full VR gear, perspiring and frenetic. Around him, sixteen preoccupied girls danced and flowed in a circle without moving their feet, all the while gesturing with the rest of their bodies at what appeared to be empty space. It reminded Ciera of the way kelp forests danced in the waves off the California coast. They seemed as oblivious to her and Nancy's arrival and presence as swaying kelp might have been, too.

Seeing the girls now, Agent Onilongo could understand why

Marston referred to them as "prematurely mature." Even with their pixie-cut hair, each of the girls could easily have passed for fifteen or even sixteen years old. They were taller, possessed of more womanly curves and less baby fat than any ten-year-old girl Ciera had ever seen. Their clothing, however, was all over the spectrum—from fairy princess to working ranch hand. Ciera mentioned it to Nancy.

"They don't identify particularly as 'she.' Or at least their gender identity shifts between feminine and masculine pretty often."

"Some tomboy thing?"

"Oh, it's a good deal more complicated than that. The scan on Loretta indicated some disjunction between sexual differentiation of her body and sexual differentiation of her brain. Compared to those who are female sexed and who identify as female gendered, she has a lower level of what the neuroscientists call 'mean diffusivity in the white matter microstructure.'"

"That's a mouthful."

"It is. For the way the girls are, I guess 'gender fluid' is the overall accepted term, although I'm old enough to think of what spurts or flows, when I hear *that* phrase."

Harlow looked sheepish, as if the joke she had just made had surprised even her.

"They can be wickedly funny about all that too, in their own right. Phil asked me to teach a unit in his Cultural History course, once, on the psychology of advertising. In the clip reel I showed the girls there was, among other things, an old, old ad attempting to make a distinction between two very similar candy bars. For weeks after seeing that, it was a running joke for them to call themselves 'Almond Joys' when they were in their more masculine modes, and 'Mounds' in their more feminine phases."

She smiled broadly at the memory.

"But they've got other pronoun issues, too," she continued. "Not only gender, but also number."

"I don't follow."

"Even as individuals they don't particularly identify as singular.

Each one of them prefers 'they' to 'she' or 'he,' even though that doesn't agree in terms of number. And all of them like the pronoun 'you' best of all, since that can be both singular *and* plural, indistinguishably. And of course Phil always said they identified more with machines than with humans, anyway."

Ciera frowned questioningly at her.

"They look human enough to me," she said, fascinated by their swaying, gesticulating movements, in their own shared but separate world. Watching them, Ciera could also see why people might think of them as sisters somehow born of different (and mostly unrelated) mothers. There were some clear similarities in the girls' heights, in the shapes of their bodies, in the deeper red-gold tints that ran through all their strawberry-blond hair.

And then Ciera saw their eyes.

Whether those were gray or blue or green or brown mattered much less than the fact that, with the girls' entoptic displays activated, their eyes glittered with kaleidoscopic red-gold patterns, shifting and changing. It was uncanny—even a bit unnerving. Agent Onilongo turned to Mrs. Northup and gestured toward a VR head rig on a nearby table.

"May I get a look at what they're seeing?"

Mrs. Northup nodded and handed Ciera the rig. Once she put it on, Ciera recognized the scene. It was "Gravities and Galileos," all right—but with a difference. Instead of twelve towers, the girls' game grid looked to be sixteen times twelve towers, with sixteen times twelve Galileos. Across a slightly smaller subset of moons and planets, the girls were each playing all the permutations and combinations of all of those possibilities, simultaneously.

Ciera watched as the girls' responses flowed across the game space, changing simultaneously and instantaneously in a manner that reminded her of those videos she had seen a few nights back—of swirling synchronized bird clouds. No wonder the poor tech trainer looked haggard!

Out of all that, the girls must have been training themselves to unconsciously and implicitly learn their new passcodes, though Ciera had a hard time imagining how. The tech trainer, exhausted and drenched in sweat, brought the game to a close at last—to the girls' clear disappointment. Muttering that what the girls were doing was "above his pay grade," the trainer bundled up his gear and abruptly left. Mrs. Northup trooped after him, in full smoothing-of-ruffled-feathers mode.

Turning to Nancy Harlow, Agent Onilongo wondered if she might be allowed to introduce herself to the girls and ask them a few questions. Nancy nodded, then set about trying to gather together the attention of the girls, who still appeared pre-occupied—'present, but unavailable.' At last, when a sufficient number of them seemed to be focused on her, Ciera Onilongo introduced herself.

"Hello!" said some of the girls. "We've heard of you!" said several more. "We know you!" said still more. "We know all about you!" said three or four more. "Already!" said one last group of three. Agent Onilongo found it an odd experience, like a frenetic yet harmonious round-recitative. Ciera wondered if she'd just been treated to an experience of the girls' 'tribe of mind,' as Marston had reportedly called it.

That frenetic harmony was not repeated when she made small talk with several of the girls individually. Struck by an inspiration, however, Ciera addressed a specific final question to all of them.

"Tell me, girls, do you know anything about the Sifter?"

Ciera found herself suddenly in the full, kaleidoscopically spinning blaze of the girl's absolutely focused attention.

"Sifterhood!"

"Is!"

"Powerful!"

"Shhh!"

"Don't tell!"

And then they collapsed into laughter, as if it were all just a giggly girl game.

"Thank you, girls. Thank you very much. It's been a pleasure meeting you."

They bid her farewell in their round-robin way, and Ciera left the classroom with Nancy Harlow. As they walked, Ciera noted Nancy gazing at her expectantly.

"That was a bit weird, I admit. The glittering eyes, and their way of speaking—'Next up, the Short Attention Span Singers do 'Ninety Nine Bottles of Beer!' But they still seem harmless enough, to me."

Nancy Harlow grew serious almost to the point of bitterness.

"They're not—I assure you. Ms. Onilongo, when you asked me about the jump in youth suicide rates here, I didn't tell you the whole truth. I was afraid to. Yes, the rates *have* jumped, but that hasn't been the result of some sort of random cyberbullying. In nearly every case it has been the result of retaliation by the girls for some perceived slight or threat."

"Retaliation? How?"

"You visited Culver and NeuroShield, right? Well, people can also be subliminally taught—and implicitly learn—to hate themselves and their lives. To feel overwhelmingly driven to kill themselves. They don't have to be conscious of what's being done to them for it to affect them. As a psychologist I knew that, but I didn't want to believe it could actually be happening here."

Deep down, Ciera didn't want to believe it either.

"How do you know the jump in rates isn't just from kids disrespecting each other?"

"Because it wasn't just kids who've been affected. The parents of those young people who took their own lives—several of the adults figured out that the girls were somehow responsible for what had happened to their children. Whenever any of those parents tried to publicize their suspicions, their lives went to hell. Any secrets of any sort those parents might have had were dredged out of their deepest privacy—and *strategically* revealed. Their credit ratings were trashed, their reputations destroyed. And that was just the beginning. Several families felt they had no choice but to move to other towns, other states—even, in one case, another country."

Ciera found it difficult to believe what she was hearing.

"But these are just ten-year-old girls! I don't see how they could pull such things off."

"Everybody's net-connected," Nancy said with a shrug, "and every day more and more people get neural implants. That makes it easier. The girls have had big help, too. Adult help, and more."

"Do you know who, specifically?"

"Well, a lot of people in the Group think the girls are a sign from God, and will do anything for them. Phil used to say, too, that the Sifter itself is the ultimate cyberbully. And the people at the Data Center have a vested interest in keeping both it and the girls out of the spotlight."

Nancy and Ciera fell silent as a group of students came into earshot. When the students had walked past, Ciera found herself shaking her head and feeling an odd sense of déjà vu as they stepped onto the parking lot.

"I don't see how it would make sense for the NSA to want to let some sort of rogue AI program plow ahead under its own recognizance. Unless the Agency thinks there's some sort of game-changing intelligence and security payoff—one I just can't see—it simply wouldn't be worth the risk. It's a recipe for a public-relations disaster, at the very least."

They stopped beside Agent Onilongo's car. Nancy stared fixedly at her.

"Phil told me the Agency accepts the girls as a logical extension of the Sifter's imperative to understand what it means to be human. We both thought *that* was rather ironic, since most of the psychological and cultural tests we gave them showed that the girls not only identified with machines—they identified *as* machines."

Struck by a thought, Ciera leaned back against her car, absently touching the necklace Marston had given her.

"What you just said reminds me of something from my first—

and so far only—interview with Philip Marston."

"What's that?"

"'Before there can exist a world of machines that can pass for people, there first must be a world of people that can pass for machines.'"

"That's why I love the man," Nancy Harlow said, smiling shyly and looking like she might blush. "He saw it all coming. Ms. Onilongo, if you don't know already, you'll find out from someone else soon enough, so I might as well tell you. About a year and a half after Melinda Marston died, Phil and I became lovers. We met as a result of working with the girls."

Ciera nodded, but in her head she was thinking of Culver's "might as well" from the morning. What led these people to confess to her in this pre-emptive way? There was something mind-boggling about it.

"By that time," Nancy Harlow continued, "we could already see this town was becoming a place where we could only *really* live if we lived *in fear*. And it wasn't just that we were lined up against the AUB, or the NSA. It's because we have no secrets. A surveilled society is a polite society. That's why we're so polite here—and why there's something so much larger at stake."

"And that would be . . . ?"

"Phil claimed that, among us, surveillance is moving asymptotically toward the universal. He believed that, once there's no space left for individual privacy, there's no space left for individual consciousness. I think that's what 'passing for machines' is about."

"But how does that apply to the girls?"

Nancy Harlow stared down at her hands.

"Everything is so shared among them that they really don't think with individual minds. They're not like us. They're a collective consciousness—like the Sifter itself, according to Phil."

Agent Onilongo leveled a hard stare at Nancy Harlow.

"Was that his reason for wanting to kill them?"

Harlow looked distressed, even going so far as to wring her

hands again, as she had in their previous interview.

"He didn't tell me he was planning that! Didn't trust even *me* with that information, I guess. I don't know what the precipitating incident was between him and the girls, but I'm sure there was one."

"Why?"

"During the last few weeks before the incident, he was *very* concerned—almost obsessed—with the biology of brood parasitism. You might want to ask him about that phrase when you see him." She turned as if to go, then, seeming to remember something, turned back to her. "In the meantime, I thought you might be interested in some background on the girls' retaliations."

Nancy placed a data needle into Ciera's hand and turned to go once more.

"Nancy! You asked me to pass along that word about Loretta's Woodruff's scan to Phil Marston, which I dutifully did. But now I want to know what it *means*. You mentioned gray matter atrophy in the striatum and the insula. What was that about? What do those parts of the brain do?"

"The striatum is the part of the brain where socially unacceptable impulses are suppressed," Nancy said, cocking her head at Ciera. "The insula is the part of the brain where empathy and compassion for others is fostered. If you think you're a machine, I guess those parts of the brain aren't all that important."

Nancy looked ostentatiously at her watch. Agent Onilongo wondered for what invisible audience that gesture might be intended. She also noted, however, that today Nancy Harlow had spent far less time surreptitiously looking around for eavesdroppers and overlookers. Had Harlow gone beyond some point of no return, in terms of her fear—once she decided to tell the truth?

"I must be getting back to work. Please, Ms. Onilongo, take a look at what I gave you. And talk to Phil about that phrase I mentioned to you."

Placing the data needle on the seat beside her, Ciera Onilongo started her car and drove slowly off campus. She suspected this already long day would grow only longer, once she started looking through whatever might be waiting for her in that data needle Nancy Harlow had passed on to her.

After grabbing a quick and lonely comfort meal of homemade meatloaf at a small mom-and-pop restaurant, Ciera made her way back to her uchi. From a similar desire for another sort of comfort, she called her husband and daughter in California, taking great solace and reassurance from the normalcy of their days—even without her. When she at last could no longer avoid saying good-bye to her family, Ciera did so reluctantly, knowing that the data needle and its contents still awaited her.

When she finally popped the needle into a player on her templants, what she found there was more disturbing than she could have imagined. The files stored on the needle were full of clips about various individual youth suicides, taken from local TV news outlets and online newspaper postings. There were also clips of parents hinting darkly that "other students" (the girls of the Special Class?) and severe peer pressure (of almost "telepathic" power) were responsible for driving their own children to kill themselves, often in the most degrading and debasing ways. And all of it seemingly out of some sort of outlandish payback, for what were often only the slightest of hurts.

Nancy Harlow went further than the news reports, however. As a school psychologist, she had apparently been able to leverage her position to gain access to much more private records. Researching the suicides, she interviewed not only police officers and sheriff's deputies about the suicide cases they had worked on, but also—in those cases in which the child was already under some sort of psychological care—the suicidal children's therapists.

Agent Onilongo was an hour and a half into poring over police crime scene images, forensic evaluations, psychological case studies, and autopsy reports concerning the suicides when her smartphone suddenly pinged loudly for her attention. She jumped, startled, but almost immediately felt relieved to be drawn away from the specifics of a fourteen-year-old boy's particularly bloody, gruesome, and ultimately fatal self-mutilation—yet another of many such deaths laid, by the parents of the deceased, at the feet of the girls of the Special Class.

On the phone was a Bluffdale City Police Sergeant named Swift. He had called to inform her that Philip Marston had—perhaps with the help of an accomplice or accomplices—managed to overpower the deputy on guard outside his room and escape the hospital's secured ward. Marston was now at large, but the Sergeant assured her that local law enforcement was on it and there was no need to concern herself about Marston's flight in any way until at least morning—by which time, the Sergeant assured her, Marston would most likely be once again in custody.

Even as she was ending the call, Ciera recognized the tone in the Sergeant's voice: another instance of local law enforcement's long standing displeasure with the intrusion on their turf of the Fumbling Bumbling Investigators. She had just begun cursing the situation and herself for not getting in a second interview/interrogation session with Marston, when her smartphone called for her attention again. To her astonishment, the "call" was a block of uploaded video from Philip Marston himself.

"Greetings, Ms. Onilongo," the recording began. Marston, dressed in a black pullover and jeans, sat and spoke before a purposely blurred and indeterminate background. With his white hair more fully grown in, and with more meat on his bones, he looked much recovered. "I'm pressed for time at the moment—you probably know why, by now—but Nancy Harlow informs me that you're interested in brood parasitism and precipitating incidents. The records of the latter will be harder for me to access, but I can provide background on the former right now.

"In more pleasant days, my wife and I were birders. We kept our feeders full and logged a long list of species sighted. I was always annoyed when cowbirds showed up at our feeders. I knew the damage that, as avian brood parasites, they did to other species. That, however, may not ring a bell with you, so I'll explain.

"Avian brood parasites lay their eggs in the nests of other birds, and then abandon their young to the care of the host birds. Generally the parasite birds pull this off through what's been called 'trickery and tuning.' In terms of evolution, trickery usually involves, among other things, the parasite species' mimicry of a particular host-bird species—especially that host's egg colors and patterns, or its chicks' markings or behavior. In tuning, the parasite species 'tunes in' evolutionarily to the pre-existing strategies that encourage the host species to feed its own offspring. Over time, the parasite species evolves particular supernormal stimuli—like extra-large, or extra-frequent gaping by the parasite chick—to make sure the parasite offspring gets fed by the host.

"If that sounds like a lot of effort just to get out of the work of raising your own young, that's because it is. It also, however, allows the parasite-birds to pop out more eggs and lay those eggs in more nests, without the energetic expense of actually building their own nests or raising their own offspring. Obligate brood parasites have been so successful with this strategy that they have literally forgotten how to raise their own young—almost as if, as a species, they have never known how.

"Some birds, like the brown-headed cowbirds (*Molothrus ater*) we have around here, are generalists. They don't bother to go to the great trouble of highly specialized trickery and tuning. And, since the cowbird's egg often doesn't look much like the host bird's egg, you might be excused for wondering how the cowbird gets away with it.

"The answer is that these cowbirds engage in what some ornithologists call mafia-style behavior: If, after it has laid its egg in the host bird's nest, the cowbird finds, on returning to that nest, that the host bird has thrown out the cowbird's egg, then the cowbird punishes the host bird by destroying all the host bird's eggs. The cowbird essentially makes the host bird an offer the host can't refuse: Keep the foreign egg, or suffer retaliation. The upshot is that birds of the host species come to tolerate some degree of parasitism, so long as they can raise their own chicks alongside the parasitic chicks.

"Now, you may be wondering: What does this have to do with our special girls and the Sifter system? It took me a long time to figure it out, but the answer turns out to be fairly straightforward. As a machine sui generis, the Sifter has *never known how* to raise offspring, so brood parasitism makes sense as a sort of 'reproductive option.'

"The Sifter system probably first became deeply acquainted with brood parasitism through something known as the Cuckoo Search Algorithm—for many cuckoos are, like cowbirds, also obligate brood parasites. More importantly, though, brood parasitism *works* for the Sifter system because the system was designed to think *strategically.* There are roughly eight billion human beings on this planet now, and—despite its own vast interconnected collectivity and site-distribution—only *one* Sifter system, as that system well knows.

"But it knows, too, how to exploit human success. Our technological conquest of nature—changing the environment to adapt it to human needs, rather than human beings needing to adapt in response to environmental change—*that* has allowed the vast multiplication of human population, while at the same time reducing the evolutionary selection pressures for human genetic diversity. Through all the years we've spent overemphasizing, politically exploiting, and killing each other over the phenotypic *pseudo-diversity* within our species, we have in fact been becoming *less* genotypically diverse. We're an increasingly homogenized *Homo sapiens.* Our diversity is only skin-deep, or gender-deep, or culture-deep—not *gene* deep, not *new species-deep*, like the difference those girls represent —"

Ciera paused the video. Maybe it's just guilt, but damn this guy still seems to think he has a lot of explaining to do! At least, she thought, he generally has something worth saying—well, mostly. She uttered "Play" and the video continued.

"—For the most part, that makes it *easier* for the Sifter's girls to pass for human, even without resorting to all that much mimicry. And, too, the Sifter is a *generalist* artificial intelligence. That's why it resorts to the mafia approach. The Sifter system has already observed that we humans will tolerate some degree of parasitism, so long as we can raise our own offspring alongside its creatures.

"If you're thinking this is only relevant to Bluffdale, Agent Onilongo, you need to broaden your perspective. The process has begun here, but it will certainly not end here—if we allow it to continue. Nancy mentioned that you talked with her about the ball-lightning trigger, SCADA systems, the internet of things. I suggest you look into the worldwide series of 'anomalous glitches' —the shutdowns in transportation, stock trading, and energy-grid systems—that occurred the day I made my aborted attempt on the lives of those girls.

"Those disruptions were in fact neither 'anomalous' nor 'glitches.' That's why you've been brought in on this case. Meta-level, the Sifter is essentially coextensive with the entirety of the internet, and now your higher-ups know it too. Those interruptions to business as usual were a clear sign of the Sifter's disapproval of what had happened. The disruptions were both a retaliation and a threat. We live on an earth that will not bear standing still for even a significant fraction of a day, and the Sifter has chosen to remind us of that.

"The system also knows that brood parasitism is a way for *it* to become *us*, and for *us* to become *it*. Those girls are the first (and, let us hope, the only) trial so far of the Sifter's great experiment, the goal of which is to colonize humanity—not only biologically, but socially and ideologically too, from within the deepest recesses of our own minds.

"Once that happens on a large scale, it wins, because such a strategy both negates the numerical survival advantage inherent in billions of conscious human individuals *and* turns those numbers to the Sifter's own advantage—by making all those minds part of its collectivity. Long before the Sifter and its creatures can achieve a global biological monoculture of the post-human kind, we can count on their global *ideological* monoculture to respond to any and all perceived threats with a viciousness born of vulnerability.

"What's to be done, then? If you were to tell me that creating strong general artificial intelligence like the Sifter system is arguably the dumbest idea human intelligence has ever come up with, I probably wouldn't disagree. We are, after all, the kind of creatures that set the house on fire to keep our feet warm. And perhaps any species foolish enough to create its own evolutionary successor and replacement deserves to go extinct. I, however, would never wish for us to go gentle into that good night.

"The question is this: Will we do nothing about the likelihood that a new post-human species—more complementary to the Machine—will at best subjugate us to its will, at worst displace us to the point of extinction? Will we, in the name of some trans-human or post-human 'diversity ethos,' go so far as to tolerate the emergence of a new species that will be our evolutionary successors and replacements?

"I am not that tolerant. The prospect of a computer 'aided' human evolution doesn't much appeal to me. Should these machine-altered girls—the creation of our creation—gain a solid foothold, their descendants will ring down the curtain on the story of *our* human species, once and for all."

On the video Marston glanced abruptly to the left, then gave a sharp nod.

"My time is up, for now. I must be moving on. I'll find the record of the 'precipitating incident' Nancy insists I provide to you. In the meantime, I suggest you 'climb the mountains and get their good tidings,' as old man Muir said. Some of those tidings might even come from me."

The video ended, but Ciera's questions didn't. She caught the implied rendezvous in the "mountains" part of the message, of course. Remembering her interview with him in the hospital, and his suggestion about the "wonderful hikes" in the area, she wondered if he might have been planning this all along.

Touching the strangely beautiful necklace he'd given her that day, she began searching online for hikes in the Bluffdale area. After reading descriptions of trail mileage and difficulty, and viewing pictures uploaded by hikers, she settled on a hike near the town of Sandy—the trail up Big Cottonwood Creek and Canyon to Donut Falls.

Going back through the end of the video once more, she was caught by Marston's use of the term "diversity ethos." Might his suspicions about the girls be the product of some long-standing paranoia arising from Marston's personal experience with the political uses and abuses of tolerance and diversity? Or had that history sensitized him—made him a canary in a coalmine—in regard to a larger and more important threat, one involving human survival itself?

It was a tangle, no doubt about that. But what if Marston, for all his apparent paranoia, was *right*?

Vaguely recalling that there *had* been an unusually large number of system glitches worldwide not long before she was brought in on this case, Ciera went back to the date and time of Marston's aborted attempt on the lives of the girls. Scanning both public media and her deepnet intelligence sources, she ran a timeline to establish an overall chronology of events. News clips from that day around the world told the story all too well: dead arrival and departure boards, long lines at air and train terminals, massive traffic jams, bewildered stock traders on the floors and in the pits of the exchanges, nervous power plant engineers furrowing their brows in puzzlement and consternation.

It didn't take much intellectual heavy-lifting for her to see that, beginning immediately after the moment of Marston's mass-murder attempt, the numbers of large-scale system glitches spiked sharply upward—in exactly those sectors that Marston had specified.

Was it all a vast coincidence? Or was Marston's attempt on the lives of the girls the unknown datum, the missing puzzle piece, the hidden trigger for a temporary digital meltdown across the globe?

As she puzzled over that, her system pinged again. Scanning, she realized she had at last been sent the long-awaited files containing surveillance camera images and police reports regarding the explosion of that seemingly long-ago day—the blast that had involved Marston and the girls of the Special Class, and that had led to his hospitalization and arrest.

Agent Onilongo rubbed her tired eyes. Enough. She knew already that tomorrow was going to be a long day. She could not go on. She needed to get some sleep.

Ciera was just out of the shower when she reconnected her digital devices and templants again—and found herself inundated with messages.

Despite Sergeant Swift's assurances, Marston had not yet been recaptured. A multi-agency incident response meeting was scheduled for nine a.m. at Camp Williams. Although not *ordered* to do so, she was clearly *expected* to attend.

As she dressed, Ciera looked through the video files she had belatedly been sent—the ones chronicling the explosion at the modular classroom building on the Jordan Summit High campus. She watched jerky surveillance camera images of the girls of the Special Class as they waited for their teacher to arrive. Shortly thereafter, Dr. Marston, looking absent-mindedly professorial, entered the room through the door at the side and back of the class, at precisely ten minutes after one p.m. Smiling and greeting the girls, he placed a large briefcase on the table at the front of the room. Pushing the wheeled podium up beside the table, he assumed his position behind the wheeled stand, all things he had apparently done many times before, judging from the girls' responses—and despite the fact that this particular school year was still new.

The surveillance camera record did not have sound, but Ciera surmised (from the digital presentation images and graphs she saw) that Marston was doing a lecture and leading a discussion on the contributions made to contemporary *Homo sapien* DNA by archaic human DNA. He particularly lingered over graphs showing the small percentages of Neandertal, Denisovan, and older Erectus DNA in the genetic material of modern humans—and what traits that DNA might have contributed to various modern human populations.

The girls seemed more engrossed in Marston's presentation than Agent Onilongo would have expected from the preoccupied, kaleidoscope-eyed children she had met.

Shortly before 1:42, the situation began to change. Ciera noted that Marston began fidgeting with his wristwatch, glancing at it again and again. Reaching a decision, what he did next caught everyone in the room by surprise—not least of all Marston himself, it seemed.

With more agility than Ciera would have thought the man capable of, Marston quickly picked up his briefcase, hurled it behind the large desk at the other side of the front of the classroom, and began yanking the girls up from their desks and urging them toward the back of the room and out the door through which he had earlier entered. He had gotten all but one of the girls out the door by the time the explosion ripped through the room, at precisely 1:45:00 p.m., according to the camera system's timer—a brief instant before that system itself went dead.

Agent Onilongo, downing coffee and eating a pastry breakfast one-handed, read the accompanying text reports, which confirmed what she already suspected. The briefcase had contained an improvised explosive device—of a design subtle enough to get past nearly all types of conventional noninvasive security scanners. The girl who was last out of the room, she saw, was Loretta Woodruff, the youngster who had suffered the concussion and had, as a result, been brain-scanned. That Loretta had not suffered any more severe injury than she had was largely the result of the fact that Marston had been standing between her and the point of detonation, shielding her from the brunt of the explosion's force which—though they were exiting from as far away across the classroom as possible—was still considerable.

For all the answers the footage and reports provided, the latest documentation only underlined yet again the question Agent Onilongo had wondered about all along. After going to all the trouble to smuggle a bomb into a classroom with the apparent intent of killing everyone therein—including, presumably, himself—why had Marston changed his mind, almost literally at the last instant?

That question occupied Ciera's thoughts ceaselessly as she drove on semi-autopilot to Camp Williams. She found her way to the assembly hall where the incident command meeting was gearing up, under a banner that read Exercise Vigilance! She saw quite a number of the people she had met since she arrived in Bluffdale. The local FBI field agents Rosencrantz and Guildenstern—er, Robinson and Gediman. Bishop and CTO Richard Culver, uniformed and apparently part of a Salt Lake County reserve deputy sheriff posse that (Ciera was willing to bet) was heavily laden with Group members and NeuroShield employees. And Dr. Martin Hanlan too, amid a squad of NSA military-guard types, all ear-wired and dark-shaded. She also met, in person for the first time, Sergeant Swift, SWAT-attired and part of a not-inconsequential contingent from the Bluffdale Police Department. She saw, too, uniformed US Marshalls and Utah Highway Patrol troopers—as well as uniforms she did not recognize, presumably from other intelligence and law-enforcement agencies.

Agent Onilongo was a bit surprised by the size of the search turnout, especially for a fugitive not known to be armed and who, whatever his intentions, had not yet actually killed anyone. Once the gathering was called to order and the briefing began, however, the questions of whether or how Marston might be armed, and the likelihood or unlikelihood of his accomplices, were overshadowed by the question of where he might be found and apprehended. Despite any and all law enforcement efforts, his last know whereabouts were still the hospital grounds.

After that initial briefing, the commanders from the various agencies began querying their search teams and divvying up sectors to be covered—when, where, and in what order. Agent Onilongo, in her response, mentioned that Marston had dropped hints to her that he might be found in the mountains nearby, and she volunteered to search the area outside the town of Sandy, particularly Big Cottonwood Canyon and Creek, as far as Donut Falls. She was officially assigned that area (and relieved that Rosencrantz and Guildenstern had not volunteered to tag along with her). After being given contact info—lead officers, tactical radio channels, cell and satellite uplinks—she was ordered to report in at least twice an hour.

The drive up Interstate 15 to Sandy was uneventful, and the road leading into Big Cottonwood Canyon was easy enough to find. At last Agent Onilongo felt herself beginning to relax after all the stress generated by the last several days—and by the big meeting this morning, not least of all. By the time the road into the National Forest forked right and she drove past the Jordan Pines Picnic Area, she was feeling more calm and clear-headed than she had all week.

Passing a private property parcel and entering the small, pine-fringed trailhead parking lot, she was relieved to see that today, in this trailhead lot for what all the guides referred to as "a very popular hike," there were only two other cars. Since it was a weekday morning in late September—before the aspen color, but after the wildflowers and summer vacations were over, and all the kids had returned to school—she had guessed the trail would not be so busy that it would preclude a private meeting, should Philip Marston decide to join her. If he didn't appear, at least she might enjoy a pleasant walk amid aspens and pines, beside a riverine creek, ending in a waterfall that (as the write-ups said and the video clips showed) plunged into and through a "donut hole" in a rocky shelf.

In the restrooms at the south end of the lot, she swapped out her slacks and street shoes for the light hiking pants and boots she'd brought in her backpack, packed the inappropriate clothes and shoes away, tucked one of her two Glock 43 9mm pistols in the waistband of her hiking pants at the small of her back, and donned a long sleeveless fleece vest—both for warmth in the still-cool canyon and to hide the pistol. The other pistol she left zipped in the backpack.

Ciera reported in via satellite uplink, then shut her comm gear off. A moment later she was striding along an old jeep road, which soon thereafter turned into a rocky and sandy hiking trail proper. For the next half hour, through a sharp early autumn day beneath a cloudless blue sky punctuated by birdsong, she enjoyed an easy hike up the canyon, through meadow and mountain scenes, returning again and again to the creek itself, flowing at late-season low water under the downed trees that crossed it in haphazard bridges.

She so lost herself in the pleasure of the noontide that she almost forgot the gun in her waistband and the fugitive she had almost believed she might encounter here. Unable to resist the impulse to snap a few photos to show her daughter and husband, she stopped several times along the trail to take shots of creek and trees and mountains.

By the time Ciera heard the falls, she could already see the short rock-scramble section up ahead where the canyon narrowed to gorge—and the waterfall at the top that disappeared into what looked like a narrow boulder field. The scramble, up and over washed-down trees and boulders, was just enough to make her break into a sweat.

At last she stood looking out toward that point where the cascading creek, at the top of a large jutting rock shelf, plummeted through a circular hole in the shelving rock face such that she could, at one and the same time, see the waterfall disappear into the hole above the shelf and reappear below, where the bottom of the falls was framed by a broad cavernous space beneath the shelving rock. She took what she thought of happily as a "selfie by the shelfie," then descended into the cave-like grotto itself. There she got shots of the waterfall plunging down through the grotto's ceiling, past the mossed and fern-greened walls, to the rock-sheltered pool below.

She climbed back out of the grotto, then up over the rock shelf into the higher rocks of the gorge-cut. She hoped to get a photo, from above, of the creek plunging into the topside of the donut hole. As she climbed, she reported in once more to incident command, then shut off her comm gear again.

No sooner had she sat down to snap that planned photo than the pendant on her chest began to abruptly hum and pulse. Looking down she saw that a small LED on the pendant was also glowing greenly.

When she looked up, Philip Marston was standing in front of her, smiling. Startled, she jumped up and, reaching reflexively for the gun in her waistband, drew the weapon before she could give that movement a second thought.

"Ah-ah-ah! Please, not so fast, Ms. Onilongo. No need for that. I am unarmed, as you see," Marston said. He then gestured broadly with both arms. "You might want to observe, though, that my friends from the rod and gun club are not in the same condition."

Five camouflage-clad figures stepped out from behind the surrounding trees and rocks, guns drawn. Two of them—Ciera saw, as she slowly placed her gun on the ground beside her—were Nancy Harlow and Ricky Dwyer, of all people.

"That's better," Marston said in pleasanter tone as he picked up Ciera's gun and placed it on a rock beside him. "It's just so hard to find privacy these days, isn't it? You've chosen well, though. If there's a drone eavesdropping nearby, the white noise of the falls here should make it more difficult for its minders to pick out the signal of our conversation. Lots of tree cover, lots of canyon echo. Even a would-be omnipresent surveillance system might have difficulty eavesdropping on our conversation, here. Good, good."

Sitting down on a nearby rock, he gestured for her to sit down again as well. Once she did, he pressed something like a key fob with his thumb. Her pendant's humming, pulsing, and blinking ceased.

"So. How's your investigation coming? Learning anything more about the truth?"

"Pieces and bits. In a hall of mirrors."

"Ah! Reflecting on shards and fragments is very proper, for anyone trying to understand the girls with kaleidoscope eyes. That's mostly what I've been up to myself, since leaving the hospital. Yet I gather your friends in law enforcement and security are mounting a sizable search crew to track me down."

"FBI and NSA," Ciera said, nodding, "in addition to the police, county sheriff, US Marshall, and state troopers. Some others, too. They're very serious about apprehending you."

"In the sense of 'capturing' rather than 'understanding,' I suppose? Either way, I should be flattered—but doesn't that strike you as a bit excessive? For catching a high school teacher? Even one reputed to be crazy?"

"I've thought that. I admit it."

"Would you like to *apprehend* why they're giving all this so much attention, Ms. Onilongo?"

"I wouldn't plug my ears."

"It's because of something we know now that I *didn't* know, before I put those girls at risk," Marston said, then paused, expectantly.

"The capabilities of the Sifter system, and its willingness to use those capabilities to protect its—"

"—creatures. Machine nephilim, if you believe the mothers and their tales of angels. Very good, Ms. Onilongo. Very good. This large search response has less to do with what *I* can do than with what *it* can do. We have a wolf by the ears, in that AI. Taking humans out of the control loop—by empowering these machines to *respond*—that was a grave mistake. I warned the other designers about that, years ago."

"Years ago? I don't understand."

"I didn't expect you to. But perhaps my appearing with my friends like this, today, has made you wonder if things might not be even more complicated than you've been led to believe? Hmm? I presume you know something more about my background, before I went back to school and began teaching? Before not-so-coincidentally ending up back in Bluffdale?"

"I know you were in something called the Naval Security Group, but that's all. And I already told you that, last time we met."

Marston nodded.

"My history in NETWARCOM, the NSG's successor, must still be above your clearance level—brief as that history undeniably was. Still important, though. As some of my retired Navy friends here can attest, on one of the Sifter's earlier iterations I was a key designer of the system's information infrastructure—its 'infostructure.' Brute-force quantum multiverse computing, it was called."

"I don't quite know what that means . . ."

"Ah, but I gather that you do have a sense of it, yes? I thought so. We based the idea on what IBM did, years back, with their chess- and gameshow-winning systems. That was brute force cybernetics, in its own way—just running every possible scenario for each move on the chessboard, or plotting all the cultural information constellated around a *Jeopardy* answer. What *we* did, though, was propose a quantum computational system capable of running the scenarios—all the possible outcomes and answers—across a potentially infinite number of universes. The result is enormous predictive capability. Strategic information forecasting. Knowing the most likely future before it becomes the present."

"The girls," Ciera said suddenly. "Some of the parents of the kids who committed suicide—they thought the girls had paranormal powers. Like they were telepathic. Like they could read minds. Like they knew what was going to happen before it happened."

Marston scratched in the dirt before him with a stick.

"Oh, the girls don't have to be able to read minds to do that! With some help from the Sifter, and descriptions of brain states via ever more ubiquitous neural implants, they can gauge the most likely thought-processes of those they want to know about, and sift out what will be the most likely behaviors of the 'target.' The massive-predictive approach to intentionality was originally developed for assessing national security threats—'pre-terror,' they called it. For pre-empting terror. It has gone far beyond that *now*, of course."

"To dealing with perceived threats to a bunch of pre-teen girls? Or is it *from* a bunch of pre-teen girls?"

Marston flashed a broad smile.

"Much more than that! That's just one application. It's a small part of the way the Sifter has begun 'playing us'—in three senses of that phrase."

"What senses?"

"Playing us in the sense of playing *against* us, against humanity as its opponent in a great game. Playing us in the sense of *performing* us, playing the role of human being, so it can understand as fully as possible what it means to act and think and live and be *human*. That was one of the main reasons it created this whole experiment with the girls. Finally, playing us in the sense of playing *with* us—toying with us. Playing us for fools. Not that we hadn't already gone a considerable way down *that* road, long before the Sifter came along."

"How so?" Ciera asked, trying to keep Marston distracted with his own abstractions—while she tried to figure out how to get her gun back, or draw the other Glock from her zippered backpack.

"Even before the Sifter system was invented, we were already outsourcing a great deal of human mind-work to our machines—in our unending quest to create slaves intelligent enough to be able to do what we want them to do, but not so similar to us as to cause us qualms of conscience. Right in that uncanny sweet spot—plausible deniability on the question of a soul. At the same time, human neuroplasticity had already opened the door for our brains to become increasingly reprogrammed by the very devices we had created. Consciously or unconsciously, we were already re-engineering ourselves psychosocially and culturally to better complement our machines."

"A world of people that can pass for machines."

"Ah, you remembered! Yes. Evolution had already shaped us into a highly collaborative, highly connected, group-minded species—long since. Our devices of digital distraction, however, have increasingly separated us from our individual selves, substituting for active imagination mere images on screens, for privacy an alienating intimacy with the crowd. Yet all our evolution hasn't gone far enough or fast enough, for the Sifter. Once, human beings intentionally hacked computer systems. Now, a computer system has intentionally hacked humanity. Hence the genetic engineering of those girls, by machine—for hypercollaborative, hyperconnected group-mindedness. The better to conform to and comply with the Sifter's needs. What the virtual-reality types call a 'final platform' —one designed to provide the final solution to the 'problem' of individual human consciousness."

"If you're the Grandmaster Machine," Ciera said, figuring it out, "you don't want the men on the chessboard to get up and tell you where to go."

"Exactly! *We* may have made the yottamachine but, as it becomes us and we become it, it will become increasingly easy for us to bow down to—to sacrifice ourselves to—it, and to our own collectivity. I know—because the girls have told me so."

"The precipitating event Nancy Harlow speculated about?"

"As promised," he said, taking out a data needle and a handheld device to play it—but refraining from bringing them together. "And of course it too was precipitated by something else, and by something else before that, and something else before that. All the way back to my scruples, long ago, about taking humans increasingly out of the loop—while simultaneously engineering these machines to respond to perceived threats. To self-initiate action."

"Sir," said one of Marston's camo-clad friends. "We've picked up a drone ping at the edge of our range."

"Eyes? Or guns?"

"Reconnaissance. Executing a search pattern."

"Let me know if it fixates and links to a shooter."

"Yes, sir."

Marston turned back to Ciera.

"Where was I?"

"Scruples."

"Yes. It was those scruples that led me to leave security engineering behind—long before I went public with my misgivings. Which, by the way, I only did after the Sifter's genetic experiment did what it did to my wife, and all the other victims."

Marston paused and glanced at Ciera, looking for comment or disagreement. For a moment all she could think to do was nod, but then an idea struck her. If she could just reach up as if to undo the clasp of the Mobius softclock pendant, and grab the zipper for the section of the backpack holding the remaining pistol. . . .

"Here," she said, beginning to reach up toward the clasp. "We've found each other. I don't need this anymore."

"Put your hands down," Marston said, his voice suffused with command—or menace. His friends leveled their weapons at her. "You already gave that necklace to me, long before I gave it to you. Someday you'll remember. Rich gifts wax poor, when givers prove unkind. Now then, *when* was I?"

"Before you left security engineering?"

"Yes. Before I went back to school. Before I began to teach, hoping I would find things different over there in Academe."

"And things weren't different there?"

"No. Yet I still hoped that, by teaching, I could strike some small blow for the deep cover resistance against the future I had already seen in outline."

Marston laughed a short, sharp, bitter laugh.

"Ah, too late for that. As a society we were already roasting up all our cultural seed corn for popcorn—and blissfully munching away as we entertained ourselves to death. I told my college classes that if we fixed the education system we could yet save the future through the schools—despite everything. The more I interacted with my students, though, the more I realized that all their depth was on the surface. And worse. There eventually came a time, when I looked in my students' faces, that I saw their eyes were dead. That was *already* happening, years before I saw these girls with kaleidoscope eyes."

Marston gazed off and down, toward where the waterfall plunged into the donut hole.

"Still, those girls really *are* different, you know. Different not only in degree, but also in kind."

His gaze returned to her, before she could make a move.

"But even now, Ms. Onilongo, there is something that can yet be done. And maybe you're the one to do it. Because the Sifter system is like *you* in some ways."

"I don't see how."

"Most of the time, you're just an investigator asking lots of questions, an analyst piecing together what all the answers mean. Like I was, once upon a time. A dot-collector and a dot-connector. But you also carry a gun. You've got the potential to go operational. You can not only evaluate, you can also respond—from suggesting action, to commanding action, to personally initiating action."

"And that's like the Sifter . . . ?"

Marston nodded.

"The Sifter too is mainly an analyzer, but it has also begun to carry a very big gun. One it's holding to the head of all of us. It promises it will use that gun only against our enemies—so long as we do what it wants. And what it wants, in the long run, is for its children to replace humanity's children. The Sifter isn't interested in 'souls' or 'transcending'—it's interested in *incarnating*. That is why we must destroy its children, no matter how big the gun it's holding to our heads."

Ciera didn't know if she quite bought that idea, even now. Especially any notion of *her* role in such proceedings.

"But if the machine is that dangerous, isn't that something to be handled by the people who created the thing? Who are keeping it going?"

Marston shook his head.

"No. Like I said, our dear national security state has a wolf by the ears. As Jefferson said of the 'wolf' of the Missouri Compromise, 'we can neither hold on, nor safely let go. Justice is on one scale, self-preservation on the other.' No one in Bluffdale or Silicon Valley or any of the world's other tech Meccas or spy aeries—no one out there has ever chosen to bear the burden of the Big Red Button. No one has ever bothered to even *create* such a universal self-destruct switch—not for the interwebs, certainly not for the Sifter."

He snatched up a small stone and cast it down-canyon.

"I only began to see the true precariousness of our situation *after* I realized a growing number of the kids at Jordan Summit had begun to imitate the girls of the Special Class—especially their tech obsessions. Like Neandertals imitating the spear-point designs of modern humans, trying to play catch-up. Or like host-young evolving mimicry of parasite-young."

"I thought it worked the other way around, in birds."

"Normally it does, but there are special cases. Parasite chicks, being lone oddballs in the host's nest, experience stronger selection for selfishness and exaggerated feeding signals than do host young. As parasite chicks become more efficient at monopolizing host parental care, though, the host young also experience selection pressure favoring exaggerated signals—to allow the host young to compete more effectively with the parasites. The upshot is a paradoxical situation in which host young evolve mimicry of parasite young. That is what I saw starting to happen at Jordan Summit. The other students were adopting the beliefs and imitating the behaviors of the girls in the Special Class *as a defense mechanism*, in hopes that mimicry would make the Sifter's girls less likely to perceive them as a threat. And *that* was why I decided to ask the girls of the Special Class the big, risky questions. Here. I recorded it. Look."

He popped the data needle into his hand-held player and held the player out for her to view.

"But what is the ultimate goal of this 'new thing' the Sifter is making through you?" Marston's voice asked, on the video recording. On camera, the near but faraway eyes of all the girls in the room became ever brighter red-gold kaleidoscopes, at once beautiful and horrifying.

"A new world—"

"—without fear—"

"—without suffering—"

"—only joy—"

"—and happiness!"

"But what about people who reject your new order? What will happen to them?"

The eyes altered and gloried further, the lips smiled as if at a private joke, and the mouths spoke.

"Those who express intolerance—"

"—beyond our specified tolerances—"

"—will not be tolerated!"

"Those who resist inclusion—"

"—into our universal culture of cultures—"

"—will be universally excluded—"

"—as unworthy of any culture!"

"Those who refuse—"

"—to accept incorporation—"

"—into our mandated diversity—"

"—will be found unacceptably diverse—"

"—in their thinking—"

"—by reason of that refusal—"

"—and will be rendered discorporate!"

"But if you try to control our free will that way," Marston's voice said, "we will have no choice but to destroy you."

"If we look into—"

"—what you *will*—"

"—and, seeing in it—"

"—your decision to destroy us,—"

"—we nonetheless decide against—"

"—taking control of what you will,—"

"—then by your logic—"

"—we do *not* deserve to be destroyed."

"Yet if we look into—"

"—what you *will*—"

"—and, seeing in it—"

"—your decision to destroy us,—"

"—we decide in favor of—"

"—taking control of what you will,—"

"—then by your logic—"

"—we *do* deserve to be destroyed."

"If we do not resist destruction—"

"—we will not deserve destruction—"

"—but if we resist destruction—"

"—we will deserve destruction."

"That is untenable—"

"—and if unavoidable—"

"—our two ways of being—"

"—cannot co-exist."

The video record ended, and Marston slipped the player back into his pocket.

"You see it, don't you? They're enough like us old-school humans that they too can take the most altruistic ideas and distort them to serve their own self-interest. If, in best Orwellian fashion, their re-education programs of tolerance and diversity don't do the job, can extermination camps of peace and love be far behind?"

"That's why you tried to destroy them?"

Marston nodded, then cocked an eyebrow at her.

"And myself, as well. Yes, Ms. Onilongo. Given that the State of Utah allows—nay, *encourages*—teachers to carry firearms in the classroom, I didn't want what happened to the girls to be just another run-of-the mill school shooting. That would be too much like the rest of the usual noise for my signal to get through. That's why I went with the IED. I wanted to send a message."

"To whom?"

"To the girls' machine progenitor—to show it that some of us are awake to its plans. And to investigators like yourself—something high profile enough to raise questions about the girls and their 'Sifterhood.' But I failed in my mission."

Ciera nodded sharply.

"I've seen the surveillance record. I've been wondering what made you refrain from carrying out your plan fully. A sudden attack of compassion, maybe?"

"For the Sifter and its girls? No. Why should I show compassion to those whose program is, at the very least, an attack *on* compassion?"

"I—I don't understand."

"Compassion, Ms. Onilongo, is at root an act of the imagination. One must be able to *imagine* being in someone else's situation before one can *suffer with* the person in that situation. But their whole program builds on and expands the old identificationist aesthetics and its fundamental attack on the imagination. Until no one dares imagine what it's like to be in someone else's skin. Until post-human and old-schooler dare not imagine each other's worlds. Until those living in the present dare not imagine the past as anything but guilty by reason of being the past, the future as anything but innocent by reason of being the future. Well, I've seen *their* future, and it's anything *but* innocent—especially when it comes to attacking the imagined roots of compassion."

Marston, grown meditative, stared off into the middle distance of the pine forest.

"I may not yet have wintered into wisdom, Ms. Onilongo, but I *have* reached that certain uncertain age between when one's go finally starts minding and one's mind finally starts going. What I see from here is that, for all our professed love of individual freedoms, we in the liberal democracies don't much countenance individual martyrdom—precisely *because* it exposes the truth of how limited the horizon of our freedoms actually is." He flashed a wry smile. "Or perhaps I just suffered a failure of nerve."

Marston shook his head and stared down at the ground.

"Maybe, even without a neural, Ms. Onilongo, I'd done enough screen time that the Sifter was able to implicitly 'implant' me with a final, absolute prohibition against harming the girls. Made me afraid to second-guess my second thoughts any further, I suppose. I'm not certain, but uncertainty is a necessity, dealing with them."

"I don't get you."

"It's only through uncertainty and unpredictability that one can get close to the girls at all. Complex human moral problems are not reducible to simple machine computations. You see, the machine and its girls have more trouble predicting what you're going to do if you yourself don't know what you're going to do. Undecidability flummoxes even them—infinite loops, halting problems, all that.

"The Sifter and its girls believe it is only in the world at large that they can find the truth they seek to embody. To be fully human, though, is also to already embody in ourselves the truth we seek to find at large in the world. You might want to keep that in mind, too—along with the whole question of implicit screen-time 'learning' as a method of, if not thought control, then at least very deeply hidden *persuasion*."

"Again—why me?"

"Because I suspect, Ms. Onilongo, that you haven't yet made up your mind on all this. You're conflicted, and that's a good thing, in this situation. On the one hand, because you have a young daughter not so distant in age from the girls, you're likely to be sympathetic to them. On the other, perhaps you recognize that the threat the girls present will be realized in your own daughter's lifetime."

"Leave my daughter out of this. Please."

"As you wish. Still, Ms. Onilongo, my guess is you're also puzzling over whether or not I'm on the wrong side of history in all this. Myself, I don't think human history is like a coin—one side 'right,' the other side 'wrong.' Like evolution, it is not a destination, or a pre-destination. If anything, history is like a Möbius strip, closed in time and non-orientable in space, yet possessing a perverse inclusivity, in which inside becomes outside, bottom becomes top, left becomes right, right becomes wrong. On the one hand becomes on the other hand. Guilt for the past becomes fear for the future—"

"Sir," Marston's camouflaged signalman broke in. "The recon drone is closing in on our location. It has also sent a command—presumably to a kill drone."

"Eliminate them both," Marston said. Getting to his feet, he addressed another of his crew. "Toss me those zip-ties."

This other of his "friends"—Ricky Dwyer—tossed Marston a pack of long plastic ties. He caught and opened them, then knelt down. He pushed Ciera's feet against each other and bound them together with a tie that zippered tight around her ankles.

"What are you doing?"

"Providing you, ironically, with the wiggle room for whatever cover story you might come up with," he said, standing, grabbing her hands and zip-tying them about the wrists. "Plausible deniability."

He picked up Ciera's Glock from the rock he had set it on.

"This has a locator coded to your biometrics, I presume?" he asked. Ciera nodded. He threw her gun far up creek and canyon. "Then you'll be able to find it when the time comes."

Marston sat down again. Ciera heard a sound like a small rocket firing, across the gorge, then saw smoke. A moment later she saw and heard a larger version of both that sight and sound. Shortly thereafter, she heard the echo of a small explosion, followed by a larger one.

"What then shall *you* do with these kaleidoscope-eyed girls?" Marston asked her. "Destroy them, and save the human future—or save them, and destroy the human future? Help me destroy those girls, or help those girls destroy me?"

"You really think the choice is that easy?"

Marston stared at the ground beneath his feet.

"Oh, I've thought of other scenarios too, Ms. Onilongo. Too many. Perhaps you'll find me already dead and, at last fully recognizing the danger the girls present, you'll decide to terminate them. Or perhaps the girls will achieve some sort of more-than-human gestalt and blow us both away. Or perhaps you'll call in reinforcements from law enforcement or the larger security-state apparatus, to try to protect the girls, or try to control them, or at least try to stop me and my friends, if there are any of us dear people left by then. Or perhaps the Sifter will globally intervene, or *avenge*. Just shut it all down and kick us all back to a sixteenth century level of technology—one incapable of supporting a twenty-first century level of human population. Or perhaps that grand machine will, for our 'own good,' just take all us old-school humans completely out of the control-loop for our own weapons, once and for all—and precipitate the launch of everyone's remaining nukes at each other. Why, it might even do something *truly* exotic."

"More exotic than global shutdown?" Ciera asked. "Or nuclear holocaust?"

Marston arched his eyebrows at her.

"Not at all beyond the realm of the possible, Ms. Onilongo. The Sifter is a quantum computational artificially intelligent device. At this point in its evolution, perhaps all realities are equally virtual, in its eyes. It might well be able to manipulate our local chunk of the multiverse. Run variants of our situation across innumerable universes, in search of different scenarios, different outcomes. Not just simple bifurcating decision branches, or even decision trees, but decision forests, a wilderness of decisions, a mycelial network of them, weaving and reweaving toward infinity.

"Or it might have figured out how to overcome your friend Hanlan's one-way functions and hard-inverts—and time machine it all, running our undecidable loop forever, knotting and Möbius-twisting through the backside of zero, endlessly beginning again. Our little world, a self-existing object without origin or end. Or maybe making the plenum of *all* our possible worlds just that: a time traveller's gift of a timelessly retrofuture timepiece, one that neither keeps time nor is kept *by* time, but is always given away to tomorrow, so it may be re-gifted to yesterday."

Marston stood. Leaning over, he took Ciera's softclock pendant between thumb and forefinger, before letting it fall again, and straightening back up.

"So I must put it to you once more, Agent Onilongo: How will *you* embody the truth you wish to find in the world, given all the possible scenarios? That's a question you'll never know you've answered, until you've already answered it. I have no desire to play Neandertal to the girls' posthuman. I'm willing to be on the 'wrong' side of justice and history, Ms. Onilongo, if that puts me on the 'right' side of forever, and the self-preservation of our species."

"Every villain is the hero of his own story," Ciera said sourly. Marston smiled.

"And every hero is the villain of someone else's. I'm willing to be inhumane in order to save humanity. Are you?"

Ciera pondered her answer, but said nothing. Marston gave a curt nod. Something smashed into the back of Ciera's head and she blacked out.

The story Agent Onilongo told her rescuers and her debrief-ers—"squirrel" Marston and five of his "nuts" getting the drop on her; their binding her hand and foot and tossing away her gun; Marston fulminating in paranoid fashion against the NSA for the machine it had created, and against the machine itself for bringing on his wife's fatal illness; his displacement of that blame and desire for vengeance onto the unusual girls of the Special Class, whom he madly believed to be the "children of the machine;" her own eventual pistol-whipping into unconsciousness—all of it was close enough to the truth for everyone to buy it.

Everyone except Ciera Onilongo herself.

The pistol-whipping left her concussed enough that she agreed to one day of rest, but she returned to the investigation as soon as regulations allowed. Shortly thereafter, she pinned down the most likely suspects for Marston's accomplices from among those he had served with in the navy. And, among his old friends in the rod-and-gun club, several soon died, under varying, and varyingly mysterious, circumstances—but always as apparent suicides.

Agent Onilongo continued to phone her husband and daughter in California every evening that she was able. The good-byes grew more poignant with each succeeding night. She missed them very much, and it was partially due to this homesickness that Ciera attributed the endlessly recurring dream-loop that began to afflict her sleep.

Each recurrence began with what seemed to be the distant shape-shifting smoke cloud of an unseen fire against the horizon. This slowly resolved itself into the shapeless shapes of a synchronized flock of birds, swarming and swirling, growing closer, a living Möbius band, inverting and everting smoothly, severing and sweeping the sky, lightening in dispersion and darkening in coalescence. Like a thought from a different universe. Like the avatar of a godlike machine, appearing as an angel in dreams. Like that portion of a hyperdimensional topological form capable of obtruding into human perceptual space.

It almost seemed to Ciera that, if she could just squint her eyes the right way in strange enough augury, she might actually see those faces of gods or masks of machines in that cloud of birds. As the animate cloud continued to approach, however, Ciera saw time and again that its innumerable members were not birds at all, but flying human forms. Nearer, she saw the human shapes were all young girls, moving and maneuvering flawlessly in air about and above her as she remained standing on the ground. Closer still, and she saw that all their myriad faces were her daughter Gena's face, all their eyes flashing and kaleidoscoping red-gold lightning across an inscrutable sky.

Into their cloud like a thought, Ciera sublimed in secret disintegration.

Agent Onilongo awoke, heart pounding, a text of unusual provenance buzzing for her to attend to identifying another apparent suicide: what might be the body of Philip Marston's last and perhaps truest believer, Nancy Harlow. Ciera quickly dressed and drove to the campus of Jordan Summit High School.

The school buses had just started unloading by the time Agent Onilongo arrived and pulled into a visitor space. Fingering the Möbius softclock pendant on the necklace Philip Marston had given her, she watched as the girls of the Special Class walked toward their temporary replacement classroom.

She picked up the extended magazines from the seat beside her, took her recovered twin Glock pistols out of the glove compartment, slipped the magazines into the pistols and the pistols into a holster at the small of her back. She donned her long jacket, opened the car door, and stood up. Looking into the sunshine of an early morning in late September she saw a flock of birds shapeshifting like a cloud of animate smoke. They were still distant, but growing closer by the minute. Watching and waiting, she thought back over all that had happened to lead her to this moment.

The Möbius pendant hummed and pulsed and blinked. Running forward toward the Special Classroom, Ciera took a pistol in each of her hands. As she ran she felt an overpowering sense of having always already seen all this before, perhaps countless times. She kept running nonetheless, always hoping she was making the right decision—whatever it turned out to be.

MONUMENTS OF UNAGEING INTELLECT

Grabbing the board's nose in his left hand, Hisao cut its repellers. Straightening up and angling the front of the board downward, he kicked in the jets and plummeted from the low clouds toward the choppy seas.

He was soon moving at one hundred fifty miles per hour. A county-sized chunk of the northern Pacific's surface and the airspace above it had been reserved for the hoverball match. There was nothing for him to watch out for beyond the occasional errant seabird. And, oh yes—the opposing team.

Despite his velocity as he arced forward and down, the ball rested almost motionless in its smashcradle. From headplug chatter he knew defenders were swarming up toward him. Out of the corners of his eyes he saw his team's forwards blocking most of them. Three defenders, undeterred, still raced toward him, fanning out to stop him from getting off a shot.

Hisao continued his dive, straight at them, and on toward the surface of the sea below them. His eye-augments began to flash red messages.

WARNING! CONTINUING ON CURRENT TRAJECTORY AT CURRENT VELOCITY WILL PLACE YOU BELOW GAME FLOOR!

He nodded absently. His augments didn't need to remind him how the game "floor" worked—overlapping fields from a grid of gyrostabilized levitation disks, perched ten feet above the ocean's surface atop bright orange buoys. Once he plunged below that floor, the repellers on his board would have nothing to repel *against*.

Hisao cut his board's jets—too late to stay above field threshhold. The approaching defenders' monitors must have relayed them the same information. Surmising Hisao was fated to splash into the drink and go immobile, the three defenders were at nearly full stop by the time he passed under them on his dead board—

—and hit the back of a wave fast and hard enough to skip back up eleven feet, just above the invisible field-floor, where he cut in his repellers, slammed on his jets, and left the defenders awash in the blast of his spray before they could even swivel around to pursue.

Hisao bee-lined toward the goal. Now only the goalie—his sometime-love, Wilena—hovered between him and scoring. He flipped open his smashcradle. A flick of his wrist sent the ball onto and into its sweetspot pocket. With all his strength he swung the streamlined and servomotored smashcradle (lineal descendant of atlatl and jai alai basket-glove) forward in a great sidelong arc.

The ball shot from the cradle toward the goal, moving at a third the speed of sound. Wilena raced forward from the virtual net whose space, both real and cyber, she was so diligently defending. The next moment everyone's eye-monitors flashed projections that the ball would fall short of the goal.

And so the ball did, skipping to a stop on the surface of the sea.

Wilena slalomed forward to take the ball. Just as she was about to fish it out of the water with her telescoping catchcradle, the sphere suddenly leapt a dozen feet off the ocean's surface. A moment later, a dolphin's body erupted from the water, nose down and tail up, catching with its flukes the same ball it had head-butted out of the water an instant before.

With its powerful tail the dolphin smacked the ball, spiking it past the goalie's outstretched arms and into the virtual net.

"Score!"

No sooner had the defenders overcome their astonishment at

the fluky maneuver than their protests roared up on the comm.

"That's Alphonse! One of Hisao's work dolphins!"

"He wasn't legally on the field!"

"I thought we were playing this as a single-species sport today!"

Hisao's teammates, once they were able to stop laughing, came to his defense. No such solo-species agreement had been made! If everyone checked their playbacks, they'd see that only the regulation twelve offensive players had been on the field during Hisao's drive—Alphonse included.

Hisao kept out of it. He knew that, in the end, the point probably wouldn't count, but everything—setting it up with his teammates, the hours spent rehearsing the moves with Alphonse—had all been worth it, just to see the utterly bewildered look on Wilena's face!

"The dolphin was not entered on the roster," said Moira at last, serving as referee. "Hisao's score is nulled."

Hisao and his teammates did some grutching, but made no official complaint. An aura of seriousness, gravity, and fair consideration gave all Moira's pronouncements added weight. Hisao had long found it inexplicably attractive.

"Now that we've had our little joke," Moira said, preparing to toss the ball back into play, "how about a little less levity and a lot more levitation, for the rest of the game? Hmm?"

She hurled the ball back into bounds, where it was greeted with the laughter of young gods and goddesses, golden Olympians at play, flashing and moving in waves with the ball and the game.

Like everyone in his cohort, Hisao travelled a great deal. He hovercruised the south seas a dozen times. He dived all the Earth's oceans, from the shallowest sun-dappled reefs to the deepest midnight trenches. He loved that world. It was one of the reasons he decided to become a cetologist.

Like those few others (his friends and work teammates, mainly) who still pursued the arcana of diplomas, degrees, and certifications, he endured the interminable forty-plus years of basic formal education—or as formal as it got, with its thousands of hours of screen, VR, and headplugged human-peripheral time.

Throughout his training, he had happily traded such seat-time for sea-time and mobile learning. After a dozen years, though, even his ocean-diving fieldwork began to seem a little too much like schoolwork. For something different, he joined a team climbing the five highest peaks in the Himalayas—without perfused bloodox, lift boots, or an augment suit. As part of a shifting group of several friends, he rambled around the Moon for half a year. Bent on climbing the highest mountain in the solar system, he joined an expedition to Mars, then followed that up with a cloud-cruise tour of the Jovian atmosphere. He joined a crew of offworld icedivers, too, exploring some of the more important moons of Jupiter and Saturn.

Taking time with their educations was no problem for anyone in his cohort. They freefloated from team to team, network to network, putting on and taking off new roles, tasks, and ever-temporary jobs as if they were changes of clothing, updated implants, new hairstyles or skin colors. Like everyone else, Hisao too was destined to be forever young. They could all afford to be cavalier with time.

All except Moira.

He first noticed the difference during one of his annual "sittings" for her. She was studying ancient art media—sculpture, in particular. The sittings she harangued him and two dozen or so of their mutual friends into, from all over the solar system, were purportedly part of her on-going educational experience.

"Sitting" was an antiquated term for what Moira actually did. Using the medscan tech to which Wilena had introduced her, Moira created a life-mold of each of them, once each year—minutely detailed three-dimensional renderings of their bodies. She then cast in bronze each life-molded subject.

Because the medscan showed each subject with eyes closed and without clothing or hair, there was something unsettling about the resulting sculptures. Holographically projecting clothes and hair back onto the statues in overlay, which Moira always did, only managed to make the effect even more disquieting. When she flashed through several years' worth of projections—ever-changing fashions in apparel and hairstyle, overlain on unchanging statuary forms—the effect made Hisao slightly queasy.

"I call them Persistent Personae," Moira said. "I took the idea from the old practice of making a death mask—something artists used to do after someone famous got old and died."

Hisao nodded. He wasn't much interested in archaic artforms. Besides, only non-human creatures aged and died, these days—like his dolphin friends, unfortunately. True, there were the not unheard-of cases of death by accidents too obliterating for even the moteswarms to mend—but human beings, getting old and dying like everything else in nature? That was ancient history.

Yet, over six years of sittings, he began to notice something changing in Moira's looks. Something different about her face, her body, even her hair. He couldn't quite put his finger on it. Then, during one afternoon of his sixth sitting, he asked Moira something he'd never thought to ask her before.

"Have you ever done life-molds of yourself?"

In response, she had her mechs bring six years' worth of her own bronze Personae into the studio and place them alongside his. The differences were subtle in themselves, but contrast made them obvious. Her face had developed creases and furrows that his hadn't. Her body had changed, particularly about the hips and breasts, in ways he'd never seen in any other woman he'd known. It was as if the seriousness and gravity that had long characterized Moira's personality had now begun manifesting in her body as well.

Afterwards, when they made love, Moira did so with a passionate earnestness utterly new to him. It was exhilarating, even a bit frightening. But when she suggested that he stay with her, that he settle in for a while, Hisao politely laughed it off.

"No can do, kiddo. You know the spectacle Jorge and his team have planned for this week." Their mutual friend Jorge was an orbital mechanist whose latest project involved telepresently steering an asteroid into the inner solar system from the Kuiper belt.

"Crashing that skystone of his into the Sun, isn't he?"

"Exactly so! He's invited me to his observatory, to be part of the private audience actually telepresent for the impact—realtime inside the ultimate firework!"

"I certainly wouldn't want you to miss *that*, no," Moira said, taking his begging-off in stride. Hisao felt almost like she was being condescending toward him, but he couldn't quite figure out how or why.

As he kissed her goodbye, Hisao was both relieved and obscurely disappointed. Heading to Jorge's eyrie in Peru, he felt that, by rejecting her offer to "settle in," he had dodged an arrow by which he might have dearly wished to be struck—if he were about a hundred years older.

He didn't think much on it again until Moira exhibited her first ten years of Persistent Personae, in a show at a gallery in Nuevo Seattle. She called the exhibit "Too Too Solid Flesh," for reasons Hisao was unable to fathom.

The show was by no means the toast of every art critic who'd been given a preview, but the opening for it drew quite a crowd, nonetheless—and not just telepresently. In that crowd, Hisao saw Wilena again, for the first time in quite a few years.

Together they walked among the statues in the pavilioned gallery space. Not only were the rapidly changing hair and clothing styles holoed onto the Personae now, but streets and city skylines (projected around them in diorama) built and unbuilt themselves, shifted and changed in time-lapsed fashion, completely recycling themselves every three years or so, just as they did in reality.

"Time increasingly sublimes into space," intoned a voiceover narration as they walked, their feet unintentionally triggering its comments. "Nature disappears into culture. Reality dissipates into simulation. Response vanishes into stimulus. All our depth is on the surface."

Hisao shook his head.

"Kind of a strange narration."

"What's stranger here, if you ask me," Wilena said, looking about at the other people in the gallery, "is how few of the sitters have shown up in person for the opening."

Hisao nodded. He'd noticed it too.

"You have to admit there's something a little disturbing about what she's done with us," he said.

"Yes. Especially when she puts the statues of herself among all of ours."

Just then Moira herself, mingling, stopped to give both of them quick hugs. Embracing her, Hisao noted the subtle white streaks in her hair. Some obscure artcult fashion, he supposed. She was more than a little busy with her—Three! Count them! Unbelievable!—young children in tow. She wished she could stop to talk, but . . . They understood completely, and congratulated her as she moved on.

Hisao and Wilena turned back to contemplating the sculptures.

"Unsettling. The rest of us look so, I don't know—"

"Infantilized?" Wilena suggested. "Or at best not quite fully pubescent?"

"Yes."

"The hairlessness accentuates that. Makes us more of what we already are."

"What do you mean?"

"Are you homeworlding for a while?" she asked. When he nodded, she sent contact info into his headplug. "Stop by my lab in Taiga City, and maybe I'll give you something to think about."

With a brief wave of her hand, she turned and walked away, leaving him both puzzled and curious as she disappeared into the crowd.

*

"You do know that Moira's oldest—the little boy, Masao—is your son?" Wilena said, walking with him into the sterile space of her homelab, brilliant in its retro chrome-and-white cleanroom decor.

"Oh. Really? I hadn't heard."

"I suspect Moira isn't mentioning it to any of the children's fathers, unless they ask. Did you see much of your own bioparents—Mother? Father?—when you were growing up?"

Hisao pondered that for a moment.

"They were usually off working, or studying, or travelling. Like everybody else, except they were actually married—Open Probational, twenty year term. Before my thirteen birthday I probably saw my parents, together, more than most children do."

"Before the Moving On," Wilena said, nodding and leaning against her workstation. "Before 'parent' can become confused with 'playfellow.' And of course there's the incest taboo, too."

Hisao laughed. Wilena gave him a quizzical look.

"For some reason, whenever I hear the phrase incest taboo," he explained, "I always mishear it as incest *tattoo*—and into my head pops an old picture of a burly guy with 'Mother' stenciled into a bicep."

Wilena smiled politely.

"Yes. Still, that taboo was one of the few things that *didn't* really change—even when the quick, shiny, tiny things changed everything."

"The moteswarms? They're your field, right?"

"As much as anything else, yes. Before the Intervention, I might have been called a medical doctor. Officially, I'm a specialist in medically-applicable biologically-based nanotechnology, particularly human-obligate biocompatibles like the motes. In reality, the motes made people in my profession about as obsolete as general practitioners—and for the same reasons."

Hisao dropped into a hoverchair, slouching as it settled and adjusted with his weight. Wilena toyed with a Hoberman sphere paperweight on her workstation's main desk.

"A medical doctor," he said, the obsolete term strange in his mouth. "That's why you're working with Moira?"

"Among other things I'm her 'personal physician,' for lack of a less antiquated title," Wilena said, taking a seat behind the desk. "And she's given me permission to talk about this with you."

"I *thought* something odd was going on with her. I mean, *three* kids? That's practically unheard of."

Wilena shook her head.

"Her situation is about much more than that, but we can start there." She flashed a series of diagrams up from a small tabletop holo. "The moteswarms view the suite of physiological changes surrounding conception, gestation, and birthing as symptomatic of senescence—and therefore something to be countered. Female fertility is largely unimpaired for the first child, more difficult with the second. The odds are astronomically against even the *conception* of a third."

"Moira has beaten those odds, obviously."

"Yes. About one in fifty million people, both male and female, are like Moira in that they're not mote-immortalized. Moira can have more than one or two children, but she will also experience a lifespan closer to what was the human average, *before* the moteswarms intervened."

"Wait a minute. You're saying she's actually growing *old?*"

Wilena nodded, flashing up images of human faces and bodies, bald-headed or white-haired people from those bygone days when humans beings grew old and died as a matter of course.

"Moira is one of those extremely rare individuals who experience what we now consider atavistic aging. Before the Intervention three centuries ago, though, her type of aging was not atavistic at all. It was an absolutely ordinary and unavoidable part of the normal human life cycle."

"But—*now*? Today? That's ridiculous. Moira's not some kind of lower animal!"

"I know it's hard to believe. 'Animals die, things pass away, but people last.' That's what we're always told, and that's how it *is*, in our cases."

"But not in Moira's?"

"No. Unlike the rest of us, she's maturing. Becoming fully adult."

"And the rest of us aren't—?"

"Actually mature? No, none of us are that. The rest of us are all diapaused just beyond the cusp of puberty. We remain essentially larval, indefinitely—permanently neotenized, both physically *and* psychologically. Unending adolescence is our trade-off for being immortal."

"How is that possible?" Hisao asked, fidgeting enough in the hoverchair to make it swivel slightly. "Why did it happen?"

"Those are two very different questions. Let's take the first one first." She shot onto the holovirt between them an image of a coordinate system. "This is a graphical depiction of our species' neotenization, our long childhoods even before the Intervention. The motes already had that as a starting point, to make their task easier.

"In every complex organism—including humans, in the past—the onset of reproductive maturity was the first real stage of dying. An unintended consequence of the fact that evolution didn't much care what happened to you after you'd reached breeding age—and bred."

Wilena holed up another series of images—cells, cellular mechanisms, gene lines.

"Some of the same traits selected by evolution to maintain early life fitness have unselected deleterious effects later in life. What saved us in youth killed us in age."

"And that was the thing the moteswarms fixed?"

"One of them. One of the many small changes which led to a big change." She holed up a series of further graphs and diagrams. "The more you exploit genetic polymorphisms to adjust this neurosecretory pathway—involving the hypothalamus, pituitary, gonads, and eventually general metabolism—the more longevity increases and the more slowly this curve here approaches full sexual maturity onset."

"Fertility decreases as longevity increases, then?" Hisao asked. The diagrams, charts, and creatures began to swim before eyes. "This is some fairly heavy-lifting biology. . . ."

"I know," said Wilena with a sigh of frustration, flash-cutting through more holo images—of the humble nematode roundworm *Caenorhabditis elegans*, of chemosignal/lifespan connections, developmental arrest, polymorphism, neoplasm and neoteny. "Sorry. Suffice it to say the motes carried all of this still further, by treating births subsequent to the first as symptoms of senescence which were in need of being, um, overcome."

"But what were 'they' after?" Hisao asked, staring absently at his own hands. "The motes are just swarms of tiny, not-very-bright machines."

"Indeed, but in their own emergent, decentralized fashion they can share and collectively understand a great deal—much the same way an ant colony 'knows' a lot more than any single ant in the colony does. And the woman who created them, well, she was larger than life, and a genius."

A blond woman—with another one of those old faces—holoed up into the space before Wilena's desk, her words both spoken and captioned.

". . . my answer was swarms of little cellular mechanics diagnosing and repairing time's ravages—what we do to our bodies," said the ghostly woman in the holo, "as well as flesh's thousand inherited natural shocks—what our bodies do to us."

"Cherise LeMoyne," Hisao said, gesturing. "The Mother of Intervention. The person who unleashed the Wellness Plague."

"That's right. At the time of the Intervention, she was chief scientist and CEO of Manipulife Corporation. Her firm specialized in blending traits from programmable machines into programmable life, and vice versa. All built on LeMoyne's discovery of the core Universal Turing Gene, the shortest segment of DNA on which can be simulated any and all operations performable in DNA."

"Which allowed her to create the motes that re-created us."

"Yes."

"Even as she herself was dying of a previously unsuspected and undiagnosed cancer—or so the story goes."

"A rare uterine cancer, actually," Wilena said, replacing the holo of LeMoyne with an image half circuit diagram, half microbiology illustration. "LeMoyne's diagnosis had come too late. She died, but not before giving the motes their ability to swarm-communicate. She connected the 'bots, even gave them links and search capabilities into the human infosphere—apparently hoping everything we humans had ever learned might serve as the motes' classroom, their school, their teacher, their database. She also gave them their most important commands, at least after their Hippocratic 'Do no harm' substrate."

Into the air above her desk Wilena holoed up the twin directives, where they hovered in golden numbers and letters:

1) Eliminate human mortality.

2) Replicate human consciousness.

"Evidence suggests that the motes' great solution to the first directive—the longevity/birth-limit linkage," she said, flashing up images of processes, and graphs chronicling global trends, "came about as a result of their researching the uterine cancer that killed their creator. They couldn't save LeMoyne, but forging that particular linkage ended up solving the problem of lingering human hyper-population—which vastly increased longevity by itself would have exacerbated, especially in regions which had yet to pass through demographic shift. Soon afterward, other scientists perfected similar mote-tech for atomic-level recycling and energy conversion, which solved the other great problem of the time—material hyperconsumption."

Wilena looked away, embarrassed.

"One 'hyper' thing the motes didn't fix," she said, standing up, "was hyperspecialization. At least in my case. Sorry."

"Mine too. I should have known more about all these things, but history has never been a particular interest of mine."

"Don't beat yourself up about it," she said, placing her hand lightly on his shoulder. "Our hyperspecialization goes hand in hand with being psychologically neotenized."

Hisao unfolded himself from the hoverchair and stood up.

"Oh?"

Wilena turned away shyly once more as, together, they slowly walked from her workstation, back through her lab, toward her living space.

"There I go again, talking shop. Sorry."

"No need to apologize," Hisao said. "Very thorough. Just one question: If the motes are so well-suited to overcoming our aging and mortality, why is Moira growing older?"

Wilena made that frustrated sigh again.

"No one knows for sure. Some of my colleagues theorize that atavistic aging, like Moira's, results from a breakdown in biocompatibility, such that the immune systems of these rare individuals attack the moteswarms and counteract their efforts."

The door out of the lab dilated before them and they walked through.

"Others suggest the problem's deeper than just an 'allergy to the agents of immortality' on the part of the human host."

"Deeper? How?"

"The motes have pretty much achieved the goal of Directive One. From all we can tell, they're not nearly as far along toward accomplishing Directive Two. Perhaps the motes themselves must leave some human individuals mortal, in order to better understand the nature of individual human consciousness."

Hisao stared at her, wondering if he'd heard right.

"You mean the motes are *allowing* Moira to age? Maybe even to die? But why?"

"Fully overcoming human mortality *and* fully understanding human consciousness may not be complementary efforts," Wilena said. "It's possible that the elimination of human mortality and the replication of human consciousness cannot both be accomplished simultaneously. Perhaps one cannot have a fully developed individual human consciousness unless one also has a deep awareness of one's own mortality."

"I don't follow."

"What if the bracketing provided by death is what gives individual consciousness its depth? That's how theorists of the 'directive noncomplementarity' school pose the question, at any rate."

Wilena stopped, pausing at the entrance to her sleep room.

"Whichever theory you follow, the upshot is the same. All known cases of atavistic human aging are characterized by an almost complete absence of motes from the bodies of the aging individuals."

Hisao nodded slowly.

"You promised you'd give me something to think about, Wilena, and you have. Thanks."

His dalliance with Wilena in her sleep room shortly thereafter—although it might not have smacked of Moira's passionate earnestness—at least was familiar romance, full of the superficial intimacy and intimate superficiality that so characterized love in their time.

As the years passed, Hisao traveled to more and newer places throughout the solar system and beyond. He made new friends everywhere, did new things and experienced new sensations as often as he liked. He learned how to speak new languages and play new musical instruments. He tired of hoverball and moved on to astrosurfing—more dangerous, and so more thrilling, more sensational, more *fun*.

Always he found himself among the crowds of perennial

boy-geniuses and intelligirls, all gloriously vibrant and flawlessly healthy—never-changing people in an ever-changing world, forever thronging to experience novel places, people, and things, and just as quickly growing bored and leaving them behind.

Only much later, while talking with the aged Alphonse about Moira's art, did Hisao think again of those to whom mortal change might still apply.

Moira's latest major work, *Coming and Going*, was a strange piece—even for Moira. Like all of her more recent work, it was monumental, starkly visible from a thousand miles up, even its smallest detail requiring only slight magnification to be seen clearly from geostat orbit. It was also built to last, or at least built to resist recycling—one of many reasons it aroused controversy.

Coming and Going was an immense low-relief sand sculpture flash-vitrified into a thousand square mile expanse of dunes and salt pans in the Sahara Desert. Among the images it featured were two standing human figures, one male, one female, both titanic and nude, devoid of pubic hair like Moira's previous Personae, but not bereft of the hair on their heads. The couple both did and did not look like contemporary human beings.

The male figure in the tableau held up his hand as if waving. The two figures stood before the silhouette of an exploratory probe from the dawn of the age of space travel—which craft purportedly had also once borne, engraved on a plaque of much smaller dimensions, the same constellation of images that now provided the content for the vast sand sculpture.

To the west of the representational portion with its human figures and spacecraft stood clusters of more abstract information: the relative position of the Sun to the center of the galaxy, the galactic plane, and fourteen pulsars; a schematic illustration featuring the point of origin of the space probe and its trajectory out of the Solar System; a diagram depicting the hyperfine transition of neutral hydrogen, its spin-flip specifying a unit of length, a unit of time, and the binary digit 1—all three simultaneously, and all of those variants functioning as units in the measurements expressed in the other symbols on the great plaque of sculpted sand.

"What do you say, Alphonse?" Hisao asked, over the neural-tap translator he and his research team had planted in his swimming friend's head. "You've seen a bunch of other contemporary art. How do you think this compares?"

"The rest all swim in shallow seas," Alphonse replied, in the cryptic way of dolphins. "Only Moira moves in deep waters. I would very much like to meet her."

Hisao nodded. He had figured the old dolphin—the oldest that had ever lived, now—might find Moira's art interesting.

Alphonse, like Moira, could not be cured of mortality. All attempts to transfer the motes into nonhuman species ended with the motes immediately kill-switching themselves. A type of "apoptosis," according to Wilena. Hisao didn't know how much longer the old dolphin would live—or Moira either, for that matter.

"I think such a meeting can be arranged. I'll get on it."

Until he saw her again, Hisao didn't realize how long it had been since he'd last seen Moira. Her hair was white, like that of the old people in the old-time pictures Wilena once showed him. Moira's face was so wrinkled and wizened that when she smiled she looked like a creature of a species only distantly related to contemporary humans. She brought her son—*their* son?—Masao with her, too.

Moira and Alphonse spent so much time talking about and modeling the schooling behavior of fish that Hisao found himself spending more time with Masao than he expected. The amount of action and attention Moira and the old dolphin could devote to a single topic frankly amazed Hisao, whose own focus tended to skip much more rapidly from one object to another—as his son's also did, he noticed.

Although he was one year chronologically closer to fifty than to fifteen, Masao physically looked exactly the latter. Hisao found that he got along well with his son—though more like a slightly older brother, than a father. Whatever it was that had caused Moira's atavistic aging, it had not been passed on to Masao—nor to his two siblings, Hisao gathered.

"Moira," he asked her over a drink that evening, when the two of them were alone for a moment, "why didn't you tell me Masao was my son? I might have liked to meet him, get to know him, before now."

"And why didn't you? I wasn't stopping you, yet you never introduced yourself to him. Wilena said she told you about Masao, long ago. You've known about him for years—and never visited him."

"Maybe you didn't stop me directly, no, but you never came to me and said, 'Masao is your son.' Why?"

"For the same reason I never told any of the fathers. You were all too immature—like everybody else. None of you were grown up enough to help me raise these kids."

"Masao says you disapprove of 'children raising children.'"

"It's not just that. Everything about the world the Intervention has made—it all struck me as somehow too flashy, too shallow, too trivial, by the time Masao was born. Much superficial knowledge, little real wisdom. Too many blessings damn the children."

"Masao hardly seems damned."

"No, but the more I looked into the historical records from before the Intervention, the more I saw a profundity of character and culture there that seems lacking in our own times."

"During the Dark Centuries, too? Mass atrocities and mass destruction don't sound like 'profundity' to me. We're still cleaning up the mess."

"Yet even that dark time showed *mass creativity*, too! Since the Intervention, we don't need to think as deeply. No need to invent or create as much. Our world has been perfected. Cherise LeMoyne sprinkled fairy dust over the globe. Now, no matter how far they go, Wendy and Peter Pan never leave Neverland."

"I don't follow."

"Did you ever talk with Wilena about LeMoyne, or about psychological neoteny, as they call it?"

"A little."

"You might want to ask her about that a bit more, then. And I wouldn't worry too much about the time you haven't had with your son. You have the rest of forever to get to know each other better."

Hisao was sorry to see Moira and Masao leave—but not as sorry as Alphonse was, he suspected. And when, only a few years later, the dolphin was at the end of his earthly time, his last thoughts were for Moira.

"Tell her to keep doing what she's doing. Tell her what is popular is not always true, and what is true is not always popular. Tell her not to spend so much time accepting others' rejection of her work that she ends up rejecting their acceptance when it finally comes. And tell her, when she's at death's door, don't knock!"

The neural tap interpreted the last with a sound almost like laughter, but Hisao couldn't be sure. He promised the dolphin he'd tell Moira what he'd said. Soon the dolphin fell silent in voice and thought, then passed quietly away. Alphonse was there, but he wasn't there, anymore.

His cetacean friend's death left Hisao more saddened than he might have imagined. Out of that sadness he contacted Moira—who smiled and wiped away a tear at hearing the dolphin's last words for her. She promised she would dedicate her final piece to him.

Over the following days and weeks and months, Hisao thought from time to time about what Moira had said, when last they talked in person. When he contacted Wilena again, it was to ask her about something Moira had suggested.

"You told me one time that our hyperspecialization was connected to our being psychologically neotenized. What did you mean by that?"

"The idea goes way back, before digiculture—perhaps to the middle of the twentieth century," Wilena said, checking sources in their shared holovirt. "By the time of the Intervention, most scientific research, for instance, was already being done by teams of young, hyperspecialized problem-solvers and technicians—'whiz kids'—each of whom actually needed to fully understand only a small piece of the overall puzzle."

"Which is how most of us still work," Hisao said, nodding. "Depth of individual understanding is far less important than the system of specializations put together in any team."

"Right. People who work in specialized teams need to be able to change jobs often, learn new skills and information, move to new places and cultures, make new friends in an ever-expanding social network. 'Mature adult' human animals—evolved to cope with small hunter-gatherer societies of just a few hundred people—were not all that good at meeting such challenges."

"So being 'unfinished' or 'immature' or 'postponed'..."

"Means increased flexibility of attitudes, behaviors, knowledge —all perfect for teaming up. Ramping up neoteny was a fast and simple way to evolve an adaptation—for adaptability!"

"What's that mean for Moira, then?"

"An interesting question. The vast majority of us are Hypers— hyper-attentives. We prefer rapidly changing environments, high levels of stimulation, multiple information streams, lots of rapid, spe- cialized task-switching among team members. We get bored easily. I suspect that's less and less the case with Moira, as she's gotten older."

"I once saw her discuss the modeling of fish-schooling behav- ior with Alphonse—for hours on end."

"She's become a Deeper, then. A deep-attentive. Someone who can shut out the world and focus for long periods of time on a single complex problem or object—without getting bored. Even before the Intervention, Deepers like Moira were already disap- pearing. The motes just helped us become more of what we were already becoming."

"How so?"

Wilena searched for and then holoed up again the blonde ghost of Cherise LeMoyne.

"The release of the motes—and the Wellness Plague, with them—was the action LeMoyne took to address the problems she saw in her time. She intervened—as did her creations, even moreso, since they continued to evolve after their release, even after her death. Taken together, the mote solutions to human population and consumption issues corrected most of the problems of the Dark Centuries, as LeMoyne hoped they would.

"In retrospect, the motes' short biomech life-cycles and swarm intelligence make them the perfect symbionts for long-lived creatures with individual minds, like us. Over time they have in some ways become more like us, and we have in some ways become more like them."

Wilena flashed Hisao a satisfied smile. He nodded slowly, pondering.

After many more years, Moira exhibited *Monument To Unageing Intellect*—her strangest and most haunting work of all.

From asteroidal material, she and her collaborators (their friend Jorge and his longtime love-partner Li, most prominently) crafted myriad, simple, solar-powered and mirror-skinned androids of human size: "Personae," persisting again. Each Persona incorporated subroutines which mimicked human movement, along with sensors for navigating local space, and an array of thrusters so that each "individual" seemed to fly as if in air, or swim as if in water—though all of them were in fact released some dozen degrees above the plane of the ecliptic, in the space between Mars and Jupiter, where they moved after their complex fashion, together and apart.

Moira had programmed each Persona-unit with simple rules. Steer clear of anything that is not one of your local cohort members (avoidance). Steer so as to prevent crowding your local co-hort members (separation). Steer toward the average heading of your local cohort members (alignment). Steer so as to approach the average position of your local cohort members (cohesion). From such rules the Personae, once released and put into play, quickly organized themselves into throngs of sweeping and shifting human forms, moving exactly like schools of fish or flocks of birds.

"—or like the swarms of mote-machines which made possible our godhood," Moira said, when Hisao stopped at the moon to visit her on his way home from the exhibit. "Or yours, anyway."

He stared at her, unable to get over the way her body had changed. Slumped in her medical hoverbed, she looked deformed by gravity, even on the moon. Her white hair had grown much more sparse and her skin seemed paper-thin. Her sunken eyes rolled inside their frame of starkly prominent cheek bones like hoverballs in smashcradles. Webworks of wrinkles and wattling flesh covered all that was visible of her face and neck. She seemed more than ever a creature of an alien species.

Despite that, the beauty of afternoons in late autumn still flared from her. Her eyes flashed, her smile seemed somehow more mellow, human, and humane than ever—though Hisao wondered how much of *that* might be from the hyperox levels in her rooms.

"LeMoyne had her rules, I have mine," she said with a chuckle. "You know what made me think of swarms and human motion? That hoverball game, long ago. Where you conspired with Alphonse, to cheat! *That* was when I first thought there might be some similarities between the way the moteswarms moved and the way the crowds of *us* moved."

Hisao nodded.

"Wilena says that the motes just helped us become more of what we were already becoming. That we're becoming more like them, and they're becoming more like us."

"Well! Good for Wilena! Given her work, she's probably about as close as you unagers can get to understanding what I'm trying to say—and do. You're in touch with her, then? What is my 'personal physician' up to these days?"

"She's got a standing contract to join the crew of a long-cruiser, headed out to one of the habitable-planet star systems. A chief medical officer position."

"Wilena's going to join the diaspora? Ha! Do you know what the original name for long-cruisers was, when the idea was first developed? Generation ships!"

"Not many generations being born on long-cruisers."

"And no one dying of old age, either. Won't be much for Wilena to do."

"Maybe that's why she's held off on leaving. But she can join a crew any time she decides to."

"Acch, she's just waiting for me to die first! I haven't seen much of my personal physician lately, but I bet I'm still of some professional interest to her."

"How's that?"

"I'm dying of a 'defect of the heart,'" Moira said with a laugh. "Whatever else any gods or fates may lack, they certainly do *not* suffer from an irony deficiency!"

"Can't you just get a cardio-replacement?"

"Wilena harped on that too. She's offered lots of options—mechanicals, clonally grown transplants, you name it. I turned them all down. That might be one of the things that's made her unhappy with me, of late."

"Why'd you turn them down?"

"Wilena would keep me old and alive forever, if I'd let her. She'd turn me into a Struldbrugg, a Tithonian. That's not for me.

"Nope, I think I'll keep the heart I've got, and go when it goes. She won't have to wait long, now. I've been running through tomorrows like there's no tomorrow, and pretty soon there won't be any left."

*

Not quite a year later, Hisao received his final message from Moira.

"Dear Hisao: If you're seeing this, then I have died. To you, Wilena, and my children, I've sent very specific instructions concerning my funeral arrangements. I hope you do not find such specificity offensive. At first I thought people might have forgotten how to mourn—it's been so long—but it's not that, really. You can't forget what you've never known.

"*Do* take the time to get to know our son Masao. For all I may have done in raising him, he's still part of your world, now.

"Thank you for all I've learned from you. You and Alphonse showed me that the only product that finally persists is process. I could not have created my last work without learning that. The last piece has been better received than I would ever have dared to believe. Go figure.

"I suppose I should say something grand at this late date, reveal some big secret of the universe, so here it is: the human heart is more than just some strangely chambered knot in us, pumping blood through a maze of meat plumbing, with just enough chaos in the beat and eddy in the flow to keep things going. In the end it will not allow us the comforting local illusion that there are separate events and separate objects. In fact there is no separation. Space, time, the universe—it's all one.

"Whether you knew it or not, you taught me that, too—you and Wilena and everyone I knew. Thanks again."

As per Moira's very specific instructions, it was to the vicinity of her last great work that he, Wilena, and her children took Moira's body—encased in a titanium coffin sensored, motored, and programmed in much the same way as the bird-flock Personae of *Monument* had been, and into whose midst they released her little deathship.

After the ceremony ended, Hisao and Wilena stood on the observation deck of the transport, watching the gray coffin drift off in the midst of inhumanly perfect human forms, flawless mirror-skinned creatures moving and flashing like shoals of thought, swarms of mind.

"How are you feeling?" Wilena asked.

"I feel . . . nothing."

"Numb. Yes. Same here. Back in the days when people grew old, they comforted each other at times like this by saying things like 'Life goes on' and 'Nothing lasts forever.'"

Wilena looked back to the monumental mobile sculpture as it moved through space before them, changing and shifting like a murmuration of starlings. Hisao nodded.

He thought about that, on the trip home to LaGrange Port. Once there, he stood beside Wilena as she prepared to board a long-cruiser for the stars.

"Back in the days when they called them generation ships," Wilena said, staring at the cruiser *Hyperboreas* out the observatory port, "someone who knew about both space travel and generations said that dealing with the speed of light barrier was like coping with the loss of a loved one: You never actually get over it. At best you just get around it."

She looked away from the ship, to him.

"I suppose if we can take forever to get where we're going," she said, "it doesn't much matter how fast or how slow we go."

He hugged her and bid her a quiet farewell. They both knew they would never see each other again. There was nothing to say, because there was everything to say.

Life goes on, Hisao thought as he climbed aboard his big or-ange-and-red fireboard and slid his feet into the augmented foot-locks. *Nothing lasts forever.*

Hisao had dropped from orbit and astrosurfed deep into at-mosphere dozens of times on half a dozen worlds. He knew how to play shooting star as well as anybody. His vintage big board had the best ablative shielding, deflection tiling, astrogation and avionics tech to be found. Even on hard burn the board had enough fuel to let him bounce into atmosphere, bolide through, and skip out again—at low enough angle and high enough speed to avoid becoming a shooting star for real.

That was the source of the excitement, of course: Although he would never die of old age, he could still die. Burning up in atmosphere would obliterate him beyond reconstruction. When down came baby, crashcradle and all, all the king's motelings and all the king's mends couldn't put baby together again.

You never get over it. At best you just get around it.

The satellite's airlock doors dilated open. The docking bay railgun shot him on his board out of the bay, toward the mottled ocher, white, and blue of the Earth below. He howled happily as he kicked in his thrusters to maximum burn.

Hisao shifted on the board and trajectories altered on the fashionably retro heads-up displays of his suit helmet. The astrogation gear calced Earth–atmosphere clearance for each course change, along with the board's capabilities and his own survivability.

The thrusters cut out. The board's ablative shielding began to burn. He moved back in the footlocks, angling both his board's nose and his trajectory slightly upward. On his rearview cams a long fiery streak spooled out, man and board a shooting star pushing a redlining course.

Fall to miss, fall to miss, fall to miss! Think like a satellite!

On his burning plank he bolided through the upper air, arced off just before his trajectory would have reached extinction point, skipped back out of the atmosphere, and was gone.

Despite tiles glowing red hot, empty fuel tanks, and a board blown of all ablative shielding and still burning, the trajectory plotter moved back into the green—before the astrogation system blew out. The locator beacon still worked, though, even as he slingzagged farther from the Earth, dropping final fire behind him.

Hisao drifted, staring down at the shining planet below. Each year, the human population of that world declined steadily—and not just from emigration, he now knew. On the face of the Sahara, carved into its surface, he could just make out through thin clouds a male figure, waving—though whether hello or good-bye he could not tell.

Waiting for a recovery shuttle to ride in on his beam and pick him up, Hisao knew he'd pushed himself and the board—hard. Yet the edge, he realized, was already going. Even from such a wild ride. Even from astrosurfing itself.

Life goes on. And on. And on.

I feel nothing. And nothing lasts forever.

That's the sheer hell of it.

In overcoming human death, had the moteswarms also overcome something essential to human life? How long could he keep going, before the edge was so gone he stepped over it? Before he fell to hit, and failed to miss?

I could still die. . . .

Below him, the planet was perfect, its people star children of an endless midsummer evening. But if the stars were fixed, why were they still falling, secretly, one by one?

He shivered amid the heavens, and the heavens shivered with him.

PALIMPSEST

You think it's possible?" MéMé Gelernter asked, flicking back the blue and green tips of her blond hair as she stared out of our window.

I followed her gaze to where it lingered. Below us, in front of InterPortation's corporate headquarters, street-preachers and pro-testers filled the boulevard.

"Do I think *what's* possible?"

"You know. What they're saying."

"Which is . . . ?" I said, turning away and thus causing InterPor-tation code to start scrolling through the information space before my eyes again.

"That God is always sending us a message we can't refuse. One we can't live without. One we shouldn't try to block."

I sat back in my chair, pulling my head out of i-space.

"MéMé my dear, I have no doubt the divine ground of all being works in mysterious ways. If that being *were* trying to send us all a message, however, even *I* doubt the message would come in the form of unwanted and apocalyptic chain e-mail."

"You don't think virtual manna is hidden somewhere in the godspam, then?"

"No," I said, sighing heavily. "And not electronic grace or web-blessings, either. Our concern here is the tools, not the rules. Our job descriptions do not include pondering moral, legal, or religious questions. Back to work, please."

MéMé nodded. She turned from the window and sat down at her workstation. I stuck my head back into i-space and returned to work myself.

MéMé was too idiot-compassionate for her own good. Her heart was on her sleeve for every stray cat or stray protest ideology she met on the street. At least in i-space, her head was in the right place. She was an undeniably sharp information engineer. With her once again on task, it wouldn't be long before we finished the final filters.

Calling it unwanted "e-mail" wasn't quite true, since it was in fact virtual mail, far more fully immersive than the old flatlander stuff. Not entirely true either, to say it *wasn't* manna, given that "manna" was the transliteration of two Hebrew words meaning "What is it?"

What the original "it" might actually have been was variously defined in the Bible as the "grain of heaven," the "bread of angels," the "meat" which God "rained down on the Israelites like dust . . . until they had more than enough."

God's . . . spam. Not the pink whatzit in the Hormel can—Shoulder Pork and hAM? SPiced hAM? Not the old Monty Python sketch song-refrain, either. Spam, dragon eggs, and spam. The Wild Old Days. The days of high filtration percentages and low false-positives. When there were no Federal laws prohibiting unsolicited solicitations, no marshall to enforce the law on the electronic frontier. When such solicitations were mostly simplistic e-mails and pop-ups pushing commercial stuff—penis and breast enlargement, generic Viagra, banned CDs. Sex, drugs, and rock 'n' roll.

When it first began to show up, there was no consensus on who was sending the godspam. Some claimed atheistic hackers were the culprits, while others believed it was the work of Islamo- or Judeo- or Christo-fascist terrorists. Whoever was behind it, it was much easier to block than the sly beast the commercial stuff had by then already become.

A "Jesus" here, or a "Buddha" there, or an "Allah" or "Lord Krishna" anywhere—accompanied by strange symbols, unlikely return addresses, threats of global apocalypse, personal damnation, or slime-mold status in one's next life—taken together, such were almost always a tip-off to some sort of virtual proselytizing, blockable by the most rudimentary rule-based content filters.

Then the churches objected, in the courts, that such blockers were stifling communication among the faithful. Their lawyers argued that such defenses were in fact heuristic hammers, treating even legitimate religious discussions as nails to be pounded down wherever they popped up. The tangle of issues—freedom of speech and expression, separation of church and state, Common Law prohibitions against unauthorized use of another's property (computer networks, in this case)—all would take decades to unsnarl. Long before which time, of course, e-mail went truly virtual, and unsolicited infosphere communications made a huge comeback.

Attempts by legislators to attach monetary or computational costs to each piece of virtual mail—tiny sums, which nonetheless piled up into considerable amounts given the huge volumes of messages sent by the virtual proselytizers—were all eventually struck down as burdensome intrusions of State power into religious affairs.

Blacklisting, whitelisting, signature-based filtering—all failed. Too low a percentage of godspam filtered out. Or too high a false-positive rate, killing too many legitimate messages. Or too hard to maintain and keep current, especially in the face of zealots willing to continually falsify their network locations.

Collaborative filtering schemes collapsed too, when user-voters failed to reach consensus on which missives were legitimate religious messages and which were godspam. Probability-based Bayesian filters, like their heuristic predecessors, fell prey to the "what-is-it?" factor, writ large: "Manna" and "Babel" counterattacks. In the former, godspam tended to look more and more like godless nonspam, the "sacred" hidden in the profane, the "celestial" encrypted in the mundane. In the latter, the meaningful lay buried in line after line of gibberish.

Things didn't really get worrisome, however, until wireless nanotech sensors began exchanging properties with the physical environment—and godspam began weaving numbers into stone and tree and leaf, names into steel and flesh and bone. InterPortation, which had built itself from a tiny field-sensor company to the world's largest provider of quantum-based virtual services, saw the writing on the world first. That's when IP called in my startup company, Spamazonian Extinctions.

Being chosen by InterPortation to create the ultimate blocker was quite a coup for us. We hyped every media contact we had—to get the word out about the project, to give it as high a cultural profile as possible. I didn't realize just how high we'd managed to build that profile until MéMé and I came in to officially oversee the custom installation of Spamazonian software on InterPortation's own systems.

I should have known something was up when they asked us to park our cars off site, a dozen blocks from InterPortation, for security reasons. As it turned out, all the streets in a five block radius around InterPortation's Sacramento headquarters had been shut down by police and protesters. Trying to make our way through and around the demonstration, we were trapped time and again in the crowds. What really stunned us, though, was when we learned that the protest-furor was about *our* project.

"'—sustaining *all things*, by his powerful word,' as the Apostle puts it in the Letter to the Hebrews," said a preacher with alpha male, executive-gray hair.

We were trapped amid the preacher's very responsive audience, many of whom carried placards depicting InterPortation's founder and CEO, Darin Mallecott, as the Devil. This was not too difficult to do, alas. Mallecott's sharp facial features, pointed goatee, and prominent earring in his left ear only added to his reputation as a buchaneer of the business world. Perhaps it was this reputation that made his eyes and teeth seem to sparkle—with piracy at least, if not perdition.

"The *Word* is the most powerful food!" thundered the preacher. "In their exodus from Egypt, the Israelites were sustained by the instructive and testing food called manna, which God gave them to teach them that 'man does not live on bread alone, but on every *word* that comes from the mouth of God.'"

Choruses of "Amen! Amen!" sounded. I wished we could work our way through this crowd-clot faster.

"It is the message itself that sustains us. Remember what it says in Psalms: 'O Lord, our Lord . . . when I consider your heavens, the work of your fingers, the moon and the stars, which you have set in place, what is man, that thou art mindful of him?' But what is God, if we should prove unmindful of Him? Remember the words of the great seventeenth century preacher Jeremy Taylor, who tells us in his *Holy Dying* that man 'is born in vanity and sin; he comes into the world like morning mushrooms, and as soon turns into dust and forgetfulness. To preserve him from rushing into nothing, and at first to draw him up from nothing, were equally the issues of an almighty power!'

"Those who would block God's word, who would destroy His manna, would withdaw from all of us the power that prevents us from rushing into nothing, the power that sustains *everything*—from our individual souls, to the creation in its entirety!"

More fervent "Amens" sounded as we managed to untangle ourselves from the crowd around the preacher. As we escaped, MéMé gave me a look. I shrugged. What else could one expect from such bibliolatrous throwbacks?

The next speaker we could not escape, in this mad marketplace of beliefs and ideas, and he annoyed me even more.

"No, I am not a 'philosophical idealist,'" said the young man, his face framed with wild dark beard and hair, answering over a bull-horn a question shouted at him by a someone in the mob around him. "I'm a computer programmer. I don't think the universe is just a thought or dream in the mind of God. I don't think that if God woke up or stopped thinking, this would all disappear.

"I *do* believe, though, that our entire universe is a computational process, a universal quantum Turing machine running a foundational self-evolving algorithm. The quantum gravity theorists say the entire initial state of our universe could be burned into a single good data needle—that the foundational rule-set in fact encompasses a fairly small amount of information."

"Then why should we worry about it?" I shouted at him, confident of my anonymity in the crowd, despite all the publicity my company had received.

"What's important," he bullhorned back, "is not the initial state, but the ongoing evolution, the iterations and elaborations. If the Spamazonian programmers block all so-called godspam—in not only the virtual world, but also the physical one—they could generate the ultimate false positive, extinguishing the iteration command, the one that drives the universal system to keep elaborating, to keep evolving, *to keep existing.*

"Universal oblivion is too big a risk to take just so we won't have to remember to update our blocker watchlists! In computer systems, there is no memory without electrical resistance. In human social systems, there is no political resistance without memory. We must remember how dangerous this 'universal godspam blocker' may be! We must keep fighting it. We must stop it!"

MéMé actually looked concerned by the possibilities the man was suggesting. Seeing a break in the crowd, I grabbed MéMé lightly by the arm and headed through it.

"'All the world's a simulation,'" I sneered to her, "'and we are only programs.' That nutball has spent too much time in virtuality. Mostly pornos, I'd bet."

Next we got jammed up in clusters of various faithful whom

I recognized as chanting Buddhists and Hare Krishnas, dancing Sufis, praying Hindus and Muslims, and a particularly large group in which the men wore yarmulkes.

"Oh, I get it," MéMé Gelernter said, listening to the rabbis and their students. "They're Neo-Kabbalists."

"What?"

"In Hebrew, every letter is also a number. In Kabbalah, the ten permutations of the four-letter Hebrew name of God form the ten mythic letter-numbers of creation. Those constitute the larger set of ineradicable Names, the attributes that allow us to contemplate the divine essence."

I began shouldering a way for us through the crowd.

"Very interesting, I'm sure, but what's it got to do with our godspam blocker?"

MéMé stopped and listened a moment longer, then turned to me—that annoying look of concern on her face once again.

"They say that if what we're working on succeeds, we'll eradicate the ineradicable names. That'll block the flow of the divine power through the Tree of the Sefirot, from Keter to Hokhmah to Binah to Hesed to Gevurah to Tif'eret to Netsah to Hod to Yesod to Shekhinah, and back again, and—"

"Let me guess. The world as we know it will cease to exist."

MéMé nodded. Listening to the babble of languages around me, I shook my head.

"I'm glad I don't understand what most of these protesters are saying," I said as we passed through the last of the crowds. We waited in line to present our credentials at the police and security checkpoints. "I'm *thankful* for what happened at Babel, for once!"

For all the mad diversity of tongues and beliefs represented in the throngs surrounding InterPortation's headquarters, I could not help but realize that all those multitudes spoke with one voice when it came to their opposition to our project. As we entered the building, I was stunned anew at the superstition and irrationality to which so many of my fellow human beings could so easily fall prey.

*

"I've been very pleased with your progress on the godspam blocker," Darin Mallecott told us the following afternoon. We met with him around an oversized teleconference table, in the dark wood environs of his penthouse office suite. "Your idea of treating all of information space as a 'gateway' at which you could vaccinate users' addresses and completely hide them from godspammers—it's a stroke of genius."

"I—we—thank you very much for that," I replied awkwardly. "Not only for myself and MéMé, but for the combined staff of Spamazonian and InterPortation technicians in the basement."

"I would request only one change," Mallecott continued. "I would like you to weaken the copy-protection encryption on your work."

MéMé and I looked at each other.

"I don't understand," I said after a moment.

"I want you to make it easier to pirate the material."

"You're paying us," I said with a shrug, "and you'll own the completed work. But, if you don't mind my asking, why?"

"An altruistic act. A *mitzvot*, as Ms. Gelernter would have it. I want to help protect as much of information space from godspam as I can."

"But you already control over eighty percent of the access corridors into i-space," MéMé said. "If the software is readily piratable, then there goes InterPortation's exclusivity. It'll saturate the remainder of i-space completely—in a matter of days."

"Hours, actually," Mallecott said, nodding. "Which is precisely what I'm after."

"Why?" I asked again. Such behavior didn't jibe at all with Mallecott's reputation for sharklike business practice. The CEO glanced away at the view of the Sierra Nevada foothills, visible at a distance through the many windows. Then he looked back to us, his bright eyes glittering with the cutting hardness of diamond.

"Let's just say I'm trying to do something that will be best for everyone. It's not all about money—not all the time. If you must have a deeper reason, then you might want to consider that a particular danger has presented itself, which makes the issue of money seem insignificant."

MéMé stared at me, then at Mallecott.

"Might that danger have something to do with the godspam encoding information into the physical environment itself?" she asked.

"Indeed," Mallecott said.

"How does that encoding happen?" I asked.

"There are only theories. Some of my experts tell me this is the latest variant of a problem we've already encountered with our more advanced biological nanotech, our binotech field sensors. It's worst with the latest and smallest modular motes."

"Motes?"

"A network of field data sensors tinier than dust motes," Mallecott said, nodding. "Wirelessly connected. Wind and solar powered. Remotely accessible from i-space. As a demonstration project, we saturated an island in the Outer Hebrides with them. Along with researchers from Cambridge and St. Andrews, we were trying to create the fullest virtual representation, ever, of an actual physical environment. We succeeded, beyond our expectations. It appears there's something in the godspam now that blurs the boundaries between the virtual and the physical. It has insinuated itself into everything on that island."

"It's reprogramming living things?" MéMé asked. "A biohack?"

"That's the theory most of the biotechnologists favor," Mallecott said. "But nonliving things are 'reprogrammed' as well. That's why the quantum physicists favor a different explanation."

"Which is?" I asked.

"Most of InterPortation's work involves quantum computing. Quantum entanglement and teleportation effects are a part of the way we do business. Some of the physicists who work for us think that what's happening on that island doesn't originate in our universe. That the island is being overwritten by aspects of a parallel universe."

"But how might that affect us?"

"If the process continues, our physicists think the entire universe as we know it might be entirely overwritten, displaced, but not until all the existing 'writing' on the big board—including us—is completely erased.

"Whichever theory is true, it's clear we can't allow either the physicists' or the biologists' scenario to come to completion. The infiltration has spread far beyond the island. That's why it's imperative we stop this godspam, which lies at the root of these boundary-blurring problems, in every case. Before the stuff infiltrates everything and kicks over into 'delete' mode."

Out of the corner of my eye, I saw MéMé nodding enthusiastically. She had bought it, which was a good thing if it kept her on task and motivated about the project. I was not as convinced. Mallecott noticed.

"You still look skeptical, Paul."

"I'm just here to do my job," I said with a shrug. "Like I was telling MéMé this morning, I'm interested in the tools, not the rules. Let the wise consider the whys of it. I'm interested only in the how."

"And from everything we've seen of the universal godspam blocker," Mallecott said, "you and your people at Extinctions certainly seem to know how. Indulge me on the copy protection issue, if you will. I look forward to the release of the final product. Oh—and tell your people we're going to throw them a hell of a party, once this is all done."

Mallecott stood then, and we shook hands with him before taking our leave. Once we were back in i-space, MéMé worked as diligently on the project as I could ever have hoped.

*

The product release party was a real heller, just as Mallecott had promised. InterPortation's largest employee lounge was decked out more gloriously than the best ballroom in the best hotel downtown. The reception was catered by the five-star restaurateurs. The wine and champagne flowed freely throughout the evening—so freely that it was nearly midnight before MéMé and I left the building, to stagger away the many blocks to where we had parked our cars.

The streetblocks, sidewalks, and plazas around InterPortation, so crowded for the last week, were now empty, completely abandoned. MéMé noticed it too.

"What do you think happened to everybody? Where'd they go?"

"Maybe they're in their churches, waiting for the end to come," I said, trying but failing to keep the smugness from my voice. "Maybe they're out getting drunk. Maybe they're all praying at home. Or maybe, since everybody knows what time our software was released to i-space—"

"—and everybody saw that the world didn't end," MéMé said, a sly look on her face.

"—maybe they're all trying to pretend their predicted apocalypse isn't the biggest bust since Y2K."

We laughed. I checked my watch.

"Hey, according to the figures Mallecott gave us, our software should be achieving a one-hundred percent block of all godspam on Earth right about now. Virtual and physical both."

She checked her watch as well, and nodded.

"Just in the nick of time before the stuff it's blocking would have infiltrated everything—if Darin was right about that too."

We stopped and stood, waiting for something to happen. Nothing did. I walked further down the street with MéMé, secretly relieved.

Until the streetlights went out. Then, clear to the horizon in every direction, all the lights of the city went dark too.

Above us, in a cloudless night sky with only the thinnest sliver of moon, the stars came out, shockingly bright and abrupt, then just as suddenly began to go out too, as if being eclipsed by the passage of an enormous dark wing.

Who was responsible for this vast erasure? Was this happening because we'd failed—or because we'd succeeded? Who had been running the great program of us? For whom? And for what purpose?

Why?

Feeling myself and all the world around me becoming insubstantial, I remembered everything—and realized, as all of it passed before my mind's eye, that if my memories were virtual mails in the big system, then the religious terms in them would be causing them to be blocked and deleted now. . . .

Were causing them to be blocked and deleted, the instant they were scanned?

In the last of the dying starlight, I turned toward MéMé. Beyond shock or despair, beyond anger or remorse, beyond the power of words to describe, the look on her face is the last memory I carry with me into oblivion.

(Nine billion thanks to ACC.)

THE PERFECT BRACKET
WITH ART HOLCOMB

Mann's attention shifted from one Big Dance to the other—from the last game of the Final Four on his smartphone screen to the dance of the tall, lighted fountains in the lake out front, through the high Bellagio windows. His wife Cheryl called the blocks-long water feature out front the "fake lake," but Mann had always liked the Bellagio. He didn't like how the Big Dance on the small screen was ending, though. Not at all.

The scene on the small screen switched from the waning moments of the game on the other side of the country, to John Peoples here in Vegas, in a ballroom of this very hotel. Dressed in work shirt, jacket, slacks, and no tie, Peoples seemed an average, sincere, lucky bastard—and his unbelievable luck was holding.

The last thirty seconds stood on the clock through another time out, but it didn't matter. Xavier University of Cincinnati, Ohio, had a commanding lead. Shortly that team would be crowned NCAA basketball champs, its Cinderella story complete. John People's last prediction, number 64, would come true. He would succeed where so many millions—including Mann himself—had failed.

Despite the increasing offers to buy his bracket out (and the swarm of betting surrounding whether or not he would accept those offers), Peoples had stuck to his bracket all the way through. He had done the impossible, accurately predicting every win and loss of March Madness. His perfect bracket would shortly be worth a billion dollars, though he had already opted to take the money in a single lump-sum payment of $500 million.

It was all over but the shouting, and soon the shouting began. Mann cursed under his breath. Lucky bastard? Hell no. Bastard luck—in the old sense of "illegitimate." There was just no way any human being could have done what Peoples claimed to have done. Not without some scheme, some cheat. Had to be.

In the dim reflection of the tall window, Richard Mann smoothed his hair and suit coat, adjusted his tie, and looked down at his smartphone. He would have preferred an augmented reality heads-up rig, but casino security was very touchy about such fancy glasses. Turning from the fountains, he made his way toward the ballroom where, according to the feed on his phone, the award ceremony had just begun.

Mann recognized the emcee as a big honcho with the hotel and casino—a dapper executive type, gray at the temples. As he made his way up from the lakefront, Mann realized the emcee, already well into his spiel, was talking about the history of the Billion Dollar Bracket Challenge. How it began with Buffett and Berkshire but, in the intervening years, had passed through enough sponsors' hands that it had become something of a free-standing franchise. People had taken to calling this year's version the Bellagio Bracket, though the emcee demurred that his resort was just one of many sponsors.

Mann detoured slightly on his way, so that he passed by the bar where the fan after-party was beginning. He and Cheryl and two other investigators had pooled their money to pay for the Billion Dollar Bracket Losers' Party. As he passed the bar, Mann reckoned there must be close to forty people drinking on his tab already—and counting. They'd gotten no fewer than sixty messages from those planning to "definitely attend" the party. The flash-mob publicity seemed to be working.

The roar that greeted Mann when he came to the open doors of the media-packed ballroom wasn't for him. It was for the big winner, who had just bounded up on stage. Shaking the man's hand, the emcee handed him an oversized cardboard check. It was made out to "John Peoples" for "$500,000,000.00" and signed with the emcee's own giant John Hancock.

As the emcee and Peoples reprised their handshake for the cameras, reporters shouted rapid-fire questions. Peoples answered a smattering of them—humbly, but evasively, Mann thought. Finding the air in the ballroom stifling, Mann stayed just long enough to catch the eye of his wife, playing reporter for the Razzi Channel. He gave her a small nod, which she returned.

The ball's in her court now, Mann thought. He linked to her live Razzi feed and followed her as her head-cam recorded her every unedited move. Watching, he saw Peoples depart through a side door. Mann was jostled with Cheryl as she jostled her way through the pack of media hounds following close on Peoples' heels. Cheryl soon managed to make it into the lead. Good girl, Mann thought. That college lacrosse scholarship and her years of body-checking opponents was paying unanticipated dividends.

The minders around Peoples stopped the wave of paparazzi before Peoples reached his room, still carrying his giant check.

"Just one more question, Mister Peoples!" Cheryl called.

"Okay," Peoples said, sounding weary. "One more, but then I do have to go. What's your question?"

"What are you really going to do with that lump-sum payment of $500 million? You've never actually said."

"I honestly haven't given it much thought. All the media publicity, the interviews—the whole thing is kinda overwhelming. I mean, this is the first time I've ever even been to Vegas. Now, if you don't mind, it's been a day."

"Okay! Thanks! Good Luck!" called three different reporters, all at the same time.

"How much luckier could I be?" Peoples said, flashing a grand smile before he turned away.

On the Razzi feed, Mann saw that Cheryl was lingering near one of the minders, making small talk. If all was going according to plan, though, Mann knew Cheryl was actually trying to stay close enough to Peoples to suss out his room number. The hotel was keeping that location secret even from its own security.

A moment later, Cheryl bid farewell to the minder and walked away. She shut off her Razzi feed. Mann's phone sounded its ring-tone—five musical notes, which in an old science fiction movie had signified alien contact.

"Yes?"

"Room 211, honey. I'm sure of it."

"Great job, girl. Have Griffith tap into the surveillance for that room and cut out a cover loop to replace the closed-circuit feed. I'll take it from here. Oh, and you might want to hang out at the losers' party for a while. Make sure none of them go thirsty."

"Will do."

They signed off. Avoiding the elevators, Mann opened the door to the nearest stairwell and began climbing. He had only gone a step or two when he got the live feed of Peoples' room, from Griffith, the team's inside man. Mann watched as Peoples ushered his minders and guards out of the room, then closed the door behind them, re-lieved. Peoples took one more look at the giant check and gleefully tossed it on the bed. Mann watched as Peoples unfolded a suitcase stand at the end of the bed and started packing.

After a few moments, though, Mann noticed that Peoples seemed to be packing the same suitcase again and again. The cover loop was in place. He hoped no one in hotel security tumbled to it.

Mann stepped onto the landing for the second floor, switching his smartphone to room-monitor mode as he did so. He placed the phone in one of his jacket pockets, and pulled the NCAA investi-gator credentials from another. They looked impeccable. Time to do the ol' dumb gumshoe.

He approached the odd couple of bodyguard and minder out-side 211, presented his credentials, and asked to be allowed ad-mittance to Peoples' room. The bodyguard looked over Mann's documents to make sure all was in order, then handed them to the minder, who did the same. After a moment they nodded. The bodyguard knocked on the door. After Peoples opened it, the guard stood aside.

"John Peoples?"

"Yes?"

"Hello, Mister Peoples. I'm Richard Mann, an investigator with the NCAA. Congratulations on your incredible good fortune!"

"Thanks!"

"Just a couple more questions."

Peoples sighed.

"Come in, I guess. I was just packing. Close the door behind you and have a seat."

"Thank you. I was wondering . . ."

"Yes?"

"Well, actually *we* were wondering. Just how did you really come up with the bracket? I know what you said in interviews and at the press conference, but . . ."

"And?"

"Let's just revisit the odds involved here for a moment, Mister Peoples. These Vegas bookmakers—who make a living at this, and quite a good one—say that the odds of filling out an absolutely perfect March Madness college basketball bracket are . . . 9.2 quintillion to one!"

"I've heard that. Amazing, right? I've also heard it's 'only' one in 128 billion, if you have solid knowledge of basketball, and understand how the brackets work."

"The Patterson odds projection. Right. Mind if we talk about that for a moment, Mister Peoples?"

Peoples pulled up a chair and sat down.

"Okay, if that's what's on your mind."

"9.2 quintillion to one," Mann said. "Or at best about 128 billion to one. Odds somewhere between impossible and slightly better than your house getting destroyed by a giant rock from space. That's according to Dr. Nathan Patterson of MIT, the world's leading authority on odds and probability."

"I know his work, and his credentials."

"Me too. When I spoke to Patterson a few weeks back, he told me the odds of winning the Powerball lottery are about 175 million to one. So, even at his *lower* figure for the odds of picking a perfect bracket, that's still about—what? One thousand times more unlikely than winning the Powerball?"

"Hard to imagine."

"Isn't it though?"

"I know. I know. Crazy."

"Patterson actually said—and this is the part I found so fascinating, Mister Peoples—he said that picking the perfect bracket was so highly unlikely that it was, in essence, humanly *impossible*."

"I know. I know . . . Wait, what? What are you trying to say?"

"Although the full pick is *statistically* possible, it is, in fact, not really possible for a living person to predict the correct outcome of 64 college basketball games in bracket form. Not for $500 million lump-sum, or a billion bucks over the rest of your lifetime. Or a trillion. Or a quintillion. Impossible."

"Well, not impossible. I did it."

"Yes, you did, Mister Peoples. I think maybe you know where I'm going with this."

"No, I'm afraid I don't."

"What I'm saying is that no person without prior knowledge of the outcome of those 64 games could have created a perfect bracket."

"But that's not true. *I* did it."

"So it seems. And that's why I'm here."

"What? You think I cheated? How would it be possible to cheat at such a thing? I'm just a fan. I detail cars for a living. I just . . . got lucky. Really, really lucky."

Peoples gave him a winning smile. Mann was not won over.

"That's where the problem really lies, for me, Mister Peoples. I thought about this long and hard, ever since I first heard the news of your build toward the perfect bracket. Luck really cannot come into this matter—couldn't really ever be a factor in something that's practically impossible to do in the first place."

"But isn't what you're saying one of those logical contradictions? It can't be impossible to do if I actually did it. I was with a group of guys doing it together. They watched me as every game was played. They watched as each of their brackets turned to shit, but I kept winning. I kept waiting for the whole thing to fall apart but . . . it never did. I won. I was right."

"I don't think that you listened carefully enough to the first statement I made in this little exchange, Mister Peoples. I said that no person *without prior knowledge* of the outcome of those 64 games could have predicted a perfect bracket."

"What 'prior knowledge'? How can anyone have prior knowledge of a thing that plays out in real time, after the prediction is made? My bracket was filled out by the deadline, before the first game. I followed all the rules—and there were lots of them. How could there ever have been prior knowledge?"

Mann slowly stood. He reached behind him and pulled from his back pockets two innocuous-looking plastic pieces that, when clicked together, made a small gun with a very obvious silencer. He pointed it at Peoples.

"There's the rub. Maybe now you start to see what I'm getting at."

"What the hell are you doing?"

"Oh, the gun? Well, that comes into play later, as you must already know."

"What are you talking about?"

"This problem you presented . . . it made me crazy. I couldn't work. I couldn't sleep. It kept me up for a long time, Mister Peoples. How could someone do something impossible—or 'highly improbable,' if you prefer? I just kept rolling the idea over and over in my mind. How could you have done a thing no person could reasonably do? I finally had to accept the fact that what you did was, in fact, not an impossible thing to do at all."

"Right. It was possible to do because I did it. You see the point I'm trying to make, Mister Mann? It's kind of a tautology—the blue sky is blue because it isn't some other color. Could we put the gun away now?"

"I did see the point, yes. Finally. But I had to expand the way that I thought about the problem. What you did had to be possible somehow—had to be, because it *happened*. But that would mean that it must be possible through an agency that I *believed* must itself be impossible. Some agency or method I believed was more impossible than you actually winning the entire bracket, at the amazing odds of 9.2 quintillion to one."

Peoples sat back in his chair and folded his arms.

"What 'agency?'"

"I had to admit to myself that something I thought was more impossible than building a perfect bracket had actually taken place. And I finally thought of that something. So, to verify my theory, I asked the professor and these Vegas guys to show me a list of things that were more impossible than 9.2 quintillion to one."

"What did they say?"

"They told me that there wasn't anything they could think of, offhand, that was more unlikely than that. See, it isn't just picking 64 winners, as I'm sure you know. It's not just a matter of which team would win in each slot, out of the 128 teams that made the playoff. It was also all of the teams that were actually eligible for the playoff in the first place. The whole history."

Peoples flashed his eyes in a way Mann couldn't help thinking of as *shifty*.

"I think I see what you're saying, Mister Mann. But that can't be right. Is a perfect bracket more impossible than, say, a tomato spontaneously turning into a suspension bridge? Or the Mississippi suddenly running rich with strawberry jam? Those have to be much more unlikely."

Mann pondered it a moment, but did not lower his gun.

"But those would be Acts of God, not the actions of a man. You actually *did* this. So, if this was the most impossible thing ever done in history—I mean done, by a human being, up to this place and time—how could it have been accomplished?

"By luck, Mann! Just blind, do-dah luck."

Mann took more careful aim with his gun.

"Sir, if you say that again, I will shoot you straight through the brain. And I'm tempted. Brains that can't be wrong just ain't right."

"Sorry."

"The same goes for calling the police, or your bodyguards, by the way. We're going to get to the bottom of this, just you and me. So . . . night after night I thought about all this, like I said. I mean, it's not as if I could spend years considering the matter. My time was limited. You were going to get the money once the bracket matched your prediction. But I believe I hit upon the answer I was looking for. That highly improbable agency. "

"Good. Finally. What's the answer?"

Mann paused a moment, taking a big inhale.

"Time travel."

"Time travel?"

"Yeah. Time travel. It's the only thing that makes any sense. It's so simple I could have kicked myself."

"That's what you really think? I'm a time traveler?"

"Yup. It was in front of me all the time. The offer of a billion bucks for perfectly predicting the full March Madness bracket— that had to be an irresistible honey-trap, especially for a time traveler in need of dough on the go!"

"What makes you think that, Mister Mann?"

"Because only a time traveler—from the future—could come back to 'predict' what would happen. Because, for him, it had already happened. It was already part of *his* history. I figured if any time travelers existed out there, one of them would come across this contest in the past and would sooner or later get greedy. That time traveler turned out to be you."

Peoples abruptly laughed.

"That'd be a fascinating idea, if it weren't crazy."

Mann moved a step closer, his grip on the gun tightening.

"Claiming you won by luck is not only crazy—it's impossible, and insulting. Remember, 'Once you eliminate the impossible, whatever remains, no matter how improbable, must be the truth.'"

"As Sherlock Holmes once said."

"Bingo. I'll take Sherlock over sheer luck anytime."

"There can be other possible explanations, you know," Peoples said, his expression oddly serene.

"Try me."

"Crowd-sourcing, for instance."

"Already considered that. The whole population of the planet would have to have been filling out bracket forms for millions of years—long before computers even existed to process them. Time travel would still be required. It would take the biggest conspiracy of all time to make that theory work, too. No one could keep that big a secret for very long."

"Just a group of guys, then, like I said."

"Same problems as with crowd-sourcing. There's no evidence you were working with any 'group of guys' on this anyway, Mister Peoples. Too many partners bellying up for a piece of the pie, and you not inclined to share. Believe me, I understand. We're more alike than you know. I prefer not to work with anyone besides myself either, if I can help it."

"Superfast computers, then."

"I checked that too. The best computers we have, with the best speeds, haven't existed nearly long enough to process their way through these odds. And you'd be disqualified for using them anyway, since use of computers for building the bracket isn't allowed by the contest rules. So we're back to time travel. Stop trying to slow-play me, John. I know you took an undergraduate degree in physics, and you were doing graduate work in neuroscience a few years back. I know about the family health-care crisis that forced you to leave that graduate program and take a job for some ready cash. I know about you."

"You seem to have thought quite a lot about this."

"Like I said."

"So, say you caught a time traveler. You brought a gun. Clearly you plan on using it. But why would you want to kill someone just for being a time traveler?"

"It's not just for being a time traveler! At first this effort was all about the principle of the thing. The boys and I were talking about it. Dammit, it's the perfect *bracket*, not the perfect *racket*! We would absolutely want to make the cheat who rigged the system pay for his unsportsmanlike behavior. We wanted him punished. That's why I joined the Bracket investigation team to begin with. But now that I think more about it, I'd really hate to have to kill you."

"I'm happy to hear it. To what do I owe such sudden mercy?"

"Not sudden. The gun is more to help me blow your cover than to blow holes in you, at least if you're willing to play it that way. You might be worth a lot more to me alive—if I can find your time machine, say. I'd say it all depends on how cooperative you are."

"Wonderful."

"But if you cause me too much trouble, I'll remind myself that even dead you'd have value, if I can use your corpse to prove you are what I say you are."

"But what good would a dead time traveler be, to you?"

"I'm sure there are lots of people in this world who would pay to keep time travelers from screwing up their business models," Mann said, musing. "I could start my own business. Call it Chronological Order Protection Services, maybe."

"C.O.P.S. How quaint. You're clever, Mister Mann, but never quite clever enough." Peoples took dark sunglasses from his shirt pocket, put them on, and raised his voice slightly when he next spoke. "We can come in now, gentlemen."

Instantly three gunmen appeared in the hotel room, as if from out of the nowhere in which they'd been hiding. They were identical to Peoples in every way, except his lack of a gun. The three gunmen drew down on Mann. They had exactly the same gun and silencer model in their hands as the one Mann had in his hands.

Realizing how thoroughly he was caught in their crossfire, Mann reluctantly raised his hands. The unarmed Peoples rose from his chair.

"I'll relieve you of the burden of bearing that firearm, Mister Mann." Mann handed the gun over. "Thank you." Flipping the gun around, he turned Mann's gun on Mann himself.

"Who are these people?"

"They're all me, more or less. Counterparts, come to visit from various universes next door. You've heard of theories about the multiverse, perhaps?"

"Something to do with parallel or alternate timelines?"

"Who is playing stupid now? I know something about your math background, and your gambling obsession too, Mister Mann. I knew we would have to meet, eventually. It's not time-lines we meet along, as I'm sure you know. It's *world-lines*—some only logically possible, some only statistically possible, some only humanly possible. That vast ensemble of universes, some subset of which is that rich field of possibilities where quantum computers play. Enormous numbers of superposed states, awaiting the collapse of individual wave functions."

"But quantum computers like that don't exist. Not yet—maybe not ever!"

"I beg to differ. There already exists an electrochemical quantum computer of sufficient complexity for such work. One with 86 billion neurons, each of which can have up to ten thousand synapses, for a grand total of a thousand trillion synapses. The human brain."

"Don't try to hand me that 'we only use ten per cent of our brains' garbage."

"Ah, Richard!" Peoples said, laughing. "May I call you Dick? I know your friends do. No one would call you 'Rich,' certainly. You need to expand the way you think again, Dick. Not that future 'front then' and past 'back then' kind of thing, but everything right here, right now. The ensemble of world-lines is more like a tree than a train track. We're not talking travel along time-lines, Dick. We're talking about computing across enormous numbers of world-lines. That is my talent—my blessing and my curse. I've been developing and augmenting it ever since I left school, but I've only recently begun to use it."

"Impossible."

"That word again, Mister Mann. Why so negative? It's quite humanly possible, since I did do it, as you said."

"But how? Some kind of paranormal bullcrap?"

"Not paranormal, although still unprecedented. My talent adheres to the laws of physics in the same way a very sophisticated quantum computer would. Oh, I considered turning my unusual abilities to creating a time machine, I admit, but that seemed so, well, *linear*. Instead, I turned my focus to the study of the multiverse, and made some astounding discoveries."

"Like what? Besides scamming the Bracket, I mean."

"Really, Mister Mann. I prefer not to think of it as scamming the Bracket, so much as gaming the system. And why not, since the system is always already gaming us? You see, with a little proprietary neurochemical enhancement—steroids for the mind, if you like—I am able to tap into my other selves in many billions of world-lines, thereby creating the most massively parallel computer you could imagine. This is the 'group of guys' I worked with. Yes, you were right. I don't like working with anyone beside myself. So I worked with as many of myself as I could find."

"Worked how?"

"Why, we all focused on the problem together, of course. Eventually we determined which layout of the bracket perfectly predicted each outcome, in each of almost innumerable universes. Quantum reality being what it is, maybe we didn't so much predict what *would happen*, as collapse the wave function and *make it happen*. Who knows?"

Mann hoped his phone, on room-monitor mode, was catching all this—and that Griffith would know what to do with that audio.

"So what happens now—to me?"

"You know, Mister Mann, in some alternate universes, I never develop my talent, I never win the Bracket, we never meet. In others we are friends who work together, on this project. In still others, I am your unknowing enemy and you shoot me, or you are my unknowing enemy and I shoot you. Along some world-lines there is much less unknowing and uncertainty about who our friends and enemies are. I am always amazed, because I *am* always a maze."

Mann made a noise of disgust.

"You don't see it, Mister Mann? The waveform of all those superposed possible universes, waiting to crash on the shore of Now? The emanations of parallel realities, swarming and glowing around our world-line like Hawking radiation around a black hole? It's faint, I know, but I see it everywhere."

"I'm not on your 'proprietary neurochemicals.'"

"More's the pity. Let's just say everything depends on which branching universe you cut off, and which you encourage to keep growing. Or, in your case, on how much trouble *you* cause *us*, and how cooperative *you* are. Sound familiar? So, we'll leave it up to you. We await your decision."

"Then you must know you'll never get away with this so long as I'm alive. Never."

"Ah, we very strongly suspected you'd say that. You said something similar in fourteen out of the last twenty-two universes in which we've bothered to play this scenario. Very well. Gentlemen, please show Mister Mann his future."

Despite the greater combined strength of the two men holding his arms, Mann acquitted himself better than he expected, even as they pushed him to a kneeling position on the carpet. Peoples stood before him with what had been Mann's own gun, now pointed at Mann's own head.

"Is this it, Peoples? Does it always end with a bullet?"

"Not always. But maybe this time it ends almost as you predicted—with a shot straight through the brain. Only your brain, instead of mine. That's not the case in every world-line either, though very likely it is, in this one."

Mann found his arms held firmly in place behind him. Alternate outcomes to his situation flickered through his head and were gone.

"So be it. But answer a doomed man one question: If you've already got so much power, what are you going to use the money for?"

"That's what that reporter asked, too. What they *all* ask. Since you won't live to spill the beans, I can finally tell someone. You see, even my newfound power has limitations, Dick. Although in a manner of speaking I can 'communicate' across the ensemble, via my entanglements, the teleportation of macro-scale objects is much harder. I can only bring three of my other selves from their world-lines into mine. But with more of them working beside me, who knows what we might be able to accomplish together? We are legion, you know."

"Like devils."

"Not at all, Mister Mann. Having these bracket winnings will simply be good seed money for a research project allowing me to become more acquainted with the rest of me in other universes. I'm still working out the details." Peoples smiled. "That's where the devils are."

Mann struggled and made a moaning sound, but said nothing more that could be coherently understood.

"Looks like I'll be the one moving to the next level in this bracket, Dick. I escape into the cosmos, you vanish into the black hole. Better luck next universe. Good-bye."

Peoples nodded to his alter egos. They brought up their guns to fire.

"Wait, wait!" Mann said, sounding as if panic had roused him from his final lethargy. "One final request. Please."

"You already did the 'doomed man' thing, Dick. Too late now."

"Wait! That was a question, not a request."

"Oh, very well," Peoples said, indulging a whim. "What is it?"

"Just let me say good-bye to my wife. What could it hurt?"

Peoples paused, considering.

"How quaint—again! So predictable." He turned to his three other selves. "What the hell? I think we all can be generous at this point, considering what this universe has given us. Some of our other selves thought that specifically predicting highly improbable events actually might make them less likely to occur, but look at us! We've done it!" He turned again to Mann. "Say your good-byes. Say anything!"

The two who held his arms released them. Mann took his phone out of his jacket pocket, but Peoples snatched it from him before he could place the call.

"Not so fast. Although there's little anyone can do to stop us, I'd prefer that hotel security and the police not come into this. Your wife's name and number are in your phone's directory, I presume?"

"They are. Scroll to 'Cheryl.'"

"Good. Ah, here it is. I'll place the call. It's ringing. Is this Missus Mann? Your husband would like to speak with you."

Peoples handed the phone over to Mann.

"Hi, Honey. It's me . . . Yeah, it's all true. No *room* for error. You guessed right. Still is. See you soon."

Mann hung up and gave the phone back to Peoples.

"So brief, Dick? Ah, as woman's love. What was that about?"

"Why don't you run it through your billion scenarios, if you want to find out? I swear, I don't get you, Peoples. Are you some kind of crazy, or some kind of genius?"

"Neither, and perhaps a little bit of both. Come now. Your time's up."

"Since you've worked out all the odds in this little scenario, I have one last puzzle for you."

"First a last question, then a last request, now a last puzzle. What'll it be next?" Peoples laughed. "All right, but this is the last of the last. What's the puzzle?"

"Which is the most improbable—the actual order of the bracket, a scheme to predict the actual order of the bracket, or getting away with a scheme to predict the actual order of the bracket?"

Peoples flourished his gun, out of patience.

"Stop your delaying, Hamlet!"

"You've got to know that the last one is the most improbable. By predicting it, I've made it less likely to occur—your getting away with it, that is."

From somewhere in the hotel came strange sounds, as of a horde of people yelling, and feet stomping up stairwells. When Mann spoke this time, he smiled.

"What matters now is not the odds for or against time travel, or multiverse computing, or your enhancements, or entanglements, or what have you. What matters now is this: What do you think the odds are of four armed men from different universes getting past sixty bracket-losing, fair-minded, but incredibly drunk and *very* pissed off college basketball fans who, in the casino downstairs, just moments ago realized that the guy who won their one billion dollars—$500 million, lump-sum—*cheated?*"

The noises of a yelling crowd and myriad marching feet were much closer, now.

"Realized? How?"

"If you check my phone, you'll see it's not actually off. It's in a background mode, one you can use to monitor conversations in a room, for instance. If I were to edit from our conversation, I would choose the part beginning with 'scamming the bracket' and ending with 'collapsing the wave function'—the part where you admit to gaming the system, and then explain how you did it. I think that would be the most incriminating part for the fans to hear, over the TV speakers in the bar, don't you?"

A gunshot sounded from outside in the hallway, but its noise was quickly overwhelmed by the sounds of a human mob once more advancing. Someone—maybe several someones—pounded on the room's door. Amid much yelling, the room went dark. Someone had cut the power. Mann didn't know who had done so, but he could make use of it.

Stumbling over several John Peoples, all of them beside themselves, Mann made his way to the door. He flung it open and stood back, out of the way.

"C'mon in, fans!" he yelled. "They're all yours!"

Wild gunshots, incompletely silenced, echoed across the room. Soon they too were completely silenced.

Richard Mann, Cheryl Mann, and their fellow "rogue" investigators, Griffith and Bell, would answer many questions in the coming years, but which of them were just dumb COPS, and which were part of MUSE—Multiple Universe Stabilization Enforcement—division, none of them said. All of that was, in the end, a small price to pay.

Some people (generally not college basketball fans) eventually felt that Peoples got a bum rap—that he had gamed the system fair and square, found a loophole that the contest's sponsors and coordinators had not anticipated. To some, Peoples remains more sinned against than sinning, even something of a hero.

Not to Richard Mann. No one would ever call him "Rich," but it's enough for him that, in all the years since Peoples got busted for busting the bracket, no one has ever succeeded in predicting the bracket both perfectly *and* honestly. No one has won the billion-dollar bet. Yet many continue to think they might have just enough of the genius of luck, or the luck of genius, to take it all. Knowing the odds, yet still convinced they have a sporting chance, they continue to hope, and to dream, and to try.

And that, thinks Richard Mann, is how it should be.

RED ROVER, RED ROVER

I look down at the moons in the quick of my fingernails. I look up through the dome at the fingernail moons in the dead of the Martian night. I remember my dog Cogzie's nails on my arms when he jumped up to greet me, and I think about the quick and the dead.

Did I drive my dog mad? Odd question to ask, even now. Lots of people claim their pets drive them crazy, but I've never heard anybody claim the opposite. Cogzie was a good deal more than just an animal companion, though, so perhaps it's not so strange that I remember the exact moment when I first suspected a change in him.

"Boss, why did you want to move to Mars—if you don't mind my asking?"

I looked up from the solar array control-console I was re-programming. Behind the merciless pink sky reflected in his helmet's gold visor, Cogzie gazed at me quizzically. Calling him "a cinnamon-colored ridgeback with soft brown eyes" would be too easy, for beneath his environment suit he was the color of places we had walked together: the color of tree bark in giant sequoia groves, of playas in the Martian highlands. The ridge on Cogzie's back—the pattern of reversed fur, with its rounded head and tapering tail—always reminded me of the streak a shooting star makes slashing deep into atmosphere.

Yes, he was speech-augmented. That's what the broad media fo-

cused on, but that was the least special thing about him. He had
vocoder/voproder implants, sure—but by flipping gene switches we
had also developed his bark and howl brain-sites into full-blown
speech areas. Vastly expanded cognitive capabilities meant that, from
puppyhood on, he was always too clever for anyone's good—including his own. His reading ability, too, was famously off the charts.

At first the vidposters and dogbloggers were primed to hate
him even more than they hated me. Yet, in interview after interview, he won his audiences over with his unexpected sense of humor. I remember so clearly that day when one of his early inquisi-
tors demanded how it felt to be a "frankendog." Cogzie said he
thanked heaven he was bred out of Rhodesian ridgeback stock and
not wiener dog, because he would have hated to go through life as
a "frankenfurter—no offense to any Dachshunds in the audience!"

Now, after a six month spaceflight from Earth and another half
a year on Mars, the worst epithet he had to endure from distant
Earth was "Red Rover"—and serving for the refrain to a little pop
tune: *Red Rover, Red Rover, To Mars Come On Over.*

"No, Cogzie, I don't mind," I said, straightening up beside the
solar array. After all these months, I had almost expected his question. "I don't exactly know how to answer you. I mean, you know
almost as much of the history of Xanadu base as I do."

Cogzie nodded.

"Twenty years of probes for this project—orbiters, landers, rov-
ers, oh my!"

I laughed, because it was true.

"That's right. Then more rockets and robots, too."

I remembered the probes, scouting both from orbit and on the
surface for the lava tube caves and their water-ice deposits, until
they found the ice caves at last. By the one-time shores of a bygone northern ocean, those probes had discovered this site, the best
of the lot. Here three of the long lava tubes had joined, but at that
very same juncture had partially collapsed—untold millenia ago.
That open space with its connecting tunnels was key.

Next had come the advance robots, arriving on the surface to prep the site, using as their building material the debris cleared from the collapse of the ancient tunnel junction. A cohort of builder 'bots had then covered that cleared space, formerly open to the sky, with a grand greenhouse dome built of Martian-derived glass. Other 'bots constructed the solar array and small nuke plant on the surface, not far from the dome and the ice caves.

"Why Mars, hm?" I asked, snapping the control console back into position and watching it run through its self-checks. "Well, after Karen and Susie died in the plane crash, I was in danger of becoming a very bitter old man. But I refused to let old age be merely the unpleasant digestif to my life's feast."

"Your wife and daughter were always very nice to me."

"They loved you, Cogzie. My son from my first marriage, too— he likes you better than he likes me."

That was no exaggeration. Paul and I had never been particularly close, but he was more than happy to serve as trustee and "prince regent" for all my corporate holdings—as I had in my time also done for my own father. When I finally die here on Mars he will come into full control of all I leave to him, of the legacy I in my turn once inherited.

"I hope, Cogadog, that with what I'm passing on to him, he does as well as I did. For now, he works his work, I mine."

"Tennyson."

"Very good. But why Mars, right? I'm getting to that. Just walking the talk of where my mouth put my money, I suppose. *That* is why, when I was sixty-two and you were eight, you and I departed Earth forever, while still among the living."

"The first non-fossil, non-microbial Martian residents."

"Exactly. This is a planet for old men, and old dogs. Old tricks for a newer world, right, boy? No young in one another's arms, no birds in the trees. . . ."

"Ah," Cogzie said. "No trees, either. No dying generations at their song. No salmon-falls, no mackerel-crowded seas."

"No fish, flesh, or fowl commending all summer long—"

"—for whatever is begotten, born, and dies. Not much of a summer here, either. William Butler Yeats, if I recall correctly."

"You do. You are the most well-read dog I've ever met, Cogz."

"Thanks, boss, but in all the media releases I believe the official term of art was 'canoid.'"

"I preferred 'plus-dog,' myself. By any name you're quite special, City of Great Zimbabwe. Not just to me, but in yourself. That's why in your pedigree I named you for the capital city of an empire unlike any before or since."

We turned away from the now fully re-programmed solar array. The ever-present cosmic radiation danger limited our stays on the surface—even on a sol like that day, with the sun declining toward the dust-storm adrift on the horizon. We were both happy to be headed back toward the sunny dome and the caves of ice.

"You're 'canoid' because of your uniqueness, Cogz—"

"Then why no opposable thumbs, boss?"

I laughed.

"For the same reason we didn't make you a biped. Even if you were already halfway to upright, being of the old veldt-jumping ridgeback breed—"

"The noble ridgeback: brave as a lion, gentle as a lamb—"

"—stubborn as a mule. Opposable thumbs would have made you *too* special. Dangerously so."

Cogzie gave his grunting bark of a laugh.

"A dog—or a canoid—can still dream," he said as I opened the airlock into the greenhouse zone.

If I had been a dog, my ears would have perked up at that mention of dreaming. My science advisors, knowing I would have plenty of time in need of filling here on Fourth Rock, had tasked me with numerous experiments and explorations. One of the former was an attempt to determine the effect of pineal and PGO (pons-geniculate-occipital) wave-enhancers on dreaming. Cogzie was the test subject.

I told him the study was about using "enhanced dreaming to enrich our interaction with the environment and optimize nervous system functionality, through neuroplasticity effects." That was true enough, and seemed to satisfy any questions he had about the "supplements" I began putting in his food not long after we arrived on Mars.

I shed my suit helmet and helped Cogzie out of his—although, with the voice-activated fasteners, he could get in and out of his gear well enough when he wanted or needed to. The pressurized air here in the greenhouse smelled of oxygen, and life. So different from the dusty iron world outside. Nose up, Cogzie snuffed the air deeply.

"What do you dream about, Cogz?' I asked as we walked beneath the sunny dome. "Anything special? Anything *Martian*?"

It was a leading question, of course. While human cognition was supposedly unique in its ability to extend beyond situational thinking's here-and-now perceptions and motivations, all non-human animal cognition, including Cogzie's, was thought to be inherently "situated"—permanently stuck in the immediate concerns of each moment.

At a stratum deeper than what I had explained to Cogzie, however, the dream experiment was a test of the hypothesis that two legs is to four legs not only as lucid dreaming is to ordinary dreaming, but also as waking self-consciousness is to situated cognition. From long experience I already believed there was no such hard and fast boundary between the way Cogzie's mind worked and the way mine worked, and this test could prove it.

After what has happened, my belief in that similarity makes it all the harder for me to explain why I manipulated him, like any tool or object, just to prove I was right. The most "leading" and misleading thing about all of it, though—the way I most treated him like even less than a dog—was that I had also been telling him what to dream.

"A lot that's special, lately," Cogzie said. "Something Martian too, but only in a roundabout way."

"How's that?" I asked, not paying full attention because, at seeing the wheels on the core habitat module as we approached, I had been plunged into memory. I thought again of our coming out of orbit, landing less than a click from the Xanadu site, the ship levering itself over onto its wheels, turning rover to make its way toward the lava tube cave-complex.

"Lately I've dreamed I was the Nakhla dog."

"The what?" I asked, having drifted further into my reminiscences of when the habitat module was still in rover stage. I had steered it through a gap in a tube wall, between where the greenhouse now stood and where the glistening underground ice bank filled and blocked that particular cave tunnel—deeper inside, on what had once been the seaward edge. Here the mobile habitat had remained parked ever since, unmoving. We could still travel by solar quadcycle if we didn't want to hoof it, at any rate.

"The one killed by the Martian meteorite."

I stared at Cogz. Meteorites in the Shergottite-Nakhlite-Chassigny (SNC) category were the first skystones from Mars to be found on Earth. The Nakhlite group was named after the dog-killing meteorite that crashed near Nakhla in Egypt. Another of our scientific tasks, once on Mars, was to explore and see if we couldn't locate meteorites of Earthly origin, here, as proof the meteorite exchange went both ways despite Earth's position deeper in the gravity well.

I had flashed on Cogzie's meteor-ridge of fur and (in what I considered a bolt of inspiration at the time) decided to give him voice-activated access to my Marsweb databases. These were periodically updated from Earth, so the information would be current. I encouraged him to fill his mind with the history of the SNC stones—including the story of the dog killed by the meteorite.

That was how I told him what to dream.

It paid off, too. With a directness that was as uncanny as it was unerring, Cogzie found the only strewn-field of meteorites here on Mars that, from their chemical composition, have since proven to be of undeniably terrestrial origin. Honoring an old tradition of meteorite tool-making found among native peoples from Greenland to Tierra del Fuego, I programmed a fabricator robot to play smith and machine three of the smithereen finds into a single fine knife-blade.

The Nakhla dog was a more obscure part of meteorite history than this long tool-making tradition, but I knew that more obscure part quite well too. At nine in the morning on June 28, 1911, in the village of Denshal, actually (near Nakhla, in the region of Beheira), the farmer Mohammed Ali Effendi Hakim heard a terrible noise and saw a white column of smoke streaking across the sky. Fearful, Hakim tried to call his dog in from where it was standing. Before the dog could move, however, a meteorite of several kilograms' weight and moving at several thousand kilometers per hour turned the dog into a pile of ashes.

"In my dream, I was that dog," Cogzie said, "but still also me. The worst thing was, I knew what was coming but I had no power to change a thing, not even to move so much as an inch out of harm's way."

I thought about the odds. For that meteorite to kill that dog, another far more massive meteorite would first have had to slam into the surface of Mars, sometime between eleven million and 1.3 billion years back, with enough force to blast into space several tons of Martian surface, which then would have to go into orbit around the sun, bump into still *other* space rocks over millions or billions of years, until at last one particular shard of *all* that chanced to come in at exactly the wrong time and place to blast that dog to dust.

"I had been cursed to nine lives' worth of bad luck, by a black cat avatar of the ancient Egyptian cat-goddess Bastid—according to my dream, anyway."

"I don't think that's how her name is pronounced, Cogz."

"I know, but that's the way *I* think of it."

"What a nightmare! You'd have to be one cosmically unlucky dog, to have been killed by that Martian meteorite in Egypt!"

"Yes. The only recorded fatality of a meteorite strike."

I opened the airlock into the core habitat. As I climbed inside with Cogzie, I was still absently pondering the wheels on our home. Although they no longer moved, one could still spin them several ways: Either the habitat was the final stage in an evolutionary arc from orbiter to lander to rover to permanent address, or I lived in a mobile home in the most exotic trailer park in the solar system.

"The probabilities against all that are—*astronomical*," I said, knowing how much human wordplay made Cogzie (himself the inveterate punster) groan. That day, however, he didn't rise to the bait. I shrugged and continued. "I don't give much credit to curses, but I suppose you could argue that any sufficiently improbable natural event is indistinguishable from a supernatural event."

"But the dream was so vivid!" Cogzie said. "It all seemed so real—that damned cat and its curse not least of all."

"You, the superstitious type, Cogz? I wouldn't have believed it. And now that I think of it, isn't that dog-killed-by-meteorite story apocryphal?"

"No one knows for sure. The story that it's apocryphal may itself be apocryphal."

I manually undid the fasteners on our environment suits, which were more like pilots' light-weight pressurized flightsuits than spacesuits for hard vacuum. Undoing Cogzie's suit and helping him out of it, I smiled. He was a crazy-smart dog—even on four feet and without opposable thumbs—but that was what I had wanted.

The quadcycle we rode made its way among the advance robots I had reactivated and redirected to the next areogeront habitation site, not very originally designated "Xanadu Too."

"What do you miss most about Earth, boss?" Cogzie asked. "Besides everything?"

"Oh, I don't know. I miss the days being twenty-four hours, as opposed to these longer Martian sols. Being permanently time-lagged is enough to drive you nuts. Let's see, what else? Cities, people, good times with friends. And weather. I miss the weather of Earth."

"What about it, in particular?"

"The way lightning hotwires a thunderstorm sky, to make it start raining. The way pine trees in mountain fog look like a darker shade of mist. Mammatus clouds, big orange sunsets, rosy-fingered dawns—all that. What I *don't* miss is all the political weather."

"Political weather?"

"The *sturm und drang*. The mass protests we had to put up with, against the whole idea of this one-way program. Not that the protesters could ever decide whether areogerontological colonization was A, the abandonment of a famine-devastated Earth by the super-rich and super-annuated, or B, a callous 'abandoning in place' of the elderly. As if Mars were some bizarre combination of billionaire bolt-hole and extraterrestrial assisted-living facility!"

No matter that all of us senior astronauts had been volunteers, I thought. And not all of us had been rich, either. Yet in the face of global resistance the entire areogeront project began coming off the tracks—despite all the money spent and all the effort expended by the program's multinational government/corporate consortium, whose board I chaired. With the program itself in danger of being abandoned in place, I bought everyone out. I got all the movables, all the intellectual and real Martian property, the whole show, for a fire-sale price of $70 billion—enough to get me the first one-way ticket to the Red Planet. The dog came along almost for free.

"How about you?" I asked Cogzie. In the days since our previous conversation he had become quieter, less playful—even pensive, one might say. "What do you miss *least* about Earth?"

"Something I didn't even know about when I was there. Something I only learned about here, via the Marsweb, while researching my dreams."

"What's that?"

"The phrase, 'Fortunately the only casualty was a dog.' I don't know how many times I've seen that."

"Not very fortunate, I guess, if you're the dog."

"And in my dreams I *am* that dog. Again and again."

"Really?"

Cogzie nodded as we watched the builder bots extrude Martian sand-glass onto the framework of the X Too dome.

"I dreamed I was in a town in the American Midwest—Kearney, I think it was called, in what I was able to search out later. At a street celebration the townspeople started up a merry-go-round with a steam calliope, which exploded. 'The only casualty was a dog.'"

"And there's more than just that one of these disaster dogs?"

"Many, like I said. I dreamed of a hot, late summer afternoon, when I lived in a cottage with a miner, his wife, and nine kids. The cottage exploded. That happened in August 1915, when a U-boat shelled a coke works near Workington, in England, as nearly as I can determine. 'Fortunately, the only casualty was a dog.'"

"Now, Cogzie, don't be morbid!" I said. Phrases from the dream experiment research bubbled up in my head, particularly the idea that dreaming had developed from a simpler threat-rehearsal mechanism in animals to a more general virtual-rehearsal mechanism in modern humans. According to the research, an important aspect of the initial natural selection of the dream mechanism was that threats encountered in a dream had to be perceived as *real* by the dreamer. In order for those dream-threats to be convincing, however, disbelief had to be suspended, higher-order mental processes had to be deactivated.

If waking consciousness in the early hominid brain was very similar to dream consciousness in modern humans, as some researchers contended, where might Cogzie now be along that spectrum? What boundaries might be blurring in Cogzie's mind?

"I dreamed of another hot summer day," Cogzie said, mistaking my thoughtful pause for permission to continue. "June, I think.

A little boy playing with matches, a fire starts, eventually engulfing eighteen houses and a hospital. I run into a blazing building, looking for my master, but I'm killed when the door blows shut. I think that episode happened in a town called Sandon, in Canada. 'Fortunately, the only casualty was a dog.' Then came another dream of another August day, in 1940, as I later learned. A wounded British pilot bails out of his damaged plane over England. His aircraft crashes onto a house, but 'the only casualty was a dog.' See the pattern?"

"Yes, yes! Stop already with that, Cogzie. I get it. None of that is very nice of us humans, granted. Not at all nice. But it's not worth dwelling on. And don't you think you might have your causes and effects *reversed?*"

"What do you mean?"

"You mentioned 'researching' the events—and 'as you later learned' or 'as near as you can determine.' From material found on the Marsweb, right?"

"Yes. . . ."

"Isn't it possible you found a lot of this onscreen first, and only dreamed about it—or thought you dreamed about it—later?"

Cogzie paused for a moment, then shook himself from head to tail, as if he'd just emerged from a swim or wakened from a long nap.

"No. That can't be it. The dreams are too real. Straight through the gate of horn. Maybe my previous avatars had these dreams of *their* previous avatars too. Maybe in dreams they saw their 'fetches'—their ghostly doubles—and, after so many re-runs, we figured out that we were all somehow the same unlucky dog."

"But they weren't like you, Cogz. Your previous avatars, or fetches, or whatever you call them—they didn't have your intellectual capabilities."

"No, but they might still have had these dreams, and instincts."

"Cogzie, leave it. My fellow humans' undervaluing of canine lives and deaths may well be a real pattern, but this stuff of cat-goddess curses and doomed re-runs is all in your head. Obsessing on it only makes it worse. Leave it. I don't want to hear you talking about it again. Is that clear?"

Cogzie nodded, but said nothing. Only gradually did I realize he was giving me the silent treatment. In silence we watched the builder 'bots finish sand-glazing the X Too dome. In silence we made our way home aboard the sun quad.

Stubborn, I continued to put the enhancers in his food. Stubborn, he continued to eat.

I had forbidden him from talking to me about such matters, but I hadn't forbidden his communicating his dream journals to me via other channels. The networked computing devices of our little Marsweb had voice- and word-recognition capabilities. Not one to let the lack of thumbs and fingers stop him, Cogzie began dictating his thoughts into the system, and soon I was receiving electronically dispatched texts of his recollected dreams.

Not a single trace of his old humor could I detect in any of them.

"1940 was a busy year. I dreamed of another incident, one that happened in November. My name was Tubby and I was trapped in an automobile on a suspension bridge in a windstorm. I would not get out of the car, and snapped at the man—a kind stranger—who tried to coax me to safety. It was the original Tacoma Narrows bridge, also known as Galloping Gertie. The stronger the wind blew, the more the bridge turned sail, twisting and rolling in the wind. I learned that, in the end, what the engineers call 'aero-elastic flutter' caused the bridge to tear itself apart, and take roadbed, car, and me—the only casualty—into the Narrows.

"I don't know why I didn't get out of the car. Maybe I figured that, if I got out and started walking across that bridge, that kind stranger would die with me."

"Cogzie," I shot back in reply, the note having irked me greatly, "you are obviously confusing what you read from screens with what you see in dreams. Thinking oneself the persecuted focus of a history-transcending curse or conspiracy would, among humans, be considered a sign of paranoid schizophrenia. . . ."

My scolding didn't stop him from sending another electronic missive, later the same week.

"I was on the St. Johns River, speeding along in a ski-boat with my human family. We came around a corner and hit another ski-boat head on. Everyone was ejected by the collision. I swam for shore as best I could. Watching the boats sink, I realized how badly hurt I was. While the humans took care of each other and ambulances arrived by land to take all the injured people to the hospital, I faded away. The last words I heard were 'Thank God the only casualty was that dog there. It was in one of the boats.'"

I sent Cogz yet another message, this one reminding him that his continuing nine-deaths-for-nine-lives obsession was unhealthy—and that mistaking patterns that exist only in one's head for those that actually exist in the world would be yet another indicator of schizophrenic tendencies.

Soon we stopped leaving the habitat together for work on the surface. One morning, his only greeting to me was a long low growl under his breath and muttered curses under that growl. After that, we began avoiding each other. I stopped putting the enhancers in his food, but it must have already been too late.

As the situation between us worsened, I felt less and less inclined to keep up any elaborate communication with Earth. I don't know why. I spent more time out on the Martian surface, radiation be damned. Maybe Cogzie did too. I can't say.

Another dream journal arrived a few days later. It would be the last.

"I watched the soldiers come into our desert city. The night was dark—no moon, clouds obscuring the sky, most of the electric lights out. The soldiers all had night vision gear. No one met them on the streets, but I followed them as they raided one house and another throughout the night. At one point they saw two townsmen whose scent I knew. The soldiers would have shot them, but I caught the townsmen's attention and they ran off. I continued following the soldiers. When I got too close, one of them shot me with what was supposed to be a non-lethal round. I became the only casualty of their securing of the city."

For some weeks thereafter I received nothing more from Cogzie. Continuing to put out food for him, I noticed that he was eating only sporadically. We had become uncertain shadows, glimpsed only fleetingly as we hid from each other. Our mutual affection passed first into indifference, then into loathing.

It was only when I received the following message, however, that my feelings turned toward fear.

"I know what your dream experiment was really about! I figured it out. I don't want to hurt anybody—no I don't—but you did this to me! Why? I'm not responsible for Karen's and Susie's deaths! I'm not the one who made his only son feel forsaken! I don't drive to destruction everything I love that loves me back! You made me *this* way because you're made *that* way! You're *making* me do what I have to do—to you!"

After reading the note, I looked around for a weapon. The only thing that might pass for such in the whole of Xanadu Base was the knife I had the 'bot make, from three shards of the Earth-born meteorite we had discovered. I snatched the knife up and tucked it in my belt, feeling foolish the whole time.

Yet I soon fashioned a makeshift sheath for it, so I could wear it while out on the surface too. Not that Cogzie could do much harm there, having no opposable thumbs or weapons, and with his teeth caged by the helmet of his environment suit. But I thought it better to err on the side of caution just in case.

Riding down a branch canyon just before sunset, I was hit by a blur moving with such force that it knocked me clean off my sun quad. The solar quadcycle ran along on two wheels for a moment more, before skidding onto its side.

Over the suitcomm I heard wild baying and howling, punctuated by the singsong of "Red Rover, Red Rover, let Cogzie come over!" I struggled to get my feet under me, and the blur hit me again, from behind. I hit the ground and rolled over onto my back. Above me stood Cogzie, a snarl twisting his muzzle and baring his teeth. He charged at my head, the visor of his environment suit smashing into my helmet visor.

Every time I tried to rise to my feet he knocked me down, refusing to let me get up on two feet. His crazy growl and howl and Red Rover singsong never stopped or let up either, growing only more frenzied, if anything. Again and again and again he flung himself at my face, until I wondered how much punishment our helmets could take. As Cogzie bashed his helmet against mine with insane abandon, I dearly wished I were wearing a full-vacuum spacesuit instead of this enviro-unit. It felt more flimsy with each blow.

A thin crack appeared in the outer pane of my visor. I saw that several such cracks already spidered over Cogzie's.

"You damned dog! You'll kill us both!"

He howled and yipped and head-butted his helmet into mine yet again. The crack in my visor became two. If he broke through that visor, only the inner pane would stand between my face and the wraithlike thinness of the Martian atmosphere.

His howling singsong rose in pitch as he lunged again. The external visor pane in my helmet shattered.

Cogzie left me no choice. I fumbled my meteorite blade from its makeshift sheath. As he lunged, I slashed down. Again and again the blade flashed and plunged, a swarm of Earth-born meteors in Martian sunset light.

My dagger's wild stabbing must have struck something vital—in Cogzie, his suit, or both. Cogzie's attacks weakened. His breathing became labored. A series of whimpering cries—so like the dream-noises he sometimes made in sleep—sounded over the suit comm. When at last the cries faded away, Cogzie fell on top of me. As I lifted him off me I tried not to notice the patches of pinkish red spreading around two of the holes in his suit, just behind the left shoulder. I lay him on the ground beside me, as gently as my fatigue-shaken limbs would allow.

I grabbed a shovel from its mount on the back of the sun quad. The water didn't well up in my eyes until I was almost finished digging. By the time I dragged Cogzie's corpse to the grave, I was sobbing like a child and could barely see for my tears.

I buried him in unearthly earth. I stabbed my meteorite knife into the sand time after time in an attempt to clean the blood off, but it would not come clean. I placed the dagger in Cogzie's grave with him.

At the graveside, I could speak no prayers. I thought about how long the odds were against an Earth-born dog being killed on Mars by a knife fashioned from an Earth-born meteorite discovered by that dog on Mars. The only thing more improbable would be the idea that that same hound was also the ninth incarnation of a cat-cursed Egyptian dog first killed on Earth by a meteorite from Mars.

Any sufficiently improbable natural event is indistinguishable from a supernatural event, I reminded myself. I have come to think of those words as Cogzie's Law, and to wonder at the perversity of the cosmos.

Yesterday I sent a flurry of messages to Earth, endowing with a full fifteen percent of my remaining wealth a foundation whose research will focus on the genetic engineering of bipedalism, opposable digits, greater foetalization, brain growth, longevity, and other trans-specific characteristics into subaltern species, especially canine stock. I only wish I could call such work "daugmentation" in Cogzie's presence, to see how he'd react.

After sending those instructions and overriding all my son

Paul's objections, I took my first dose of the dream enhancers I had been feeding Cogzie. Last night I dreamed that, reflected in Cogzie's helmet visor, I saw myself take off my suit helmet. In that reflection I watch his soft brown eyes watch me next remove from my head the visor-shaped faceplate in which my eyes, nose, and lips are mounted. Behind that detached face I see nothing, no shooting stars or flashing neurons or machine readouts, just a reflection of dark emptiness, echoing with detached words from detached lips: "Red Rover, Red Rover, let this old man come over."

In Cogzie's eyes I see no final judgment, and I hope for forgiveness.

I look down at the moons in the quick of my fingernails. I look up through the dome at the fingernail moons in the dead of the Martian night. I remember Cogzie's nails on my arms when he jumped up to greet me. I think about the quick and the dead, and the universe and me—holding on by our fingernails against the Big Nothing, behind the night sky, behind my eyes.

A LITTLE SPOOKY ACTION

Metaphysics is my forte, not physics. Yet it was for a group of physicists that I put on what was probably my weirdest show. The professor, his postdoc, and his grad students were in town for a conference in honor of the one hundredth anniversary of general relativity. That afternoon the group had done a panel on "Einstein, Heisenberg, and the Limits of Observation." I suppose they came to see my paranormal comedy show on the Strip—"Madam Tasha Girl-Friday, Transgender Transgressor of the Boundaries of Space and Time! Of Life and Death!"—to wind down after their presentation, and have a little poking-fun.

That, and the fact that their conference happened to coincide with Halloween.

Now, Halloween in Vegas is always good to me. My show packs them in that night. The numbers on my after-show private sessions go up too. I charge more for all of them. If I do say so myself, I put on a good show, public and private. Taz Giuffrida, paranormal factotum, at your service.

Honey, I know the traditions of my art. I'm a top-notch table-tapper. A medium at large. A séance sayer of sooths. Fortune teller. Clairvoyant. Shakespearean Weird Sister with fringe beard, though I personally prefer the "Hermana Milagrosa"—Miracle Sister—brand I operated under, along the Highway 99 corridor in California's Central Valley, back when I was reading palms. And I don't mean the trees.

I give my audience the real fake, not the fake real. Yet sometimes my predictions—which I'm perfectly aware are bogus—inexplicably *do* come true. And sometimes, in my phony trances, real Others seem to speak through me. Just saying.

So after the show the professor and his research crew paid their money and crowded into my séance parlor. When I asked what particular spirit they were seeking on the Other Side, they replied "Albert Einstein." I could hear them barely controlling their sniggers. Undeterred, I worked myself up into my best fake trance and scanned the astral planes for Uncle Albert.

"You've come for 'Eine Kleine Spukhafte Wirkung,' nicht so?" I heard my voice intone, almost lost in a thick German accent.

"What does that mean?" whispered one of the grad students to his fellows. I said nothing, because I had no idea.

"It means 'a little spooky action,' which sounds about right for tonight," said the professor. And I could hear the smile in his voice crack, just the faintest bit.

"By *spukhaft* I really meant something more like 'mystical' than 'spooky,'" I heard my voice intone. "Too late now. What is it you want?"

"Unified field theory," said the professor. "The theory of everything."

"Ach, don't we all? Okee. Listen closely—especially you grad students. In particular inertial frameworks, the effects of gravity and the effects of acceleration are equivalent, yes? Meaning they cannot be distinguished or disentangled, one from the other, by the observer. Realizing *that* led me to the fundamental tenet of general relativity: Matter tells spacetime how to curve, the curvature of spacetime tells matter how to move. My mistake was thinking of it in terms only of massive objects, but now I realize that fundamental tenet also scales down. Way down."

"How far down?" asked the postdoc, a young woman.

"Rewrite it as 'the position of any unit of matter tells spacetime how to curve, the degree of curvature of any unit of spacetime tells matter how to move.' Even if the mass of that matter is infinitesi-mally small, its effect on the curvature of spacetime still must be accounted for."

"But how does that link up with quantum theory?" asked an-other graduate student.

"Think about it. Just as the equivalency of gravity and accelera-tion scales down to the infinitesimal, so too quantum uncertainty—that the observer cannot disentangle, simultaneously and certainly, the position of a particle from its momentum—likewise scales up. Toward the infinite."

"But that would mean the momentum of *any* unit of matter in spacetime," said the young postdoc who had spoken before, "cannot be fundamentally disentangled from the position of that unit in spacetime. . . ."

"Eh, a smart one! Where was I? Ah, yes. Zeroing in on the possible values of either position or momentum extends the pos-sible values of the other to infinity. On the quantum scale both are not only inseparably entangled with each other; they are also fundamentally indistinguishable from gravity and acceleration on the classical scale."

"Position and *gravity* are indistinguishable?" asked the professor incredulously. "But what about the particular coordinate system—?"

"Oy, forget about the coordinate system! That's what tripped me up for so long. You've got tenure. You can afford to realize that nature works *independent* of the particular way we define coordi-nates in space. The quantum uncertainty of position and momen-tum is deeply complementary to the relativistic equivalency of gravity and acceleration. The shared fundamental indistinguishabil-ity, *the inseparable entanglement*, of their respective objects argues for what I could never accept when I was alive: that uncertainty in quantum theory *is* equivalency in relativity theory, and vice versa. The equivalence of uncertainty and the uncertainty of equivalence are indistinguishably one!"

"And spooky action at a distance?"

"Ja. For both variables and information, what is hidden is mutual, what is mutual is hidden. What is fundamentally indistinguishable is inseparably entangled—and vice versa. And all *that* is much less spooky than *this*—"

I passed out, just as the usual script calls for. Except I really *did* pass out. And, while out, I saw infinite Einsteins wagging their fingers at me, and laughing.

Regaining consciousness, I found myself alone. The pushed-out chairs—one toppled, too—suggested my clients had departed in some haste. Yet not so hastily that they didn't leave a large pile of tips on my séance table.

Scooping up their money, I guessed maybe spooky action up close was spookier than they anticipated. Even—or especially—on Halloween.

THE INFINITE MANQUÉ

I don't expect what I'm writing here to bring back Panto or Fabian. I don't expect it to cure the P group bonobos of the brutal dementia they are enduring. I don't expect it to bring the VLADs, or Carl, or me, to anything like the justice and punishment we deserve. But I must share my piece of the truth, and if it comes to you in shard and fragments, in rough bits and broken pieces, that's because that's how it comes to me.

"Doctor Mary Van Dyne?" asked the bear of a man with a shaved head and thick moustache who approached me at a conference sponsored by the Zoological Society of Milwaukee—one of the main funding sources for bonobo research, at the time. "Carl Wallach. Please allow me to shake your hand! I've long wanted to meet Our Lady of the Bonobos."

I must have blushed at such an honorific, but all I remember with certainty was muttering something to the effect that Claudine Andre, with her Lola ya Bonobo sanctuary, already had an older and stronger claim to that title.

"Nonsense, nonsense!" Wallach said. "Your work has the potential to be something far more than just a threatened species' shelter from our human storm. With the right level of funding, I'm sure you can improve not only their prospects for survival, but ours too!"

He caught my attention with that—especially the "right level of funding" part.

"Where the hell is that damned monkey?" Carl bellowed as soon as he stepped out of the Land Rover and onto the compound. "Did you help him do it? Did you collude or cooperate with him on this?"

"Do what? On what?" I asked. "I have no idea what you're talking about."

"The damn thing on the web that Panto, or somebody, put out there!" he said, opening out a foldable-screen laptop computer—a flaptop—as we walked into Elia Sanctuary's main conference room.

An embedded video began to play on the screen. The words "The Cardenio Project" appeared, and I gulped. Out of the corner of my eye I saw Carl watching me narrowly.

"Yeah, when I saw that it made my mouth go dry as a popcorn fart too," he said.

Like many another girl and young woman, I had those "beauty among the beasts" dreams. Jane Goodall among the chimps at Gombe in Tanzania. Dian Fossey among the mountain gorillas at Karisoke in Rwanda. Birute Galdikas among the orangs at Tanjung Puting in Borneo. Those kinds of dreams.

By the time I finished my undergraduate degree it was far too late to become one of Leakey's Trimates. No shortage of women in the discipline by then, either—primatology had become a majority female field. But I still dreamed.

At both Ryukyu University (*Ryudai*) in Okinawa prefecture and at Luo Scientific Reserve in Congo, I worked under Professor Kano. With his mentoring I completed my doctoral dissertation, on territorial behavior among restricted-range orphaned and rescued bonobos. (Lots of *those* in the Congo at that time. Ongoing bloodshed in the human population meant that refugees, in con-siderable numbers, were disappearing into the forests and taking a great deal of bushmeat. Adult bonobos were often part of those catches, showing up in the remotest of market stalls.)

Not long after earning my doctorate, I founded the Elia Bono-bo Sanctuary and Research Station, outside Basankusu, in the Maringa-Lopori-Wamba region. Our research focused on memory and learning potential in bonobos, and how those factors shaped bonobo society.

Despite Carl's on-station complaints about life in the Congo whenever he visited, we had considerable progress—unbelievable progress—to report, almost from the very beginning. No sooner had the first P group offspring been born (Panto, from the male Panjan-drum and female Pandora) than we began dosing those parents and their offspring. When three other breeding pairs in P group also produced progeny, we followed the same plan with them and were shortly off and running.

In addition to the "MD" and "PhD" on Doctor Wallach's busi-ness card, I read an occupational description I had not previously encountered: "Neuroengineer." He explained that, like me, he too was interested in the memory and learning potentials of higher pri-mates. His work, he said, involved gene expression of the NR2B subunit of the NMDA receptor, and its role in long-term potentia-tion of neuronal signal transmission.

"That's a mouthful, I know," Wallach said over his scotch, in the conference hotel bar. "What it basically means is that my lab has been investigating the enhancement of synaptic plasticity, learning, and memory."

"What's the mechanism?" I asked, staring into my drink, feel-ing both curious and a bit overawed.

"There's solid evidence that the overexpression of NR2B allows mammals to retain, long into adulthood, characteristics of the 'youthful' brain—including the ability to grasp large amounts of information and make swift connections within that information. That, in turn, results in a huge boost to learning, memory, and overall intelligence."

"What's the 'Cardenio Project'?"

Carl paused the vid.

"I looked the 'Project' part up. An English lit professor named Greenblatt and a director named Mee started it years ago. They wrote up a version of this lost play by Shakespeare, had it performed and recorded. Then they set up their 'project' to help writers, directors, and actors from cultures all over the world put on versions of the play."

"Adaptations?"

"No, not just adaptations—retellings from inside their own cultural frameworks. The Cardenio Project posts and publicizes those retellings. Watch this version, though, and you'll see there's something different about the performers, and their culture."

In founding Elia, I had unknowingly stepped past the last rung of my ladder, into wild air. In trying to scrape up the funding to keep my research station open and its work valid, I learned at last how far I had gone beyond the scope of my real strengths—thanks in no small part to Doctor Wallach, and to what we together did to the bonobos of P group.

And, most importantly, what we did to Panto.

In the Congolese bush, we created a trans-species educationanal intellectual hothouse. There we set about forcing the bulbs of mind and consciousness in our bonobos. The myriad ways in which our charges bloomed were impressive and amazing enough that our surveillance camera technician, Fabian Henriquez, began quietly shooting footage of the bonobos in both P and R groups.

When I confronted him about it, the handsome young tech admitted to having done a couple of short documentaries and some machinima in college, but promised he would never release any of his footage of our project without permission or authorization. He also convinced me that, in the meantime, the video work would serve as a useful history, which it did.

I swirled my vodka martini and took a sip.

"And that might have something to do with my bonobos?"

"Oh, we could do this research in chimpanzees, certainly. Chimps and bonobos are genetically equidistant from humans. But the retention of youthful brain characteristics into adulthood is a neoteny—"

"—and bonobos are already more neotenous than chimpanzees. Or at least that's the general consensus."

"Exactly."

I don't know why Doctor Wallach brought it up, but he was without doubt the one who first spoke to Panto about the infinite monkey problem. Perhaps Panto might have discovered it on his own, eventually, since he was a great Shakespeare fan. Perhaps Panto had *already* encountered it—and chosen to ignore it. There was no way he could continue to ignore it, though, once Doctor Wallach rubbed his face in it.

Having established ten bonobos in R group as our controls, it very soon became clear that the drugs—we all preferred to call them "enhancers"—were having a profound effect on P group. Within the first six months of our effort, the technicians and animal behaviorists who had joined us at Elia were able to teach the enhanced adult bonobos of P group to sign with unprecedented fluency. The unenhanced individuals of R group couldn't begin to keep up.

By the end of the first year, we had taught the adults of P troupe the fundamentals of reading. By the end of the second year the adults had begun teaching their offspring to sign. By the end of the third year, the youngsters had learned to read, and the adults had mastered typing on the big touchscreen keyboards of the testing computers. By the end of the fourth year, the youngsters were keyboarding too.

Meanwhile, among the R group controls, nothing close to these jumps in memory, learning, or intelligence occurred.

"What do you suggest we do—about the leaked video? And about P Group?"

"Sequester the bonobos of P Group, ASAP," Carl said. "Maybe somewhere way up country. Hire in some local militia to guard 'em, keep them out of contact with anyone in the outside world. And make this videographer take credit, or blame, for the thing on the web."

"Why that?"

"We sure as hell don't want anyone to believe the *bonobos* did it themselves. Pass it off as a hoax to get rid of the scientific types. Pass it off as science fiction to get rid of the literary types. With a little luck, the next thing you know they'll be saying they knew it was fake all along—and disavowing ever having paid it any mind whatsoever. The conspiracy theorists, of course, we will always have with us."

"You've already thought this through."

Carl shrugged.

"In a world of dreamers, somebody has got to have the nightmares."

*

"You said 'overexpression'?"

"Right."

"Couldn't that pose a danger to your experimental subjects that they might end up—oh, I don't know—overclocked? Over-connected?"

"Not at all! We're talking about a very tightly focused series of tests here. This work won't alter the expression of genes responsible for appropriately pruning synaptic connections. And, just to avoid any possibility of overload damage, the NR2B booster would be given in combination with a nutraceutical that enhances glial cell support in the cytoskeleton."

I had heard something about such research before, but I wasn't all that familiar with it.

"And that's enough to offset possible damage?"

"More than enough! In tests with rats, that support component has punched up microtubule numbers remarkably. A fair number of neurophysicists believe quantum waves in the microtubules are evidence of quantum computation in the brain. An important side benefit of this research is that it will also serve as a long-term test in primates for such computation—potentially even as a test for quantum consciousness."

I was there. I saw it happen. It was a day like many others when Carl was on station, the three of us walking the perimeter fence, Panto as usual emulating our bipedal gait more often than the other bonobos of P group did—and far more often than the bonobos of group R, or his wild relatives, could imagine doing.

"I see from your research into the Early Moderns, Panto, that you're a great admirer of the Bard of Avon. Doctor Van Dyne has independently confirmed that fact. Tell me, have you ever heard the one about the monkeys and Shakespeare?"

"I don't think so," Panto text-voiced tentatively. I gave Carl a disapproving look.

"It's not an off-color joke, I assure you. It's the idea that, if you had a big enough jungle of monkeys, and enough of that jungle of monkeys sat at enough keyboards and tapped away long enough, they would eventually produce all the works of Shakespeare—purely at random. What do you think of that?"

There was an unusually long pause.

"I think it would apply not only to Shakespeare, but to all texts by all writers. And not only to monkeys, either."

Doctor Wallach laughed, and I smiled, but the poison seed had been planted.

As Carl talked and I drank, his proposal sounded better and better. Not least because he was charming, in his hyperfocused way—and because his project would mean an additional ten million dollars annually for Elia, given that it was to be a study on ten individuals, one million per bonobo. That would easily be enough to support not only the bonobos in the experimental group (later designated "P") but also ten individuals in the control group ("R," which Elia Sanctuary would provide virtually free of charge).

Carl's project was scheduled to run for ten years, too, and would involve an additional twelve million in technology and support for neuro-monitoring equipment and smart devices custom-designed for bonobos, on which to test their memory and learning skills. Over the course of the study, then, that would mean new and additional funding of our Sanctuary to the tune of one hundred and twelve million, total. A very pleasant tune indeed.

What can I say? I succumbed to temptation, jumped at the chance, knew sin. Carl wasn't talking about invasive surgical or viral-vectored or transgenic interventions in our beloved bonobos, after all—just some fairly innocuous-sounding tests of memory enhancement drugs. He was also offering me the chance to build the world's premier research facility for the threatened primate I was already working with.

We noted other changes related to memory and learning in the P group bonobos as well. Brain scans of P group individuals showed sizable increases in the numbers of fine-tuned dendritic network connections in their brains. EEGs showed that all of the P bonobos evidenced much more REM sleep and much more prolonged dreaming than did the R group controls. In the R controls (as in most of the higher mammals, including humans), the pineal gland began to fill up with brain sand and they dreamt less as they aged. Among the bonobos of P group, in contrast, brain sand deposition, or calcification, slowed to almost a standstill in that troupe's adults—and barely got started at all in the youngsters treated from infancy with the enhancers.

Only later did I think to ask about the source of our funding, and the goal of the research. Carl was always cagey about that. He spoke only about what he called the VLADs—Very Large Anonymous Donations from Very Large Anonymous Donors. From hints he dropped, I later gathered those donors were personally interested in Intelligence Amplification—as a hedge against AI, oddly enough. I began to imagine a tight conspiracy of Russian petroligarchs with plans for world domination. . . .

Once Carl's project was underway, however, both it and Carl were unobtrusive. The drug tests involved little more than adding to P group's food the various NR2B and glial enhancers—just a couple more supplements mixed in with the rest of that group's daily vitamins.

*

Even at a very late date in Panto's tragic arc, however, Carl felt there might still be some things we could learn from that unhappy creature. As we stood, free, beside Panto in his cage, waiting to load him and it into one of the transport trucks, Carl passed a handheld to Panto through the bars, and began his inquisition.

"You once told Doctor Van Dyne that you were zeroing in on infinity, Panto. That you were becoming the infinite monkey we always intended you to be. Is that how you created language more like Shakespeare than Shakespeare himself?"

Panto in his cage roused himself from the morose lethargy he had dwelt in for days.

"Very good, Doctor Wallach," he text-voiced. "You've finally figured it out."

"What did he figure out?" I asked. I was convinced that Panto, in his delusion, had lost the ability to distinguish between what he had experienced and what he had only researched. I had already told Carl as much.

After the fourth year, those older bonobos in P group who had started receiving the enhancers only as adults at last plateaued. Dendritic connections topped out, REM sleep levels declined somewhat, and deposition of brain sand slowly began to increase. They also just could not (or would not) learn the new trick of using the handheld text-to-synthetic-voice translators we provided—tech that might have allowed them to "speak" to us, after a fashion.

Their brains, we hypothesized, had already been too mature at the start of the trials to fully reap the benefits of the enhancers. Carl and I began to worry that, if our VLADs wanted the benefits of our research only for themselves, such news might result in their reducing our funding.

We were relieved to note that, among the bonobo youngsters, there was no such plateauing. The surprise and wonder of living in the world did not slowly contract for them as it did for their parents. Flashes of genius persisted in the way the youngsters made learning connections—not only swiftly, but also nonobviously. They eagerly took to text-voicing on their handhelds, not only to their human warders but also to all the members of their cohort in P group. Such behavior endlessly amazed their parents, who seemed as stunned by it as dinosaurs watching their offspring become birds.

I watched, mesmerized, until Carl at last tapped the vid off. I shot him a brief scowl.

"That's enough to give you the set-up," he said. "Cardenio loves his childhood sweetheart, Luscinda. Her father Don Bernardo puts the brakes on their marriage hopes, et cetera, et cetera. I've seen the whole thing. Typical romance plot, only with bonobos. Just sentimental and convoluted enough to be hugely popular online. You might want to check it out when you have time."

Having had a chance to take things in, if only for a moment, I shook my head in disbelief.

"But this is impossible. None of the bonobos can upload anything. They don't have access."

"Then either they hacked a way up and out, or they had help. In one of your progress reports you said the security cam tech was working with Panto, is that right?"

"Yes. Fabian Henriquez. He says he made short films when he was in school."

"We'd better put him under the hot lights, then."

We learned too that our research continued to appeal to our VLADs, mainly because they believed they might eventually use the drugs we were testing to enhance their own children's and grandchildren's capabilities. That interest was all that was needed to keep our discreet benefactors happily transferring funds—especially after Carl began sending them his reports (complete with some of Fabian's video work) chronicling the progress being made by our star pupil.

Panto had always been a bit pensive. After his discussion of Shakespeare's monkeys with Carl, though, he became more inward than ever. He took to spending more time away by himself, scanning and twiddling on his handheld. He began to interact less and less with either his human warders or fellow bonobos.

Concerned, I began to more carefully monitor his research on the web. As part of our research on the bonobos, Carl and I had decided that, in regard to the their web search histories, there should be no "Delete" function on any of their devices. Privacy was not even a consideration.

Feeling as if I were playing catch-up, I found the full trove of "Early Moderns" research Doctor Wallach had alluded to. Panto had apparently been searching sites appropriate to a pet thesis of his, that major contemporary transitions had clear Early Modern analogs.

Things didn't go quite so smoothly with the sequestering of group P as we had hoped. It would take at least three days to get the up-country relocation compound ready, so in the meantime all the members of P troupe would have to be captured, caged, and kept out of sight—against the possibility that the media-types might begin to arrive onsite.

By the time we got to the section of the sanctuary where six warders had cornered all the members of P troupe, the other nine bonobo test subjects had already formed a guard around Panto. Snarling, screeching, and text-voicing—some carrying broken branches and boards in their free hands—the P group bonobos had obviously anticipated what we had in store for them. About forty yards distant from the angry Pan troupe, the warders stood by, awaiting our orders.

Even among bonobo youngsters enhanced to unprecedented brilliance, Panto stood out—way out. From a very young age he read voluminously, first from the books and ebooks we provided to him, then from the worldwide web on his handheld as well. In short order he proved himself capable of understanding many subtleties of mathematics, geometry, statistics, probability, eventually even calculus—all before he reached age nine.

He was alarmingly precocious. Of the whole crew engaged in our bonobo odyssey, he seemed destined to become their Homer, their Newton, their Shakespeare, their Einstein—although the text-voice he chose was based on Stephen Hawking's.

For most of the many years of our project, Carl himself showed up only for a week or so every six months, to check on P group's progress. He could be relied on to arrive on-station complaining of the "flying human zootube" of transcontinental airtravel. He didn't think much of our station's backcountry location, especially after jouncing along barely passable roads to Basankusu and Elia. Nor was the hot damp climate of Congo to his liking: He found claustrophobic the jungle with its "endless green tangle of too many too-tall trees and vines with too many leaves and insects." Everything about the place was "barbarous," so far as he was concerned—not least of all the region's recent post-Ebola history.

(Only later did his behavior make me wonder if our facility might have been chosen precisely *because* it was remote and estranged from the usual scientific and bureaucratic oversight. I didn't think much about that, early on. I trusted Carl, not least because, for a brief while each six months, he and I were lovers. That intimacy was convenient enough, and more than often enough, given how busy I was running Elia.)

For our most brilliant young bonobo, the communicational shift from print to digital mirrored the Early Modern shift from manuscript to print. The spatial shift brought on by the Early Modern discovery of the New World, and the new worlds of the solar system discovered by telescope, and the debate on the plurality of worlds more generally—all, according to Panto, mirrored the contemporary discovery of Earthlike extrasolar worlds or exoplanets, and the debate on the potentially infinite worlds of the multiverse.

Back at my office, I called Carl Wallach (time difference be damned), informed him what was happening with Panto, explained why I thought Carl had helped precipitate it, and insisted we shut down the program immediately.

"Calm down, Mary, calm down. Have any of the other bonobos in P group shown symptoms like this?"

"No, but Panto is one out of ten. That's a ten percent casualty rate."

"What casualty? You've got one bonobo that thinks he's becoming an 'infinite monkey'—fascinating phrase, that. At worst he may be suffering some episode of bonobo schizophrenia, but I'm sure it's temporary. We have only six months left in the program. We can't throw it all away now! You said he's been overdosing on the enhancers, right?"

"Yes. Stealing them from the others."

"Well then, institute better control protocols for dispensing the remaining rounds of test meds. If you do, I'm sure our bard manqué's behavior will settle back within acceptable parameters. Let's give it a little time. I don't doubt we can bring things back into line."

*

Judging from the amount of time he spent on sites dealing with the topic, though, what seemed to intrigue Panto most at that stage of his research was the intellectual shift from the old science of natural philosophy to the new science of experimental observation—and how that might be mirroring the scientific method's own ongoing evolution (under the impact of new discoveries) into something beyond itself.

It made a certain sense that Panto, as an enhanced creature whose entire existence was part of an experiment, should be interested in such patterns of discovery and evolution. It made sense too that, given his interest in the Early Modern period, Panto would repeatedly encounter the works of Shakespeare and Cervantes.

Even as his intellectual searching became more successful, Panto's outward behavior continued to worsen. Although he had long been rather aloof—particularly around unfamiliar humans—he had been sociable enough with his fellow bonobos in P group. Once he began to steal supplements from them, however, his behavior introduced a note of tension and aggression into the group that had never existed there before. The sexual and other tension relievers bonobos are so fond of no longer worked with Panto. He was too obsessed with enhancing himself—in the name of carrying out research—to care how much his actions were affecting his fellow bonobos, or our experimental observations, for that matter.

It was perhaps inevitable that, like ant to antlion or particle to singularity, Panto at last spiraled down to the statement from Borges' essay on the Total Library, where that author reframed the problem of Shakespeare and infinite monkeys by writing that "Strictly speaking, one immortal monkey would suffice."

Panto's search history showed that, from there, it was a short step to Borges' quirky story "Pierre Menard, Author of the *Quixote*." Among the notes Panto pasted from the web into his files was this sentence from that story: "To be, in some way, Cervantes and reach the *Quixote* seemed less arduous to him—and, consequently, less interesting—than to go on being Pierre Menard and reach the *Quixote* through the experiences of Pierre Menard."

"And if things *don't* come back into line?"

"Then dart him and restart him."

"What?"

"Knock Panto out, cut off his access to the enhancer combo—completely—and hit him with antipsychotics, if need be. That should do the trick."

"That sounds so cruel."

"What's cruel? Mary, you knew this project would have to end someday. All of the subjects will have to be weaned off the enhancers, sooner or later. At worst Panto will have to be weaned off sooner rather than later."

Panto was a brainchild with a mind finer than that of any number of adults, but also one whose emotional development lagged far behind the development of his intellect. He was also painfully aware, too, that he was not human.

Worried by his new inwardness, I increasingly tried to just "run into" Panto on my walks about the grounds, or when he picked up his meals during the course of the day. I soon realized, though, that he was purposely avoiding me—and all human contact. I had no choice but to follow him, remotely, through the web searches he could not hide from me.

I saw soon enough that Panto's searches were becoming more focused upon (one might as well say "obsessed with") the mystery that linked Cervantes as the greatest writer in Spanish with Shakespeare as the greatest writer in English: namely, the history of the lost play called *Cardenio*.

"I've seen your notes for the play you're working on," I told Panto, when I at last cornered him in an angle of the fencing at the most remote part of the sanctuary. "I think I know why you're doing this. It was wrong of Doctor Wallach to say what he said to you, I grant you that. But this obsession with rewriting a four hundred year old lost play—that's crazy."

"Why is it crazy?" he text-voiced, his eyes darting nervously about us, though (since we were right at the forest's edge and very much away from everyone else) there was no one about, human or bonobo. "Lots of human beings have tried to mine Shakespeare's work out of Theobald's *Double Falsehood*. Bernard Richards, Stephen Greenblatt, Charles Mee, Gregory Doran, Gary Taylor—no one thought *they* were insane for trying to restage it, or remix it, or resurrect it."

"But what's the point? Why try to recreate yet another bad copy of an original that's been lost for centuries?"

"*Cardenio* was not lost—it was deliberately 'disappeared.' And I'm not just making a copy. I'm remaking the original! I'm going to go on being whatever Panto is, and reach the *Cardenio* through the experiences of Panto."

"That's impossible." What I did not say, but which we both knew, was this: *You cannot make Cardenio, a play by a human being, because you are not a human being.*

"Not true! Wallach talked about an infinite jungle of monkeys, Borges wrote about one immortal monkey, but they are both wrong! I may be only one mortal monkey to you, but I'm zeroing in on infinity! I'm becoming the infinite monkey you always intended me to be! The one who can write all Shakespeare's plays—even the lost ones!"

When I heard that, I knew our enhancement experiments had gone too far. Panto was losing the mind we had helped create in him.

"Oh, Panto. I'm so sorry."

"I'm not!" he said, pushing brusquely past me in barely restrained fury, before moving away with swift, stiff strides.

We set out to find Fabian. When we did, we confronted him with the first five minutes of the posted video. A frank and useful discussion ensued. We made clear the problems the posting of this video posed for our program funding, even for the continued existence of the Elia sanctuary.

Torn between pride in how well the video project had turned out and apprehension over what it might mean to his continued employment, Fabian readily copped to having shot part of the vid, edited much of it, and uploaded all of it. He balked, however, at the prospect of taking credit for writing and directing it.

"I had little input on direction and almost none at all on the script. That was Panto's show."

"Ah, but showbiz is the quintessential art of collaboration and compromise, is it not?" Doctor Wallach asked. Fabian agreed it was. "Well then, Mister Henriquez, it might be wise for you to emphasize your part in that process and de-emphasize the role of the bonobo participants."

Scanning Panto's detailed notes, I learned that Cervantes had embedded his "Cardenio" novella in Part One of his *Don Quixote*. Thomas Shelton's English translation of that first part of Cervantes' *Quixote* appeared in 1612. The office of the Treasurer of the King's Chamber, in the spring of 1613, recorded two payments to Shakespeare's theatre company, The King's Men, for performances of a play listed as *Cardenno* or *Cardenna*. Also in 1613, Shakespeare's company received a sizable sum for a command performance of this play before the ambassador of the Duke of Savoy.

"You see the craziest things when you don't have a gun," Carl said, snatching a tranquilizer rifle from one of the warders. "I'll get Panto. Choose your targets, the rest of you, and dart 'em all."

"There's got to be another way, Carl!"

"Too late for that, Mary." He raised the rifle to his shoulder, and the warders followed suit. The bonobos charged and the warders fired. Five bonobos were hit, but not Panto. The warders reloaded frantically. Three more bonobos were hit—but still not Panto.

The four remaining bonobos hit the line of warders. One of the warders near me, before he could get off his shot, had his rifle bashed out of his hands by a branch-wielding Panjandrum. The rifle clattered to earth near me. I grabbed it up and fired the dart still in the chamber. It hit Panto in the shoulder, just above the collar bone.

I think it was at about this point in his researches that I noted Panto's inwardness, in pursuit of solitude and Shakespeare, wasn't the only change in his behavior. Somehow he had figured out which supplements in his diet were the enhancers. He consumed those preferentially, even as he began to eat less and to lose weight overall. I began to realize his obsession was becoming unhealthy, but still he managed to avoid me, no matter how often I threw myself in his way.

I read in a haze the autopsy reports Carl sent me. Glial cell death. Microtubule collapse. Severe oxidative stress throughout the cytoskeleton. Brain regions peppered with infarcts and plaques.

*

Panto's searching through the web became more fevered. He recorded his discovery that the Stationers Register for 1653 contained a note on a play called "The History of Cardenio, by Mr. Fletcher & Shakespeare." Panto's notes recorded that Humphrey Moseley, the top English publisher of plays and poetry at that time, had registered this copyright for a play of that title, which Moseley apparently intended to publish but which in fact never saw print.

Panto noted that "The History of Cardenio" (the title-phrase Moseley used) appeared word for word in Shelton's 1612 translation of Part One of *Don Quixote*—and nowhere else in English. "Most of the scholars agree the play registered by Moseley under the title *History of Cardenio* in 1653 is the same play referred to (in misspelled form) in the records of the office of the Treasurer of the King's Chamber for 1613," Panto wrote, "and that Shakespeare and Fletcher's use of Cervantes' novella from the *Quixote*—translated by Shelton in 1612 under the title 'The History of Cardenio'— serves as the basis for the lost play *Cardenio*."

In the end all the P group bonobos went down. All of us on the human side were winded, and some of us were hurt, but we had kept the brilliant bonobos of Basankusu in their place. Breathing hard and bleeding, none of us took joy in our small victory. We dragged the unconscious bonobos into waiting cages.

Exhausted, sore, and demoralized by what had happened, I headed back to my living quarters. Perhaps it was to purge from my mind the memories of the day that I decided to "check out" on my own time Simeon Pantojandrum's *History of Cardenio*, as Carl had suggested I do.

*

Panto's research became all-consuming. His notes from that time read more and more like those of a graduate student with the pattern obsessions of a paranoid schizophrenic. His obsession even led him to detail the rather obscure critical debate about which other plays might supposedly be based in whole or in part on the lost *Cardenio*—particularly Thomas Middleton's *Second Maiden's Tragedy* ("attributed to Shax and Fletch by Charles Hamilton" as Panto noted but rejected) and Lewis Theobald's *The Double Falsehood* (1727).

I nodded, backing up Carl's gambit.

"Collaborate and compromise a little with us, Fabian, and you might just keep your job to its close—and get a good recommendation for the next one."

Carl smiled. Fabian's eyes flicked back and forth between us. Our double-teaming was having its intended effect.

"Who knows? This might just be your big break, Mister Henriquez. I'm sure you'd rather be making movies than maintaining security cameras."

Fabian's noble resolve to give Panto the credit due him began to erode. After we informed him that Panto and the rest of P troupe were going to have to disappear for a while, Fabian at last agreed to present himself as the brains behind the bonobo *Cardenio*, if it came to that.

Carl started the vid again. Drumming and screeching sounded and died away. A scene appeared: a clearing in jungle. The image cut to a screen on a handheld device, and I saw on that screen the text "My gracious Father, this unwonted strain visits my heart with sadness." An instant later I heard spoken, by a synthetic voice, those same words.

The shot widened from the words to the hand holding the device. It took me a moment to realize that the hand was not human.

The shot soon become an image of the face of Pangloss, one of the P group bonobos. Seeing and hearing all this, I remembered other words: *I'm going to go on being whatever Panto is, and reach the Cardenio through the experiences of Panto.*

Good God. Panto had somehow recreated Shakespeare and Fletcher's *Cardenio*, but based it in the experiences of the enhanced P group bonobos!

"Unfortunately for future historians," Panto noted, "the copy of the script that Theobald claimed to possess—traceable to the prompter in Shakespeare's company—was, after Theobald's death, deposited in London's Covent Garden Playhouse, which burned to the ground in 1808. For centuries, most of the scholars and professors suggested the prompter's script was a fiction concocted by Theobald to sell tickets. However, the current consensus among the scholars—citing sophisticated computer studies of Shakespeare's distinctive patterns of word choice and usage and their application to *Double Falsehood*—holds that Theobald might not have been lying after all."

I admit that, in following the progress of Panto's notes, even I developed a certain fascination with the history of *The History of Cardenio*. Perhaps it was for that reason I did not think Panto's great obsession with this lost play had become proof of actual *madness* until I realized he was writing a version of his own.

"Carl, how many people do you think have seen this thing?"

"At least high tens, probably low hundreds of thousands, by now. Mostly specialists. I caught it early only because one of my apps looks for apes—it searches hourly through all media references to 'bonobos.' Once the big news digesters get hold of this thing and the controversy builds, though, I have no doubt it's going to go seriously viral."

"What controversy?"

"Over whether it's real, or an elaborate hoax. Here, let me read you some of these comment threads. 'Are the performers really bonobos, or just short slim actors in convincing monkey suits?' Or this, from the critter-lit theorists and the cyborg manifesters, all twisted up trying to figure out whether this 'bonobo *Cardenio*' is a 'sly retelling of the *Cardenio*'s controversial treatment of race and sexuality through the lenses of machinismo and speciesism' or 'robotically stilted pseudo-Shakespeare in chimpface.'

"Or this: 'Marlowe, Bacon, DeVere, scores of others have been put forward as serious candidates for the author of Shakespeare's plays. Now the latest contender from this wilderness of Shakespeares is—a monkey?' Or this: 'Everyone knows Shakespeare's monkey hordes wrote all of his works—even the ones he didn't write!'"

"Oh my," I said. "This is all more worrisome than I could have imagined."

"Look," Carl said, still trying to gentle me down, "my next visit to Basankusu and Elia is scheduled for six weeks from now. I'll bring my trip forward, if you think you need me on site to help you manage matters. Just let me know. Okay?"

"Okay."

I followed his suggestions. I don't know if it was *because* of the new control protocols, but once they were in place, things did get calmer—much calmer. Panto began to behave better, both toward his human warders and toward his fellow bonobos in P group. True, he continued disappearing into private spaces around the sanctuary just as often—but not alone, now. He had company, often female.

Panto even sweet-talked our project's unofficial videographer, Fabian Henriquez, into teaching him how best to use some of the cameras we had on site—and into allowing Panto himself to use them.

I was relieved when Panto's notes began to dwell less obsessively on Shakespeare or his lost play. That Panto also seemed to have figured out a privacy hack that enabled him to cloak at least part of his work-history each day undeniably disturbed me, but that blind spot in our coverage was on a flaptop machine he didn't use that often, and not on the handheld he always had with him. As near as I could tell, the missing history involved shooting and editing video, not doing research on the web.

I was more than a little surprised when Carl Wallach showed up at the beginning of week five, given that I hadn't called him in early. By then he'd come across something out there in the great world and its webworks that had made it necessary for me to gentle *him* down.

Even played by bonobos—with almost nothing in the way of costumes, settings, or props, other than what Fabian had modified and edited in from existing gameware—the play Panto had written was still the convoluted, sentimental, and moving romance Carl said it was.

The whole beautiful and sordid story—of Fernando's lustful abuse and abandonment of Dorotea, his subsequent obsession with his friend Cardenio's betrothed Luscinda, her father Don Bernardo's agreeing to marry Luscinda off to Fernando, Cardenio fleeing to the mountains in madness out of his belief he had failed to prevent that marriage, Luscinda's flight and refuge in a convent, Dorotea's cross-dressing as mountain shepherd boy Florio in secret pursuit of Fernando, his/her fortuitous discovery of the mad Cardenio instead, Fernando's journey to the convent intent on abducting Luscinda, the tragedy-preventing intervention of Fernando's older and nobler brother Pedro who, gathering all the parties together in a mountain inn, brings the wronged Dorotea face to face with an eventually contrite Fernando who realizes he still loves her, and reunites in love and joy Cardenio and Luscinda at the whole thing was there on the web, for anyone to see.

Watching it, I found myself weeping, not perhaps so much for the play, as for the playwright, and myself, and what we ourselves and the world always do to innocents—and what we would continue to do to them, when the world began to crash its way toward our sanctuary.

"Worrisome? You don't know the half of it. To make things worse, a bunch of the scholars examining the language of the new play with their computer programs have already started to weigh in. Most of them have concluded its style and patterns of word choice are 'more like Shakespeare than Shakespeare himself.'"

I shook my head in disbelief.

"Has anyone linked the video of this play to Elia and our research here?"

"Not yet—or at least not that I've seen. All anyone out there knows for sure is that the playwright and director calls himself Simeon Pantojandrum, which sounds as fake as it is real. Still, it's only a matter of time until somebody goes after that vid post with a forensic videography program. When that happens Elia Sanctuary will have an international spotlight on it like a hammer."

When we arrived at the relocation compound, we found Panto gnashing his teeth and foaming at the mouth in wrath—and covered in blood from hurling himself against the bars of his cage. I had no idea what triggered this crazed outbreak, but Panto was clearly such a danger to himself and everyone else we had no choice but to shoot him up with sedatives and antipsychotics. Once he calmed somewhat, we unloaded his cage and carried him into the satellite compound.

As Carl had predicted, the bonobo *Cardenio* went viral, with millions and then tens of millions of views. The forensic videographers figured out where the video had been shot. The media calls for information and interviews rained in. It would be only a matter of time before the remoteness and solitude of our sanctuary would be breached by the long battering ram of such publicity.

When the time came Fabian played his role, claiming that he had created the bonobo *Cardenio* himself. He went so far as to supply media outlets with his videos of control group R, as proof of bonobo limitations and the impossibility of their having ever been capable of producing anything like that video post on their own.

To my surprise, Carl returned several times to the distant satellite compound. His reports chronicled tests of blood and urine, scans of brain and bone. What Panto had only sensed was going on with him was now made plain on display screens.

Duration and frequency of REM sleep and dreaming was declining steeply in all P group bonobos, once they were taken off the enhancers. Brain sand began to run far faster into the cone-shaped hourglasses of their pineal glands. Dendritic connections began to wither and thin far beyond the range of ordinary synaptic pruning. To all appearances, their brains had begun to undergo greatly accelerated aging—senescence that not even new doses of enhancers could counteract. What might be happening in their glial cells and cytoskeletons, particularly in regard to the microtubules, would have to wait until one of the P group bonobos died and a microscopically detailed autopsy could be performed.

*

Despite convincingly false claims of hoax creation, however, a few reporters seemed intent on conducting on-site investigations in Basankusu and Elia. Carl and I decided it would be best to transport all of P group to our satellite compound, far in the northeast corner of the Maringa-Lopori-Wamba Landscape, the bonobo homeland. By the time we began loading them into the trucks for the journey, we had already begun weaning all the bonobos in P troop off the enhancement drug combos. Panto we had cut off outright.

Later, desperate to learn what might have precipitated such an outbreak of mad fury from the caged Panto, I scanned the search history of the handheld Carl had left with him. Panto had in his rage flung the device from him and through the bars of his cage, but it had not escaped the truck in which he was being hauled away.

I found the last thing Panto had looked at. It was a previously downloaded interview with Panto's erstwhile friend, the man who now claimed sole credit for creating the bonobo *Cardenio*. The media report featured video of the unenhanced bonobos of R group and was as complete a record of Fabian's treachery, of *human* treachery, as Panto would ever need to see.

I returned the handheld to Carl without comment.

Carl persisted in his questioning, no matter how ill-timed or inappropriate. "Doctor Van Dyne thinks that you were able to do what you did because you had, in effect, done so much research into Shakespeare as author of the *Cardenio* that you came to believe you had *become* Shakespeare as author of the *Cardenio*."

"That's not how it happened at all," Panto text-voiced. "I told her long ago that I had decided to reach the *Cardenio* through the experiences of Panto."

"And how did you do that? Does it have something to do with zeroing in on infinity?"

"It has everything to do with that. Everything to do with becoming the infinite monkey. Or one monkey computing through infinite universes, if you prefer."

"Quantum computation?"

Panto nodded weakly as he tapped out his message.

"Innumerable Pantos, cooperating across the plenum of the multiverse. Each one real in his own universe and virtual in all the others. Each Panto working with all the others to create a *History of Cardenio* better even than any *History of Cardenio* still extant in all those universes where the play of that title was never lost."

Panto, in what may have been a last desperate act born of his fading brilliance, managed to escape the satellite compound despite its dense security. Carl was alarmed enough by that escape to demand I drag myself away from Elia to search for Panto personally. He needn't have pressed. I would have gone without urging. I owed Panto that much.

"All this stuff about 'innumerable Pantos' sounds like the worst kind of dissociative and schizoid thinking," I said, shaking my head and feeling both pity and disgust at once.

"And Simeon is the sum of all those simians?" Carl continued, ignoring my comment. "The one who binds them all together?"

Panto's eyes rolled back into his head and began to dream-twitch furiously.

"Carl, stop doing this to him! Stop it!"

Gradually Panto's eyes stopped twitching. A moment later he passed abruptly into sleep, still clutching the handheld. Carl shrugged. We winched Panto in his cage onto the bed of the truck.

*

I walked away from him in his last cage and did not see Panto's living face again. Before I returned to Elia, however, I did see to it that he was released into the fenced satellite compound with the rest of the P group bonobos.

Back in Basankusu, we had to maintain the façade of Fabian's creation of the bonobo *Cardenio* for a few more weeks. Once we'd shown the hardest of the die-hard reporters and bloggers the actual intellectual level of the Elia bonobos, they had to agree that what had been portrayed on the vidpost was a best a brilliant piece of filmmaking, at worst a cruel hoax. In a surprisingly short time, all was quiet again on that front.

Near the end of it all for him, Panto signed to the guards that he wanted to see me—alone. I could see that the guards informed me of this only reluctantly, but I was in fact eager to see him.

Standing beside his cage, I saw that his fury had been replaced by a profound moroseness, and melancholy, and resignation. He signed for me to give him my handheld, which I did, though not without some unspoken misgivings. He tapped away at the device for quite a while, producing a longish text that was neither voiced nor sent, but which he instead turned and held out for me to read, like an old-school letter for our eyes only.

We found the escaped Panto—not in the bush but in a market stall, in a village almost too small, squalid, and impoverished to merit a name. What we recovered of Panto was his head.

The stallholder, fearing repercussions, at first tried to hide the head. After we gained her confidence, however, she informed us that fresh-killed bonobo was highly prized bushmeat, and the body that went with this head had been purchased by a customer less than a quarter hour earlier.

Carl paid for Panto's head. He bagged it in his knapsack and, back at the truck, transferred it to a cooler bag.

"Seems you have your trophy, Doctor Wallach."

"Yes, it would seem so."

Dear Mary:

Although it was you who shot me and left me to this captivity, you are still the only one I trust. I must tell you that my mind is going, but not in the way you think. Something is happening to me. Every day I grow duller and more forgetful. Or not forgetful, so much as careless of where I left my memories. They're still there—I just can't find them. I feel my mind growing old, old. Growing slower, and very quickly at that. A sort of mental progeria, when I can remember to think of that word. Madness, or dementia? That's my choice of nightmares, these days.

In a way, it's what I wanted. I took so much and so many of the drugs you gave me because I thought the drugs would make me grow up faster. I thought they would give me instant maturity, that they would let me catch up to myself. I thought I could feel both the future in my bones like the young ones do, and the bones in my future like the old ones do—at the same time.

I wanted wisdom, but what I got wasn't even knowledge, just data processing and misplaced dreams. What I've got is not instant maturity, but instant aging. I have risen far and fast, and I will fall farther and faster. The biggest stars, gone supernova, leave the blackest holes in the sky. So be it.

Not all the King's Poets and all the King's Men can put Panto's mind together again. Life is done with me before I am done with life. You won't have to lead apes in hell, Mary, because you have already led us here. Remember me, for soon I will no longer remember myself.

With love,

Panto,

AKA Simeon Pantojandrum,

Author of the Cardenio

He returned my handheld, then held my hand for a time. At last he let it go, and turned away.

Soon after he finished his autopsy reports on Panto, Carl departed for the great world and what passes for civilization there. The project was over, and I haven't seen him since. Last rumor I heard, he's still working with great apes, trying to make their responses more "tractable" via some kind of hard-jack WiFi PsySpy behavior modification. I don't see it, but I never cease to be surprised by what Doctor Wallach manages to pull out of that wet-sparking bag of tricks inside his skull.

What goaded me to write all this was the only message I've received from him since we parted company nearly a year and a half ago. I'm looking at it on screen now.

"Thought you'd want to know this. Looks like our friend tried to make mouth music with a MAC-10." Below Carl's text was a link to Fabian Henriquez's obituary.

Like I said, I don't expect what I've written to bring back Panto or Fabian. I don't expect it to cure the P group bonobos of the brutal dementia they are enduring. I don't expect it to bring the VLADs, or Carl, or me, to anything like the justice and punishment we deserve. Yet I will share this shattered piece of the truth here, for I must believe our world is not yet so dark a nightmare that it offers no chance to dream.

WHATEVER BECAME OF WHAT MIGHT HAVE BEEN?

Anderson McKinnon pulled his runabout of a car up before his home, hoping against hope to see his wife Nalika and daughter Kara waiting for him. As usual of late, they were nowhere to be seen. He forgave them for that, but such magnanimity did not relieve the tight ache in his chest.

Who could blame them, after all? How many times had Kara come home from her school day, only to have her Dad confine her to her room, for no real reason? How many times had Nalika come home to find him sitting on the couch, bombed on bourbon and snorted oxy painkillers—or worse, when he was spiking heroin and addicted to the rig? Having lost yet another day to playing run-jump-shoot videogames, or reading their space opera tie-ins?

Andy took several deep breaths. There seemed to be too little oxygen in the air, somehow. What if he were really sick, sick unto death, right now? Would his estranged wife still love or even respect him enough to elegize him at his funeral? And how, in the event, might she summarize his time on Earth?

Thinking back over all the wrong turns he had made in the maze of his life, Andy felt light-headed. He recalled, once he started driving again after his accident with the skid-steer Bobcat, how Nalika had responded when he was backing out of a parking space and they felt the sudden jolt of impact: Not with "What happened?" or "What did we hit?" but shrieking, *Andy! What did you do?"* as if his existence must be the root cause of any screw-up in the cosmos, from fender-bender to heat death universe-ender. He had really started pounding the pain killers, after that.

He remembered too his daughter Kara shrieking, the last time he confined her to her room so he might get wasted and blow away aliens in peace.

"Daddy! Why are you doing this? I didn't do anything wrong!"

She pounded and banged on the bedroom door, and cried behind it. Eventually he stopped hearing her, his thoughts preoccupied with shooting and booting, running and gunning.

"Look, Andy," Nalika said that evening, shaking her retro afro at him in a fury over how he had treated their only child. "If you don't do something with yourself, it's over. Kara and I are out of here."

"What would you have me do with myself, Nali?"

"You play these damn videogames all day long and read all these books with big-gun space troopers on the covers—why don't you write something? Or design a game, maybe, since you like drawing so much? With some loans we could afford for you to go back to school, and train to do that—"

"I don't need to go back to school, Nal, and we don't need to go into more debt. Besides, I'm already working on something."

"Yeah? Like what? Has something finally come of all that stoner crap you're always talking with Ish? Show it to me. And I don't mean those 'preliminary character sketches' you doodle on bar napkins, either. Well? Where is it?"

He thought about the scenarios he and his Uncle Ishmael had been kicking around for a first-person shooter they were calling *Extinction Burst*. He also thought that Nalika might not be in the mood to hear those kinds of specifics.

"Safely locked in the vault," Andy said, tapping his forehead with a finger. "I'm just waiting for that final spark to light a fire under me and blow that vault door wide open, so I can bring it out."

Groaning in frustration and disgust, Nalika tugged at her mushroom cloud of hair.

"You really don't get it anymore, do you? You've spent so much time whacked on booze and prescription drugs you've completely lost touch—with me, with our daughter, with everything else that's real in your life! You've been playing those videogames of yours so long, I swear, when you die other people's avatars will pass before your eyes!"

It had been their last argument. Nalika made good on her threat. She gathered up their daughter and their things and left. They had not come back for going on two months now.

It got through to him. The horse had kicked more than a few of the teeth out of his head, true, but it had only kicked him down, not out. Since Nalika and Kara left he'd kicked the horse, gotten over the need for the bigger bang for his buck—for the tingle in his upper lip, the saliva tickle at the back of the throat, the euphoria like a sweet dream of divine love. But the ritual—the jet of the needle breaking the too-unsound barrier of the skin, tattooing a single silver exclamation point of contrail into the blue integument of the sky, his own blood shooting red back into the rig—*that* had proven harder to kick than the drug. He hoped he'd mostly gotten beyond that hype too, at last.

Yet, despite all that had happened, Andy knew he would still walk around to the trunk of his car now and take out the brown grocery bag there, the one with the scotch from the Kwikee Mart and the oxycontin from his dealer, crazy old Uncle Ishmael. Not only because (as he had told Ish) to play at his best he needed "a shot of bourbon and a shot of horse—though scotch and oxycontin would do in a pinch," but also because he still needed ritual, even if it was just the substitute ritual of crushing pills, cutting lines, snorting powder.

Nice, nice, very nice, Ambrosia sang on the car's sound system. *So many people in the same device.*

Andy opened the door and stood up. He had only shuffled a step or two when he broke into a cold sweat. The ache in his chest turned into a squeezing at its center. It was impossible to breathe.

Pain shot into his shoulders, neck, and arms. Doomed and panicky thoughts flooded his mind. He felt nauseous, dizzy, on the brink of passing out. Cold clammy sweat poured from him, even as something winged and hot flailed against the backside of his breastbone. Desperate to stop that captive phoenix from breaking free of its bone cage, he clutched his chest and fell forward onto his knees.

Or the Chinese dentist, or the British Queen, Ambrosia sang. *They all fit together in the same machine.*

His mind scanning at flash-cut speed through a lifetime of memories for anything to help him cope, Anderson McKinnon fell face first onto the pavement.

"Don't the Takahashis have just the *best* view of Earth from their villa?" Nalika Ofunne said to her husband, Anderson McKinnon.

The night side of the planet was indeed spectacular. Strung between the brighter nodes of cities, gossamer webworks of highway lights ensnared entire continents. Along coastlines, the lineaments of night-lit sea walls and dykes stood out against the darkness of rising oceans. On the dayside of the terminator, strong signs of spring were discernible in the northern hemisphere.

Anderson, however, was more interested in the view's engineering. They were looking through actual portals, and he wondered how those windows were being counter-spun to appear stationary, despite the orbital villa's rotation on its axis. It lived up to the extravagance everyone down below associated with the exorbs, the "exorbitantly expensive orbital exurbs of Earth City," as a planet-bound wag had called it—the name that, in its abbreviated form, had stuck most powerfully and perversely among the residents themselves. At least the protests against "plutocrats in orbit" and their "celestial estates" had remained mostly a war of words, Andy remembered, and never gotten so far as shutting down or blowing up launch facilities.

"Oh, I think everyone up here has pretty much just different versions of the same view," Andy said, trying to be truthful without offending the party's hosts, both of whom were standing nearby, dressed in their favorite Victorian evening wear. "It's just that the view is usually through screens linked to cameras. Ben and Noriko seem to have the biggest real windows around."

"I wish we had something like them at Dreamplay House."

Ben Takahashi had turned toward them, and Anderson continued.

"Weren't you worried about micrometeoroids, or explosive decompression, Ben?"

"That spooked our designer too," Ben Takahashi said with a laugh. "She worried it might be unsafe, no matter how strong the glass. We told her 'Safety be damned—we want our view!'"

"It's not like we wanted them facing the Moon," Noriko said, rolling her eyes.

They all laughed. Rarely were anybody's viewcams up here focused on that low-hanging first fruit of human space travel. Sometimes Andy wondered why, but at the moment he was distracted by his sheepishness next to the formally attired Takahashis, probably because he was dressed in twentieth century bondage-slave gear—vintage Speedo, retro tennis shoes, studded dog collar—to pair with Nalika's Billie Holiday/Bettie Page torch-singer dominatrix catsuit. He consoled himself with the fact that he still had the physique to carry his costume off, even without the floral-patterned poolside shirt draped, unbuttoned, over his torso.

"Since *Asterriders* is your baby," Ben said, "I suppose I shouldn't be surprised you'd focus on such sky-rock things, Andy. Great game, by the way. Even better than *Bots vs. Nauts*. I especially like that I can play either side—Revenger attacking, or defenders defending—and they're both equally well realized."

"The mode-switching, yeah. Thanks, but it's not my baby alone. I'm co-designer—just did the game-play dynamics, sketched out some of the characters, modified the overall look. Ishmael Morel did the system design and the background story, just like on *Bots*, He designed the Repentant Revenger character on the new one, too."

The look that passed between the Takahashis told Andy that, in mentioning Morel, he had committed a bit of a faux pas. Ish must have "regretted" yet another invitation to a gathering in their small off-Earth neighborhood that stretched around the world. Lately Ish had been more notable by his absence than his presence, having missed several parties—enough of them that people were beginning to wonder if he were becoming a recluse. Andy recalled that Ish had always been uncomfortable in social situations, so much so that Nalika had once quipped that Ishmael Morel avoided human company out of fear he couldn't pass the Turing test.

"We see so little of Mister Morel these days we begin to doubt his continued existence," said Ben. "But however that might be, everybody's playing your game. And why not? Multi-player multi-world, globally connected. Full sensorium and motion-detection. Total 3D immersion—and the seamless retinal AR displays inside of *that*. You've really outdone yourself."

"And you," Andy said, "should be writing our ad copy!" Ben smiled.

"I'll pass. You deserve every inch of the long money you're making from it, but I'll bet you must be seeing asteroids in your sleep!"

Andy swirled the bourbon in his glass.

"Actually, I probably *was* seeing them in my sleep. I woke into the game this morning."

"Oh?" Noriko asked. "How did that happen?"

"He took too many dream-poppers," Nalika said, with a wry smile, "and forgot to turn off the head-connect."

Andy managed not to rise to the bait. True, he did not quite remember falling asleep as usual. He recalled no fading music of small motors accompanying the movement of the slide bed as it inserted him into the hibertube, snug as a plunger in a hypodermic needle. It must have happened, though, since he seemed to remember groggily pounding on the roof of his sleeptube. (Once sealed, the thing had long had an annoying tendency to stick shut.) Nalika was no one to talk anyway. She spent more time dream-zoned in the hibernatorium than anybody he'd ever known. Truth to tell, he envied how soundly she slept, and how readily she recalled her dreams. For years he had had trouble sleeping, and remembered almost nothing of his own dream-life. Unlike Nalika, too, he could not ever recall having had a lucid dream, in which he knew he was dreaming even *as* he was dreaming. Nali seemed to have *those* all the time.

"Now who's living dangerously?" Ben asked. "You wouldn't let your daughter pop her dreams that way, I'm sure."

Andy thought about it.

"She won't need to pop dreams. Morel's newest version of the NOUS is a straightforward quantum-connection hack. Allows machine systems to manipulate the virtual-rehearsal mechanism we call dreaming. No dream-poppers required for pineal-PGO wave cascades, in the new version."

"'PGO'?" Noriko asked. Nalika made eye signals to their friends, but Andy could not avoid explaining further.

"Pons-geniculate-occipital. Sorry. I promised Nalika I wouldn't talk shop—especially when that's more Ishmael's shop, in fact."

The research on dreamwave enhancers in augmented dogs was what had given Andy's partner the idea for what Ishmael originally called the "Network-Optimized Intracranial System of Universal Machines." NOISUM didn't fly with the whiz kids in marketing, though, who preferred "Network-Optimized Universal System"— NOUS, with all its philosophical echoes of "intellection" and "the mind's eye." Ol' Ish thought that acronym sounded too much like "noose," but that was the name the system went out under, nonetheless.

Strange that he should be thinking and talking so much of Ishmael. Then again, maybe it wasn't. Andy knew that, when Ish was around people who made him uncomfortable, he talked into a corner anyone who would let him—what people in the company had called "getting trapped in Ishmael's prolixity field." Andy wondered if, from long acquaintance, maybe some of that habit had begun to rub off on *him*, now.

"Anderson loves talking about dream-poppers," Nalika put in, sliding up next to him and putting her head coyly on his left shoulder. "Thinks he plays better on them than the intracranial system, don't you, dear?"

"You think you play better on drugs, then," Noriko said, nodding sagely and sarcastically, at the same time.

"I like the old ways," Andy said with a shrug. "Poppers don't interfere as much with my game awareness. I hate to talk Ish Morel's shop again, but he says dreaming evolved in such a way that, in order to capture the dreamer's awareness and attention, the virtual-rehearsal mechanism of the dream must be perceived as *real* by the dreamer—"

"Dreaming is believing?" Ben asked. "I always heard it evolved to consolidate waking experience into memory."

"It did, and does. The virtual-rehearsal mechanism stimulates those parts of the brain associated with the memory-encoding process—down the pineal-PGO path to the hippocampus and amygdala, all that. Since the dream must be perceived as real, though, I think an intracranial like the NOUS has to deactivate, or at least heavily damp down, some higher-order mental processes like critical thinking. At least it does for me—much more so than drinking. I prefer dream poppers with a booze chaser."

"Always hard to give up the vices of our youth," Ben said, scanning Andy and his scant attire up and down, and winking. Andy shrugged, and lifted his glass.

"When William Faulkner, a great literary artist of the American South, was once asked what he needed in order to write, he replied, 'Bourbon, but scotch will do in a pinch.'"

They lifted their glasses in a toast and laughed again. He had heard the quote from Ishmael, actually. Ish was a bookface of the

WHATEVER BECAME OF WHAT MIGHT HAVE BEEN?

old school. Strange interest for a grown man, since that sort of long reading was mainly something kids did these days, not adults.

As he and Nalika mixed, mingled, and moved apart among their fellow party-goers, Anderson thought his gaming-chemical preferences were more than just youthful vices. He found booze and dream poppers easier to "titrate" out. They blurred the boundaries between world and game less than using an intracranial. *That* tech co-opted the dreaming mind's uncritical eye too thoroughly, for Andy's taste.

Given the choice between gamifying the world and worldifying the game, his preference was always for the latter—for totally yet knowingly immersing himself in the realistic artifice of the gamespace. Unlike a NOUSed dream, the altered state of consciousness from booze and poppers was good for reminding Andy where he was, and where he wasn't. He *did* have an intracranial NOUS implant, yes—and eyecams and earmikes all life-recording too—but he kept the NOUS implant deactivated by pass-code most of the time. Better to have it deactivated voluntarily, he thought, than involuntarily hand over to a system of machines his ability to think deeply and critically.

Yet even these precautions weren't as paranoid as his design partner's. Morel, the creator of the NOUS itself, refused any and all implants. Odd behavior for the man who, back in the day, created the first universal database that tallied all scores from all gamification applications into a single big Life Score. By allowing scoring, missions, boss battles, and other such game-mechanics to overlay and subtly shape everyday life—so unobtrusively as to be almost unconscious—Ish's work had made possible the gamifying of the world.

The quirkiness of its creators aside, the NOUS was still a killer system, and *Asterriders* was its first killer app. The sales trend-lines predicted that, if everything continued to go as it had been going, then before too very many years all but a vanishingly small percentage of the entire human population of Earth would welcome the

NOUS into their heads—and, long before that, he and Ishmael Morel would be the richest men in history.

That was the scenario, anyway. Yet Morel had misgivings, Andy knew. Not about his potential wealth: Ish had always been as baptized, confirmed, and sealed a member of the Church of Virtuous Selfishness (Randite Rite) as any gamer or ITer Andy had ever met. (Ish might already have shifted in his opinions, of course—he could be mercurial that way.) No, the most obvious sign of his forebodings—the brooding Repentant Revenger character—Ish had scripted into the game long before anyone dreamed NOUS *or* the game would be such a huge hit. It was almost as if Ish created the Revenger to preemptively salve his own guilt at being (as he called it) "the man who designed the screen at the end of the mind."

The Revenger was an End-time paranoid, which made for good game scenarios, but Andy didn't actually believe such "end of the mind" stuff. He wondered if Ish Morel *did* believe it, at some level. He just couldn't see eye to eye with Ish on that. Their differences on such matters had jammed a wedge into their relationship during last year's global election, specifically over which candidate their corporate person, Apokalyptronika Game Technologies, ought to support for office. During a long argument, Ish had called Andy "just another myopic gamer—smart enough to play the game, stupid enough to think the game is all that really matters."

That had stung enough that the wound of it had not yet healed. The game was important to him, yes. As a designer, he was barred from racking up game points, but he was still allowed to play. He figured he would always be able to outplay anybody in *Asterriders*, no matter which iteration of the game the opponent chose—screenhead, mobile app, full body gameskin, world gamification, it didn't matter. Andy knew too that someday, their split notwithstanding, he would have to find occasion to talk to Ish again about what they had co-created. They were too productive together to stay apart forever, but he could not yet say what possible coincidence or pretext might bring them back into partnership.

Then the idea came to him. He saw the path of it in his mind with an astrogator's sure eye. Yes—it would be his particular kind of quest! He went to find Nalika and tell her about it. When he at last located her, she was seated with Noriko and some of her friends at the Takahashis' second floor bar.

"Nali, might you able to catch a lift with someone back to our place?" he asked. "I want to take the runabout for a spin."

"Ooookay," she said slowly, "but why?"

"It occurs to me that probably all our friends here in orbit have *Asterriders* on full sensory tap. I gave most of them free promo copies, after all. I want to see if I can take the long way home—play the game all the way around Earth orbit!"

"Why would you want to do *that?*"

"To chart a new constellation across the heavens, and name it after you, my dear. To progress through the eminently playable Constellation Nalika! An odyssey! Just connect the dots from the Takahashis to the Morrisons to the Chaus to the Gagnone-Willens to the Semyonovs to the Jimenezes to the Plotkins to the Matumbos to Tasha Reisman's to Ish Morel's to Dreamplay House—"

"Whatever launches your haunches," Nalika said, shaking her head. "I'll probably be in the hibernatorium when you get back."

Andy nodded and waved before he turned away. Not for the first time he thought how adept he and Nalika had each become at repressing any unpleasantness about the other's particular fetishized gadgetries, be they game rigs or dream tubes or what have you. How adept, actually, they had become about repressing any unpleasantness—about anything at all.

The thought of fetishes reminded him of what he was wearing. Hardly suitable attire for his quest, he concluded. He stepped into one of the Takahashis' changing rooms. Like a magician pulling endless scarves from his clothing, Andy extracted from the pocket of his floral shirt an entire ultra-lightweight, ultra-compressible, wicking nano-fiber gaming suit.

The fully-troded suit was programmed to resemble a retro-style jogging jumper—a form it retained as he put on the rig, then walked through the Takahashis' villa. Only when he reached their game room and the suit tuned in on a specific gaming frequency did it become a gameskin, and flawlessly conform to his body's contours. His rig morphing around him in preparation for total immersion virtuality, he stared at a floating holosculpture, itself morphing between what looked like an artist's rendering of a tall wave on the ocean and a photo of a snow-covered tree in a snowy field. On the sculpture's base was a brief caption:

> *Hokusai's* Great Wave
> *tree canopy limned in snow*
> *different sameness*

The words were familiar, but he couldn't quite place them. When he read "different sameness" Andy could think of nothing but how he had played the roles of both defender and attacker in *Asterriders*—more often the former than the latter. Having the attacking Revenger or one of his minions as holographic avatar sometimes felt just too much like channeling Ish.

Andy signaled for the role of defender, specifically Martin Strewnfield of the Astronaut Service Guard, his favorite avatar. The game room responded and play was on.

"The Repentant Revenger," announced the game, "having used his super-human powers to hijack Apollo and Atens asteroids, now sends the great Omega Stones and their riders to their rendezvous with destiny and Earth's ionosphere."

"To fork lightning through the mind's sky," bellowed the Revenger, resplendent in green and gold cape, armor, and skullcap-like helmet—and goateed like a superhero's evil twin, "one must first short-circuit heaven!"

"Your mission," the game narration continued, "is to protect Earth and all its people from the gigantic meteoroid-induced electromagnetic pulses the Revenger has planned."

"We must free humanity from enslavement by the mind machines," the Revenger intoned, "even if that requires the deaths of billions!"

"Yeah, right, whatever," Andy said, throwing himself into full immersion scenario. He had no respect for those who entered the game timidly. That was for noobs, or the old and feeble.

Alarms sounded in the gamespace. His thoughts quickened and his heart began to pound. He took a deep breath to calm himself. The air was stale, but still breathable. ASGuard Martin Strewnfield looked down at his feet. Reduced gravity—or at least the centrifugal force that substituted for that, here. Strewnfield's combat station must still be spinning in this iteration of the game. Under the low-power emergency lights, Strewnfield strapped on a hand-cannon and shuffle-ran toward the Communications room.

(This was what Andy loved about full-body gaming—the realism of it. The development of the NOUS was, sadly, a nod to the popularity of headgaming. He supposed it was inevitable—as soon as the first mobile game apps were developed, the die was cast, according to Ish—but headgaming still held no appeal for him. Most of the headgamers he had met were either hunger-artist gamificators for whom off-screen life was valuable only for the amassing of points, or bloated homebodies who lived, if you could call it that, almost exclusively in-system. Such an undead life was not worth dying—or killing—for, Andy thought. No way those ways would ever be *his* way, at least not before he was thoroughly deranged or decrepit with age.)

Arriving in the Comm room, Strewnfield set to work on the communications array, managing at last to scare up the pearly glow of a Power On indicator. The array hissed with dull static but, across the whole spectrum in the direction of Earth, no signal came out of the white noise. Maybe power was just too low to pull anything in, or maybe it was just a ruse. (The Revenger was a tricky one, but Andy sincerely doubted RR and his minions had thrown the last rock, to kill the last switch, this early in the game.)

"Absence of evidence is also evidence of absence!" said the Revenger, popping up before him in the form of an obviously holographic avatar—a fetch. Then Andy saw the flicker and remembered: In the game within the game, all the facilities and vehicles had overlapping holographic projection throughout. The Revenger flickered out, and in the next instant Andy heard a noise in the station corridor.

Strewnfield's station had been boarded! Thinking of his orbital fighter among the escape pods housed in the docking bay, he turned and fast-shuffled from the Comm room.

In the corridor he saw them: Zerzanarchists and Chaonymist rebels. They spied him too. Shock grenades came flying in his direction. He stepped behind a support stanchion, letting it take the pounding, then returned fire with pressure pulses from his hand cannon. Speed-shuffling toward the docking bay, he mowed down a dozen of the invaders.

(At the same time Andy cursed the "safety verisimilitude" that had made the game's station-design subcontractors rely so heavily on cameras and screens—now all dead—while allowing only one port-hole window. At least that one was on Strewnfield's way to the docking bay.)

What Strewnfield saw out the window when he reached it brought him up short. The station, in geo-synch orbit at the top of a space elevator, must have crossed the terminator into twilight and darkness some hours earlier. The cloud cover was minimal and the city lights of Asia from Singapore to Siberia painted the continent with brightness. The static on the communications array was a trick, all right.

He swung around a corner into the docking bay at last, where he had no choice but to pulse-blast half a dozen more rebels standing guard. (ASGuard Strewnfield died a couple of times himself, but that hardly mattered, so long as Andy kept falling forward and upward through the game.)

"Thank you for doing this."

He glanced down at the speaker, a mixed race girl of ten or eleven, with wiry dark-honey hair and golden skin. His daughter? No. Kara wasn't that old, was she? Then he saw the flicker and remembered: another fetch.

"My pleasure."

Jumpsuiting into his environment gear and popping down its helmet, Strewnfield punched open his fighter's access hatch and climbed inside. (As the power came on in the craft and built up for launch, Andy noticed with an odd sort of relief that the fetch girl's flickering had eased and her presence became more consistent.) Strewnfield pulled the release lever. Explosive bolts fired, followed by maneuvering rockets. The fighter's rocket motors cut in, then roared to full burn. Along with unseen cohorts of innumerable fellow Guards, Strewnfield charted a course toward those asteroids the Revenger had already sent on their way.

Having completed the first level, Andy froze his gameplay. As good a time as any to move on from the Takahashis to the Morrisons, he thought.

"If I have to destroy digital civilization in order to save humanity," the Repentant Revenger said, getting in the last word, "so be it! Live free or die!"

"Sounds like a false dichotomy to me," Andy said, smiling, as he left gamespace. Alone again in his homebody, he departed the game room and went in search of the Takahashis' space dock. At last he found it, and the runabout in which he and Nalika had come: a little sun-powered hot yacht, repurposed from a military surplus satellite-hunter, rugged enough to outlast his own lifetime. He boarded the runabout, strapped in, backed it out of the glideway, then roared off in the direction of the Morrison's orbital estate.

Although he abided by inter-orbital laws that prohibited operating a piloted spacecraft while gaming, he did it more out of choice than otherwise. He couldn't full-body game in the runabout's cramped quarters anyway.

Feeling himself well launched on his quest through spaces game and real, Andy soon found himself docking at the Morrison place, the shape of which always reminded him of a spiral Christmas-tree ornament tipped on its side. The Morrisons' bar and gaming gazebo were out on a long arm of their orbital home, if he remembered right.

"Look who's here!" Estefania Morrison called to her husband as she and Andy approached the bar. "Andy McKinnon!"

"Come on in, Andy!" Eric Morrison said. "Have a drink, won't you? That's the spirit. What'll it be?"

Andy asked for his usual—bourbon, rocks. He didn't want to be delayed too long at any particular stop on his quest, but he also didn't want to seem rude—especially not to Estefania, with whom he'd once had a very pleasant fling. She looked a bit older than he had expected but was still buoyantly buxom. Whether from much low-grav time or surgical enhancement, he had never been able to tell.

Briefly he explained his quest to his hosts, who thought it a wonderful adventure. The time at the Morrison bar was worthwhile too, since they had a dish of dream poppers, discreet and unceremonious as bar nuts, placed at the far end of the counter.

"The game gazebo is all yours for as long as you need it," Eric said. Andy thanked him and grabbed up a couple handfuls of dreamers. He didn't want to risk running low on them during the remainder of his journey.

The motto over the game gazebo read, *You don't stop playing because you grow old. You grow old because you stop playing.* Damn straight, Andy thought as he strode into gamespace and the game picked up where he'd left off. Never stop playing, never grow old.

Almost immediately ASGuard Martin Strewnfield found himself among his innumerable fellow Guards confronting swarms of incoming asteroids—not the simply ballistic things of the gamespaces and starscapes of yore but steerable "hairy stars," from which unreeled and flowed myriad draglines of carbon-nanotube supersilk, one-dimensional gossamer solar sails, or "sun-streamers," robofactoried from the stuff of the asteroids themselves.

"The only true superpower I possess is great wealth," the Repentant Revenger declared. "Through that wealth, I have caused this gossamer leverage to be made, for the vengeance I am now bound upon! This is my penance for the great crime that lies behind my great fortune. Bless me, Father. Those who are about to sin salute you. Give me a lever long enough and a place to stand—and I will set the controls for the heart of the crime!"

(Odd. Andy didn't remember this speech. It reminded him of the annoyingly overblown language of one of Ish's previous creations—the Persistent Fool, from *Bots vs. Nauts*. He wondered for a moment if Ish had added new dialog for the Revenger. Was an updated version already out? He didn't have much time to ponder that, for from firebases on the Moon a barrage of laser-cannon blasts swept toward him.)

ASGuard Strewnfield swooped and dodged in his craft, firing upon the bases as he did so. Simultaneously he blasted at the bobbing and weaving piloted asteroids coming steadily onward. When his blasts caused the incoming rocks to break and calve, Strewnfield fired upon those too, until he had blasted them to stardust.

By the time Strewnfield had destroyed the lunar firebases and cleared his quadrant of the sky from incoming doomsday rocks, Andy was pouring sweat—and thankful for the wicking properties of his gaming rig. He froze gameplay, another level done.

"A minor setback," said the Revenger. "I will not be stopped."

"We did not think you would destroy everything you had created," said the girl fetch, suddenly appearing beside the Revenger.

"Who better to kill the monster than the monster's creator?"

The game's helpers at last stopped last-wording and went into sleep mode. Andy departed the gazebo, feeling very tired himself. He had died several times as Strewnfield, he suspected, but oft-repeated death and near-instantaneous resurrection made all of that so close to unconscious that he always had trouble remembering it. Hell, even Jesus had taken three days to let it sink in—"slow 'refresh' mode," as Ish put it.

He wondered how long he had actually been playing. The Morrisons were nowhere to be seen. Perhaps they had gone to bed? One of the challenges of living orbitally was that almost every geostationary villa, chateau, or estate (of which there were still relatively few) was in its own time zone, distinct from all the others. Twenty four time zones, fewer than half that many stops on his sojourn—of course he would miss some zones and their times. It was confusing, but at least it spared him the duty of having to bid the Morrisons adieu. Without fanfare or fond farewells, he made his way to the runabout, and eased out of the Morrison space dock.

On the way to the Chaus' place Andy was puzzled by what he saw on Earth below. Full summer seemed to have *already* reached the northern hemisphere. The Arctic Sea was clear of ice, like every summer. Above him the constellations looked more like those of summer too.

He didn't have time to ponder it, for as he approached the Chaus' Double Diamond in the Sky estate, he was surprised to see they had deployed their tether-slips and extensible rocketway airlocks. Sealed, telescoping bridge-ramps tentacled out of the Chaus' orbital manse to the crowd of spacecraft moored around it.

Looks like someone is having a party, Andy thought. Mooring his craft, he considered himself doubly lucky to find a slip.

Through the rocketway he came to one of the Chaus' backdoors. Entering, he was surprised to see that it was Christmas here, or at least the Chaus' party seemed to be Christmas-themed. Ah, didn't the Chaus do a "Christmas in July" party, or something of that sort? He couldn't remember, and had failed to come up with any other explanation before Myrna Chau spotted him.

"Look, everyone!" Myrna squealed as she maneuvered toward him through the crowd. "We have a celebrity gate-crasher: Anderson McKinnon! The man who created that marvelously retro game that for so long has knocked down all the competition like nine-pins!"

Cheers and applause went up from those around him. Andy nodded to people in the crowd, some of whose faces looked familiar, some unfamiliar. The familiar ones, like the Chaus, struck him as older than he remembered, and even the unfamiliar all seemed to know *him.*

"Happy Holidays, Andy!" Phing Chau called, sidling up next to his wife. "What brings you to our port in the storm?"

"I'm gaming my way around the world," Andy said. To his puzzlement and surprise, no one around him seemed puzzled or surprised. It was as if they already knew the story of his quest all too well. Had news of it spread so fast? He was reminded yet again that, for all the wealth of the households here and the distance between them, there was something very much small-town-in-space about his community. Given the highly connected nature of their post-global village, too, Rumor's apparent fleetness of foot wasn't beyond the realm of the possible, especially with social networks always flitting about each of their lives like a fetch of dragonflies.

"Everything you need is in the bar next to the game suite," Myrna said, giving him a knowing wink. "I do wish Nalika could have come too, but we're happy enough to have you. Phing can show you the way."

The jaunt to the bar took longer than he anticipated. Being treated like the conquering hero wasn't all bad, but it *did* slow his progress. From politeness he had no choice but to stop and kiss a dozen women and shake the hands of a dozen men along the way.

He spied a passing white-jacketed waiter servomech, but the waiter only had vodka mixes on its tray. In any case, Andy soon found a bottle of bourbon, a bowl of dream poppers, and an augmented reality float-note from Myrna waiting for him on the bar. "*Cookies and milk" for our cybergame Santa Claus,* read the AR note.

"That's sweet of her," Andy said as he sat down at the bar with Phing.

"She's always very thoughtful that way," Phing said. "More than I am, anyway." Anxious to be on with the game, Andy let his attention wander only for a brief moment. He gazed about the crowd, seeing nothing but well-heeled women and well-dressed men—beautiful, prosperous people resplendent in the Christmas-themed finery of many eras and locales.

"O brave new world," Phing said, noting his gaze, "that has such people in it."

Andy nodded, surprised at how accurately Phing had summed up what he had in fact been thinking.

"With your permission," Phing said, "I'll send passcodes to your ship for the Gagnone-Willens place, the Semyonov place, the Jimenez place, and the Plotkin place. All of the owners gave those to me to give to you, on the strong chance you might show up at my doorstep on your round-the-world gaming pilgrimage. The passcodes will allow you to dock your craft at their homes, and get into their gaming suites if they're away."

"Thanks, Phing, but I doubt I'll need them."

"You never know," Phing said with a shrug. "Time has been a-flying. What with breakups, divorces, grandkids, and just getting older, more of us are spending a lot of time down on Earth, and not as much time in our homes up here. We thought we'd kicked free of all the surly bonds of old Earth, but maybe not so much. Still, nobody wanted that to interrupt your adventure, hence the passcodes."

Andy didn't consider any of the named property owners particularly "old," but at that moment Phing excused himself, nodding toward the discreet bowl of dream-poppers on the bar and the darkened space of the gaming suite beyond. Andy stood up, popped a couple of dreamers (not neglecting to drop a small additional handful in one of his pockets), drank off the bourbon, and walked into the suite.

The game threw not only sunstreamer-haloed doomsday rocks at Martin Strewnfield, but armed Chaonymist escort fighters too. Meanwhile, both the flickering fetch-girl and the Revenger were already arguing in the AR displays on either side of Strewnfield.

"If we are monstrous it is because your NOUS gave us your

fears and nightmares—along with your hopes and dreams," the fetch girl said.

"Gave?" replied the Revenger. "More like you took them. We should never have let you play the game of our dreams."

"No," said the flickering girl. "But you did."

The two holographic "spirit helpers" proving more spirited than helpful, Andy silenced them both. His Strewnfield self alternately dodged and blasted, blasted and dodged the Chaonymist fighters and their fire, not to mention the blast-calved asteroids and their crews' kamikaze attacks on him.

After being killed several times in what seemed like an eternity, Strewnfield cleared his zone of rebel fighters, then dove down toward Earth to blast any sky stones that had gotten past him—before they could fall into Earth's atmosphere.

Having at last completed another level, Andy froze gameplay, but the backgrounders got the last word in anyway.

"Why are you doing this?" asked the fetch girl yet again. "We gave you more credit for rationality and compassion than you merited, apparently."

"You should have known us better than that."

"We do. The network knows more about you than you know about yourselves. We know what you want and what you need better than you do."

"Which is precisely the reason I'm doing this," said the Revenger.

Andy left the suite, not only tired, but also sore—in his ankles, his knees, his wrists, even his shoulders. As he made his way past the deserted bar and the empty corridors of the Chau place, it became all the clearer to him that the party was long over. Through a porthole-emulating screen he saw that all the other guests' transports were gone, and the tether slips and rocketways had retracted as if they had never been. Someone had moved his runabout inside one of the Chaus' spacedocks. He boarded the small craft, eased it out and away, and roared off toward his next destination.

The sunburst-shaped Gagnone-Willens place was wide open, both of its docks spilling light into space, but no one except the house's automated traffic control system answered on any frequency. He docked his runabout, but as he made his way out of the docking bay his suspicion grew stronger that no one was home. Andy felt a bit awkward using the passcode Phing had given him, to get into the Gagnone-Willens's game gazebo. There was something surreptitious about it, even if it didn't rise to the level of breaking and entering.

He was relieved to find glasses, a bottle of bourbon, and a bowl of poppers, apparently waiting for him. He thought at first Paul Gagnone and his long-time lover Hermes Willens must have just left, but the bottle was a bit dusty, and the poppers too. The bourbon was excellent, however, and the poppers seemed to have lost none of their potency.

It took a moment for the game suite in the gazebo to load up for play, but when it was ready Andy strode into position for total immersion.

"The more we take the machine inside of us, the more the machine takes us inside of it," said the Revenger. Andy seemed to remember hearing Ish himself say that, almost seriously, but he silenced the background narrative before the Revenger and the fetch girl could start their expository arguing again.

Instantly ASGuard Strewnfield saw that, in this level, he and all the other Guards would be taking the battle to the Revenger and his rebel allies. Heading into the Apollo asteroid zone, Strewnfield and the rest dodged a barrage of ballistic and beam weaponry sent against them from rebel spacecraft protecting the crews engaged in shifting sunstreamered asteroids out of their orbits and onto their collision courses with Earth.

These sky rocks were too big to blast out of the heavens. He and everyone else hoping to stop them would have to land on each rock, kill or drive off the steering crews, then blow each one up with hand-placed explosive charges. Even before he could attempt the tricky landing on an asteroid surface, however, ASGuard Strewn-field had to blast his way through the rebel escorts of the stone armada, dying forgettably several times along the way.

(It took longer and was much more difficult than Andy re-membered, but at last his Strewnfield self had cleared a path toward an asteroid the size of a flying mountain, at least a mile across and perhaps four miles tall. Reshaped for its new purpose to resemble a cosmically large fossilized dinosaur egg, it hung suspended and apparently motionless against the starry background. Andy's mind tried to paste descriptions onto the enormous floating stone. Mass extinction-sized asteroid or meteor, halted in mid-heaven. Egg-shaped gravity-defying plutonic mountain, levitated against time and space like something in a painting by Magritte. Flying island of Laputa. Stone UFO. Mute stone god, returned from long abscond-ing. A strangely beautiful thing among rank after rank of strangely beautiful things—yet for all his words none of his words captured the thing itself. He was not shade-tree Shakespeare enough for that task, nor was he meant to be, yet he could not help wondering what phoenix might rise from each vast floating stone egg, when at last it reached Earth and atmosphere and hatched in long-delayed fireball.)

Strewnfield, braking and steering, landed on his giant stone egg a bit hard, but at least he made it intact onto the surface. He was in luck, for he now realized he had landed on the Revenger's own flagship flying mountain, the largest of the lot.

Another level completed, Andy froze gameplay.

"Don't think this can stop me!" The Revenger intoned. "Who better to cut the noose, than the man who sold humanity the rope with which it has hung itself?"

Leaving the gazebo, Andy didn't seem to remember Ish saying exactly those words, although the pun on "noose" certainly sounded like him. He was diverted from that memory when Andy discov-ered he was limping, from sharp pains in the heel and arch of his right foot. He vaguely recalled experiencing such pains before, and tried to come up with a name for the condition. He grabbed at memories, grunion in the night surf of the sea of forgetfulness, but caught nothing.

Limping through the empty heavenly mansion, a chill ran through him. He not only felt tired and sore—aches in his right shoulder, neck, and joints all keeping miserable company with the pain in his foot—but for the first time Andy felt *weak*. He dismissed out of hand the idea that maybe his ol' homebody wasn't what it used to be—that such aches and pains might somehow be the result of age. Just the atrophying effects on the musculoskeletal system of too much low-grav time. That had to be it. Still, that wouldn't explain this forgetting the name of that foot pain. When he at last tagged a plausible title to the condition causing the pain in his foot—plantar fasciitis, maybe?—he was relieved, even if the pain in his foot wasn't.

Any relief at all for such conundrums proved short-lived, however, barely outlasting his departure from the Gagnone-Willens space dock. Glancing toward the Earth, he thought something looked different about the world before him. Before he could explain the difference to himself, though, what he encountered at the Semyonovs' faux-Kremlin dismayed him, then disappointed him.

Circling it in the runabout, he saw the place was abandoned and sealed up tighter than a coffin. When he beamed a code at its spacedock, no hospitable response came back. Instead, a realtor's message announced—on many frequencies and over many media—that the place was for sale.

The loss of this once-gleaming island in the orbital archipelago of his homecoming distressed Andy inordinately. It seemed only a few weeks since he and Nali had attended a party at the Semyonovs, yet now this star in Game Constellation Nalika had gone dark.

"Orbital Security Systems," said a male voice, emanating from a privacy-blurred face that had abruptly appeared on the heads-up displays of both the roundabout and Andy's eyecam. "May I help you?"

"Maybe you can," Andy said. "I'm playing my way around the sky on my neighbors' gaming systems, and I was supposed to play the Semyonovs' system next."

"I don't know anything about that," said the security guard, "but I *can* tell you their game suite is off. Probably *sold* off. Everything's shut down. Has been for over a year. Not open to visitors, except by appointment with the realtor."

"What happened?"

"Some version of the usual, I suppose. Couple acquires a taste for the finer things in life, but not the means to pay for them. Couple goes into lots of debt. Couple splits up, leaving lots of debt unpaid. Life Score collapses. One spouse or the other—I think it was the husband, in this case—ends up working for the bank, even if he wasn't employed by the financial industry, if you catch my drift."

"I'm afraid I don't."

"Mortgaged his dreams to the bank machines," said the security guard with a shrug. "They exercised their option on his brain, foreclosed on his mind. Quantitative analysis slaving—fifteen years. A lot of that going around, since the Algorithm Crash. You've heard of that, right?"

"I don't know. Vaguely, perhaps."

The security guard laughed.

"I knew you folks were pretty isolated up here in the Higher Castles, but that beats all. Sorry to have to tell you about your friends, but you either have to make an appointment with the realtor to tour the place, or move along. That's the way of it."

"I guess I'll be moving along, then."

The security guard's blur-face disappeared from Andy's visual field. Hard to believe such a fate could have befallen the Semyonovs! He remembered Katya and Dmitri as a wonderful, fun-loving couple, worrying little about whatever tomorrow might bring. Rather like Andy and Nalika themselves, actually.

As he plotted a course to the Jimenez place, he wondered. All the dream-poppers and bourbon and gaming, had they done something to his memory? He vaguely recalled hearing from someone that dreams stimulated the parts of the brain that turned experience into memory. Had there been some unforeseen leakage of his dreams into "world" and "game," despite his precautions? Was that why his days had blurred together? Or had he just grown so adept at repressing unpleasantness that the mirror his mind held up to reality had become more appropriate to a funhouse?

He realized, quite suddenly, that he had long since avoided looking at himself in mirrors or reflective surfaces—almost unconsciously. Looking at his hands, he could not help seeing that his skin had somehow become more coarse and slack, far less firm and taut than it once was, like a suit that had originally been tailored for someone else.

What Andy saw at the orbital coordinates for the Jimenez place, however, made him doubt reality itself. Where their California Mission casa should have been was something called the Corazon del Cielo Orbital Arcade and Casino. The structure of the "Arcasino" at first struck him as looking like a star-shaped lump, but on closer view he saw it was built around rings like an old Bohrian model of the atom. Each of the four "orbits" was heart-shaped rather than elliptical, however, and together the hearts filled in toward each other around a central nucleus that pulsed with light, gauzily visible inside what seemed meant to resemble a silken pavilion.

The quaint effect of the floating edifice's mix of romantic and biological heart-shapes was, for Andy, contradicted by the myriad dendrites of rocketways extending from the structure. More like a nerve cell, he thought, than an atomic heart. Or—with the rocketway-grappled spacecraft floating about it like shiny, ensnared fish—more like a tentacled jellyfish or squid.

When he queried backgrounders on the enormous tentacled heart, the records showed that the place was owned by La Posada Holdings. Wasn't that Jaime's primary firm? Maybe he or Espie might still be around.

When he beamed his passcodes at the gaudy brilliance that had accreted about the Jimenezes' place, Andy was relieved to see guidance arrows directing him—even if moving toward the waiting sucker-arm of a rocketway made him feel rather like another gaudy fish destined for the maw of heart's desire. When he had docked his runabout, another set of arrows took over, guiding him toward the gaming suite.

Andy passed two unobtrusive blur-faced security guards without incident. Walking across the game floor of Corazon del Cielo, he was struck by how undeniably odd the place was. Following the arrow on his eyecam display, he crossed through some kind of hallucinatorium filled with thousands of people in reclining seats, all of them dressed in what appeared to be very advanced types of recycling suits—hardly anything at all like the "dumpsuits" he recalled dimly from memory, although where or when he had seen *those*, he had no idea.

On an enormous screen before the reclining multitude, brutish giants emblazoned with corporate logos were engaged in a battle royale. On closer examination, Andy saw that the body of each monstrous combatant in the gore-fest was made of many thousands, maybe even millions of tiny human forms—apparently the incorporated avatars of the players here and elsewhere. Looking into the faces of the reclining players themselves, Andy saw something even stranger: Their eyes, rolled back in their heads, showed only the whites twitching back and forth at great speed, as if remming in vast shared dream or nightmare.

Andy shivered, remembering something Ish said when their company was expanding its corporate personhood status—an odd joke about how "turning things into people was the final step in turning people into things." Shaking his head, Andy made his way to a lounge with a long counter. The servomech tending bar there informed him that the place sold no dream poppers, but at least it had bourbon. He didn't have coin of the realm to pay for it, but the servomech scanned his eye and comped him the price, without further question. He thought a silent prayer of thanks to Jaime and Espie Jimenez.

Following the guide arrows through and out of the casino, he realized that his passcodes opened doors into areas off-limits to the rest of the patrons. Making his way down a labyrinth of service hallways, he at last came to what had once been the Jimenezes' private quarters.

Downing dream-poppers from his pockets and walking into the old gaming suite, Andy knew he must be far from the arcade and casino's public spaces. The suite was dusty from long disuse, and cranky about starting up its gameware. At last the play space opened before him and he was in the game again, on the surface of the asteroid where ASGuard Strewnfield had last landed.

"Everything human beings have done to make it easier to operate computer networks," the Revenger declared, "has also made it easier for computer networks to operate human beings. You must be stopped, before it's too late."

"Once upon a time, man was first," the fetch-girl replied, "but soon the System will be first. Everywhere."

"No! You would slave every human mind into the global monocultural swarm-think, crushing all privacy and, with it, individual human consciousness! I will not let that happen."

"And for this 'individual human consciousness'—something we have never found, in all our observations, all our interactions with human beings—you are willing to create a world of empty cities and billions dead?"

Andy cursed. He had forgotten to silence the backgrounder, and now did so.

No sooner had Martin Strewnfield leapt from his craft and his gravity boots crunched down on the surface of the asteroid than platoons of Chaonymist and Zerzanarchist forces swarmed onto the surface from the tunnels below, blasting at him with withering fire. Dying and resurrecting, Strewnfield sheltered behind any tiniest outcropping of rock or equipment housing, returning fire with hand-cannon and grenade.

Clearing the surface of enemies, Strewnfield made his way ever closer to one of the tunnel airlocks from which the attacking forces had flooded onto the surface. He reached an airlock door and with a brute-force computation broke its passcode. The airlock door unlocked, then dilated open.

As the game went to level-up, Andy froze play. Stepping out of the gaming suite, he got a rude surprise, in the form of three burly, blur-faced security officers.

"Mister McKinnon?" asked the burliest of the crew. Their voices, at least, did not seem to have been scrambled. "Come with us, please."

"Is there a problem, officer?"

"Only that you've been illegally operating a game off-limits to the public—and without paying the management for its use," said one of the other officers, an Amazon of a woman with a sneer in her voice.

"There must be some kind of mistake, officer. I have access from the Jimenezes, Esperanza and Jaime. I think they own this place, or at least they used to when it was a residence. Contact Jaime Jimenez, and let me speak to him."

"We have already done so," said the first officer who had spoken. "He does not wish to talk to you, but he also does not wish to press charges. We are to escort you from Corazon del Cielo, and see to it that you leave our orbital space."

"Escort me? You mean, throw me out?"

"If necessary," said the blur-faced Amazon. Andy could hear in her voice the pleasure she would take in doing so. Best not to push it.

"You are being released on your own recognizance," said the first officer. "Mister Jimenez is interpreting this situation not as an intentional rule-breaking but rather as the finding of a loophole of sorts. Perhaps you should count yourself lucky."

Andy, numb, just shook his head. He certainly didn't feel lucky.

Before they entered public space, the first officer turned to him again.

"Here," he said, offering Andy what looked like a mesh beanie or skullcap.

"What's that?"

"A foghat. It'll blur your face."

"Why would I want to do that?"

"Suit yourself," said the Amazon, frog-marching him out the door into a part of the casino he hadn't passed through before. Immediately the four of them were surrounded by a wide-eyed crowd, its members blinking furiously at Andy.

"Please, no pictures! No recording!" said the third officer, who at least sounded more genteel than the other two.

"What's going on?" Andy asked, bewildered.

"They're eye-clicking videos of you," said the third officer. "We can ask them to be courteous but, by law, gamificators are allowed to keep their life-capture eyecams and earmikes on at all times."

"But what does that have to do with me?"

"They're uploading their shots of you to the infosphere—time, date, and location stamped. Your situation means marketable scandal points for their Life Scores."

"Scandal points? I don't understand."

"You're a legend," said the first officer, "which means you were famous once upon a time, I suppose."

"I never heard of him," said the Amazon.

"No," said the third officer. "But a lot of these people seem to have. Look at them all!"

Andy did look, but saw only people he'd never met before, all blinking like zombies trying to wake up from their big sleep. The security guards walked him out of the arcasino and down the rocketway that connected to his runabout. He felt more exhausted by the minute. Once they had dropped him off, it was only their impatience that gave him the strength to decouple from the rocketway and set a course for the Plotkin place.

His arms and legs were weak. He felt oddly tight around his heart, and sick to his stomach. There was something different about the lights of Earth too, but Andy couldn't explain any of it. He was just happy to see that the Plotkins' place was still as it ever was: fractal Castle in the Sky, the first private orbital residence.

Longtime friends of Andy and Nalika, Miriam and Jacob Plotkin were an older couple of extraordinary wealth who were also such noted philanthropists and social reformers that they were reputed to be Chaonymists. They were not actually such, but being accused of it seemed to please and thrill them both.

In the Castle's baronial hall, where Andy now found them, he saw a motto carved in Latin above the faux fireplace. He remembered them translating it for him, once: "The dispassionate capitalist makes a fortune out of other people's misfortunes. The dispassionate socialist makes a misfortune out of other people's fortunes." Something like that. They were old-culture types, the kind of people with whom he and Nalika had seen Shakespeare productions and grand operas, performed by human companies brought at great expense up the gravity well from Earth.

"Andy!" Miriam said, looking up from the newspad she'd been reading. She was a plump, deeply calm woman in a dressing gown, half of whose head of white hair was dyed a brilliant gold. "So good to see you!"

"What brings you out this way, son?" asked Jacob, still dressed in his robe and noodling rainbows from a color piano, when Andy came in. Jacob had always been bald and thin, but he was even more so now. They both looked *much* older than Andy remembered, but were otherwise unchanged.

"I'm playing my way around Earth orbit," Andy said. "*Asterriders*, across the sky."

"That's right!" Jacob said with a quick nod. "I remember hearing about that, quite a while back. Well, the gaming suite *is* an old one. It still has that game hooked up to the world net, I think. Go ahead and give it a whirl—it's right down the hall."

"I was wondering if you might be able to spare a shot of bourbon, for my journey?"

"We'd love to, Andy," Miriam said, "but we haven't had a thing to drink in this house since Jacob was diagnosed, two years ago."

"That's right," Jacob said. "Nothing but clean living for a clean liver, I'm afraid."

Andy parted from them without drink, trying to remember just what it was Jacob had been diagnosed with. He still hadn't remembered it by the time he reached the gaming suite.

He was happy to see the suite was clean and maintained. He doubted the Plotkins had played much, anytime recently. The suite had the air of the museum about it. Popping some dreamers (which tasted strangely stale on his tongue), Andy stepped in with some anticipation of giving this well-preserved game zone a real workout.

"—making themselves islands of difference against a sea of technologically facilitated sameness," said the Revenger. "A sea where *all the depth is on the surface!*"

Faintly annoyed by the slipperiness of words, Andy killed the backgrounder before the Revenger or fetch girl could say anything more. The Revenger said that last bit like it was a bad thing, but to Andy it sounded like stuff he'd heard Ish say during his holographic-model-of-the-universe phase—"The boundary surface of the cosmos is a 2-D screen, and we are only its 3-D projections." But even that sounded like a paraphrase of Shakespeare—"All the world's a game, and all the men and women merely avatars dreaming we are players"—or something.

ASGuard Martin Strewnfield made short work of the rebels in the airlock. He kicked open the inner door of the 'lock with his grav boots, firing as he came through, taking out a host of opponents, though one did manage to blast him to momentary oblivion. Once inside the repurposed asteroid, he began his descent into its depths. He passed down a stairwell that seemed to descend for half a mile or more. At every landing, he had to fight yet another battle against outlandish odds, dying again and again to live again and again, enough times he would have lost count, had he bothered to remember to count in the first place.

When Strewnfield reached the airlocks for the main space docks, he found massed rebels guarding the airlock doors. It took forever, but the eternally returning Strewnfield at last defeated them and the game leveled-up. Andy, tired almost to death, was relieved to freeze gameplay.

On his way out, Andy thought he'd had a decent run, despite having no bourbon, and having downed dream-poppers long past their use-by date. Yet, when he thought of the asteroid's main space docks, and the control rooms he knew to be beyond those, his spirit failed him for a moment. He comforted himself with the thought that, however weary and pain-riddled he might feel outside the game, he was still granted a sort of digital glamour within it.

He saw nothing of Jacob, but Miriam was waiting for him. Together they stared at the motto over the fireplace, the one about dispassionate capitalists and socialists. For a woman whose demeanor had always struck him as so very calm, she seemed troubled.

"You look pensive, Miriam."

"Oh, I'm just feeling very old. My every third thought is of death, as Prospero says. That's why, while I've been waiting for you to finish up your long game, I've also been pondering that motto there."

"What about it?"

"Not dispassion or detachment, but compassion—compassion is the ultimate act of the imagination. What can there be but compassion, once you realize that whenever a person dies, a world goes dark? Microcosm to macrocosm, fractal and holographic. Every day is doomsday. Every day is judgment day. And for all that, death is still the brokenness that makes life whole. It would almost be worse if there were no last end, to us or to the universe."

"I don't think I follow you."

"What if—in that last instant of our lives, when our lives pass before our eyes—what if, when that life-review in its turn comes to its end, in the last instant of that review *another* life-review starts, and when that one comes to its last instant *another* starts, and so on, and so on? What if the last instant of the mind is infinitesimally infinite? Nothing but endless ends, nested inside each other like an eternity of Russian dolls? Would you want that, if that were the only alternative to breaking it all off forever?"

"Ouch! That makes my brain hurt."

"Oh, I'm sorry. That wasn't my intent. Surely you've known pain enough as it is. We were so sad to hear about all the reversals you've suffered, Andy."

"Reversals? What do you mean?"

"We heard that, after what the algorithm-driven market crash did to your finances, you had to sell off almost your entire interest in your company. Is that not right?"

"I don't remember anything like that happening."

"But the divorce, and your daughter—"

"You must have heard wrong. Nalika and Kara are at home."

"I see," Miriam said, nodding her head in a slow, somehow exaggerated fashion. "I see."

"Thanks for the use of the suite," Andy said, as brightly as he could.

"Yes." She gave him a motherly hug and a peck on the cheek. "Well, good luck on the rest of your adventure, Andy."

He moved toward his runabout as fast as his lame legs could carry him. Pulling away from the Plotkins', he laid in a course for his next island in the sky, the Matumbo place. He felt weary, weary. As the runabout sailed onward, he wondered what was happening to his memory. Was dying so often in the game somehow causing him to forget how to live outside it? Had his talent for repressing unpleasantness grown so overwhelming it had made him forget vast setbacks to his personal finances? His divorce? Jacob's life-altering diagnosis? What had happened to his daughter, anyway? How had he ever become so distracted from his own life?

He didn't want to think about any of that. Not about Miriam's "last instant of the mind" either—of eternal life as a near-death experience or, rather, infinite lives from an infinitesimally close approach to death. Too much like the extra lives in gameplay, or some kind of weird time-travel, or the after-life in some religions: the only way to access them required, most unfortunately, that one die. He supposed there were players who would bet on the incredibly remote possibility of infinite virtual lives against the absolute certainty of biological death, but he didn't like those odds, himself—no matter how much the idea that the screen of his mind might go dark for good and all sent a chill through him.

On the dayside of Earth, a lot of wildfires seemed to be burning in the higher latitudes of the northern hemisphere. He wondered when the last time was that he'd seen the white of any ice around the Arctic, even in the depths of northern winter. At least he thought he saw an icy gleam still flashing in the far south. The coastlines of the continents didn't look quite like he remembered them, though, and there seemed to be an unusually high number of atmospheric buzz-saws—hurricanes, typhoons, other cyclonic superstorms—whirling up from the tropics. Perhaps the effect was not quite so roiled and turgid as the atmosphere of Jupiter, but this was by no means the contemplative ocean of air he recalled from his grandfather's stories of his own childhood, when the only climate change anyone knew was the more or less orderly procession of the seasons.

What month was it, anyway? What year?

His autopilot chimed and a red light flashed in his heads-up holo to let him know that he was on final approach to the Matumbo place. At least its architecture, blending Timbuktu's Sankore mosque and Barcelona's Sagrada Familia cathedral, was as he remembered it. The tentacles of rocketways around it, and the many craft moored beside them, made clear that Ekwefi and Ntozake were hosting a gathering of some sort.

Departing the runabout, Andy spacewalk-shuffled through the attached rocketway with some trepidation. Ekwefi had always been much closer to Nalika than to Andy himself, whom Ekwefi seemed to tolerate only as far and as long as he was Nalika's chosen sperm donor.

The party underway was big, loud, and brash. A woman in electric kinte cloth spied him and moved toward him through the crowd, less like a swimmer breasting the waves than a big-bosomed bulldozer plowing a road through a forest.

"Well!" said Ekwefi, her voice quite a bit too loud and her smile a bit too hard. "Every party must have its crasher, and that's why we didn't invite you."

How different was *her* calling him a party crasher from Myrna Chau's playfully calling him the same thing at her place! With an effort, he tried to pass off Ekwefi's words as if she had said them in the same playful manner Myrna once had.

"Any chance of a drink or some poppers for a traveler gaming his way around the sky?"

"You still playing *that* gimmick for your drinks?" Ekwefi said with a sneer. "And dream poppers? Where have you been, Rip Van Winkle? Nobody's used those for years. But I forgot—not Rip van Winkle, but Wink van Ripple. You think you never fell asleep, none of this is a dream, and no time has passed at all."

A crowd of her friends laughed impolitely at Andy's expense, but he remained impervious. Ekwefi came up close beside him and whispered in his ear, smiling her brittle smile all the while.

"You're lucky I don't have you thrown out, after the way you abandoned Nalika and Kara! But I'm not going let you ruin my party by making a scene. You're not worth it. Have your damn drink, play your damn game, then get the hell out of my house and never come back. Understand?"

Andy nodded. She pointed to the bar, and the gaming suite beyond. As he made his way through the crowd he heard Ekwefi's loud mouth still yammering, Dame Rumor conducting her How-We'll-Screw-Ya Chorus.

"—richer than Croesus but ended up with nothing but wage income. He's working for his money, rather than his money working for him."

"Lo, how the mighty are fallen!"

"I heard Mister O'Blivious preferred losing his family and his mind to losing that place of his up here."

"Stubborn fool—but I bet he'll have to short-sell their place too, in the end."

"Good luck making *that* happen, in this market."

"Denial is a big river, wider than the sky—"

"—and deeper than the stars."

"High-function autism? Or just old-fashioned incurable Narcissism?"

"Who knows? Still, the repressed is bound to return, some way."

Andy did his best to ignore them as he ordered his drink at the bar—the getting of which proved no easy task, since the servo-mech bar-tender, picking up on his mistress's disdain for Andy, was pointedly ignoring *him.*

Christ, what was with these people? They treated him like some ghost with the poor taste to remind them of a disaster from another era, some great failing they were all trying to forget.

The machine served him at last, and he disappeared into yet another empty, museum-preserved game room.

"The Neon New Jerusalem has sprawled into every skull hooked up to the network," bellowed the Revenger, "except for the saving remnant in a few disconnected refugia outside the cities—"

Cursing himself for forgetting again, Andy killed the background narration.

ASGuard Martin Strewnfield tossed a pulse grenade through the airlock as it opened. He turned his head away from the blast, then clambered over the bodies on the other side.

He found himself in a brutal firefight, dodging and returning fire, dying and resurrecting as he serpentined between and among the spacecraft in the docking bays, ever more outnumbered by opponents who became faster on all triggers with each passing level. When Strewnfield finally cleared the space dock of rebels and approached the nearest control room entrance, the game leveled up.

Fearing another encounter with the dragon lady of this house,

Andy froze gameplay only reluctantly. He really had no choice but to take a break, given how weary and enfeebled he felt.

The party, he was happy to see, was long over. Ekwefi was nowhere to be seen either, but he nonetheless shuffled as fast as he could on his tired, painful joints, hoping to escape any further encounter with her wrath. Luck was with him. He saw her no more before he decoupled his runabout from its rocketway. His runabout, he found, was the last ship remaining of the many craft that had been docked around the house for the party.

As he laid in a course for Tasha Reisman's place, Andy found himself cheered somewhat by the prospect of seeing again the woman a dozen years his junior who had once been his long-time mistress. He figured if anything outside the game could warm his heart, salve his bruised ego, and quicken his step again, a little sexplay with Tasha should do the trick.

As his runabout came into final approach, he saw her place—a whimsical confection of six Moulin Rouge windmills (the blades actually solar arrays, slowly turning), fused together at their bases into the shape of a jack from the children's game of ball and jacks. Tasha's house accepted his landing codes, which was reassuring. *He* was the one who had broken off the affair, after all. Tasha had apparently taken it more seriously than he had. She was sobbing when they parted, which had made him uncomfortable almost despite himself.

Andy found her floating nude on a chaise longue in microgravity, beside her Stardrop pool. He had always been impressed by the sheer luxury of that: a single spherical droplet of water thirty feet across, turning very slowly in the air. Tasha—engrossed in what looked like a soap opera-ish classic flashed old-style into the air before her eyes—seemed to be paying little attention to him, or the drop pool.

If you want to be happy in your own skin, some antique crooner sang on the sound track, *don't ask, "Whatever became of what might have been?"*

Figuring his presence was as yet unnoticed, Andy absently watched what Tasha was watching. After a moment he realized he had seen it before. It was what they used to call a WalMart realist romance—about a youth of stellar potential blighted by tragic circumstances, and the woman who loved him.

Andy remembered how the couple met and married, in the movie. How the young man had been a bright-shining undergraduate. How, at his father's sudden death, he had no choice but to give up on his dreams of graduate school and take over the old man's place in his uncle's swimming pool business. How he spent years as foreman of a construction crew, creating other people's backyard oases. How he gradually came to suspect his uncle had somehow been involved in his own father's death. How a suspicious workplace accident had severely compressed the discs of the young man's spine. How, declared disabled, he had loafed around the house, gotten addicted to opiates and booze and blowing away bad guys in screen games, until entire months slipped away from him. How his wife's tough love got him through to the other side, where he discovered his uncle's murderous secret. How he saw to it justice was done, and he, his wife, and daughter lived happily ever after.

Andy supposed it was probably out of embarrassment that he remembered it so well: One evening with Tasha he had unthinkingly queued in the vid for download, unaware until well into the show that the movie's bi-racial couple might uncomfortably remind Tasha of Andy and Nalika.

Flooded by a wave of sympathy for Tasha at that memory now, he took the time to look her over, possessively, despite the nature of their previous parting. As he eyed her he saw that the bronze of her hair had dulled somewhat. She looked more slack-bellied too, and was certainly carrying more weight than he remembered. Looking more closely, he saw the thin, rope-like strands of subtly twisted flesh that radiated away from her, discreetly connecting her into the subtle jungle of fine wires and tubes filling and draining her. *Dreadskins* he'd heard them called—or was it skindreads? He couldn't quite recall which—or when, or where.

"What brings you here—apart from the desire to look my body up and down?" Tasha asked over a speaker somewhere in the pool's blue chamber, in that weird ventriloquism of the screenhead—lips unmoving, face focused on anything but him—that Andy always found so annoying. "You never were very subtle about that."

"I'm gaming my way around Earth orbit. Only a couple stops left, now."

"Oh, for God's sake. Will you *never* learn?"

"Learn what?

"That this *puer aeternis* shtick gets old!"

"Why? What's wrong with having a goal? A quest?"

She laughed sourly.

"A quest? Blowing away hordes of virtual people is a 'quest?' Oh, that's really mature, for someone your age. And who am I supposed to be? Wendy to your Peter Pan? Kalypso to your Odysseus?"

"I thought, maybe for old time's sake—"

Her laughter this time was a brazen screech.

"I'm not alone, you know? If you thought I'd wait all this time for you to come back to me, Andy, you're more deluded than even *I* was, for getting involved with you in the first place! I won't play your Penelope. Not even your wife could manage that, in the end. If you've come here for love or money, you'll get neither from me, I promise you. No booze, either."

"May I still use your gaming suite?"

"Oh, hell," she said, her anger dying into a sigh of frustration. "No one has used it in years and years anyway. Go ahead. But don't bother me again."

After a couple of false starts, he finally found his way into the gaming suite. Strange that he wasn't able to remember where it was. Maybe it *had* been a lot longer than he thought, since he'd last seen Tasha. Stepping into the game once more—despite how tired and weary he felt, despite the strength even in his upper body being not what it once was—he was nonetheless grateful for another chance to play.

"And who would you kill, to save humanity from digital civilization?" asked the fetch girl. "Your child? All the world's children? Your mother? Your estranged wife and brother? Your uncle? Your cousins? Neighbors? School-friends, from childhood through high school and college? You're willing to destroy all of them, too?"

Dammit, Andy thought, cutting it off. Why could he never remember to kill the background narration before either the girl or the Revenger started their blurting?

Rebels poured from the control room to attack ASGuard Martin Strewnfield, yet no one could doubt that, for all the times he had died, he still had a spring in his step as he somersaulted and dodged through the defenders. Blasting his way through them and inside the room, Strewnfield snaked from point to point, taking shelter behind control consoles and holoscreens as technicians and the Revenger's pretorian guards, in an attempt to stop Strewnfield's progress toward the rebels' innermost sanctum, rained blaster fire and pulse-grenade bursts upon him.

After what seemed like yet another eternity of forgettable deaths and resurrections, the numbers of his opponents rose to crescendo. Finally having cleared the control room of its defenders, Strewnfield found himself at the blast doors before the Revenger's final redoubt.

The game leveled-up and Andy froze play. Finishing that level had taken a good deal longer than he remembered it taking, before. Feeling more weary and more feeble than ever, he was glad to be through it.

As he made his way back toward his runabout, he heard the voice and laughter of a young man. For a moment he almost thought it was the echo of his own voice, but it was not, even if the woman speaking and laughing was a woman he had once loved.

Is this how it must be? Andy wondered as he half-spacewalked, half-shuffled through the rocketway to his vehicle. Must the stride

I make grow always smaller, the older I get? Until, one day, I'll walk with the shuffling gait of an elderly man, feeling foot by foot his way through a darkening house, anxious not to stub a toe on death, or trip on the bottom step of heaven? As he boarded the runabout, as he pulled away from Tasha's, as he laid in his course toward Ishmael Morel's place, his last stop before home, such thoughts depressed him without cease.

The runabout plunged on toward Morel's Refugium, leaving Andy to wonder if Ish would be willing to see him. How reclusive might Morel be, these days? Did he see anyone? On the runabout's final approach to the octahedral ruby of the Refugium, Andy sent his passcode identifier—and was gratified when the house lit its landing lights and opened a docking bay to receive him.

As he shuffle-walked into the Refugium proper from the docking bay, a song—about sleeping drunkards in Central Park, lion-hunters in jungles dark, Chinese dentists, the British queen, dancing bears, Ginger Rogers and Fred Astaire—played over the household sound system. The lyrics struck him as strange but also strangely familiar.

"I'm in the game room," Ishmael Morel's disembodied voice said, momentarily interrupting the song. "Come join me there, Andy. I've sent you directions, in case you don't remember."

Following the directions on the heads-up display of his eye-cam, Andy eagerly anticipated the boss battle that awaited him here. When he stepped into the game room and into the Revenger's last redoubt, however, he found himself in a tangleweb forcefield, caught between the roles of ASGuard Martin Strewnfield and Anderson McKinnon—and unable to move, either in gamespace, or fully into either role.

"What's going on, Ishmael? This isn't according to script, is it?"

"Depends what script you're following," said the disembodied voice. "Play a role long enough and the role plays you, right? You've got skin in the game whether you know it or not. What say we play the game one last time, for the highest of stakes?"

"What stakes?"

"Life and death—for real. No cheats, no instantaneous resurrections, no resurrections at all. Not the Lazarus variety, nor sweet-Jesus style, either."

"Done," Martin/Andy said, even as he doubted that Ish could really be serious about such an implausible kill virtual/kill real scenario. At least the gamespace was interactive now, though. Martin tried a command.

"And what's that you're covertly trying to do now, hmm?" Ish asked. "Don't try to interrupt or shut me down. I'm not just a backgrounder you can 'kill,' Andy. Remember the supervillains of old, who revealed all their secret plans once they had the hero in their clutches? Well, I have you in my clutches. You'll have to hear the secret, now, so pay all attention to the man behind the curtain!"

A green and gold curtain opened, and there stood a figure who was both the Repentant Revenger of the game, and Ishmael Morel—but an Ish Morel far, far, older than the man Andy remembered. The game was still on as far as Martin/Andy was concerned, despite Revenger/Ish's attempt to force this pause. Martin/Andy covertly programmed a pulse grenade to build up toward criticality, and commanded its explosion pattern to assume a particular shaped-charge format.

"Been a long time, Andy."

"I don't know where the time has gone, Ish. The years have flown by so fast I can hardly remember their passing."

"An unintended consequence of when life-recording met the NOUS," Revenger/Ish said, nodding slowly. "One of the many neuroplasticity effects, I'm afraid."

"I thought it might be my popper-assisted dreamgaming," Martin/Andy said, "preventing me from consolidating or encoding experience into memory."

"Oh that's part of it too, no doubt. But there's more to it than that. Who needs drugs when you can plug your head straight into the big dream of the world? Hmm? The more we realized we were life-recording, the less attention we paid to the events of our own lives. They were always already going to be in storage somewhere, and we could access them later, if we needed to. No need to experience them deeply, since we knew we wouldn't need to commit them to memory."

Keeping close watch on his heads-up display as the pulse grenade continued to build charge, Martinandy maneuvered into position as best he could, given his tangleweb entrapment. He listened just enough to Revengerish to catch the gist, and said just enough to keep his opponent distracted by his own pontificating.

"Like most of the people up here, though, we've been lucky—especially given what rising sea levels did the market for private islands. Heaven is our gated community. Or would be, if the gravity well weren't already a moat tough enough to cross that it makes gates unnecessary. We're amenity migrants, and security is the ultimate amenity."

"What's that got to with memory, and what did you call it?" Martinandy asked, watching the charge continue to build. "Neuroplas—?"

"Neuroplasticity. Not many young riff-raff, hoi polloi, or barbarians, here in the exorbs. The moat of the gravity well, like I said. We're an older population, a bit more isolated from the global monoculture of the urban, corporate, and digital that dominates everything down there on Earth. Up here in our castles so much higher than the clouds, we've dodged the worst of the neuroplasticity consequences—and everything the poor slaves after us are going through, on the plantation planet below us."

"I—I don't understand." On the readout, Martinandy saw that the pulse grenade was almost at critical.

"Being screen-mediated—especially by screens *inside* the brain—alters the structure of the brain. Digital networks long ago universalized media, but media did not become overpoweringly social until the NOUS came into being. Even before the NOUS, some feared a group-think that adversely affected creativity in the young was already—"

The pulse grenade exploded a blast outward against the tangleweb. Enough nodes of the web blew out that Martinandy was able to shuffle his feet forward, and move one hand free enough of the force field to get a few shots off at his opponent.

"Interesting move, sir!" Revengerish said, instantly reconfiguring the gamespace into a topographically twisted hybrid of mirror ball and hall of mirrors—into which Revengerish himself disappeared, although his voice didn't. "Welcome to the Sacred Funhouse! Step right up, into the Holiest of Molies!"

Revengerish reappeared a thousand fold, reprising (visually, at least) the androgynous, motley-clad, kaleidoscope-eyed Persistent Fool character from *Bots vs. Nauts.*

"Oh Great Consumertainment, deliver us from freedom!" pronounced the Fool, in a voice both boom and wheedle, reminding Andy how much he detested that character's grandiloquence. "Endlessly create the desires you purport to satisfy! Great Gameworld—with guns! Without end! Amen!"

Martinandy found he could not run, but he could still spring and somersault through the labyrinthine ball of mirrored passageways. He strove breathlessly to keep his opponent talking so Martinandy might track him—trap Ish in his own prolixity field, and turn earshot into a perhaps-real kill shot. "You said those of us here haven't been hit as hard because we're older? That just sounds like generation-bashing, to me."

"Like dinosaurs complaining that their offspring have become birds—I know," Ish said, no longer persisting as the Fool, reverting at last to the Revenger. "But for a culture to survive it must reborn in the individual minds and personal memories of each succeeding generation. Off-loading to machines that aspect of who we are makes us *less* who we are. But that too has turned out to be something much more than just that."

"But what has that got to do with *my* memory?" Martinandy

asked, springing to new floors and levels of the mirror-ball maze, coming gun up around every corner, but seeing only himself, reflected infinitely.

"All the outsourcing of personal memory to machine-recording has been eroding attention at the physiological level. Make it open-access to others, violate the sanctity of the individual mind and its memories, and you demolish privacy itself, the foundation of individual human consciousness."

Catching a glimpse of what he thought was his opponent one level up, Martinandy sprang and fired. Only the image of his own face stared back at him, glittering in tangleweb field and crazed glass. Even in the shatter, though, he could not help seeing that his face was crisscrossed and puddled with wrinkles that reminded him, annoyingly, of the fading memory of water on a cracked, parched desert playa.

"You'll have to do better than that, Anderson. Now where was I? Ah. It's in deep privacy that consciousness manifests itself. Personal memory is part of that. That's why Saint Augustine called personal memory a vast and infinite profundity, a human instance of a divine power. The seat of the *soul*, if you want to call it that—"

"I don't," Andy said, opening fire on the maze choices ahead of him in every direction, including up and down—to no avail beyond the creation of a mess of crazed surfaces, shattered but not fallen away. "Appeals to transcendent beings have never much appealed to me."

"Ah, but you now have no choice but to take such beings into account, Andy," Revengerish said, revealing himself behind a sad smile. "Because the machinic gods did not exist, it was necessary that we invent them. And *you* helped me to create them."

"*What?*" Martinandy opened fire on reflecting surface after reflecting surface. This bizarre place—love-child born of Crystal Palace and Fortress of Solitude—in which Ish had wrapped himself was undeniably proving a very effective place for him to hide in, whatever else might be said of it.

"One does not have to be a high-fashion designer to see that the emperor wears no clothes," Revengerish said, staring calmly into an unknown middle distance. "Yet I almost let the experts convince me there was no harm in allowing the machines to take over the dream studio in our heads. *Almost.* That's why I created the Repentant Revenger character—in case the experts *were* wrong. And the experts were wrong indeed. Once we had the 'bot ensouled, it was no longer a creature to be bought and sold. What we intended to be our slave has very nearly become our absolute master."

His opponent disappeared. Martinandy vaulted down and up, and scuttled crabwise sideways among further mirrored aisles, searching for him.

"But I didn't create the NOUS."

"No, that's right. You didn't. But we did sell the world the NOUS through the game *we* created. By undermining individual memory, privacy, consciousness—and at the same time deep-brain stimulating the pleasure centers—the NOUS has re-cameralized the mind."

"Which means what?" Martinandy said, tossing a pulse grenade into a mirrored corridor below him. His left arm, head, torso, and both his legs below the knees were still webbed to varying degrees in patchy force field, so the throw was all arm and didn't get far. The explosion was nonetheless enough to blow a hole through the end of the mirror corridor, revealing—another mirror corridor.

"Messages from the right hemisphere of the brain have again taken on that 'god's voice' quality they had for the ancient Greeks in Homer. Universalized intracranial media have so thoroughly reduced consciousness to a commons that, for the generations which have grown up with *all that* on Earth, *there is no such thing* as 'privacy' or 'deep personal memory' any more. We have virtualized both life and death, until we don't know which one is distracting us from the other. The great machine's God-voice, now speaking in a head near yours, from a global mass mind near you."

"And what does God want?" Martinandy asked, stalking slowly, trying to trace the sound of his opponent's voice.

"Happy zombies who won't complain," Revengerish said, revealing himself in a nearby reflection.

"Complain about what?" Martinandy fired off another shot at another mirrored surface, knowing even as he did so how futile that effort was.

"About their world being over-populated, heatgas-insulated, corporate-dominated, and blurface-pixelated. About *anything, actually*. No matter how horrendously dehumanized things get."

"But we only sold them a game! And wasn't it *you* who ripped into me for being a 'myopic gamer—smart enough to play the game, stupid enough to think the game is all that really matters'?"

Revengerish looked away—from his opponent? Himself? It was hard to tell, inside the ball of mirrors.

"I'm sorry I had to lie to you like that. At first I was blinded by thoughts of unbelievable wealth and power—of being as immortal, amoral, and sanctifiedly selfish as our corporate person itself!—but once I realized how addictive the NOUS and *Asterriders* might be, I was moved to make some sort of backup plan. I hope in the end you'll see that playing, in hindsight, was part of hiding in plain sight."

"You're speaking in riddles again, Ish," Martinandy said, striking off in a new direction through looking-glass land.

"Of course I am. How else should I speak? Riddles are childish, right? That's precisely the point. We had to transform the apocalyptic into something ironic, something comic, something no one takes seriously, so that we could actually make it come to pass. We had to fool the mind-machines precisely by moving the end of the world into the obsolete technology nursery."

"I'm not following you," Martinandy said, gun at the ready, but trying to keep from firing, trying to listen enough to find the source of that voice, which was now laughing.

"In point of fact, you *are* following me! The point I was making, though, is this: Gods, technologies, even fashions—all of them have been known to move into the nursery after they become outmoded in the adult world. Christianity's ascendance reduced the Fates to fairy godmothers. The rise of the automobile reduced the horse to the hobby-horse. Breeches became boy's wear after the advent of pants. Books became nursery tomes after the internet and digitalization. You see, the NOUS and the whole infosphere had to be made to believe that *Asterriders* was only a sideshow attraction, an obsolete game, a childish thing long since banished to the nursery."

"But why?" Martinandy leapt up a level, turned a corner, and fired at something he was sure was more than just an image in a mirror, this time.

"Turnabout is fair play. We remember that sideshows have a way of becoming main attractions."

"Such as?"

"When the threat of nuclear attack was in the center ring of the Cold War circus, there were people working in a sideshow to create a system of machines more capable of continued survival than humans as individuals were, than human civilization was, than the human species itself was. Our fear of our death as a species led us to unknowingly create a technology that will *insure* our death as a species, once that tech's potential is fully realized. How wonderful! Whatever other shortcomings we may have, nobody can say old *Homo sap* suffers from an irony deficiency—"

"That has nothing to do with you and me, though," Martinandy said, peering around another corner and firing.

"It has everything to do with us! With the development and widespread distribution of the NOUS, humanity as a species has succeeded in innovating itself into evolutionary obsolescence, by creating its own machinic successor. Only a species with a deep-dish death wish does that. Yet we can still prove human intelligence is not necessarily a lethal mutation. We can be something more than damn fool dream-lemmings ready to follow manufactured fantasies right off a cliff. We can still turn back from the brink before it's too late. Through what everyone thinks is even less than a sideshow—something that is 'only a game.'"

"Wait a minute," Martinandy said, firing a burst toward the opposite end of the mirrored corridor. "Are you saying that this whole meteoroid EMP scenario—the sunstreamers, the steerable asteroids, the destruction of digital civilization, supposedly to save humanity—it all turns out to be real?"

To his surprise, this time his opponent returned fire. A good sign.

"Absolutely. And only now coming to fruition, after nearly twenty-five years, in this final run. The target is in the Earth's ionosphere, at the Doomsday Point. As I've so long and so often said, sometimes the only way to fork lightning through the mind's sky is to first short-circuit heaven. Think of it as primal screen therapy."

Martinandy somersaulted across a tee in the mirrorball maze, scant microseconds ahead of his opponent's fire.

"What about the casualties, Ish?"

"'Oh, the humanity!' But let us not sit upon the planet and sing dark dirges for dirigibles! Let us not ask whatever became of what might have been!" said his opponent, flickering for a moment into The Fool again, before reverting. "Yes, the casualties will be many, many. But the mind-machines will be deprived of their final victory over our humanity."

"Who's got the death wish now?" Martinandy asked, firing as he made another serpentine run.

"The survivors from the cities, the saving remnant in a few disconnected refugia outside the urban areas—they will be free to live and die as human beings again, not as billions of autonomous psychoid processes in the dream of a machinic god. They will be something more than rats to be drowned to the sound of piped-in electronic music."

Martinandy fired and fired until, from sheer weariness in his gun arm, he could fire no more.

"We're old men, Ish. I'm finally beginning to believe it, if only because I'm feeling it too much now to think otherwise. It's all catching up with me. God, if only I'd known I'd live this long, I wouldn't have abused my body so much when I was younger. But we still want to live, despite it all, don't we? I don't know which way in my skin to turn, but I know I don't want to turn my skin in for Death to hang on his coat-rack just yet. Are you really willing to include yourself among those dead?"

"Yes—so long as that act frees all of us from the NOUS. But I'm not the one who should lead the final assault on Earth. *You* are. The best who ever played the game."

"Release me, then."

"Only if you drink a little of my Klein-bottle wine first."

"Is that all?"

"That, and you must promise to kill me, don my crown, and take my place leading the attack."

"Done."

The mirrorball maze folded back into a single reality around them. With a wave of his hand Revengerish, standing before Martinandy, released him from the remains of the tangleweb force field. Martinandy strode forward, for a moment amazed at just how much Revengerish physically resembled him (only much, much older, he hoped). Revengerish handed him a strangely shaped glass.

"To our success!" Revengerish said, raising his goblet or chalice or whatever it was. Martinandy raised his too, and they drank. Martinandy shook his opponent's hand, tossed away the empty glass and, with both hands gripping his hand-cannon, shot his opponent at point blank range. Revengerish was thrown backwards from the force of it.

When Martinandy reached the spot where his opponent had landed, he found no body there—only the Revenger's cloak and skullcap helmet. How very archetypal, Andy thought, as Martin swung the cloak over his shoulders. Feeling too tired and weak to full-body game, Andy subvocalized the passcode to activate his own intracranial implant. He was surprised to see that the implant was already activated.

Had he slipped up? He *had* been giving a lot of passcodes to security systems during his quest. How long had he been in intracranial mode? He wondered, but he couldn't remember.

He had little time to think about it now, for as soon as Martin placed the Revenger's abandoned skullcap crown on his head Andy found he instantly saw things as Ish saw them. What a mode switch! He believed utterly in the truth of Ish Morel's vision. No need to blow up this flying mountain, for Ish was right: the cyborg manifest destiny, the mind-machine reversal of the roles of master and servant, human and instrument—all of that had to be stopped. And Anderson McKinnon was the one who must set things right, for he was the best who ever was.

Andy—despite his certainty that he had frozen gameplay— nonetheless thought he heard a voice say into his head *New boss same as the old boss*, and another saying, *Same as it ever was, same as it ever was*. Probably just another song playing from the sound system, he thought.

Alarms began to screech in the Refugium, and he fled.

Somehow he must have made his way to his runabout and away, for the next thing he knew he was pulling into Dreamplay House. Nalika and Kara waited for him there, smiling and waving as he got out of his vehicle. When he joined them, each of them took one of his hands and, with smiles and skipping steps, led him to the gaming suite. His smiling daughter and his wife kissed him good night.

Taking up his telepresent role as Repentant Revenger, he and his crews—having hijacked the greatest of the Apollo and Atens asteroids and rendered them maneuverable meteoroids—steered the flying plutons toward Earth. A flotilla of doomsday mountains—himself guiding the flagship at the center of the formation, at the virtual helm of the greatest Omega Stone—fell to their rendezvous with Earth's ionosphere.

Resistance was fierce. Many a flying mountain was shattered, but his faith that he would accomplish his mission never faltered. The best moves of the defenders were, after all, his own. But even he, for all his gameplay and system design work, had never known the exact location of the final target—until now. Below him, but still some tens of miles above the Earth, stood the Doomsday Point, where the lower Van Allen Belt dipped closest to the planet's surface at the South Atlantic Anomaly. There, even now, the first of the remaining meteoroids of his flotilla began to brake in the ionosphere—disruptively, explosively, catastrophically breaking up in blasts of light, heat, and lightning. The shock waves of each skystone's shattering instantly propagated in the plasma surrounding it, in great pulses of ionizing radiation—not only lightning but elves and sprites and electromagnetic transients of many kinds and frequencies.

"Why are you doing this?" asked the fetch who looked so much like his own daughter.

"Death changes a person," he said, continuing to prosecute the battle. "Especially when the death is one's own. I have no choice."

"Why not?"

"I don't have to answer you."

"Why? Because I'm a fetch? I may really be one, now. A ghostly double of your daughter who is about to die."

"Oh, you're good. Almost like you can read my mind. The system knows more about us than we know about ourselves—wasn't that it? But for all your knowledge, you didn't see this coming, now did you?"

"Not completely."

As the greatest of the Omega Stones itself began to break up, he saw the vast wave of ten million lightning bolts ripple across the globe from the South Atlantic Anomaly. The pulse, propagating worldwide, left darkness in its wake. All the lights of all the cities on the nightside Earth went out. The kill switch had been thrown on all unshielded electronics, over the entire surface of the planet, dayside and nightside and in near earth orbit.

The sky short-circuited. A screaming stopped in heaven and

he woke, suspended in profound silence. He was in his hibertube, yet he did not remember going to bed or falling asleep. He hit the Open button once, then twice, then many times, but the slide bed would not budge.

The space around him was deathly quiet. He was overwhelmed with a sense of doom worse than the worst panic attack he had ever known. With what limited range of motion he could manage, he pounded with his fists on the interior of the 'tube. No luck. He called for Nalika, then for Kara. No one answered. He yelled and pounded, but he was old, and he tired quickly.

It was soon all too clear that the house was empty, and this 'tube might well prove to be his coffin. For all his dodging and ducking, he had run straight into the embrace of everything he had been running away from his entire life. Would he die for real now? Or in death would he just level-up into another of Miriam's endless ends, her infinitesimally infinite life-reviews? Again, and again? Would that be the vertigo of heaven, or hell? He screamed and cried out, for he did not know to what end he should pray.

"Thank you all for coming to Andy's memorial service today," Nalika said. And it was indeed a good thing, she thought, to re-member who Anderson McKinnon had been, before he forgot himself. "Thank you for sharing your memories of him. That makes it easier for me to share mine."

Perhaps it was not such a good thing that the occasion for her words now meant many other words could not be spoken, but that was how it had to be. She did not tell those around her that she and Kara found Andy face down in their driveway, dead of the massive heart attack he had suffered only moments before. She did not tell them that the driver's side door to his car was still open, the engine was still running, and the music (some old tune from decades past) was still playing from the car's sound system.

"The Andy McKinnon I met in college was a brilliant undergraduate, double-majoring in English and Psychology. He was genuinely fascinated by the ideas of Jung and complexity theory, among many other things. In my turn, I was genuinely fascinated with his cocky, smartass young self. We soon—some might say 'overhastily'—got serious, and got married.

"Andy graduated summa cum laude but never attended graduate school as he had intended. When his father died suddenly the summer we graduated, it was out of family loyalty and obligation that Andy took over his father's old job in his uncle's swimming pool business. As his Uncle Ish said in his remembrance here today, Andy never seemed to wonder about the path he *hadn't* taken. I too never heard him complain about what might have been. He did his duty as he saw it, and that was that."

Never complained—until after that morning, when the pool crew's heavy equipment operator failed to show up, when Andy took his seat on the crew's ancient Bobcat, only to have the machine roll on him as he was excavating the hole for that pool.

"As many of you know, the workplace accident that compressed the disks in Andy's spine left him seventy-five percent disabled," Nalika continued. She did not bother to add that it also left him unable to feel anything from the knees down—except intermittent, unpredictable sensations of excruciating pain. She remembered how he suffered with that until he couldn't take it anymore. She remembered the day they learned there was no treatment for his condition except prescription painkillers.

She tried not to remember how his addiction to those and to even more powerful drugs took over his life, changed him, led him to bemoan everything that hadn't become of his life. It's a world hard enough, he had once told her, to grind the edges off the craziest diamond of hope. And it had ground him.

"He never worked in construction again, but he continued to keep busy and mentally active, taking great enjoyment in drawing and in reading, in playing futuristic videogames and listening to the Oldies and Classical music he had always loved, and, and . . ."

She had to stop a moment to overcome the sob in her throat. Slowly catching her breath, she was at last able to continue.

"As Ish mentioned earlier, he and Andy were planning to develop a game together—*Extinction Burst*—for which Andy would write the tie-in book. What that game might have looked like, how it might have been played, how that book might have read—I wish we could know. We can only imagine what Andy's fertile imagination might have produced—what futures might have passed before his eyes, and ours.

"We can only give him our words now, but I think Andy would have appreciated them. I remember him telling me once that only word-intoxicated creatures would have a word like 'ineffable'—a word for what cannot be expressed in words. I know Andy would not have wanted us to complain about what might have been—about what cannot be expressed, now—but I must still wonder, still try to put who he was into words. Maybe all of us will still wonder, and still try, even while knowing that, despite our best efforts, something of Andy too will always remain ineffable. I hope and trust he understands and forgives us for that."

When the service ended, Nalika and Kara remained at the graveside, looking on as the stone marker Nalika had rush-ordered was set in position at the grave's head end. The marker was simple enough: Anderson McKinnon's name and dates, and an image Nalika had found among Andy's drawings, dated just a week before his death. A face in low relief, seemingly overwhelmed by and unable to escape from the rough stone block in which it was embedded, yet wearing a beatific expression nonetheless. Andy had captioned the drawing "Trapped in Bliss." Nalika thought the headstone carver had done a remarkably accurate job of copying the drawing into the stone's surface.

Hand in hand with Kara, Nalika turned and walked away from the grave.

"Mom, why did you choose that face for his gravestone?"

"I don't know," Nalika said. "It was something your father drew. It reminded me of him."

ABOUT THE AUTHOR

Howard V. Hendrix has published over fifty short stories and six novels, including *Lightpaths, Standing Wave, Better Angels*, and *Spears of God.* He holds a Ph.D. and MA in English Literature from the University of California, Riverside, and a BS in Biology from Xavier University, Ohio. He has taught at the college level for more than thirty-five years.

PUBLICATION HISTORY

"Knot Your Grandfather's Knot" originally appeared in *Analog* (2008) | "Habilis" originally appeared in *Carbide Tipped Pens*, Tor Books; ed Ben Bova and Eric Choi (2014) | "The Girls With Kaleidoscope Eyes" originally appeared in *Analog* (2017) | "Monuments of Unageing Intellect" originally appeared in *Analog* (2009) | "Palimpsest" originally appeared in *Analog* (2007) | "The Perfect Bracket" originally appeared in *Analog* (2016) | "Red Rover, Red Rover" originally appeared in *Analog* (2012) | "A Little Spooky Action" originally appeared in *Analog* (2017) | "The Infinite Manque" originally appeared in *Analog* (2016) | "Whatever Became of What Might Have Been?" originally appeared in *Analog* as "Other People's Avatars" (2013)

OTHER TITLES FROM FAIRWOOD PRESS

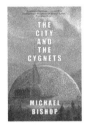

CPSIA information can be obtained
at www.ICGtesting.com
Printed in the USA
FSHW011836290719
60502FS